By K.C. WELLS

NOVELS

LEARNING TO LOVE
Michael & Sean
Evan & Daniel
Josh & Chris
Love Lessons Learned

COLLARS & CUFFS
An Unlocked Heart
Trusting Thomas

With PARKER WILLIAMS
Someone to Keep Me

Published by DREAMSPINNER PRESS
http://www.dreamspinnerpress.com

LOVE LESSONS
LEARNED
K.C. WELLS

Dreamspinner Press

Published by
Dreamspinner Press
5032 Capital Circle SW
Suite 2, PMB# 279
Tallahassee, FL 32305-7886
USA
http://www.dreamspinnerpress.com/

Love Lessons Learned
© 2014 K.C. Wells.

Cover Art
© 2014 Anna Sikorska.
Cover content is for illustrative purposes only and
any person depicted on the cover is a model.

ISBN: 978-1-62798-783-7
Digital ISBN: 978-1-62798-784-4

Printed in the United States of America
First Edition
April 2014

For two wonderful people who were with me
every step of the way for this one.

Thank you, Max Vos and Alex Vaughan.
Your advice was invaluable.

# Acknowledgments

Thanks, as always, to my wonderful betas,
Tina, Lara, Mardee, Will, and Max.

CHAPTER 1

MAYBE MUM is right. Maybe it will be third time lucky.

John Wainwright stared into his cup of coffee and tried to ignore the rolling in the pit of his stomach. The interview had gone well—at least, he *thought* it had. John didn't exactly trust his own judgment anymore. He'd thought the previous two interviews had gone well too. The fact that there were four other candidates didn't fill him with confidence, especially since two of them had been on the last interview.

All of us chasing the same jobs, he thought morosely as he stirred his coffee. He glanced at his watch. They wouldn't be calling for another hour or so, and John didn't want to catch the train back to Chester just yet.

His phone vibrated in his jacket pocket. John took it out and smiled when he saw the caller.

"You checking up on me?" he asked his brother as soon as the call connected.

Evan chuckled into his ear. "Where are we up to?"

"*We* aren't up to anywhere," John corrected him. "*I* am sitting in Debenhams in their café, having a cup of coffee while I wait to hear." He took a sip before continuing. "The interview went fine. I really like the school, and the class they gave me to teach was a nice group of kids."

"Did the lesson go well? I know you were nervous about it."

John gave a wry chuckle. "That would be an understatement, but yeah, it went well." Teaching a lesson was always the most nerve-racking part of the interview process, as far as John was concerned. It was only thirty minutes, providing the two observers with only a brief glimpse of his presence in the classroom, but John fervently hoped it had been enough. He loved the school. It had a good feel about it.

"Did you say you're in Debenhams? Want to meet up? I can be with you in twenty minutes."

John considered the proposal. His interview had finished at two thirty, and the remaining four candidates had still to be interviewed. It would be at least five thirty before anyone rang him to let him know how he'd done. *That's the best thing about teaching jobs*, he mused. *They let you know on the day.* It was only four o'clock, and he'd already wandered up and down Market Street twice, looking in all the shop windows. *And you haven't seen Evan since the wedding*, he told himself.

"Yeah, that sounds great. Will Daniel be coming with you?"

"Only if you promise not to kiss him again." John could hear the amusement in Evan's voice.

John felt his cheeks heating up. Evan was never going to let him live that down. "Ev, you *promised*," he whined. It was his own fault. The first time he'd met his new brother-in-law, he'd thoroughly embarrassed himself.

Evan laughed. "Sorry, bro, I couldn't resist." John heard him speaking quietly to Daniel. "Daniel says if it's okay with you, he'll come along."

"Tell him it's *fine*," John stressed. It would be good to see them both. "Shall I stay put?"

"I've got a better idea. How about meeting us at Via Fossa on Canal Street?"

John groaned internally. *Evan* would *want to meet in a gay bar, wouldn't he?* "At least you didn't suggest meeting at G-A-Y," he said. He heard Evan snicker. "Okay, Via Fossa it is. See you there." He hung up and pocketed his phone. A leisurely stroll down to Canal Street would mean he'd arrive shortly before his brother, which was fine. John didn't want to spend too much time there on his own. It wasn't that he didn't like

Manchester's gay village—he'd hardly ever visited the district. But just being around gay guys made him nervous.

He wasn't about to share that information with Evan. John knew *exactly* how his brother would react. He could hear the words in his head, plain as day.

Does it make you nervous because you don't like the idea of a gay guy coming on to you? Or because you might be tempted to come on to one of them?

John shivered. Nope. Not going to go there.

JOHN SAT on the wall that ran alongside the canal and watched for Evan and Daniel's arrival. July had been glorious so far, the summer everyone had been waiting for since the previous year's washout. The temperatures had climbed up into the late twenties, which was pretty damn good for the UK, and had even nudged past thirty a couple of days. Canal Street was buzzing. Crowds of people sat at tables out in the cobbled street or perched on the walls that channeled the canal as it ran through the center of the city. There was a party atmosphere in the air. It was the weekend of Sparkle, the village's transvestite event, and Sackville Gardens were full to bursting as everyone crowded in there to watch the judging for Miss Sparkle.

John glanced around at the many men, young and old, who sat drinking in the early evening sunshine. The crowd wasn't made up exclusively of males. He'd been surprised to see a group of giggling young women, obviously out on a hen night, judging by the young woman who was wearing a tiara and wedding veil. They'd clearly had a lot to drink already, John decided as he watched them stumble along the street, their high heels skittering over the cobbles.

"That's becoming a regular sight around here."

John jerked his head up in surprise. Evan was standing beside him, looking over the top of his sunglasses at the party of girls. John got to his feet and hugged him. Daniel stood at Evan's side, his long black hair tied back and sunglasses perched on top of his head. Both men were smiling.

"I didn't hear you," John said as he took Daniel's hand. Daniel ignored it and gave him a brief but warm hug.

Evan's smile widened. "That's because you were too busy watching the show," he said, indicating the departing group. "Some of the guys who drink here regularly say there are more and more hen nights down on Canal Street." He shook his head. "Why do some women like hanging out with gay guys?"

"Maybe they feel safer," suggested Daniel. "They're not likely to get hit on, are they? And it's not often you see fights breaking out. The girls can concentrate on having a good time."

"Let me get you two something to drink, seeing as you're still impoverished students." John winked.

Evan chuckled. "You haven't got that job *yet*, bro."

John's smile faded. "Don't remind me." He hadn't thought it would be this difficult to get a teaching job, especially when other students from his teacher training course had literally walked straight into jobs as early as March or April.

Evan put his arm around John's shoulders and squeezed. "It'll be fine. Maybe this is the one. You and Daniel find a seat, and I'll get us all a drink. Lager okay?" John nodded, and Evan disappeared into Via Fossa. John took a look around and spotted a group of three men who were just getting up to leave.

"There," he prompted Daniel, and the two men pushed quickly through the crowd to grab the table before anyone else reached it. They sat back on the chairs and sighed simultaneously. Both men burst into laughter.

"So how is married life treating you?" John asked him. "It's been, what, nearly seven months?" He grinned. "Evan hasn't driven you up the wall yet?"

Daniel's face creased into a lazy grin. "I have *no* problem handling your brother, believe me." There was a gleam in his eye. "He knows how to stay on my good side."

John wasn't sure what to make of that statement until he remembered something he'd seen on their wedding day—a very distinctive piece of jewelry Evan had worn around his neck, a black choker made from chain links, joined at the front in a little gold spring clasp. What had made it so distinctive was the tiny charm in the shape of a pair of handcuffs that hung from the clasp. John had only glimpsed the choker toward the end of the reception when Evan had undone his shirt at the neck.

And he's wearing it today.

John had read enough to have a fair idea of the significance of the choker. Not to mention the way Evan and Daniel acted around each other. There wasn't anything overt in their behavior, but it was obvious who wore the pants—and maybe wielded the whip, for all John knew—in their relationship. He wasn't about to mention it. That would open up the door to a conversation John was definitely *not* prepared to participate in. It was bad enough that both Evan and Daniel knew he wasn't 100 percent certain he was straight.

Evan exited the bar and look around for them. John raised his hand in signal, and Evan's face lit up. He edged his way precariously through the tables with the three pint glasses and joined them. Evan sat down at the table and then raised his glass.

"To you, John. Here's hoping you find what you're looking for."

John gave him a sharp look, but Evan's expression was guileless. John raised his glass in acknowledgment and took a drink. The lager was cold and refreshing.

"So, tell us about the school," Daniel said after taking a long drink.

John put down his glass. "It's in a deprived part of the city—in fact, it's only a ten minute walk from the center. The area is rundown, and the school is set in the middle of a council estate."

"Wow. That's a little different from the first two jobs you went for," Evan commented. John had to agree. His first interview had been in a Church of England primary school where the governing body had clearly provided a lot of money to furnish the children with the best facilities available. The second had been very similar. "What made you go for this one, John?"

"I liked the ethos of the school," John admitted. "They're committed to helping every child who walks through their doors, regardless of their background or level of ability." The school had looked good on paper, and John's first impression as he'd walked around and glimpsed into the classrooms had only reinforced his belief that this was where he was meant to be.

"What are the teachers like? Did you get to meet many of them?" asked Daniel. John could tell his brother-in-law was genuinely interested.

"Well, I got to have a chat with them in the staff room during the lunch hour—those who weren't out supervising the kids, anyway. I have to say, they seemed very young."

"Says you at the lofty age of twenty-four," Evan said with a snicker.

John shook his head. "I only meant to say that there didn't seem to be any older members of staff, *you* know, really experienced teachers. The ones I saw could only have been teaching for a few years at the most."

"Is it a new school?" Daniel asked.

John huffed. "Hardly. There's been a school on that site since 1906, according to the plaque near the entrance. Okay, so the original school was knocked down and rebuilt a couple of years ago, but they wouldn't have gotten rid of all the staff, would they?"

Daniel shrugged. "You wouldn't think so." His gaze was affectionate. "You really want this job, don't you?"

John nodded slowly. He had a really good feeling about it.

"You said on the phone the interview went fine. No tricky questions, then?" Evan asked before downing half his pint.

John smiled. "None that I wasn't prepared for, at any rate." The interview had been conducted by the head teacher, Brett Sanderson, along with two governors. Both Brett and Mary Lacey, the teacher-governor, had observed John's lesson. John sighed. "The worst thing was being interviewed first."

"What about the competition? Any really strong candidates—apart from you, of course." Daniel winked.

John had to smile at that. "Two of them I'd already met before at the last two interviews. There was one really pushy guy, though. Kept asking lots of questions as we did our tour of the school. It was difficult to get a word in edgeways." John had disliked him immediately. "And he's probably got the job," he added gloomily.

His phone vibrated in his pocket. He chuckled as he withdrew it. "This will be Mum, wanting to know if there's any news." He glanced at the screen and froze. Definitely not Mum. His fingers trembled as he connected the call. "John Wainwright."

"Mr. Wainwright, this is Brett Sanderson from Ardwick Primary school. Are you able to talk right now?"

"Yes, certainly, Mr. Sanderson." John watched both Evan and Daniel straighten, their eyes fixed on him. "And please, call me John."

"John, I'd like to offer you the position." John's mouth dropped open, and he stared at Evan in astonishment. Evan gave him a questioning look and put his thumbs up. John nodded eagerly, and Evan's expression of joy was a delight to see. "John—are you still there?" John was convinced there was the tiniest hint of amusement in that cool voice.

"Yes—yes, I'm still here. Thank you very much, Mr. Sanderson." John did his best not to sound flustered.

There was a dry chuckle. "We're a pretty informal bunch here, John. I'm Brett, all right?"

"Yes, Brett." John could hardly believe it. *I got the job!* "What's the procedure now?" He was trying hard to keep his cool, but he felt like dancing, his heart was so light.

"School closes next week for the summer, so it might be an idea if you came here on Monday morning and got some details about the class you'll be taking. I warn you, they'll be a challenge." Brett paused. "I hope you're up to it."

"Yes, sir—I mean, Brett." John couldn't have cared right now if the class was comprised entirely of kids who liked juggling chainsaws and throwing knives around the classroom. *I've got a job....*

"Shall we say first thing Monday, then? You can spend the whole day with us. We should be able to sort out everything then."

"That sounds great," John said. He couldn't stop grinning. "Thank you again, Brett, for this opportunity."

"You don't need to thank me. I happen to think the best candidate got the job. And, John? Welcome aboard." Brett's voice was deep and firm.

"Thank you. I'll see you Monday." John hung up and stared at the phone in his hand. *Wow....*

"Congratulations!" Evan was up out of his chair and hugging John tightly, Daniel not far behind him. John's mind was already reeling. There was so much to think about. He'd need to move out of his parents' house, for a start, and find somewhere to live before the new term started in September. At least he'd be closer to Evan. And clothes—he'd need to make sure he looked the part. So many things to consider....

"John? You need to stop and enjoy the moment."

John turned to Daniel, who was studying him with an amused grin. John gave him a sheepish look. "Yeah, I suppose you're right. Though as soon as Mum and Dad hear about it, Mum will have a load of questions to throw at me." His main concern was his accommodation. Much as he loved living at home, he was excited at the prospect of being on his own again. University had been a lot of fun, and John was anxious to have his freedom back.

"Never mind enjoying the moment," Evan said with a smirk. "If he knows what's good for him, he'd better ring Mum."

John pulled out his phone with a sigh. No use putting off the inevitable.

His mother's shriek of joy was deafening. "That's fantastic news! Oh, I had a good feeling about this one." John didn't want to remind her about her previous good feelings. "So I guess we can tell you what your present is!"

"Present?"

She laughed down the phone. "Of course. We wanted to give you something practical, so Dad and I are giving you the deposit and first month's rent on your new place, wherever you end up living. Providing you don't want to live somewhere really pricey, that is. Think what you'll be able to afford on your salary."

John smiled. It was the perfect gift. "Mum, that's great. Thank you, and please thank Dad for me." Not that he wouldn't give his thanks personally when he got home.

"Can I have the phone for a sec?" Evan asked. John handed it over. "Mum, don't expect John home tonight. Daniel and I would like to take him out to celebrate, and then he can stay at the house with us. Sean and Michael aren't home yet from Spain, so their room is empty—he can sleep in there." Evan looked at him questioningly. John nodded with a grin. A night out with Evan and Daniel sounded like a great idea. Evan listened for a minute. "Yes, Mum, I'll be sure to take care of him. Not that he isn't capable of taking care of himself." He handed the phone back to John with a grin.

"Now have a lovely evening," his mum urged. "And don't drink too much." John could hear his father in the background, saying something about "For God's sake, Christine, let the boy enjoy himself, why don't you." John chuckled. He said good-bye and then pocketed the phone.

Evan was almost bouncing on his seat. "Oh, we're going to have fun tonight." His gleeful expression made John a little wary.

"Just what are you planning?" He stared pointedly at Evan, who arched his eyebrows in an expression clearly meant to convey innocence. *Yeah, right….*

"You're going to come home with us and we'll feed you," Evan said with enthusiasm. "Josh and Chris won't be there. They've taken Mark, Josh's Dad, away for a holiday. Josh had to insist. That man works far too hard." John had met Josh and Chris at the wedding, along with Mark. Mark Saunders had been in a wheelchair, as he'd been recovering from a gunshot wound.

"They all needed a break after everything that's happened," added Daniel, his face serious.

John racked his brains for a moment before recalling that Josh had been kidnapped by his sadistic ex-boyfriend. Mark was the detective inspector who'd found him.

"How is he?" John had liked Josh. He'd seemed a pleasant guy who clearly adored his now-fiancé, Chris. "And have they made any plans yet for the wedding?"

Daniel shook his head. "They're in no hurry, they say. Josh will be starting the second year of medical school in September, and Chris has one more year of his degree left. And as for how Josh is, ask Evan. Josh seems to confide more in him than in me." His brow creased into a slight frown.

Evan reached across and took his husband's hand. "Don't be like that, babe. Who was it Chris turned to when *he* needed advice, hmmm?" He fixed Daniel with an earnest stare.

Daniel sighed. "You're right, of course. I've just had the impression that Josh has been a little… cool with me recently." He stroked Evan's hand, his gaze lowered.

John tipped his head to one side. "I thought you all got on famously in that house of yours. Trouble in paradise?"

Evan shrugged. "I think Josh has been through a horrific experience. It's bound to have left its mark, yeah? And maybe some time away on the Isle of Wight will help him—help *all* of them." He shivered. "Anyway, enough of that—you just need to concentrate on having a good time tonight." His eyes glittered. "And we are going to give you a *really* good time."

"It's your idea of a good time that worries me," John muttered under his breath. Evan chuckled, and Daniel patted John's shoulder. They picked up their pints and sat back, relaxing in the early evening sunshine. John sipped his pint and tried to ignore the butterflies in his stomach. *How bad could it be*, he thought. Then he remembered. If Evan was in charge, heaven only knew what the night had in store for him.

Oh, brother….

CHAPTER 2

JOHN TOOK a drink of his gin and tonic and then glanced around. Babel was certainly a popular club, judging by the number of men who crowded onto the dance floor and propped up the bar. The music had a heavy, percussive beat, and it went right through him, making his body tingle. Evan was at the bar next to him, eyeing the dance floor wistfully. Daniel was already swaying in time to the music.

"Oh, for God's sake, go and *dance*, you two!" John said with exasperation. "It's clear you both want to."

"What—and leave you all alone?" Evan grinned. "We're your chaperones tonight, remember." But still his gaze drifted to the gyrating men under the pulsing lights.

John folded his arms across his chest. "This may be a gay club, but I certainly don't think I'm about to be *molested*." He glared at his brother. "Go. Dance. *Both* of you." He took another mouthful of his drink and smiled. "I'll be fine. I'm having a good time watching the floor show."

"If you're sure." Evan was up on his feet even as the words left his mouth. He grabbed Daniel's hand. "Dance with me… husband?"

John's chest tightened at the expression that crossed Daniel's face. There was so much love in that gaze. *Oh, to have someone look at me like that….* Daniel put down his glass and was tugged toward the dance floor, Evan beaming at him with delight. John watched as Daniel put his hands on Evan's waist and pulled him close, Evan's arms around his husband's neck as they locked eyes with each other. It was obvious that no one else existed for the pair in that moment as they swayed to the music, their movements slow and sensual.

John walked around the edge of the dance floor, admiring the firm bodies of the club's occupants. He leaned back against the wall and watched the dancers. That heavy beat persisted. There was something almost... primeval, even *erotic* about it. He closed his eyes and let the music flow through him. He let his mind wander as he imagined strong arms around him, a firm chest pressed against his....

With a shock, John opened his eyes. *What the fuck?* He hadn't expected his thoughts to go off in that direction. He mentally shook himself. *You are* not *going to go there, okay?* He reached for his drink, which he'd placed on the ledge behind him, just as someone collided with his foot. He jerked his hand uncontrollably, and the gin and tonic went *everywhere*.

"I'm sorry, are you—" The words died in his throat as he caught sight of the older man who'd tripped in front of him.

The man straightened and glanced at his shirt, then raised his gaze to John, the faintest smile twisting those full lips. He was about thirty, with dark brown hair, blue eyes, wide shoulders—and a *very* wet white silk shirt.

In horror, John wiped his hands over the man's chest in a pitiful attempt to remove the excess liquid. The shirt was now transparent. He could make out a thick mat of hair beneath the fabric, not to mention a silver ring through his left nipple. He swallowed and withdrew his hands hastily.

"Oh, don't stop, baby, please. Not on *my* account." The man's voice rumbled out, deep and rich. He grinned at John, then grabbed John's hands and placed them back on his chest. John stared at him openmouthed. Twinkling eyes met his. "Now doesn't that feel better?"

John had to agree. It felt damn good. The silken fabric was smooth, wet and clinging. He couldn't believe how bold he was being as he explored the contours of the man's chest with intrepid fingers, hardly daring to breathe.

His new friend was almost purring. "*Much* better. So let's make it perfect." He cupped John's head with both hands and slowly drew him closer. John's heartbeat was erratic as he closed his eyes and surrendered.

Two warm, soft lips met his. His heart was pounding as the man slipped his tongue between John's lips and leisurely explored him. *God, it feels so good.* John kept his eyes closed as the kiss continued, the man's tongue thrusting slowly but insistently into his mouth, and John loved every second of it. Until he felt his hand stroke down John's back to cup his arse and squeeze him firmly. The kiss came to an abrupt end.

"Oh, your arse feels good. It would feel even better if I slipped my hand into your pants and stroked a finger across your hole. Let me?" that voice whispered into his ear, warm breath tickling him.

John gasped and opened his eyes wide. The man's eyes were glazed with lust, and he was gazing at John expectantly. John pushed at the firm chest and tried to back away, but the wall prevented his retreat. He gulped, and his new friend stared at him.

"Oh, wow." The man stepped back. "You really *are* new to this, aren't you?" John blushed furiously. The man got up close, his breath wafting against John's cheek. He locked eyes with him. "You're a virgin, aren't you?" The words were barely a whisper.

John's eyes widened. "N-no. I had a girlfriend."

The man grinned. "But you've never been with a man, have you?" His gaze drifted slowly down to John's crotch, and John was suddenly painfully aware of his erection, pressing against the zipper of his pants. That grin widened. "Oh, but you want to, don't you, baby?"

"Max. Why am I not surprised to see you here?"

John jerked his head to the right to find Evan and Daniel standing beside him. Evan's arms were folded across his chest, and Daniel had his arm draped around Evan's shoulder. Both men were watching the scene intently. Daniel was smirking. Evan's expression was a mixture of amusement and concern.

"Evan, do you know this guy?" John's new friend asked.

"Max, meet my brother, John."

Max quirked his eyebrows. "Your *brother*? You have *got* to be kidding." He chuckled. "God, the genes that must run in your family." He returned his gaze to John. "You have a sexy mouth, John—not to mention a *very* tempting arse." He stepped back even farther and shook his head. "And here was me thinking I'd got lucky." He cupped John's cheek. "I take it you don't want to play?"

John struggled to find his breath. "Not… not tonight, thanks," he managed to croak.

"Pity." Max leaned forward and kissed his cheek, his lips lingering for a moment. He whispered into John's ear. "You change your mind, you'll find me at the other end of the bar—stroking my hard-on in anticipation." He winked lasciviously. Max moved away slowly, after giving Evan and Daniel a brief nod.

John scrubbed a hand over his face as he watched Max walk toward the bar with a sexy roll of his hips. *Talk about sex on legs….*

"A-*hem.*"

The sound of Evan clearing his throat brought John sharply into the present. He stared guiltily at his brother. John was at a loss what to say.

"I think we need to have a little talk, bro." Evan's tone was kind, and John heaved a sigh of relief. "But not here, it's far too noisy."

"How about Via Fossa?" suggested Daniel. "It'll be quieter. Or else let's go home." He gazed quizzically at John. "Unless you want a drink while we talk?"

Suddenly, a drink sounded like a very good idea.

"Via Fossa," John said at last. He wasn't ready to go back to their house just yet. And maybe it was time to be honest.

JOHN STARED into his third gin and tonic of the night. The conversation had been light since their arrival in the bar, but he could tell Evan was itching to say something.

He took a long drink and faced his brother. "Okay—out with it."

Evan arched his eyebrows. "Out with what?" Daniel was smirking into his pint.

"Come on—you know you're dying to say something." The suspense was killing John.

Evan snickered. "I'm still reeling from the shock, to tell you the truth." He tilted his head. "You going to tell me that was another experiment?" He took a drink of his pint and locked eyes with John. "Or are you finally ready to admit it?"

John swallowed. There was no escaping it. "Okay." He took a deep breath. "I'm gay." He gulped down several deep breaths. "Don't suppose I can really deny it, not after that."

"That's the first time you've admitted it to yourself, isn't it?" Daniel asked in a low voice. John gave him a grateful look and nodded. "Feels good, doesn't it, to finally get it out in the open?"

"Yes," John breathed. God, it did. "I can't believe I did that. Kissing a total stranger…." His words trailed off.

"Max is pretty full-on," admitted Evan. "And *very* sexy." Daniel hit his arm lightly, and Evan's blue eyes widened. "Ow! I was just saying…."

"Well, don't," Daniel said shortly. Evan leaned closer to his husband and stared into his eyes. His hand was at his throat as he fingered the choker.

"Only yours—*Sir*," he said, so low that John only just caught it. But there was no missing Daniel's reaction. His pupils enlarged, and his breathing quickened. Evan reached across to stroke Daniel's arm, trailing his fingers over his bicep. "Later, I promise, okay?"

Daniel nodded with a shudder. A shiver ran down John's spine as he observed the couple. The way they were with each other….

He studied his drink. "Can I say something here?" He raised his head and regarded his brother-in-law. "I'm really sorry, Daniel, for what happened the first time we met. It's been on my mind lately."

Daniel smiled. "John, honestly, it's okay. Especially if it helped you to realize the truth about yourself." He lifted his glass. "Congratulations. You just took your first steps into a new world."

"What am I thinking? Daniel's right." Evan got to his feet and pulled John to stand. He wrapped his arms around him and held him tightly. "Congratulations, bro. You just came out."

John's face was hot against Evan's cheek. He put his arms around Evan and hugged him. "Thank you. I'm glad I've got you for a brother."

He could feel Evan's smile. "You might not say that when I try fixing you up with Max." Evan chuckled.

John pushed free of his embrace and shook his head. "Sorry, but you're not fixing me up with *anyone*, is that clear? I have to be really careful now."

Daniel frowned as Evan sat down. "What do you mean?"

"I mean, I'm now a primary school teacher. I've got to be squeaky clean."

It was Evan's turn to frown. "I don't understand."

John guffawed. "Come on. You must have worked it out by now. Being gay is almost synonymous with 'child molester' in some people's books." Both men stared at him, eyes wide. "You can't *both* be *that* ignorant of what goes on in the press, surely. A gay teacher? Working with little kids? Think, guys. What would the parents say if they found out?"

"You're serious." Evan studied his face.

What planet do they live on? "Of course, I'm serious. Why do you think people kick up a fuss about scout leaders who are gay? I'm *deadly* serious. I may have just come out, but as far as my job is concerned? I'm right back in that closet and *staying* there, thank you very much." John's heart hammered. Much as he wanted to take more steps into the brave new world he'd only just discovered, he knew common sense had to take precedence.

"I'm not sure I could live like that," Evan said, and his face clouded over.

John gave him a gentle smile. "*You* don't have to, little brother. But *I* do. All right?" He watched as Evan's expression changed to one of grudging acceptance. "Thank you. And thanks for bringing me here tonight."

"Much good it's done you," murmured Evan.

John shook his head. "But it *has*," he insisted. "I've finally accepted the fact that I'm gay. God knows I've been dancing around the issue for long enough. So be happy for me," he pleaded.

Evan stared at him for a moment and then nodded. Daniel edged his chair closer and put his arms around John's shoulders.

"We're here for you, whenever you need us, okay?"

John could have kissed him. The sincerity of his words rang out. "Thank you." John felt so lucky to have these two men in his life. "But I think I've had enough for one night. Can we go home now?"

Evan laughed. "Yeah, I can understand that. You've had quite the night, eh, bro?" He winked. "And I think Max enjoyed it too."

John's cheeks were red hot. "Let's... let's not mention him again, okay?" But he touched his lips as he recalled the feel of Max's mouth on him. Damn, the man could kiss.

Push it from your mind. Dwelling on it won't do you any good.

Except John didn't want to do that. In spite of everything he'd said to Evan and Daniel, he knew deep down that he didn't really want to go back into his nice, safe closet. He wanted more of what he'd tasted with Max.

JOHN ROLLED over in the large bed and peered at the LED alarm clock beside him. It showed 2:00 a.m. in glowing red numerals. He closed his eyes and tried to slip back into the velvety blackness of sleep. Until he heard....

There was no mistaking the sounds that emanated from the room below. Evan and Daniel were having sex.

John's first thought was to stuff his fingers into his ears, because damn it, that was his little *brother* down there. But he couldn't resist. He lay there in the darkness, listening to the muffled low moans and cries that seeped up through the floorboards. There was no doubt who was fucking whom—not that John had ever had any doubts on *that* score—as he listened to Evan begging Daniel to fuck him harder. And it wasn't as if this was John's first exposure to gay sex. Now and again he'd ventured onto the Internet in search of porn—more often when he'd been at university, less frequently now that he was back home with his parents. Straight porn had left him fairly.... He supposed *cold* would be a good way to put it. It certainly hadn't got him stirred up. *And surely* that *should have been a clue.*

But his first look at gay porn... *that* had been a different story. John's skin had tingled and warmth flooded his body as he'd watched two men fuck for the first time. And he'd come within minutes, he'd been so aroused.

Why the hell did it take me so long to admit I'm gay? John had been in denial for nearly two years. Every time he'd had the urge to seek out gay porn, he'd wrestled with himself, pushing down hard until the feelings subsided. And to this day, he had no idea why he'd resisted. Maybe it was because he was afraid his family would think he was copying Evan—though Evan had been out since his late teens. He remembered the day his sixteen-year-old brother had sat there at the kitchen table with their parents, calmly telling them he was gay—and then he recalled his older brother Aaron's expression. Aaron had obviously known. John couldn't deny feeling more than a little hurt that Evan hadn't confided in him—not that he could have stayed hurt for long. Evan had a way of getting under the skin, and John adored him.

That's probably why I've been remembering kissing Daniel that day. I must have really hurt Evan. His brother had been so generous. John hadn't deserved to be treated so kindly, not after he'd treated Daniel so abominably. And then to force himself on Daniel like that, all in the name of experimentation. Kissing Daniel had confirmed in his own mind what he'd tried so long to deny—and continued to deny, even to his brother. *Until today.*

A low cry shattered the silence of the attic bedroom, and John realized that Evan had just come. He reached down under the soft cotton duvet to palm his hard cock. John closed his eyes and focused on Max, the feel of that firm chest under his fingers, those lips pressing insistently against his, that tongue thrusting slowly into John's mouth, that hand squeezing his arse—and Max's voice in his ear, his dirty talk burning him up with the images it created in his head. John had been so incredibly hard. It wouldn't have taken much to have him coming in his pants. As if touching Max hadn't aroused him enough.

John squeezed his cock, but it wasn't enough. He reached out to switch on the lamp and pulled open the bedside drawer. *Bingo*—Sean and Michael had left lube. He worked the pump and coated his hand with the thick liquid and then wrapped it around his now heavy, turgid dick. He pushed up with his hips, sliding his cock through the slick fist, his movements increasing in speed. John pushed out a low moan as he tugged at his dick, Max's image foremost in his mind. He imagined Max carrying out his promise as he insinuated his hand into John's pants and slid a single finger down his crease to circle his hole. John shivered, and his hips bucked with increasing frequency as he arched up off the bed. *Close, so close....* And then that imaginary finger pressed slowly inside him.

With a shudder, John came, his cock pulsing come over his fist, body trembling as his orgasm bulldozed through him, his mouth wide in a silent scream. He lay there as the remnants of his climax slipped from him, dissipating into nothing. He pushed back the duvet and reached for his pants, for the cotton handkerchief his mother had forced him to take that morning. John wiped away the sticky fluid and deposited the sodden handkerchief on the rug beside the bed. He dropped back onto the mattress and stared at the ceiling, his thoughts still on Max.

That was my first real kiss. John was forced to admit that the kiss with Daniel didn't count. Daniel hadn't exactly been a willing recipient, whereas John had been all too eager to accept Max's attentions. He knew the likelihood of ever meeting Max again was extremely remote. No way would he ever go back to Canal Street. The chance of being spotted there was too great a risk. The thought made his heart ache. For a moment, he wondered what sort of life he was condemning himself to. *Do I really want to give this up? When I've only just found out how wonderful it feels to be kissed and held by another man?*

With a sigh, he switched off the light and lay back on the pillows. It didn't matter how wonderful it had felt. On that path lay danger.

CHAPTER 3

JOHN HURRIED along the street, his backpack bouncing against his shoulder blades and his shirt slightly damp with perspiration. He'd meant to arrive much earlier than this, but his intended train had been canceled—goodness knew why. Thank heaven the railway station was fairly close to the school. He paused at the school gate to take a breath. The playground was empty—obviously the school day had already begun—and the only signs of life were the faint murmurings of childish voices that floated through the open windows. John glanced at his watch. It was already nine thirty. *This is going to make a great impression*, he thought gloomily. Now breathing more evenly, he turned in at the gate and went toward the main door, labeled Reception.

John had seen photos of the original school building—built in 1906, all red brick and huge sash windows—but the newest incarnation looked nothing like that. Walls of glass, with a two-level playground. He'd liked the classrooms, which were spacious and well equipped. He pushed open the glass door and turned left to the reception area. A kind-faced woman in her fifties greeted him with a smile.

"Good morning. It's John, isn't it? I remember you from the interview day."

John beamed. "Yes. Thank you for remembering, Mrs.—" He racked his brains for the name of the receptionist, but she waved her hand.

"Oh, I don't expect you to know my name. You were rather busy, I seem to recall." Her eyes twinkled with good humor. "I'm Emily Taylor, and I'll expect you to call me Emily, except in front of the children, of course. Mr. Sanderson is with a parent right now, but please, take a seat and I'll come and get you as soon as he's available." She opened the logbook on the counter in front of her and gave him a pen. As John signed his name and arrival time, she filled out a name badge with a red lanyard bearing the word Visitor. Once he'd hung it around his neck, she indicated the comfy-looking seats facing the reception area. John nodded in acknowledgment and sat down. He'd intended to be there an hour ago. *Bloody trains....* He opened his backpack and took out his notebook. The previous night, he'd written down a list of his requirements. He didn't want to forget anything important.

John couldn't think of anything else he needed to add to his list, so he put down the notebook and looked around at the reception area. The walls were covered with work by the children—pictures, short essays, photos—and the name of the school was emblazoned across a large, colorful banner. Below it was the school's mission statement—it was the acronym TEAM, with the words Together Everyone Achieves More spreading out from it like rays of sunshine.

The low murmur of voices made him turn his head toward the source. Brett Sanderson was walking out of the office with a scruffily dressed young woman, barely in her twenties. Her eyes were wet and reddened. Brett was talking to her in an undertone, but John was able to pick out a little of what was said.

"You did the right thing coming to tell me, Anna. At least we can be extra vigilant, now that we know what to expect." He handed her a tissue, which she took gratefully. She dabbed at her eyes. "And I promise you—if we see *anything* suspicious, we'll call you *and* the police. All right?" His expression was kind.

The young woman sniffed and nodded. "Thanks so much, Mr. Sanderson. 'Ee's a good lickle kid an' 'ee doesn't need this crap in 'is life."

"Agreed," Brett said with a tight smile. "And if you have any more visits like this morning, you *must* go straight to the police. Promise me, Anna." He pinned her with an intense gaze. She nodded, swallowing. John noticed for the first time the darkening skin on her cheekbone. She shook

Brett's hand and gave John a cursory nod as she went to the reception counter to sign out. Brett watched her exit, his expression suddenly sad. When she'd left the building, he turned to John and walked toward him, holding out his hand.

John got to his feet and grasped the hand in a firm shake. "Mr. Sanders—*Brett*." He remembered just in time.

Brett gave him a half smile. "Well saved, John. Come on into my office, and we can talk." He glanced in Emily's direction. "Emily, any chance of some coffee—and maybe the odd biscuit or two?" He winked, and Emily laughed.

"No problem. I might even manage to find those chocolate-covered biscuits you're so fond of."

John couldn't help smiling. There was clearly a rapport between the two. He followed Brett into the large office, which was sparsely furnished. There was a small desk in the corner with a computer monitor and keyboard and a bookcase behind that with lots of box files and folders, but the room was dominated by the large oval wooden table that John remembered from Friday's interview. Two chairs had been pulled out, and Brett sat in one of these. John took the other.

"That sounded pretty serious," he couldn't help commenting.

Brett nodded. "Yes, actually, it was. Anna Meadows has a little boy in Year One, Wayne. He's six years old and the most adorable child. Anna's husband, Carl, has recently been freed from Strangeways Prison and is making life very unpleasant for her. He used to beat her, and she put up with it for far too long, until friends persuaded her to go to the police. When she finally took out a restraining order, things got ugly. He got arrested after a brutal attack on her."

"That's awful," murmured John. "And now he's out?"

Brett dipped his chin. "Carl turned up this morning and tried to force his way into the house. He claimed he wanted to see his son, and Anna wouldn't let him. He managed to land one blow before she was able to call for help. Luckily, her next-door neighbor was home, and he grabbed Carl while Anna fled into the house and called the police." Brett's gaze met John's. "You *did* know about the area when you applied for the job, didn't you? There's a high rate of unemployment here and an equally high rate of crime and drug use."

John knew. "And yet this school manages to provide its pupils with a sound education. I checked out your latest OFSTED report." He smiled. Checking out the government's official schools inspection reports was pretty much standard practice when applying for a job these days.

Brett scowled. "As if spending one-and-a-half days in school is enough to provide the inspectors with an adequate picture of all we do here." He sighed. "School inspections used to be so rigorous. The whole system needs overhauling, if you ask me." He huffed. "Anyway, let me get off my soapbox. Anna came to warn us to keep an eye out for Carl, in case he turns up here and tries to take Wayne."

"Sounds like she's thinking clearly. Have you spoken with Wayne's teacher?"

"I was going to do that as soon as Anna left. You can come with me, if you like. I don't think you met Georgina Bryant on Friday. I'm pretty sure she was out that day." He got to his feet and walked to the door, John following him. Brett led the way along a wide corridor with classrooms on either side. The walls were festooned with colorful work, and there was hardly any space left. A year's effort, displayed for all to see. John knew it would be a case of All Change as soon as the school closed its doors at the end of the week. Displays would be taken down, getting ready for the next academic year.

Brett arrived at the last classroom on the left and peered in through the glass porthole. He smiled. "Story time." He opened the door quietly and slipped inside, John close behind him.

In the corner of the classroom was an area surrounded by bookshelves, and on the floor was a large green carpet, on which were seated about twenty small children. They were staring in rapt attention at the elderly woman who sat in front of them, an open book in her hands. John listened as she related the tale of Kipper, a cute little dog who was searching for his teddy bear. Brett walked across to stand at the edge of the carpet. John stood behind him to one side.

She glanced up at Brett's approach and seemed startled. She recovered quickly and smiled at the class. "Children, look who's come to visit. What do we say?"

Twenty heads swiveled to look in Brett's direction. John was pleased to see the smiles that lit up their faces as they chorused, "Good mor-ning, Mister San-der-son."

"Good morning, children." Brett gave them an affectionate smile. "Now, do you think you can all sit quietly while I talk with Mrs. Bryant?" He gave them an expectant look.

"Yes, Mister San-der-son." The chorus of youthful voices was delightful to John's ears. Mrs. Bryant gave the children a stern look and then got up to join Brett. He spoke with her in whispers, and both turned to look at a little boy who was sitting at the edge of the carpet. John understood Brett's description of Wayne as adorable. The boy had the biggest brown eyes and a shock of curly brown hair. Mrs. Bryant nodded thoughtfully as Brett continued to whisper. At last they parted, and she came back to the carpet to retake her seat. Brett slipped quietly from the room, beckoning for John to follow him.

Brett closed the door behind him and let out a sigh. "So that's done. Let's go have that coffee, shall we?" The two men walked back to the office, and sure enough, a tray with two mugs of coffee and a plate of chocolate biscuits awaited them on the table. They sat down once more, and John took a sip of coffee.

Brett leaned back into his seat and studied John intently. "I'm glad you were able to spend the day with us. By the time we're done, you'll have everything you need to get started in September. I've put together a USB drive with all the information about your class. You'll be taking a Year Six group, and there are twenty-two pupils in the class."

"Will I be able to see them today?"

Brett pursed his lips. "I'd like to say yes, but I can't introduce you to them yet, not until you've cleared the CRB check. Procedures."

John nodded. He'd expected as much. The Criminal Records Bureau check was mandatory for anyone whose work involved contact with children.

"I don't have to remind you about keeping this information safe, do I?"

John shook his head. Most schools had strict rules about letting pupil information pass beyond the school boundaries. "Are there any pupils I need to know about in particular?"

Brett folded his arms across his chest. "There are a few pupils with special needs, and as far as we can, we'll provide a learning support assistant to work with you in the classroom. Their statements are available on the drive, along with detailed notes from their teacher this year. Which brings me to the most important thing we have to discuss."

John looked into Brett's deep brown eyes, which regarded him intently. "Yes?" He wondered what was coming.

Brett took a deep breath. "You've probably noticed that this is a fairly young staff. Georgina Bryant is our most experienced teacher, and she's retiring at the end of the week. Now, she is usually the NQT mentor, but her retirement leaves me with a bit of a problem. The rest of the staff has only been teaching for a couple of years, three at the most. Three years is plenty of experience, but for a newly qualified teacher, I happen to think that calls for a mentor who's been in the classroom for a while."

John was inclined to agree. He wanted his mentor to be able to advise him on anything that might possibly occur—especially as he wanted to pass his newly qualified teacher year with flying colors.

Brett cleared his throat. "So what I am proposing is that I am your mentor for this year."

John widened his eyes. "Will you have enough time for that? Surely as head teacher, your plate is pretty full already."

Brett shrugged. "There isn't an alternative, so we will make the best of it. Normally, that will mean meeting with you once a fortnight and observing you teach as regularly as I can. I'll have two assessments to complete on your progress, the first one being due by Christmas." He peered at John. "I will make it clear now. You are going to pass. Is that understood?"

"Yes," John agreed earnestly. He'd come this far; there was no *way* he was going to fail now.

"Which brings me to your interview lesson." Brett took a drink of coffee.

John jerked his head back. "Was… was there something wrong with it?" His heartbeat quickened, and his stomach churned.

Brett waved his hands agitatedly. "Oh, no, nothing like that, believe me. I'm sorry to have given you that impression."

John sagged into his chair, his mouth suddenly dry. "Then what...."

Brett heaved a heavy sigh. "John, that lesson was nothing short of brilliant." John's mouth fell open. "Your planning was excellent, thorough, and detailed. Your resources were well thought out and beautifully prepared. The pace was perfect, and you planned for a variety of activities. And the children responded to your enthusiasm."

John's cheeks glowed as he listened to this unexpected praise. "Thank you," he murmured.

"But...." John straightened. "My point is, you can't do that every day, John. You'll burn out by Christmas."

John stared in astonishment. "But... if that's what the job requires...." He was at a loss.

Brett shook his head vehemently. "John, you've obviously got what it takes to be a really good teacher. I'm just suggesting that you work to live, not live to work. Don't spend every night and the early hours of the morning in lesson preparation. *And* all the weekend. Try to find the right work/life balance. Do you have any hobbies?"

John certainly hadn't expected this. "Well, I like reading, going to the cinema...." He couldn't think of anything else to offer.

Brett regarded him steadily. "Get yourself some interests. Something that helps you switch off the school brain." He smiled, and John noticed for the first time how it reached his eyes. A genuine smile.

"And do you do the same?" John had to ask. To his surprise, Brett flushed.

"I like to travel," Brett admitted. "During the school holidays, I often visit different parts of the country. I try not to spend the entire week or fortnight chained to my desk. Balance, John."

John nodded. "Balance," he repeated doubtfully. It wasn't something he'd given a lot of thought to achieving. The last four years had been hard work. He'd given his studies 100 percent of his attention, and it had been worth it. Mum and Dad had expected him to work hard, and he hadn't wanted to let them down.

Brett was smiling at him again. "You're going to have an overactive duty gland, aren't you?" John cocked his head, and Brett grinned. "One of those people who don't know when to stop and relax."

God, he's got my number quickly. It was John's chief fault. It occurred to him that Brett was going to be good for him.

As if privy to John's thoughts, Brett quirked his eyebrows. "I'm going to have to keep my eye on you, Mr. Wainwright. I think I need to make sure you don't overdo it." He picked up the plate and held it toward John. "Biscuit?" John took one, and Brett followed suit. "And make the most of these. Emily usually hides the good stuff." Brett winked.

John laughed and then took a bite. He had a feeling things would work out just fine.

BRETT SWITCHED off the monitor and closed the blinds.

"Are you done for the day?" Emily stuck her head around the door. "Because it's almost five thirty and the rest of the staff have gone." She gave Brett a knowing look. "Did it go okay with John?"

Brett shuffled the folders on his desk into a neat pile. "Yes, it went well. I think he'll be good for this place. And it's about time we got a male teacher on the staff." He knew the vast majority of primary school teachers were female, as most males tended to go toward teaching the older students. "Though I'm sure his arrival will cause a few hearts to flutter in the staff room." *Mine included,* he thought wryly.

"Oh, you mean those gorgeous blue eyes, that soft blond hair, that knockout smile?" Emily's eyes sparkled. "Yes, I can see John breaking a few hearts before the first term is over."

Well, he won't be breaking mine. I'll make sure of it. Brett's heart had almost stopped when John had walked into his office last Friday. It had taken every ounce of his willpower to keep a calm exterior when he'd laid eyes on the beautiful young man. Of all the men to walk into his life right now, the last thing he needed was one who was exactly his type. And the more time he'd spent with John, the more he'd come to realize that the gorgeous exterior hid a man of great intelligence, not to mention ability and humor.

"Mary Lacey said his interview lesson was the best she'd ever seen," added Emily. "And coming from her, that's high praise indeed."

Brett chuckled. Mary was usually hard to please when it came to interviews. And Brett's almost instantaneous attraction to John made it doubly important that his was not the deciding voice when it came to John's appointment. Mary had led the vote, and the second governor present, Justin Eldridge, had been equally in favor, so that made things simpler. Brett didn't want to appear too eager to appoint John.

The decision to act as John's mentor was a difficult one. On the one hand, he wanted to make sure John had the support he'd need for the year ahead. But on the other hand, the thought of working closely with the young man, meeting with him, spending time with him…. It was going to be torture. That was the only word for it.

You're going to have to be so careful. You can't let him see how you feel—you know *that, don't you?*

Yeah, Brett knew. He'd spent the last ten years of his career making sure no one guessed that he was gay. And that was the way things had to stay. Even if just *looking* at John made him hard.

Save that for the next trip to Brighton.

Thank God school was nearly done for the year. Brett was in dire need of a week on the south coast, where everyone knew him by a completely different name and he was free to be… free. Out. Gay. The end of term couldn't come fast enough. And maybe putting some time and space between him and his new staff member would make things better. Maybe the coming year wouldn't be as torturous as he was anticipating.

Yeah… right.

CHAPTER 4

"HOW MANY more?" groaned Evan as he got back into the car. He glared at John. "And exactly *what* was wrong with that last one?"

John got into the passenger seat and fastened his seat belt. "Are you serious? Would *you* live there?" He met his brother's glare head-on. "Well?"

Evan shrugged as he pulled away from the curb. "Okay, so it was a little bit on the small side."

John guffawed. "You think? That bedroom was so small you'd have to step outside it to change your mind." He was starting to think this was a waste of a Sunday. He and Evan had looked at five places already, and not one of them was really suitable. He couldn't afford to rent a flat on his own, not on his salary, so he'd been forced to check out the ads in the *Manchester Evening News*. There were several places needing another tenant to share a house, and he'd ringed the six most promising ones. They'd left Daniel at home. He'd voiced the opinion that three people going round these properties might be too much.

John glanced at the folded newspaper on his lap. "Let's make this the last one for today," he suggested. He'd had enough. It was great that Evan had offered to ferry him around in their car, as John didn't have transport yet. *Something else to put in my to-do list*, he thought. At least there was plenty of time. They were barely into August.

"Then it might be a good idea to tell me where we're going, don't you think?" Evan grinned. "Because right now, I'm driving aimlessly."

John chuckled. "Keep going along this road, according to the A to Z." He twisted the street atlas to make sure of his directions. "We're going to turn left onto St. Chrysostom's Road, and the house is on the left." Evan gave a brisk nod and peered at the approaching road signs.

St. Chrysostom's Road turned out to be a quiet little street that overlooked a park. The houses were all large Victorian edifices, with small, neat gardens at the front. *This looks* much *better.*

"Now this is nice," murmured Evan. "We'll have to park in the street, but there are parking bays all the way along." He leaned forward over the steering wheel. "Which number are we looking for?"

"Fourteen," John said after checking the ad. He pointed to an empty parking bay. "There, Ev."

Evan swung the car into the space and switched off the engine. As they got out of the car, he glanced around. "Nice quiet neighborhood," he noted with a satisfied expression. "How far is this one from your school?"

"Maybe a twenty-minute walk." John had tried to find places within walking distance of the school, but nothing *too* close. He didn't want to be forever running into his pupils when he wasn't in school.

They walked up the short path to the heavy front door and rang the bell. Moments later, the door opened and a young man appeared, casually dressed in jeans and a T-shirt. He was possibly in his mid to late twenties, with short black hair and brown eyes. He seemed surprised to see John and Evan.

"Hi, I'm John. I rang about the room." John held out his hand, and the young man took it with a firm shake. "Was it you I spoke with on the phone? Martin?"

"Yeah, that's me. Is it for both of you?" Martin asked with a hesitant smile.

John grinned. "God, no. This is my brother, Evan. He's just my chauffeur for the day."

Martin's face relaxed. "Ah, I see. Come on in." He stepped to one side and let them push past him into the wide hallway with its high ceiling. Evan was looking around with an appreciative expression.

"This reminds me of our house."

John knew what he meant. It was about the same size, with a wide staircase, rooms on both sides of the hall, and what looked like a kitchen at the end of it. "How many bedrooms are there?"

Martin closed the door behind them. "Four, if you don't count the attic."

"It's a beautiful house." John had a good feeling about this one. He only hoped the bedroom lived up to his first impressions.

Martin's smile was definitely less hesitant. "Thanks. It was my grandma's house." He flicked his head toward the stairs. "Want to see the room? I'll have to ask that we keep the noise down. Stuart only got in from New York this morning, and he's sleeping."

John arched his eyebrows. "New York?"

"Yeah, he's a flight attendant with Virgin. He's been away for the last three days, and if he doesn't get some sleep right away, he's a real bear. So we let him sleep as much as he can." Martin led the way up the stairs, John and Evan close behind. At the top of the stairs was a bathroom.

"How many people live here, then?" John whispered.

"Normally there are four of us. Me, Stuart, Den, and Alec. Den's firm moved him to London last month, hence the vacancy."

"All guys?" Evan said under his breath to John. There was that characteristic wicked grin.

Martin opened the second door on the right, and they entered a large, sunny room. John looked around at the double bed, wardrobe, and chest of drawers. Even better—there was a desk under the window. *Perfect.* The room felt spacious, and the large window looked out over the park. John couldn't hold back his smile.

Martin stopped in the middle of the room and turned to face them with a serious expression. "Look, I'd better say something now before we go any further. Stuart, Alec, and I are gay." He met John's startled gaze. "I only say this because it's been an issue with some of the prospective tenants." He kept his face straight and waited for John to speak.

John was lost for words. It was the last thing he'd expected to hear, as Martin hadn't given off any signals. *Or maybe I just don't have a gaydar like Evan.* He opened his mouth and then closed it. Evan chose that moment to step in.

"Oh, trust me, that is *so* not going to be a problem." He winked at Martin, whose face broke into a delighted smile.

"Really?"

Evan nodded and held up his left hand, where his white gold wedding band gleamed in the sunlight. "Uh-huh. We left my husband at home today." His face shone.

Martin grinned. "Husband? Excellent!" He stepped forward and gave Evan a quick hug and then regarded John speculatively. John swallowed, but Evan put his arm around his shoulders.

"You'll have to forgive this one. He only came out a fortnight ago."

"Wow." Martin's eyes widened. "Congratulations. Gay brothers—fantastic!"

John spluttered. "Evan!" He could feel the flush that crept up his chest and neck until his cheeks were glowing. Both Martin and Evan chuckled.

"What—you weren't going to tell him?" Evan seemed incredulous. "Well, if you're going to live here, they should know." He cocked his head to one side. "You *are* going to live here, aren't you? 'Cause you'd be a fool to turn *this* one down." Martin chuckled. Evan turned back to Martin. "Are you in a relationship with either of them? Of course, it might be *both* of them, for all *I* know." He waggled his eyebrows.

Martin almost choked. "Oh, God, no. We're all single."

"Could you make any more noise, Martin?" a voice grumbled.

The three men turned toward the door to see a tall, tanned young man wearing a dark blue silk robe tied around the waist. He ran his fingers through tousled blond hair and yawned widely.

"Oh, sorry, Stu." Martin's expression was extremely apologetic. He gestured toward John. "This is John. He's here to look at the room." John gave Stuart a quick nod.

"An' are you goin' to be movin' in?" Stuart asked, midyawn.

John looked at Evan, who nodded encouragingly. "Yes," John said decisively. Evan was right, of course. This place was perfect.

Evan's smile grew. "Fantastic. Then we'll get out of your hair, Stuart, and let you sleep." Martin murmured in agreement. Stuart groused under his breath and shuffled out of the room.

"He'll be much better when he's had a few more hours," Martin told them. "Let's go downstairs and talk about boring stuff like rent." He led the way, and they traipsed down the stairs, John caressing the polished banister as he did so. The house already felt comfortable.

Ten minutes later, he was sitting in a sunny lounge on a comfy couch with a cup of coffee in his hand. The rent was reasonable, and all the bills were split evenly between the four tenants. There was a landline phone, but it seemed that they shared the line rental, as each of them had a mobile.

"What about food?" John wanted to know. "Do you all have separate shelves in the fridge or something?"

Martin chuckled. "God, that takes me back to being a student." John had to agree. "We each have a cupboard, and we tend to share the cooking. Can you cook?" John nodded. "Oh, that's good. We take it in turns to cook dinner, and we share the bills for that. Anything else you want is up to you. And don't worry about space in the fridge—it's one of those huge American monstrosities. There's *loads* of room."

John took a sip of coffee. "I know Stuart works for Virgin. What about you?"

"I work in a men's clothing store in the city center. I'm the assistant manager."

John was impressed. "And Alec?"

"He's a paramedic. He works out of the Royal Infirmary." Martin regarded him quizzically. "What about you, John?"

"I'm about to start my first teaching job in a primary school in Ardwick."

Martin let out a low whistle. "Ooh, ankle-biters! I don't envy you." He gave a lopsided grin. "So, are you happy with the place?"

John gave a contented smile. "Oh, yes." He could already see himself living in the quiet house, especially if Stuart and Alec were as easygoing as Martin. "Are there any house rules I need to know about?"

"Not really—we're a laid-back bunch, and as you can see, we're well house-trained." Martin's eyes glittered. "However, if you bring a date home, please ensure the rest of us are not subjected to whatever goes on behind closed doors." He winked. "We'll only get jealous."

John gulped. A date? Suddenly, his insides were quivering—just as a warm hand came to rest on his arm. He looked up to see Evan regarding him with affection.

"One thing at a time, eh?" Evan said quietly. "There's no rush."

John gave him a grateful look. No rush. What mattered now was to sort out his move and get settled in before the start of term. *Plenty of time to think about dating when I've been teaching for a while.*

And then he shivered. This was all so new, with so many things waiting just over the horizon to be discovered and experienced.

Yeah. He could wait.

"YOU BEEN watching the parade, Rob?" Tim, the barman, asked Brett as he placed a pint on the bar in front of him.

"Yes. I think there was an even bigger crowd than last year." Tim nodded his agreement and then walked off to the far end of the bar.

Brett loved Pride. The atmosphere in Brighton was electric, and the opportunities for hooking up were so numerous as to be unbelievable. Nevertheless, he avoided the cameras as much as possible. No *way* did he want pictures of him appearing on the news. Not that it was very likely, but Brett didn't believe in leaving anything to chance.

He took a long drink of his pint and surveyed the hotel bar. There were men of all types seated at the tables or standing at the bar. Tim was chatting enthusiastically with a small guy who was leaning toward him in a very telling way. From Tim's body language, Brett could tell the client's interest was definitely reciprocated. And as if to prove him right, Tim suddenly reached across the bar and cupped the guy's face, stroking his cheek gently. Brett couldn't help grinning. He knew who'd be in Tim's bed tonight, with any luck.

"You having a good time, Rob?"

Brett turned around to face Elliott, the hotel owner. He was a tall bald man with a muscular physique. Brett had been coming to Elliott's hotel for more years than he cared to remember, and his response to the name Rob was now deeply ingrained.

"Yeah, thanks. I can't believe I'm going home tomorrow. This week has flown by." Maybe it was a feature of growing old, but it seemed to Brett that his weeks spent in Brighton went faster each time he stayed there.

"And will you be celebrating your last night?" Elliott asked with a cheeky grin.

Brett shook his head and tut-tutted. "You know me *far* too well, Elliott." He knew exactly what Elliott meant by "celebrating." Brett had been *celebrating* every night of his stay so far—and never with the same guy twice. And yes, he'd had been scanning the room in search of anyone who captured his interest. *One last night of freedom before I go back into the closet.* The thought depressed him.

"Just to prove how well I know you," Elliott said in a low tone, "take a look at the guy who's just walked into the bar."

Brett swiveled on his stool to look toward the door—and his heart almost stopped. The tallish man who was glancing toward him could have been John Wainwright. The same soft layers of blond hair, the same piercing blue eyes…. *Oh, baby.*

And then their eyes met. The new arrival stood still and stared at Brett, a slow smile spreading over his face.

"Oh, yeah, do I know *you*," said Elliott with a chuckle as he walked off.

Brett straightened on his stool as the new guest approached, moving in a nonchalant enough manner past tables and chairs, but it was clear where he was headed. Finally, he stood at the bar next to Brett.

Tim was there in seconds, and the guy flashed him a quick glance. "Medium white wine, please." Oh, Brett liked that husky voice. But then those cool blue eyes went back to appraising him.

"Coming right up."

His new friend registered Tim's words with the briefest of nods and then gave Brett his full attention. "Hi." Yeah, that husky voice was definitely doing things to certain parts of Brett's anatomy. "I'm Tony."

"Pleased to meet you, Tony. The name's Rob." Brett gave him a matching slow smile. He wondered what the next few hours would bring. *Better make it a good one*, he thought ruefully. *It has to last you a long time.*

Oh, fuck. It was going to be a long, hard winter. Brett could feel it.

"THERE," TONY gasped as Brett's cock connected with his gland. "Oh, yeah, right there." He groaned and held onto the sheet in tight fistfuls, arse tilted, head dropping to the bed.

Brett dug his fingers into Tony's slim hips and thrust powerfully into him, dick pistoning in and out, their balls slapping together in a wonderfully erotic soundtrack. He grunted as he fucked Tony faster, feeling his body tighten around his shaft. It wouldn't be long now. They'd been fucking for hours. *God, the joys of fucking a guy in his early twenties.* Tony had already come twice and was clearly about to have his third—and final—orgasm. Brett had taken him first in the shower—*God bless the inventor of waterproof lube*—and he had come fairly quickly. Then he had Tony on his back on the thick rug next to the bed, arse in the air as Brett pile-drove into him, Tony crying out hoarsely as Brett nudged his prostate relentlessly until Tony came, his hot seed spattering his face. And finally, they were on the bed, Tony on all fours as Brett pounded his hole, edging closer to his orgasm.

"You have… the most… amazing tight arse," Brett grunted out as he drove into him. "I could… fuck you… like this all night." He closed his eyes and concentrated on the feel of Tony's arse wrapped around his cock, of thrusting into slick, hot tightness. Behind his eyes swam John's face. *Oh, fuck, yeah.* Brett let go and gave in to the hot fantasy. Suddenly, it was John's tight arse he was plowing into with increasing speed, John who was crying out as Brett filled him completely.

"Oh, God, gonna come."

And with those words, the fantasy shattered, and Brett cried out as his cock was gripped in a velvet vise. He pulsed into the condom, feeling Tony tremble as he came all over the bed. Brett dropped low to cover him with his body, their skin slick with perspiration. Tony's breath hitched as he jolted every now and again, as though tiny electric shocks spiked through him. Brett wrapped an arm around Tony's chest and held him close. He loved this part, the feeling of being connected so intimately with another human being.

But it never lasted. Within minutes, Brett was itching to get rid of him.

Why do I always feel like this? Brett longed to preserve that connection for as long as possible, but it was always the same. A quick cleanup and he knew he'd be hustling Tony out the door, even though he knew it made him seem callous and cold. *What will it take for me to want to spend the whole night with a guy?* It wasn't the first time that particular thought had crossed his mind, and he doubted it would be the last. He always gave his sexual partners what they wanted—which in Tony's case had been a damn good fucking—but as yet, no one stirred anything more in him other than the desire to get his rocks off.

Maybe I just haven't met the right guy yet, he mused as Tony stretched out on the bed next to him, unaware that he was about to be asked to leave.

And when will that be? Brett contemplated his hotel room ceiling. Okay, so thirty-three wasn't exactly ancient, but he didn't want to be still doing this another five years from now. *I want* more *than this, damn it.* His chest tightened at the thought. God, yes. Because there had to be more than just fucking. *Had* to be.

CHAPTER 5

DANIEL PULLED up in front of John's new accommodation and switched off the engine. He twisted in the seat to peer through the rear window. "Nope, we didn't manage to lose them," he said with a grin. Next to him, Evan chuckled and then mock-punched his arm.

"Don't forget, those are your parents-in-law you're talking about, and I'll tell."

"Snitch," Daniel murmured but then leaned across and kissed him on the mouth.

"Oh, do I have to be subjected to you two all loved up *all day*?" John said with a groan.

"I'd forgotten—you are so not a morning person." Evan looked positively gleeful.

John climbed out of the backseat of the car, muttering under his breath. "How can you be so wide awake when you got up so early? It's not normal." Mum had awoken him with a cup of tea at some ridiculously early hour and had then advised him to grab a shower before the bathroom got monopolized. The house was full to bursting as Evan and Daniel had stayed the night in order to be ready for the early morning start. Once everyone in the house had washed, dressed, and eaten, the process of loading the large van and Daniel's car with all John's worldly belongings had begun. And once that task had been accomplished, there began the trek from Chester to Manchester, which was about forty-odd miles, Daniel taking the lead.

Evan came around the front of the car and winked. "Trust me—*you'd* be wide awake too, if you'd woken up the way *I* did."

Daniel fixed him with a hard stare. "No sharing, please." But then his face creased into a grin.

John couldn't help his reaction. In spite of his fatigue, he guffawed. "Ooh, glad to see you've learned how to be quieter when you two—"

"John." Evan fired him a warning look, just as his mum and dad walked up behind them, accompanied by his elder brother, Aaron.

"Oh, this looks lovely." His mum stared at the house and smiled. "Do you have a key?"

"Not yet." John had arranged for one of the tenants to be home. "You know, as nice as it is to have you and Dad bring all my stuff in a van, you didn't have to, you know. I'm sure Ev, Daniel, and I could have managed on our own." But it *had* been nice to have his parents, brothers, and Daniel helping him. Too bad he hadn't been able to say good-bye to his twin sisters, Penny and Emily. They were on holiday after finishing their first year at university. At least he'd Skyped with them the previous evening.

"Nonsense," Christine Wainwright huffed. "You'll need all the hands you can get to unload everything. And besides, I wanted to see where you'd be living."

"What she *really* means is, she wanted to make sure you took everything of yours before she turns your bedroom into her new craft room." His dad's characteristic cheeky grin warmed John.

"Sam!" His mum looked shocked. "That's not true. I   "

"Oh, come off it, Mum." Aaron joined in the fun. "You've been waiting for this day for *years*. All those lumbering, untidy boys, finally out of your hair." He winked at John. "Now you've got sweet, tidy Penny and Emily all to yourself." His blue eyes twinkled.

John looked around at his family and smiled. He was a lucky man. Growing up with two brothers and two sisters had meant life had never been quiet, but it had always been enjoyable.

"I see you brought a small army of helpers with you."

Stuart appeared at the front gate, a wide smile across his face. John shook his hand and performed brief introductions. "Are any of the others here?"

Stuart shook his head. "Martin got called into work on his day off. He's not best pleased. And Alec's at the hospital today. You'll meet him tonight. We'll be cookin' dinner, by the way. Can't drop you in it on your first day." He grinned.

"I hope it won't be an inconvenience," Sam interrupted, "but we're taking John out to dinner this evening."

John stared. "You are?"

His mum laughed. "Surprise! We wanted to have a final meal with all of us together." She fixed Evan with a firm stare. "And that includes you two. We haven't seen much of you since the wedding."

"Ooh, nice." Evan was bouncing until Daniel laid a hand gently on his arm. John watched his brother calm almost immediately. He smiled to himself. Daniel was exactly what Evan needed, it seemed.

"That's fine," Stuart said with a grin. "We'll break him in some other time."

John looked toward the van and Daniel's car with a sigh. "No putting it off any longer. Let's get to work."

STUART APPEARED at the bedroom door and surveyed the chaos. "I've just put the kettle on for tea, and there's a whole pot of fresh coffee in the kitchen if anyone wants some. Evan and Daniel are sorting out drinks for everyone."

"Oh, what a nice young man." Christine straightened from her task of inserting John's duvet into a new cover and smiled at Stuart, whose cheeks flushed. "John says you work for Virgin. That must be an interesting job, flying to all those different destinations."

Stuart gave a half smile. "Yeah, but it can be knackerin' at times too."

"Where do you want these books, John?" asked Aaron as he and Sam came into the room, loaded down with two heavy-looking boxes.

John gestured toward the bookcase to the right of the fireplace. "Just put them down over there. I'll sort them out later." He was busy putting his rowing machine back into working order. Fortunately, it could stand upended when not in use. "Is there much left in the van?"

"Nope, these are the last two boxes." Aaron dropped the box onto the floor in front of the bookcase and then straightened, rubbing his back. He glanced around the room, and his eyes widened. "Aren't you finished sorting everything out up here yet?" There was a wicked glint in his eyes.

Whatever words John had been about to utter died on his tongue as Evan and Daniel entered the room bearing a couple of trays with mugs of tea and coffee. Everyone grabbed a mug and sat down. John made sure his mum got the armchair, however. Stuart sat cross-legged on the rug beside the bed.

"How long have you lived here?" inquired Sam. He was sitting on the bed with Aaron. Evan and Daniel were on the floor in front of the defunct fireplace.

"Three years," he replied. "Martin inherited the house from his grandma and wanted to live here, but he didn't want to live on his own. I saw an advert he put up on the notices board in Via Fossa." Sam's brow furrowed, and Stuart explained. "It's a bar on Canal Street where I go drinkin' now and again."

"Ah." Evan grinned. "I was wondering how Martin managed to find tenants who were all gay."

Stuart laughed. "Yeah, but when Den moved out he decided to advertise in the *Evening News*. That was a mistake—he should've stuck with Via Fossa."

"Why?" Christine wanted to know.

"'Cause the first three or four prospective tenants looked great—until they found out we were all gay. Then they suddenly changed their minds." Stuart scowled. "You think things are gettin' better, but...." His words trailed off as he stared into his coffee mug. He shrugged. "Anyway, that doesn't matter now, 'cause we got ourselves another gay guy after all, didn't we?" He winked at John—who paled.

There was a sudden silence. Three heads turned in his direction. Three pairs of eyes focused on him.

Aaron cleared his throat. "Something you want to tell us, John?" He was smirking.

Oh, God. John had wanted to tell them in his own time. *Well, too late for that now.*

Stuart looked around with a puzzled expression, and then his eyes widened. "Oh, hell. Did I just out you?" He gave John an extremely apologetic look. "Oh, John, I'm so sorry. I thought they knew. Martin said you'd come out and—"

John held up his hand. "It's okay, Stuart, really." He turned to face his parents and took a deep breath. "Mum, Dad, I…." For a moment, words failed him. It had been so much easier with Evan and Daniel.

"Son, it's all right." His dad's voice was quiet. "It's not like we haven't been expecting it."

John's mouth dropped open. "What?"

His mum smiled at him. "John, we've suspected it for years. We did think we'd got it wrong when you started going out with that girl in your first year at university—what was her name?"

"Clare," volunteered Aaron. "Yeah, but she didn't last long."

John was amazed. He'd been struggling for two years with this internal confusion as to his sexuality—and his family had known for longer than that. Clare had been his first girlfriend, and it had been a pleasant enough experience, going out with her. He'd finally lost his virginity, but sex had been vaguely unsatisfying. When they'd separated amicably after about six months, John had been in no hurry to find another girlfriend. There had been a few girlfriends throughout his degree course, but nothing serious. He kept waiting for the sex to get better, but it never did, and he'd arrived at the conclusion long ago that he must have an extremely low sex drive. Until he'd seen gay porn and that was that.

At last, he found his voice. "You… you knew?" Evan and Daniel were regarding him with matching sympathetic expressions. His parents didn't seem unhappy about the news. And as for Aaron, he just looked smug.

His mum got to her feet and came to where he was sitting on the rowing machine. She held out her arms, and he stood up and walked into them. She hugged him tightly. "Love you, darling," she whispered into his ear. John wrapped his arms around her and hugged her closely. When she let go of him, she stepped back and gave him a warm smile. "I suppose I should say congratulations." She laughed. "You'd think I'd be better prepared, having been through this once with Evan."

"Yeah, but with Evan, you had no time to react." Aaron snickered. "He was just 'Mum, Dad, I'm gay—is there any more toast?'" Everyone laughed. Aaron got up off the bed and grabbed John in a tight hug. "Congrats, little brother." He winked. "At least you have Evan and Daniel for advice." He released him and sat back on the bed with a grin.

His dad snorted. "And the rest of their household." He met John's gaze. "Let's face it. With three gay couples in one house, you'll never be short of someone to turn to. And at least you'll be nearer to him now."

Stuart beamed. "You have the most amazin' family, John. I really envy you. If you could've seen what happened in *my* house when I told my family I was gay...." His face clouded over briefly, but then he shook himself. "Anyway, that's over now."

John could only stare at his family and new housemate in stupefied silence. He was such a lucky man.

"I COULDN'T eat another thing," groaned John, pushing away his plate. "That was wonderful." He beamed at his parents. "However did you find this place?"

His dad tapped the side of his nose. "Contacts, son. I asked around some of my customers who knew Manchester well. When I said I was looking for a good Italian restaurant, three or four mentioned this place." He gave a huge sigh of satisfaction and patted his belly. "I must thank them next I see them."

John glanced around at the busy restaurant. He loved the quiet, unobtrusive jazz that was playing in the background and the candles on every table, flickering in red flowers sculpted from glass. The service had been great too. Their waiter had been very attentive.

"That was delicious," Evan said with a contented sigh. He was seated on John's left, with Daniel at his side. The pair held hands on the table. John was pleased for his brother. Evan seemed blissfully happy with Daniel, so happy that it made John's heart ache. *That could be me one day*, he mused as he watched Daniel lean close and whisper in Evan's ear.

"Would you like to see the dessert menu?" Their waiter had appeared once more and gazed around the large table at the contented group.

Aaron rubbed his hands together. "Oh, yeah, bring it on."

His mum stared at him in amazement. "Do you have a tape worm or something? Where do you *put* it all?"

"Ew, Mum!" Aaron curled his lip. "What a thing to say at the table."

"Yeah, but she's only voicing what the rest of us have been wondering for years." His dad chortled. "The day *you* left home, our food bills were halved, I swear." He winked at the others and then turned to the waiter. "Yes, please. *Some* of us will be having dessert, apparently."

The waiter—Alex, according to his name badge—grinned and then looked down at Evan and Daniel's joined hands. "*Nice*," he mouthed. The couple returned his grin. Alex walked off to fetch some menus.

John shook his head. "Are you two a magnet for *every* gay guy in the vicinity?"

Evan winked. "No—only the cute ones." Daniel tightened his grip on Evan's fingers, and he yelped. "Hey! He's cute—admit it!"

Daniel eased off. "So he's cute—*you're* a married man." He leaned across and kissed Evan on the cheek.

"Sweetie, I may be married, but that doesn't mean I can't appreciate the floor show."

John caught Alex's eye as he handed out menus to everyone. Alex's cheeks flushed bright red, and he lowered his gaze. He stood there while Aaron and Sam perused the menu. When they finally decided on the tiramisu, Alex collected the menus and an order for coffees. John watched him walk toward the kitchen. Alex moved gracefully, in spite of his height—he had to be at least six feet tall.

"Do you find yourself noticing guys more?" asked Evan quietly.

John nodded. "It seems everywhere I look there are the most gorgeous men." He gave a tight smile. "And look is all I'm going to do—for the time being."

Evan grasped his hand. "I know what you said about playing it safe, but don't shut out your feelings. If you meet someone you're attracted to, you should go with it, explore it. Life is too short, bro. We all need to find someone to help us through it." He smiled and then gestured toward Alex with a flick of his head. "Did you like him, for instance?"

John chuckled. "Stop it. You're not going to match me up with someone, is that understood?" Evan pouted. "And besides, I think Alex is spoken for. He's wearing a collar. I saw it under his shirt."

Evan's eyes widened. "You know about collars?" His fingers reached toward his neck.

John regarded him with affection. "Yes, little brother. And you don't have to say anything. I've already worked it out about you two." He clasped their joined hands. "It's okay. It's not my thing, but it plainly works for you. I'm glad Daniel is such a good fit for you."

Evan's face was wreathed in a huge smile. He opened his mouth to speak, but Aaron interrupted him.

"When you two have finished whispering over there, and before our desserts arrive, I'd like to propose a toast—if we still all have drinks." All eyes were on him. Aaron picked up his wineglass. "To John. Congratulations on finally leaving the nest for good—and coming out at the same time." His eyes twinkled with good humor.

"To John." His family repeated the toast and raised their glasses. Everyone took a drink.

John acknowledged their wishes with a shy smile. "Thank you so much for all you did today. And for being the most fantastic family." He gazed around the table. "I am so lucky to have you all."

"Good luck to you, son, in your new career." His dad raised his glass. "You're doing what you always wanted to do. You already know it's going to be a demanding job. We wish you every success with it and hope it brings you a lot of satisfaction. Heaven knows, you deserve it."

John's throat tightened. The love in his dad's voice was overwhelming. He tried to take a sip of his wine, but suddenly, it was difficult to swallow.

Evan released his hand and leaned close. "Love you, bro. You know where we are if you ever need us. You're going to be busy once term starts, and you'll need time to get used to the job. But we're only a phone call away."

John smiled. Evan was telling him in his own way that he and Daniel were going to let him get on with his life. It was comforting to know he had backup if he ever needed it.

He couldn't wait to start his new life.

JOHN TOOK a sip of coffee and sagged into the comfy couch with a sigh. *Peace and quiet at last.*

"Families." Martin snickered. "They're great when they're around, but it can be bliss when they leave."

John laughed. "I was just thinking how nice and quiet it was." It was nine in the evening, and Stuart had already gone to bed. He was off early in the morning on the New York run again. John's parents and Aaron had left an hour ago, and Evan and Daniel had only just gone.

The lounge door opened, and a shortish young man with curly brown hair and green eyes came in, dressed in a red toweling robe. He smiled as he caught sight of John. "You must be the new guy." He held out his hand. "I'm Alec. Sorry I wasn't here to meet you earlier, but my shift just finished." His eyes lit up when he saw their mugs. "Ooh, there's coffee." He scooted out of the room in a hurry.

Martin laughed. "The coffee machine belongs to Alec. You wouldn't believe how many different types of coffee there are in the fridge. You name it—he drinks it." Alec rejoined them, this time with a large mug of coffee in hand. He plonked himself down into the rocking chair by the fire and let out a contented sigh.

Martin chuckled. "How was the shift, Alec?"

The light in Alec's eyes died. "Don't ask, okay? We had to attend a fire in Moss Side." He stared at the floor.

Martin winced. "Bad?" Alec nodded somberly. "Sorry. Let's change the subject."

Alec gave a slight shrug. "Part of the job, I know. You'd think I'd be used to it by now."

"The fact that it still upsets you just proves that you care." John couldn't keep quiet.

Alec gave him a grateful smile. "Thanks for that. I try to switch off my feelings when I'm on the job—you can't treat people efficiently if you're emotionally involved—but it's hard sometimes." His eyes hardened. "And what made this case worse was that it was arson."

Both John and Martin inhaled sharply.

"Oh, God." Martin peered intently at Alec. "You need a hug, mate?"

Alec looked at him in silence for a moment and then nodded. Martin got up from the armchair and knelt beside the rocking chair. He wrapped his arms around Alec and simply held him. John saw Alec put his head on Martin's shoulder and close his eyes. The two men made no sound. After a minute, Alec pulled away.

"Thanks, Martin," he said softly. He met John's concerned gaze. "Sorry. It doesn't happen often, but—"

"Please, don't apologize," John interjected. "I think it's great that you have people supporting you when you need it." It gave him a warm feeling. This was going to be a good place to live.

Martin returned to his armchair and picked up his coffee. "How much longer now until term starts?" he asked John.

"Only a couple of weeks. This summer has really flown."

Alec let out a quiet laugh. "Oh, I remember when I first started working full-time. It was such a shock to the system. No more long summer holidays as a student. Getting up early. Working late." He grinned at John. "You have all this to come, John."

John groaned. "Are you *trying* to depress me?" His housemates chuckled. Then John winked. "But I still get the summer holidays, remember? Teacher?"

Martin laughed. "Nice one, John." He drained his coffee mug. "We'll draw up a new dinner rota now you're here. We can sort that out when Stu gets back, though." He glanced at Alec and tilted his head. "What are you thinking about, Alec? You've got this little secretive smile going on."

Alec gave a guilty start. "Don't know what you mean." His cheeks looked hot. John was instantly intrigued, as was Martin, apparently.

"Oh, come on. Something's up."

Alec grinned. "Well, there's this new guy just started on my shift...."

Martin guffawed. "I *knew* there was a guy involved somewhere. Is he cute?"

"Cute, gorgeous, *so* sexy—and straight." Alec let out a heavy sigh. "Why are all the best ones straight?" John and Martin chuckled. "So I'm checking the ambulance with him, showing him the ropes…."

Martin burst out into a peal of laughter. "And I know *exactly* what ropes you'd *like* to be showing him."

Alec's cheeks flamed. "Martin! Don't go giving away my secrets— it's John's first night, for God's sake. Give him a while before he finds out what a degenerate I really am." He winked at John, who felt his cheeks heat up. He could guess to what Martin was referring.

"*Anyway*," Alec continued. "As I was saying… I was showing him how we restock the ambulance and go through the checking procedure, and I couldn't help noticing he had the most beautiful blue eyes." He sighed once more. "I could drown in those eyes."

Martin gave him a fond look. "Down, boy. And remember your number one rule—don't shit where you eat."

Alec glared at him, though John could tell it wasn't heartfelt. "Do you have to spoil it? Can't I at least have my little fantasies?"

"You can have whatever you want, hon." Martin smiled. "I just don't want you to get hurt, that's all."

John watched the interaction between his new housemates with interest.

I'm going to like living here.

CHAPTER 6

"YOU MUST be John."

John turned around from his task of brewing a cup of tea to address the speaker. A young woman dressed smartly in a gray skirt and white blouse stood behind him. He took her outstretched hand and shook it. "Guilty as charged. And you are…?"

"Bev Waverley. I teach Year Five." She pushed a lock of long brown hair behind her ear.

John grinned. "So you're the one I have to thank for all the info on my new class." He'd spent the last week poring over the notes on the USB drive, trying to remember as much as possible about his new charges.

Bev's grin matched his. "Guilty as charged." They both chuckled. "I thought I was the only early bird around here—with the exception of Brett, of course. No one gets here before him in the morning." She leaned closer and spoke in an undertone. "Personally, I think he sleeps here. He might even be one of those bat-like creatures, you know, from that episode of *Dr. Who*? Where all the teachers slept hanging from the ceiling in the head teacher's office?"

John let out a giggle. Somehow, he couldn't picture Brett Sanderson as some bat-like creature. "As for me being an early bird, enjoy it while it lasts. I couldn't sleep last night. First day nerves, I suppose." He glanced around at the staff room, empty but for the two of them. The little kitchen area was furnished with a kettle, microwave, and fridge-freezer, along with a few cabinets containing mugs and plates. He'd brought his own mug from home, a present from Evan and Daniel. It was an insulated mug bearing the words Keep Calm and Carry On Teaching.

Bev's expression became sympathetic. "You'll be fine," she assured him. "I hear on the grapevine that you're a knockout in the classroom."

John felt his stomach roll over. "What?"

Bev smiled. "It's a small school, and word gets around fast. Apparently, you were very impressive on your interview."

Talk about piling on the pressure. John swallowed. "Oh, I don't know about that."

"And modest too. Nice." Bev gave him an appreciative look. John wondered briefly if he was reading too much into it. *Maybe she's just being friendly.*

"I see you've already met one of your new colleagues." Brett appeared next to them, holding out a large mug with a smiley face on it. "I don't know if Bev told you, but all the staff pay toward the tea and coffee supplies. Emily Taylor is in charge of buying, and she'll let you know each half term how much you need to pay." He gave Bev a polite nod. She smiled and left the room.

"Fine. I wasn't sure how things worked, so I brought my own this morning." John couldn't see himself getting through the day without tea or coffee.

Brett glanced at him approvingly. "Good man." He went to the coffee machine, already bubbling away, and helped himself to a mug. "I usually get here first in the morning, so I put on the coffee. Glad to see I'm not the only one who thinks it's important to arrive here in plenty of time."

That did it. John was determined to make sure he got to school early every day—even if it killed him. "Do you have a staff meeting before school?"

"Yes. We meet in here at eight thirty, and I run through any notices first. Then staff members get to add things that need to be noted. The bell rings at 8:50 a.m., and by that time, you'll be out there in the playground, waiting to line up your class." Brett gazed at him intently. His voice softened. "Are you ready for your first day? Any nerves?"

John was about to reply that he was fine, but he thought better of it. Brett needed him to be truthful. "Yes, if I'm honest." He swallowed. A few hours more sleep would have helped, but that wasn't to be. He'd tossed and turned half the night.

Brett regarded him for a moment, saying nothing. Then he smiled.

"Nerves are good," he said at last. "If you'd breezed in confidently I would have been more concerned. I know you want to do a good job." He glanced up at the clock on the wall. It was seven forty-five. "How about we go to your classroom and you can show me what you have planned for the day. I can take a look and offer any suggestions, if needed."

John heaved a grateful sigh. "Thank you. That would be good." He tried to ignore the empty feeling in the pit of his stomach.

Brett's smile reached his eyes. "I was going to do this anyway. Did you think I'd leave you to fend for yourself on your first day?" He rolled his eyes. "I'm not an ogre." He speared John with another intense look. "I'm here to help you, John. Please remember that. It's my job to make sure you have everything you need to get you through this year. My door is always open to you—it is to *all* my staff—but as my NQT, you are a priority. Is that clear?"

John took a calming breath and then nodded. "Yes, Brett." It was reassuring to know his head teacher had his back.

That great smile was back. "In that case, let's go look at your planning, shall we?" He gestured toward the staff room door. "After you."

John led the way out of the staff room, his legs shaking.

Just let me get through today without screwing up, he prayed silently.

JOHN WALKED around the classroom, watching the class as they concentrated on a quick maths test designed to gauge their levels of ability. It was almost break time, and John badly needed a cup of coffee. The morning had passed smoothly enough, but he had the impression of the calm before the storm. *Maybe they're all too shocked at seeing a new face*, he mused. There had certainly been some surprised looks when he had lined up the children that morning. He was waiting for the eruption he felt sure was coming. *It can't be* this *easy*, he surmised.

He glanced at the clock. Time was nearly up. Some of the kids seemed to breeze through the work. Reassuringly, they were the ones he'd expected to find it easy. He had a seating plan on his desk with photos of each child and brief notes on levels. He'd tried to make sure each table had a mixture of ability levels, the theory being that the stronger pupils would aid the weaker ones. The learning support assistant, Mandy, had arrived promptly at 8:50 a.m. and introduced herself. She would be working as LSA with three pupils in his class, and he'd arranged for them all to be seated together with her. John had drawn up detailed notes for what he wanted her to be doing with the kids, and he was encouraged to see her respond positively to these. It hadn't been like that on his first teaching practice. The LSA at his first placement had sat next to one child and done virtually nothing the entire time.

"Okay, children. Time to put your pencils down." As soon as he'd spoken, Mandy started to collect in the papers, and he could see her checking that names had been written on each sheet. *Oh, good, she's efficient.*

A mixture of happy sighs and groans greeted his announcement.

"Sir, I 'aven't finished. Can't I 'ave more time?"

John walked up to the boy who had uttered this last question. He leaned down to speak quietly. "Philip, at the end of this year and when you go to secondary school next year, you'll have exams to do. There will be time limits on them. The aim of this test is to get as much done as you can to the best of your ability. It will show me where I can help you to make more progress. Okay?"

Philip thought about this for a moment and then nodded. "Yeah, that's what Miss Waverley said last year too." He gave John a look of satisfaction, and John felt absurdly as if he'd just passed some sort of private test. Then Philip frowned. "I find maths dead 'ard, sir." He bit his lower lip.

John smiled at him. "Then we'll have to see what we can do to help you improve your maths skills." Philip regarded him in silence for a few seconds and then nodded once more. John looked up to see if Mandy had collected all the papers. She gave him the thumbs-up. Once more, he glanced at the clock. "Okay, children, stand up please and put your chairs under your desks. Quietly, though."

The room was filled with the sound of chairs scraping over the floor as children got to their feet, eager for their break. When the noise level grew too high, John raised his hand. "Five… four… three…." As he counted down, he lowered his arm, and soon the noise level dropped as all eyes focused on his hand. By the time he reached zero, the room was quiet. John gave them an approving look and then walked to the door that opened onto the playground. The bell rang, shattering the peaceful silence, and John grinned. "Break time." He opened the door and hurriedly stepped out of the way.

Twenty faces broke into happy smiles as the children dashed out into the sunshine. John collected his mug from behind his desk and headed for the staff room. *God, I need a coffee.*

The small staff room was already full by the time he got there. Bev caught his eye and gestured for his mug. He smiled gratefully and handed it to her. There were six or seven people present. Bev brought him a mug of coffee, and he took a quick sip.

"Not everyone is here," she said. "There are two members of staff on break duty in the playground, and Brett will be out there too. He's out there every day."

John was impressed. Having seen two primary schools in operation, he'd gotten used to the head teachers hiding themselves away in their offices, with not much of a presence around the school. *Maybe they were the exception—or is it Brett?* John's first impressions of the head were extremely favorable. His advice that morning had been practical and precise when he'd looked over John's detailed planning. And John had to admit the man knew his stuff. He wasn't surprised Brett had risen to the height of head teacher so quickly. He estimated him to be in his early to midthirties, which was young for someone in his position.

"Do I have a duty day?" John asked. There was so much he still needed to know. He had to remind himself that it was only the first day. *Breathe, John, breathe.*

Bev nodded. "The duty list is up on the noticeboard. You'll always be on duty with another member of staff." She smiled. "You never know—you might end up doing a duty with me." That smile widened, and then she walked over to talk to Mandy.

"Finding your feet, John?"

John turned. Next to him was an attractive woman, short blond hair and eyes so startlingly blue they had to be lenses. "Michelle Fielding. I teach Year

Two." She grinned at him. "I see you've survived the morning. Always a good sign."

"So far." It was disconcerting that everyone seemed to know his name and he knew hardly anyone. Then something occurred to him. "Michelle, are there any other male members of staff here, apart from me and Brett?"

She shook her head. "You're something of a rarity around here." She winked. "Not to mention the fact that you're *very* easy on the eye. You're going to be a popular boy."

John groaned internally. *Oh, hell….* He took a drink of his coffee and glanced around the room. Now he could spot the approving looks of his female colleagues more easily. It was beginning to feel as if he were a gazelle who had innocently wandered into the path of a pride of lions, because there was definitely something predatory in *some* of those glances…. He gulped.

Michelle let out a wry chuckle. "You're safe—for the moment. But just wait 'til the staff Christmas do. You'll have *so* many girls clamoring to dance with you."

"What about Brett? Doesn't anyone get to dance with him?" John could see the female staff wanting to dance with the head. At about five feet eleven, with dark brown hair and brown eyes, a firm jawline, and wide across the shoulders, Brett was very attractive. And hadn't *that* thought crossed John's mind once or twice the day he'd spent in the school with Brett.

Michelle looked thoughtful. "Interesting that you should ask that. Brett's really good with the staff, don't get me wrong—he has a great manner about him and he's easy to talk to—but when it comes to Brett the man? He doesn't give much away. And he certainly *doesn't* dance with us at parties." She shrugged. "Maybe that's the sign of a good head teacher. He doesn't get too familiar with his staff." She glanced at her watch. "Oops. Time to get the kids back inside." She gave John a warm smile. "Glad to meet you, John. I dare say we'll have the chance to chat later. Good luck with the rest of your morning." She gave him a brief nod, left her mug in the sink, and walked out of the staff room.

John watched her exit, deep in thought. He hadn't expected to be the only male teacher on staff. Then an idea stopped him dead in his tracks. He assessed Michelle's remarks about him being popular among the staff. *What if one of them asks me out? What the hell do I say?* John couldn't believe he'd never considered the possibility before. It was as if being gay had put blinkers on him. Just because *he* had no interest in the opposite sex, he'd automatically assumed *they'd* have no interest in him. Well, not according to Michelle….

God, John, could you be more naïve?

He saw the time and quickly drained the rest of his coffee. *Time to go back into battle.*

JOHN SANK into his chair at the desk and dropped his head back against the wall. *What a day….*

"You survived, then." Brett was standing in the doorway, holding two mugs. John could smell the aromatic coffee. He straightened immediately and tried looking more alert.

Brett smirked. "Relax, John, you've earned it." He walked in, handed John a mug, and then perched on the edge of the desk. John could smell the woodsy aroma of his cologne. It was a warm, sensual fragrance.

Brett regarded John closely. "You did well today."

John looked up from his mug in surprise. "I did?"

Brett chuckled. "You were so busy with your class that you didn't even notice each time I stopped to have a look what was going on in here." His eyes danced with amusement. "I must have walked past this room about seven or eight times, and you were oblivious."

"Really?" *Wow, talk about focused.* "So it looked okay in here?"

Brett grinned. "You get a gold star." For some reason, this tickled John, and he smiled shyly. He took a sip of his coffee and let out a low moan. Brett chortled. "You're honored. This is my personal supply. I'm sorry, but life is too short for instant coffee."

"Oh, a man after my own heart." No sooner were the words out of his mouth than John regretted them. It felt a little too personal. But one look at Brett's features allayed his fears. Brett had clearly taken no offense. He took a drink of coffee and peered intently at John.

"So, any issues crop up today that you think need to be addressed?"

John puffed out his breath. "To be honest, I'll have a clearer picture after I've marked these." He gestured to the pile of papers sitting on his desk. "They did tests today in maths and English, and I got to hear some of them read." He frowned. "There are some kids in here with very poor reading skills, considering their age." All the children were nine years old, going on ten.

Brett nodded. "And there lies the crux of the problem. We ask parents and carers to hear their children read every day, but in a lot of cases, it's just not happening."

"I don't understand. Don't they *want* their children to make progress?" It confounded the hell out of John.

Brett's expression became sad. "You have to understand that in the majority of cases, the parents have poor literary skills too. They leave school having gone through it all in a blur, gaining few or, in some cases, no qualifications. Then the girls get pregnant in an effort to leave home and get into a council house."

It wasn't the first time John had come across this issue, but the number of kids who seemed to be in this position was alarming. "I just keep thinking of ways to help them bring their reading along, but success requires a modicum of support from the parents." He'd already begun to put together a list of parents he wanted to contact. He tapped the list with his index finger. "This has to be my starting point if I am going to change anything for these pupils."

Brett's eyes glowed with approval. "And this is why you're going to be a damn good teacher—because you care about their future." He glanced around the room at the tidy tables, the cleaned whiteboard. "John, are you ready for tomorrow? Lessons planned, resources prepared?" John nodded. "Then take my advice—go home. It's five o'clock. Day over." He speared him with an intense look. "Am I making myself clear?"

John let out a sigh. "Yes, sir."

Brett's eyes gleamed. "Good boy." He got to his feet and headed for the door but paused at the threshold and turned to face John, a wry smile in place. "Finish your coffee first, though. It would be a shame to waste it." And with that he was gone.

John leaned back and took a long drink of the delicious coffee. And then he smiled.

I got a gold star.

JOHN TURNED the key in the door and stepped heavily into the hallway. The walk home had sapped what little energy he had left, and he was ready to drop onto the couch and veg out the rest of the evening. Alec spotted him as he came out of the kitchen and grinned.

"Now *there's* a man in dire need of a drink."

John groaned. "Alec, I love you."

Alec guffawed. "Sorry, sweets, you're not my type, and besides, it's cupboard love. But I'll get you a cold glass of white wine anyway." He winked and then disappeared back into the kitchen.

John smiled to himself as he dropped his backpack in the hall and staggered into the lounge. The couch looked really inviting, and he collapsed onto it. He leaned back against the plump seat cushions and closed his eyes.

"Oh, no you don't."

John opened one eye and peered at Alec, who stood there, glass in hand. "Whaaa?"

"If you close your eyes now, you'll be asleep in minutes. And then you'll miss the delicious dinner that Stu made to celebrate your first day."

That had him sitting up. "He did? Wow. That's really nice." John couldn't get over how easily he'd slipped into life there. It was as if he'd known his three housemates for a good deal longer than a mere few weeks. "What's he made?" He sniffed eagerly, trying to get an idea. There was a hint of garlic in the air, and maybe beef. Suddenly, John grinned. "He made lasagna."

Alec chuckled. "Got it in one. Dinner will be ready in about thirty minutes. We weren't sure what time to expect you." He glanced at the clock over the fireplace. "Earlier than this, maybe." He tut-tutted. "First day and you're already overdoing it."

"Oh, it gets worse, believe me," John said with a sigh. "I have marking to do before tomorrow."

"Markin'? Already?" Stu came into the lounge and frowned at John. "This doesn't bode well." He dropped into the armchair, a glass of wine in hand.

John kicked off his shoes and moaned as he flexed his feet. *God, they ache.* "Whoever thinks teachers spend their lives sitting at a desk has obviously never been inside a classroom recently."

Alec's face lit up. "Stu, go do your stuff."

John cocked his head as Stu put down his glass and came over to the couch. He sat cross-legged on the floor in front of John and took hold of his left foot. "Stu, what the hell are you—*ooh, my God*, that's good." He couldn't hold in the low moan of pleasure as Stu expertly manipulated his foot, kneading the ball and flexing his ankle joint. "*Oh*, don't stop."

Stu laughed. "These guys *love* my foot rubs. I get to spend a lot of my time on my feet during a flight, and you soon learn the trick to a damn good rub. I was shown this by a guy I worked with a couple of years ago. Whenever we were laid over, everyone in the cabin crew would clamor for one of Geoff's famous foot rubs. We'd descend on his hotel room en masse."

"I've changed my mind," John gasped out. "Stu, I love you more."

Alec huffed. "See what I mean? Cupboard love." But he grinned. "I'll see to dinner, Stu—you just concentrate on rubbing John's feet." He got up and exited the room. Stu said nothing but continued to work his magic with John's poor, tired feet.

John eased back into the couch and let out a sigh of satisfaction. What a perfect end to his first day.

CHAPTER 7

"THANKS FOR coming in, Mrs. Welsh." John indicated the empty chair facing his desk and the young woman sitting in it, her face frozen in a mask of indifference. "I wanted to talk to you about Kimberley's reading progress."

"What about it?" Mrs. Welsh's lips narrowed. "That's *your* job, isn't it—to teach 'em to read? What's it got to do wi' me?" She folded her arms across her chest and stared resolutely at him. She could only have been about twenty-six, maybe twenty-seven. She was dressed in black leggings and a pink sweatshirt, with a few gold chains around her neck and several heavy rings on each hand. Across her knee, she draped her black leather jacket.

John bit back a sigh of exasperation. It wouldn't have been so bad if Mrs. Welsh's attitude was atypical of the parents he'd met so far. Unfortunately, it was fast becoming the norm.

"Kimberley presently has a reading age of six years and one month. Now, if she's going to stand any chance of coping in high school next year, then we need to work on that."

"What's this *we* crap?" Mrs. Welsh glared at him. "I keep tellin' yer, it's nowt to do wi' me."

John silently counted to five in his head before continuing. "Mrs. Welsh, it would be really good if you could hear her practice reading a little every night. I'm setting her reading exercises, but if you could sit with her and make sure she's doing them, then—"

"I 'aven't got time to sit wi' 'er," she growled. "I *do* 'ave *other* kids, yer know." Suddenly, her eyes lit up. "I got 'er an iPad for 'er birfday—is there an app for it that can 'elp?"

An app—to teach her daughter to read. Give me strength.... Still, it was better than nothing, and John clutched at the proffered straw before it was withdrawn.

"Maybe there are some activities I can find for Kimberley that she can access on her iPad," he suggested in desperation.

Mrs. Welsh's expression clearly communicated her satisfaction with that solution. "Yeah, that sounds good." She got to her feet. Apparently, their meeting was at an end. "When you find somefin', write it down and send it 'ome with Kimmie. She can sit and do it while we watch telly." She beamed. "See—that wasn't so 'ard, was it?" She gave a brief nod and went to the door. "Bye, Mr. Wainwright." She grinned at him from the door. "Our Kimmie really rates you, by the way. She's always talkin' 'bout stuff she's doin' in school. Never known 'er to be so interested in 'er lessons before." She walked through the door, letting it bang shut behind her.

John put his head on his arms on the desk. *Is it always going to be such a struggle?* Right now, he felt so weary.

"It won't always be like this, you know."

He jerked his head up as Brett came into the classroom and walked over to his desk, a sympathetic expression on his face.

John shook his head sadly. "Sorry, but right now, it just feels like an exercise in futility."

Brett held up his hand. "But didn't you hear the last thing she said? Because I certainly did. Seems to me you're making a difference—at least for Kimberley Welsh." He studied John carefully. "Are you all right, John?" He approached the desk and placed his hand on John's shoulder, patting it. "Only a couple of weeks until half term." He smiled kindly.

John gave a half smile. "The way *I'm* going, half term will get here and I'll collapse from exhaustion."

Brett squeezed his arm. "Remember, not all the parents are like Mrs. Welsh. Just don't take it to heart, okay?" He released John's arm and moved toward the door. "Don't forget our meeting tomorrow after school," he called back as he walked out.

"Not forgotten," John murmured, watching his mentor exit the room. He looked forward to his bi-weekly meetings. Brett had formally observed him teaching the class twice so far, and while he'd been pleased overall with John's progress, he'd made a few suggestions to make things run more smoothly in the classroom. Good suggestions, as it turned out.

John told himself his enjoyment of their meetings was down to the fact that it was good to have another male around in an environment top-heavy with females. But there was another reason. John liked being around Brett. He liked the way his eyes were so expressive when he talked. He liked the way Brett listened to him attentively, as though everything he said was of importance. And he couldn't deny he found the head teacher very attractive.

Oh, God. It feels like being in high school all over again—except this time, I have a crush on the only boy in the place, and a straight boy at that. Because that's exactly what it felt like—a schoolboy crush.

BRETT WENT into his office and closed the door behind him. The building was quiet. In fact, he was pretty sure he and John were the only people left there. Emily had gone promptly at four, as she had a doctor's appointment.

John works far too hard. Brett's thoughts were on his NQT as he poured himself another cup of coffee. So far John was working out just fine, although Brett had to make sure he didn't overdo it—John was usually one of the first to arrive and the last to leave.

He reminds me of me, mused Brett with affection. He had a lot of time for the modest, hard-working young man, who always had a pleasant word for everyone. Brett could see how quickly John had fit in around the school. Trish Stetman, the Year Four teacher, was in charge of sports and physical activity in school. She reported how pleased she was to hear that John was really encouraging his class to achieve Brett's end-of-school target, that each pupil in the Year Six group should be able to swim twenty-five meters by the time they left the school. Every Friday afternoon, John accompanied his class to Victoria swimming baths. The swimming teacher had called Brett to say what a refreshing change it was to have a teacher who didn't disappear during the forty-five minute lesson, but who actively encouraged the pupils from the side of the pool. Six children had already gained their certificates since September, and at this rate, the whole class could be the first ever to achieve Brett's target.

Yeah, you're interested in him because he's so good in the classroom.

It was the only way Brett could *allow* himself to think about John. Because if he thought about the handsome young teacher in any other way, logic went out the window and what took over was lust. Well, maybe not *entirely* lust…. In the first five weeks of term, Brett had come to see his newest staff member in a different light, and he liked what he saw. John was beginning to come out of his shell and relax around Brett, which was exactly what Brett wanted. They were starting to develop a rapport—as long as Brett kept a tight rein on his libido. Which had been almost impossible the day John had cycled into work, wearing a tight-fitting black cycling shirt and a pair of cycling shorts that left nothing to the imagination. The sight of those firm calf muscles and nicely toned arms was enough of a distraction, but seeing the tight globes of his arse, not to mention the clear outline of his cock…. Brett had disappeared very quickly into his office, staying there until he was sure John had showered and changed into his suit.

And that was another thing—John wore suits to school. Nothing wrong with that. But the *way* he filled out his suits was positively *sinful*.

God, every day is like an obstacle course, Brett thought with a groan. Thank God the half term holiday wasn't far off. He was in dire need, and he could already close his eyes and picture the delights of Brighton that awaited him. He longed to bury his dick in a tight arse, to have someone slide deeply into him again and again….

God, just get me to the end of October, he pleaded with his Maker.

JOHN HAD the distinct impression that something was on Alec's mind.

It might have been the permanent air of distraction Alec seemed to have worn like a piece of clothing for over a week. Or maybe it was the way he'd drift off into his own little world. Whatever it was, John knew he wasn't the only one who'd noticed. He'd caught Martin and Stu regarding Alec with more than a little concern.

There was only one more week until half term, and John was more than ready for the break. He'd even begun to cross off the squares on the calendar, something he hadn't done since he was a child.

"Six days and counting," he muttered under his breath as he stared fixedly at the calendar on the kitchen wall. The first thing he wanted to do with his week-long holiday? Sleep for a *whole day*.

"Did you say something?" he heard Alec mutter behind him. John turned to find Alec pouring himself a mug of coffee and staring out of the kitchen window at the garden beyond. The leaves were already turning to glorious shades of oranges and browns. But he doubted Alec was admiring the view. John thought quickly. It was a bright Sunday afternoon, and Martin had gone for a run through the park. Stu was still sleeping after a long-haul flight from Singapore. *So that leaves me....*

"Come and sit down for a minute, Alec."

Alec turned to face him. "What?"

John gestured to the chairs and took one himself. "Come sit down for a sec."

Alec shrugged good-naturedly and sat down, mug in hand. "What's up?" His usually bright eyes were a little dull, and John noticed for the first time the dark smudges around them. *Yeah*, something's *up, all right....*

"Want to tell me what's going on?" John asked, keeping his tone light. Alec was silent for a moment, opened his mouth to speak—and then closed it again.

"Please, Alec," John begged. "You've not been yourself for a week or so now. Please tell me. What's wrong?" He'd assumed it was the stress of Alec's job. There had been a few nasty accidents in the last few weeks, and Alec must have seen his fair share of them.

Alec stared at the table, his hands wrapped around the mug. The silence was beginning to get to John.

Alec inhaled slowly. "Remember me saying a while back that there was a new guy working on my shift?" John nodded, unable to tear his eyes away from Alec's earnest expression. "Well, it turns out Ian's not as straight as I'd first thought." His gaze remained fixed on the table.

"Oh, wow." John grinned. "That sounds promising." His grin died, however, as he watched Alec's face. Whatever was coming was definitely *not* good. "What happened, Alec?" he asked softly.

Alec swallowed. "We... we had sex in the back of the ambulance during a break."

John stared incredulously. "No way." Alec nodded glumly. "Was... was it a bad experience?"

Alec swallowed several times, his Adam's apple bobbing. "Oh, John, it was damn good. I let him top, which I don't normally do, but he really wanted to, and *God*, the things that man can do with his dick...."

John felt his cheeks glow. "And?" he prompted.

Alec let out his breath in one shuddering, long exhalation. "And I found out this week that he has a wife. That they're having problems... in the bedroom." His eyes sparkled, and John felt sure tears were imminent. "And that basically he was horny and I was... available." Alec gulped. "That's all I was—a convenient hole to fuck." He shivered.

"How did you find out he was married?"

Alec raised his gaze to meet John's. "She came into the ambulance bay last Monday. It seemed he'd left his lunch at home, so she brought it in for him." He sniffed. "One of my colleagues asked Ian who she was, and he told her."

"Did you confront him?" John wanted to hug Alec. He was two years older than John, but right then, it felt like he was his little brother. And at five seven, he seemed to bring out the housemates' protective sides, being shorter than the rest of them.

Alec nodded. "That's when he came out with the line about them having sexual problems. Though after seeing them together, I'm not sure I believe it now."

"You think he used you?"

"Oh, yeah. He knew I was gay—I'm out at work, and besides, anyone could have told him that—and when it comes to hiding how I feel, I'm pretty crap. I tend to wear my heart on my sleeve." He took another deep breath.

"So the way I see it, he'd figured out I was attracted to him and he decided to make the most of it. Like I said, a convenient hole."

"And now?"

Alec's lower lip trembled. "And now he looks at me like I'm dog shit that's stuck to his shoe. He's really cool to me, and working with him is very uncomfortable." A single tear slid down his pale cheek.

John couldn't take any more. He stood up and pulled Alec into his arms and held him close, feeling the tremors that shook his slight frame. "It'll be okay," he murmured into Alec's ear. He rocked him gently. Alec reached around him and placed his hands at John's back, his face pushed against John's chest. He heard the front door open and Martin's cheery whistle. Alec made as if to pull away, but John held him tightly. "You stay right there," he whispered. He felt Alec sag against him. John twisted his neck to peer at Martin, who was standing by the kitchen door, his face a mask of misery. John could understand that. Martin and Alec were close.

Martin crossed the kitchen floor to where John and Alec stood. "Come here," he said simply. Alec relinquished his hold on John and stepped into Martin's outstretched arms.

"I'll pour us a drink," John said quietly. Martin nodded as he stroked Alec's hair and held him. "You take Alec into the lounge, and he can tell you all about it." Martin released Alec, and the two men left the kitchen, Martin's arm around Alec's shoulders.

John went to the fridge and got out a bottle of wine and three glasses. His heart ached for Alec. The paramedic was a hopeless romantic, they all knew that, and to have someone treat him so abominably was plain *wrong*.

I will never get involved with a straight guy, John vowed to himself. And then he laughed quietly. He didn't have *time* to get involved with anyone. His job ate up all his time and attention. He knew he was ignoring Brett's instructions about finding a work/life balance, but surely, that wasn't a bad thing so early on in his career. Things would settle down after a term or two.

And besides, the more he threw himself into his work, the more easily he could ignore the elephant in the room—his attraction to his very gorgeous but very *straight* head teacher.

Not going to go there, he thought. *Just look what happens when you fall for a straight guy. Well, it's not going to happen to me.*

And as for the ache in his chest? Heartburn, nothing more....

God, he was crap at lying.

JOHN AND Bev strolled around the playground, their eyes on the children as they dashed all over the place, laughing and giggling. Seven or eight boys were playing football on the field, while a group of girls played hopscotch. Everywhere John looked, there were small clusters of children, and all doing something different.

"You need eyes in the back of your head to keep a watch on them," he murmured.

Bev laughed. "Yeah, break may only last twenty minutes, but it keeps you on your toes when you're on duty."

John caught sight of Brett as he walked across the playground. There was a purposeful air about him that told John something was up. He still smiled at children who greeted him as he passed by.

As he reached John and Bev, however, his smiled slipped a notch.

"Please be vigilant, you two. The police have just been in contact to say Carl Meadows made another attempt last night to snatch Wayne from his mother. If it hadn't been for a quick-thinking shop assistant at the supermarket who knew Anna, he might have succeeded."

"That's awful," muttered Bev. "Is there a description of Carl that we can put up in school so that everyone knows what he looks like?"

Brett nodded. "I've already asked for this, and the police are faxing it through. I'll make sure you all have a copy." He set his jaw. "But I must stress this. If you *do* see him, inform me immediately. Under *no* circumstances are you to try to deal with him on your own."

John took one look at Brett's expression and shivered. "He's dangerous, isn't he?" he said under his breath.

Brett met his gaze. "Yes. That's why the police contacted me. They'd been informed that Carl and some of his former associates are planning something, possibly a robbery, but they're convinced weapons are involved."

Icy fingers danced up and down John's spine. "And they really think he might come here?"

Brett's eyes were troubled. "If he's planning to take part in a robbery and then maybe flee the country, I can't see him wanting to leave his little boy behind. The police think this is why he's getting desperate. The job is about to go down, and he wants Wayne." He shook his head and gazed around at the happy children milling about. "Of course, this is sheer speculation, but I don't even want to think about it."

"We're going to have to make sure *everyone* is alert, that's all," John stated decisively, trying to ignore his quickening heartbeat. Brett gave him an approving nod.

"Exactly. And I might start by asking more staff to be out here at breaks and during lunchtime. The more pairs of eyes, the better." He took one more look around and then gave a tight smile. "I'll let you organize the children ready for going back in." Brett walked off slowly, greeting more children who ran up to him, their faces wreathed in smiles.

"Talk about scary." Bev watched Brett, her face taut. "Let's get them lined up."

John nodded and blew his whistle, bringing the break to an end. As the children flocked to Bev to get into their lines, John found himself scanning the school fences, looking for anything out of the ordinary. There were no strange faces lurking beyond the school gate, no shifty characters watching from across the street—at least, none that *he* could see.

Well, you wanted to work here, he told himself.

But that was before life took a step in an unexpected direction, wasn't it?

John shook his head. *And they say teachers have a dull life. Yeah, right....*

CHAPTER 8

"THERE'S A parents' evening coming up," Brett said as their scheduled meeting drew to a close. He shuffled the pile of papers into a neat collection and placed them back in John's folder. The school was quiet at last. The pupils had left ninety minutes ago, along with most of the staff, which was normal at the end of a half term. *Everyone eager for their holiday.* His own thoughts went to the train he'd be catching the following morning. Brighton was calling….

John jerked his head up. "Already? But we've only been back in school for seven weeks."

Brett smirked. "Let me guess. When you were at primary school, your parents had one meeting at the end of the year, right about the same time they got your school report too." John nodded. Brett shook his head. "Times have changed. These days, parents get to meet with staff early on in the year to address any issues before they become insurmountable. And then we do it all over again at the end of the year."

"Is this what the parents want?"

Brett let out a wry chuckle. "No. Most of the time we get a sixty, maybe sixty-five percent turnout if we're lucky. *This* initiative comes from the governors. They're the ones who employ us, after all—the local authority only pays the salaries." He sighed heavily. "And both the local education authority *and* the governors have to approve our curriculum."

"I take it you're not in agreement."

Talk about an understatement.... "Yes, but now's not the time for me to get up on my soapbox again. Any questions?"

John folded his hands into his lap. "Is everything in order?"

Brett straightened and cleared his throat. "Yes. Your folder is up to date, your lesson plans and evaluations are in place, and your forward planning for next term is in evidence." He grinned. "A very successful first half term, Mr. Wainwright."

John's smile lit up his face. "Brilliant." He relaxed visibly into his chair.

Brett leaned back and laced his hands behind his head. "And now you can go into the holiday feeling ready for the next seven or eight weeks. Do you have any plans for next week? Maybe go somewhere with your partner—if you have one, that is." *Shame on you, Brett Sanderson, fishing like this....*

John smiled. "No, no plans—and no partner either." He flushed. "And I *had* thought about spending some time getting resources ready...."

Brett frowned. "No." He folded his arms across his chest. "I'm putting my foot down. You are allowed a maximum of one day for your planning. The rest of the time you need to unwind." Inside, he was cursing himself. *So what if he's single? For God's sake, he's straight—and so are you, as far as he's concerned. Stop torturing yourself like this.* "Am I making myself clear?" He tried to glare, but his lips twitched with the effort of holding back his smile.

John regarded him with obvious amusement. "Yes, sir."

Brett relaxed his features. "That's better." He glanced at the wall clock. "And now it's definitely time to go home." He tried not to think about John getting into his cycling gear. He'd made the mistake of walking into the men's toilets last week when John was getting changed. One glimpse of that firm backside as John wriggled into those tight shorts and Brett's cock had been like granite. *Yeah, one day you'll do that and he'll catch you staring....*

Something struck him as John reached the door. "John, let me give you my mobile number, in case you need to speak about something before we come back." He grabbed a pink Post-it note from his desk and scribbled his number down. He handed it to John. "For use in an emergency," he said with a wink. John tucked it into his pocket. "And now go and enjoy your week off."

"I will," John replied, and he grinned. He exited the office, and Brett closed the door after him with a sigh. That smile of John's made his abs quiver and his breath quicken.

I really need to get away from here.

"ARE YOU *still* workin'?"

John spun around on his swivel chair and beamed at Stu as he peered around his bedroom door. "Just finished." He put down his pen with a triumphant sigh and stretched his arms high above his head. "All done." He gazed at the neat notes with satisfaction. *And I stuck to Brett's time limit too.* For some reason, this pleased him enormously.

"Great." Stu came fully into the room and flopped down onto his bed. "So what are you goin' to do with your first week off?" He looked at his watch. "You have eight days and… ten hours left of it." He chuckled.

John put his notes into their folder and placed it in the bookcase. "And counting," he added with a grin. "Where are the others?" Martin had a Saturday off, which was a rarity in itself. Apparently, he had one every three or four months. And Alec wasn't on 'til the following day.

"Martin's gone shoppin', and Alec went with 'im." Stu's smile dimmed slightly. "That boy needs a night out."

John had to agree. Alec came home from work every day looking drawn. "Is he still getting a load of shit from Ian?"

Stu let out a sound that was almost a growl. "Yes. I've told 'im to request a transfer to another shift. He shouldn't 'ave to put up with 'assle from work colleagues—his job is stressful enough without addin' to it."

"And is he going to do that?" John wanted to know. It made sense.

Stu shrugged. "Alec says he doesn't want to rock the boat. And he doesn't 'ave a clue what reasons he could give for requestin' a transfer. He doesn't want everyone knowin' what went on."

"Poor Alec. I can understand that." They had made sure Alec knew he had their complete support. Martin in particular had gone out of his way to be affectionate around him, and it was clear Alec really appreciated the hugs when he got home and the cuddles on the couch while they watched TV. In fact, it had got John wondering. "Is there any possibility that he and Martin…?" he let his words trail off.

Stu laughed. "Absolutely not. Two tops? It'd never work."

John stared in surprise. "Alec's a top?" Seeing Martin as a top required little effort. But Alec? He pictured the slightly built, smaller man in his head. He'd assumed that with his size Alec would be a bottom. *Shows how little I know.*

Stu guffawed. "Oh, God, don't let his size fool you. He may *look* all *"pick-me-up-in-your-arms-and-carry-me-home-with-you,"* but that guy is a total top—small but feisty. You're not the first to think that, by the way." He shook his head. "The number of guys he's hooked up with, who got the shock of their lives when they finally made it to his bedroom." His eyes held a wicked gleam. "Especially when the cuffs and ropes came out of the wardrobe." He winked.

John swallowed. *Oh, wow….*

Stu was laughing loudly now. "Oh, my God, I keep forgettin' what an innocent you are." He wiped his eyes. "I really have to stop corruptin' you."

The sound of laughter floated up through the open window, followed by the slamming of the front door.

"They're just in time for lunch." Stu clambered off the bed and went to the door. "Comin'?"

John bobbed his head and followed him down the stairs to the kitchen. Martin and Alec were emptying the shopping bags and putting away their purchases. Both men looked cheerful.

"I was about to heat up some soup, but there's enough for all of us," Martin said as he pulled the can opener from the drawer. "Interested? It's pea and ham." Both John and Stu nodded. John had just started to slice up the bread when his phone warbled. He grinned when he saw the caller.

"Ev, to what do I owe this pleasure?" He hadn't seen his brother for about two months, though they'd spoken on the phone.

"You're on holiday now, right?" Evan sounded his usual effervescent self.

"Yeah, and I just got my homework done," John said with a smirk.

"Great! So, do you want to come out with us tonight?"

"Define *us*." John had only met the rest of his brother's housemates briefly at the wedding. He wasn't sure how he felt about spending an evening with them.

"Just me and Daniel. Josh and Chris are round seeing his dad, Michael's not in the mood, and as for Sean...." Evan's voice faded. "No, it's just us." The bright tone sounded a little forced, but John knew better than to pry. "We were going to go to Babel. Want to come along? And you can bring your housemates too, if they want to come."

John thought about it for a moment. The idea was tempting. His first visit to the gay club had been an interesting one, to say the least.

"Hang on a minute," he told Evan. He lowered the phone and addressed the others. "My brother and his husband are going to Babel tonight, and they want to know if we want to go along."

Alec's face lit up. "Dancing at Babel? Count me in!" It looked as if Stu had it nailed—Alec did need a night out. He tugged at Martin's arm as he stirred the soup in the pan. "What do you say?" He made those green eyes large and round.

Martin's reaction was immediate. He gave Alec the thumbs-up, and Alec punched the air. "Stu? Gonna join us?"

Stu grinned. "Definitely." He winked at John and then flicked his head toward Alec. "Wait 'til you see this one in action."

John was intrigued. "Okay, Ev, that's all of us. Shall we meet you there?"

Evan's gleeful reaction made him smile. "Fabulous! Nine o'clock, okay?" They spoke briefly and then hung up.

"It's about time we had a boys' night out, anyway. And I could do with one." Alec's happy expression faltered, and Stu leaned across and kissed his cheek lightly. Alec gave him a grateful look.

John was positively buzzing. He wanted another look at the world he'd so far only glimpsed. *Last time, I got kissed. Heaven knows what might happen tonight.*

"I REALLY like your housemates," Evan hollered in John's ear above the din of the music that throbbed through the floor and bounced off the walls. "What a nice bunch of guys."

John smiled. "Yeah, they are." His gaze strayed to the dance floor, where Stu and Martin were clearly enjoying themselves. Alec was surrounded by a group of three or four guys, all trying to catch his attention, but he seemed oblivious. He moved sinuously in time with the music, arms high above his head, eyes closed, lost in a world of his own.

"He doesn't have a clue how sexy he is, does he?" Evan was watching Alec too. John counted silently in his head. He got to three before Daniel snaked an arm around Evan's chest and pulled him back against him. He whispered into Evan's ear, and John was intrigued to see how quickly Evan's cheeks burned bright red. John chuckled to himself. Daniel was extremely possessive of his husband.

John watched as one really tall guy pressed up behind Alec and placed his hands on his shoulders. Alec tilted his head up, and his face broke into a delighted smile. He turned to his new dance partner and let himself be held, the pair moving sensually together.

Ah. Alec likes them tall. John smiled to himself.

"Nice to see you here again." Warm breath tickled John's ear. A shiver rippled through him as he recognized the voice. He turned toward Max, whose face broke into a happy grin. "Hey, baby. You're back." He leaned forward until his lips were almost touching John's ear. Goose bumps prickled along his arms. "Want to dance?"

He was about to refuse when Max's hot, wet tongue licked around the shell of his ear, before his teeth nipped at his earlobe. John shuddered and closed his eyes. *Oh, hell….*

"Feels good, doesn't it?" Max's deep voice rumbled. He licked a trail down John's neck to the open collar of his dark blue shirt. John trembled. He couldn't help it. He opened his eyes to search for Evan, only to find the two men regarding him silently, Daniel's arms around Evan as he kissed his throat. Evan gave John a questioning look, and John swallowed briefly before giving him a hopefully reassuring smile. Evan grinned and turned in Daniel's arms.

Oh, shit. I'm on my own—without a net.

Max reached around him to stroke down his back as he began to kiss John's neck. He pressed John to him, and John let out a small gasp as he felt the hard length against his hip. But he forgot to breathe when Max slipped a hand around to his front and slid down to his own stiffening cock. Max slowly stroked the bulge through his jeans, and John shuddered.

"Just looking at you turns me on," whispered Max. "I get the loveliest images in my head." John couldn't think straight. One hand on his dick, moving up and down in a maddeningly slow motion. Another at his back but descending most definitely toward his arse.

"I-images?" His voice shook. *God, how can he expect me to think straight when all the blood in my body is rushing to my cock?* And then he froze as Max expertly popped open the button on John's jeans—and eased his hand into John's briefs. *Oh. My. Fucking. God.* Warm fingers circled his shaft. His mind reeled. *Another man has his hand on my dick. This is really happening.* His breathing grew erratic.

"Relax, baby. No one can see what I'm doin'." Max's voice was smooth as butter. "Yeah, I'm picturing me sucking this cock, for a start." That hand at his rear pressed firmly against the seam of his jeans. "And then maybe spreading this beautiful arse wide so I can fuck you with my tongue." Max chuckled and nipped at his earlobe once more.

John shook uncontrollably as the images took root in his mind. *Fuckfuckfuckfuck....* His body seemed to have a mind of its own. He felt his hips give a little involuntary roll as Max massaged his cock inside his jeans.

"Yeah, you *like* that idea," Max whispered with a chuckle. "Hell, baby, what have you *got* in there?" He glanced around the club. "I live nearby. How 'bout we go to my place and I take care of this?" He squeezed John's dick, and John let out a little yelp. Only now he was starting to hyperventilate as Max's words finally registered. And one thought started to hammer in his brain. *I don't want this. I don't want this.* He didn't know *why* he felt that way, but the panic was rising and his heart raced.

"Is everything all right?"

Oh, the relief. Martin's voice was clearly audible above the music. John looked over Max's shoulder to see his three housemates standing right behind him. Martin's gaze was fixed on him, and John could read the anxiety there.

Max paused, his hand stilling on John's shaft. "*Is* everything all right?" His eyes questioned.

John gulped down several deep breaths and struggled to regain his composure. "Actually, no." He took a step back, and Max withdrew his hand slowly from his jeans and rehoused the button. "Sorry, Max. I didn't mean to—"

Max held up a hand. "I think I took you outside your comfort zone, didn't I?" His expression was vaguely amused. "No harm done." He gave John a sweet smile. "You're not ready yet, are you, babe?" Then he leaned forward to whisper. "But when you are? Come back and find me." He stroked the bulge in his tight pants. "Because I'd love to be the first in that tight virgin arse." He leered.

The music died suddenly, and John saw Martin's eyes flash. "I think we need to go home now," Martin said in a tight voice.

Max half inclined his head at the words and then pecked John on the cheek. "Bye, hon." He winked. "See you around." He sauntered off toward the dance floor.

"Not if I can help it," muttered Martin, his jaw set as he watched Max's exit. Then his gaze was back to John. "You okay?" His hand came to rest on John's upper arm.

"Yeah," he replied shakily. "I think that was slightly more reality than I was prepared for." Martin nodded, his brown eyes still troubled.

Evan appeared at his side, Daniel close behind him. Evan seemed very agitated.

"Oh, God, I'm sorry, bro. I thought you were okay with it." He scraped a hand through his layers of blond hair. "Are you all right?"

Now there were five concerned faces turned toward him. John took a deep breath.

"Guys, I'm *fine*," he stressed. "It's just that I'm clearly... not ready to take things to the next level."

"Nothin' wrong with that," Stu said, his brow furrowed. "And it's *your* decision—no one should force you to do anythin' before you're ready." He scowled in Max's direction.

John grasped his arm. "Stu, it's okay. That wasn't the first time Max and I have... met." He caught Evan's smirk. "It just didn't feel right, that's all." As to *why* it had felt like that, he didn't have a clue. He'd been aroused; that much was true. There was no escaping *that* fact—the rigid length in his jeans was proof enough.

But there was something missing. And until he worked out exactly what that was, John wasn't prepared to take things any further. He gazed at the men who stood around him in a protective circle. *They were looking out for me.* The thought warmed him inside.

"How 'bout we call it a night?" Stu said decisively.

John liked that idea. He'd had enough excitement for one night. "Yeah, let's go home."

BRETT NURSED what was left of his pint and huffed out a sigh.

"You gonna tell me what's wrong, Rob?"

He lifted his head to meet Elliott's inquiring stare. "What makes you think anything's wrong?" He drained the rest of the cold beer and then gave him a bright smile.

"Yeah, right." Elliott snorted. "I'm not buying it. This is the third night in a row that you've sat in the bar, drinking pints and looking sorry for yourself. And God knows I've pointed you in the direction of some really stunning blokes." He inclined his head toward the window that looked out over the promenade. A solitary figure sat there, legs stretched out, fingers laced behind his head—and an unmistakable rocket in his pocket. "That guy over there has been giving you the eye for the last fifteen minutes, and you haven't even noticed." Elliott reached over the bar and placed his palm on Brett's forehead. "You got a fever or something?" He withdrew his hand and smirked.

Brett considered the object of Elliott's attention for a moment, trying not to make it too obvious. The guy had a pretty face, no denying that, and *definitely* something of interest in his jeans. But Brett couldn't bring himself to summon up the energy required—or the motivation—to get down off his bar stool and go across to strike up a conversation.

Who am I kidding? Like we'd have a conversation that would last more than a few minutes before we'd be up to my room, or his, and then there'd be no talking beyond demands to fuck him. Brett *felt weary.*

"Rob, what is it?"

And that was another thing. Brett was heartily sick of being unable to be himself. Well, that was one thing he *could* do something about.

"Elliott, allow me to introduce myself." He held out his hand. "The name's Brett."

Elliott widened his eyes as he took the proffered hand. "Well, I didn't expect *that*." He grinned. "Pleased to meet you... *Brett*." He withdrew his hand and gave a nod to his barman before pouring out two glasses of Scotch and coming around to Brett's side of the bar. "Let's sit over there." He gestured toward the corner of the bar, where an intimate little booth had just been vacated. He led the way, Brett following him, intrigued.

They sat facing each other, and Elliott placed one of the glasses in front of him. Brett stared at it for a moment, shrugged, and then threw it back in one swift movement. The back of his throat burned, and he gasped for air.

Elliott leaned against the padded bench and gave him a lazy grin. "Okay, you want to tell me why you suddenly felt the need to tell me the truth after, what, seven years of coming here?"

Brett looked at the empty glass. "I can't do this anymore." His chin dipped toward his chest, and he closed his eyes. There was a moment of silence before Elliott spoke.

"Do what? Come here? Hook up with guys? Come on, give me a clue here."

Brett opened his eyes. It was clear from Elliott's expression that he was genuinely concerned.

"Elliott, I'm thirty-three. I've known I was gay since my late teens, and I've lost count of the number of guys I've fucked. But that's all there's ever been—fucking." He shook his head sadly. "I can't keep doing this. There has to be more to life than this."

"Oh, my." Elliott leaned forward and spoke in a low voice. "You're getting broody."

Brett snorted. "Broody?"

Elliott nodded. "You mentioned your age. Maybe your brain is telling you it's time to settle down, *you* know, with *one* guy?" He snickered. "Some people have been known to do that, I hear."

Brett stared at him. "You're kidding." Elliott met his gaze resolutely. "Oh, come *on*, you of all men. I see you eyeing up every cute guy who walks in here."

Elliott gave him a half smile. "Yeah, I look—but at the end of the day, I go upstairs to be with my partner of eleven years."

Brett gaped. "Really?"

Elliott gave a slow nod. "I may flirt with the customers and do the odd bit of matchmaking"—he winked, and Brett chuckled—"but that's as far as it goes. I love him. He's all I need." He shrugged.

The simple truth of his words shook Brett. He was rendered speechless.

Elliott cocked his head. "Out of interest, have you ever *looked* for more than a good fuck? Engaged a guy in conversation? Tried to find out what makes him tick—and I mean more than working out what he wants in bed?"

Brett huffed. He didn't have an answer—well, not one he was willing to share.

Elliott nodded knowingly. "Then maybe that's where you need to start. Is there anyone back home who interests you? Maybe someone you'd like to get to know better?"

John. The thought was there in an instant.

Elliott's smile widened. "There is, isn't there?" His expression was smug. "I knew it."

Brett shook his head. "It doesn't matter. One, he's straight, and two, I'm his boss."

Elliott laughed. "Oh, he *told* you he's straight, did he?" Brett stared, and that smug smile was back. "Never assume, honey. And as for being his boss, are there no-fraternization rules where you work?"

Brett grimaced. "Not exactly. Let's just say it could be awkward."

Elliott snorted. "Find a way. If there's someone out there who might be more than just a willing hole for your cock, then you need to pursue this." His expression grew serious. "And maybe it's time to call a halt to cruising the streets of balmy Brighton." And then he winked. "Unless it's you coming back here to introduce me to your fella."

My fella. The ache in his chest as he thought of having someone at his side, someone to come home to, to share his day with....

"You've got a deal," he whispered.

*C*HAPTER 9

"OKAY, WHEN you're ready, let's get started."

The chatter died down, and all eyes turned to Brett. He smiled at the assembled staff.

"Welcome back. I trust you all had a great week off and have recharged your batteries, ready for the next eight weeks. It's going to be a busy term. November is upon us, and you all know what that means." He grinned. "Charity time."

John nudged Deb Hatton, the Reception teacher. "Charity time?" he whispered.

She smiled. "All will be made clear."

Brett cleared his throat and gave them both a hard stare. John straightened, his cheeks heating up. Brett shook his head.

"First off, during this next week you need to talk to your groups about Operation Christmas Child. I'll be talking about this in assembly this morning, but you'll need to cover it in greater detail so the children all know what they can and can't put in their shoeboxes. These need to be in school by the end of November, so we don't have much time. I've asked Bev to be in charge this year. She'll be coordinating the collection of the boxes." He gazed around the room. "We sent off seventy-seven boxes last year, folks. Let's see if we can beat that *this* year." He gave them all an encouraging smile.

John was totally lost. Operation Christmas Child, shoeboxes.... Hopefully, Brett's assembly would be helpful.

"And the next thing is, I've picked January as our school charity month. I'd like years three to six to come up with as many ideas as they can think of for raising money. We're going to have a charity day when we'll invite in the parents, carers, local businesses, etcetera, to take part in whatever activities we organize. So we need to start thinking now of different things we can do. Try to make some of them fun. One idea might be a raffle, especially if people have unwanted Christmas gifts they're looking to get rid of." There were noises of approval at this point. "Maybe a car boot sale? We need to think of creative ways of getting people to part with their cash."

"Which charity will we be supporting this year?" asked Michelle.

"That was to be my next point. I'd like suggestions from you as to where the money goes, rather than picking one myself. Please pass your suggestions to Emily." He looked at Emily, who nodded. "But I shan't be coordinating this. I'd like to ask John Wainwright to be the organizer."

John gaped. "Really?" There were snickers around him, and he snapped his mouth shut.

"Sorry to drop it on you, but I'll talk to you about it during our next meeting. I think you'll do a great job." Brett smiled encouragingly.

John was startled to hear a smattering of applause. *Oh, wow....*

"SO TELL me again. What has he got you doing?" demanded Evan.

John sighed into his phone and shut down his laptop. "Operation Christmas Child is where the school collects shoeboxes, covered in wrapping paper and filled with little gifts. They then get sent to needy kids all around the world who wouldn't have a Christmas."

"That's a great idea!"

"Yes, it is," admitted John, "but there's this long list of things you can't send. Food—except for wrapped sweets—toy guns or knives, liquids.... I've just finished putting together a presentation for tomorrow for the class, and then we're going to start collecting items. Little stuff— coloring pencils, a scarf, gloves, toy cars, soft toys, that sort of thing."

Evan chuckled. "We never did anything like this when *I* was at school."

"Brett's really into raising money for charity. You should see the walls of his office. There are certificates from Comic Relief, Children in Need…. And now he wants *me* to organize the charity day." John stared glumly at the notes he'd begun making. So far he'd had no inspiration.

"We'll put our heads together and see what we can come up with," Evan said confidently.

John had to smile at that. Trust Evan to want to help out. "Thanks, little brother."

"Well, there *is* something you could do for me in return."

John laughed. "I wondered why you were calling me so soon. I only saw you last week, after all."

"I could use your help, but it's a little short notice. Margaret is organizing one of her charity balls, and Chris said he'd help."

"Who's Margaret?" John was at a loss.

"Oh, God, sorry." Evan sounded flustered. "Margaret is the grandmother of one of my housemates, Chris. She's this really formidable little old lady who heads a foundation that raises money for disadvantaged kids. Anyway, she's organizing this ball, and Chris said he'd help her fill the last empty tables."

"How much?" John knew if it was for charity, the tickets wouldn't be cheap.

"One hundred pounds a ticket." John gave a low whistle. "I *know*, but it's for a good cause," coaxed Evan. "Daniel and I are going, as well as Josh and Chris." There was a moment's pause. "You could ask Brett. He seems to be into charities in a big way. Do you think he might like to go?"

"When is it?"

"Next Saturday—yeah, I said it was short notice. Sorry." Evan's tone was apologetic. "Maybe if you sell him on the idea of making some contacts? There'll be some celebrities attending, I think. Someone who might want to come to your charity event, a crowd-puller."

Now *that* was an idea. "Let me give him a call, and I'll get back to you. Where's the ball being held?"

"The Midland Hotel. And you'll need to hire a tux, if you're coming."

"Leave it to me. I'll see if I can get him to agree." John thought the networking idea might swing it for Brett. He also liked the idea of spending time with his mentor away from the school environment. He relished the chance to get to know Brett the man, rather than Brett the Head Teacher.

And besides, you really want to see what he looks like in a tux, don't you?

John's suddenly stiffening cock was a reminder that Brett the man was hot.

JOHN FINGERED the stiff collar of his dress shirt and wished for the umpteenth time that he didn't look like a ridiculous penguin in his tux.

Brett chuckled beside him as they waited to be served at the bar. "Will you stop doing that? You look fine—now quit fiddling." His eyes sparkled with amusement.

John sighed. Next to Brett, he felt like a downy duckling. His boss, however, looked mouth-wateringly handsome. At five eleven and with his wide shoulders and narrow waist, Brett had the height to make the tuxedo look damn good. That smooth jawline had been drawing John's attention ever since he'd arrived. He had to fight hard to pull his gaze away.

"What's wrong?" Brett's quietly uttered question pulled him from his reveries.

John let escape another sigh. "I just feel out of place, that's all." He glanced around the hotel bar at the smart men and elegantly dressed women who'd begun to assemble there. There was a serious amount of money in this room.

Brett leaned closer. "Relax. You look great." John quirked his eyebrows, and Brett nodded. "Yes, really. And we're here for a good cause, so *do* try to enjoy it, all right?" He pinned John with a stare. John swallowed, and Brett let out a brief chuckle. "Okay, so they might have more money than you or I, but they paid the same price for their tickets as we did. Now all we have to do is find someone who might be willing to help out the school." He took the glasses of white wine from the barman and handed one to John. "Have a drink—and I repeat, relax." He grinned and then took a sip of wine.

John huffed in resignation and took a drink. The crisp wine was delicious. He let out a tiny moan of satisfaction, and Brett's grin widened. John felt his face redden.

"Thanks for agreeing to this, by the way." He took another drink, hoping the cold wine would cool his burning cheeks.

Brett waved a hand. "Don't mention it. I don't often get the chance to wear a tux, and besides, you were right—it's a wonderful opportunity." He sipped his wine. "Do you know where we're sitting?"

John shook his head. "Apparently, there are name cards, but I haven't looked yet." He'd been too distracted by the sight of Brett walking into the bar, looking so drop-dead gorgeous that he'd found it hard to breathe for a second or two.

"Well, let's go look." Brett led the way into the ballroom, and John gasped. The chandeliers dripped with crystal from the high ceiling, and the light sparkled around the room. Every inch of available space was taken up with round tables, each seating six people, with a larger table in the center of the room. A small orchestra was playing softly.

"Wow." John was seriously impressed. "I've never been to anything like this before."

Brett nudged closer and whispered in his ear. "Then enjoy it." He grinned. "I'll let you in on a secret—neither have I."

For some reason, this revelation warmed John. A raised arm across the ballroom caught his eye, and he heaved a sigh of relief. "I think I've found our table." He led the way across the room, Brett behind him, to where Evan and Daniel were seated. John recognized the other occupants immediately. Evan was grinning.

"Brett, this is my brother, Evan, and his husband, Daniel." John thought he saw the slightest look of surprise cross Brett's features before he shook Evan and Daniel's hands. "And these two gentlemen are Josh and his fiancé, Chris. They share a student house with Evan and Daniel."

Brett shook hands and then took one of the two empty seats. "I didn't know you had a brother, John." He smiled. "But then again, I never asked."

"Actually, he has two," Evan interjected. "And two sisters." He gave Brett a polite smile. "So you're John's Headmaster? I hope he's behaving well." He winked at John.

"I'm *always* well behaved," John said with a warning glance to Evan. That wicked gleam in his brother's eyes was disconcerting.

"I'd say impeccably," Brett added. He glanced at the four men. "Are you all students?"

"Yes. Evan, Chris, and I are in our final year, and Josh is in the second year of medical school." Daniel looked amazing. He wore his long black hair loose, and it spilled over his shoulders in a silken curtain.

Brett leaned back into his chair. "So, four gay students, sharing the same house. How interesting. And two of you already married. At your age, that shows a remarkable level of commitment." He laughed. "I apologize. That sounded very condescending, and I certainly didn't mean it to be."

Evan's eyes sparkled. "No apology necessary. And it's six gay students," he corrected him. "Two of us couldn't be here tonight. And they're married also."

"That's wonderful." Brett arched his eyebrows. "I mean that in all seriousness. I'm impressed."

Evan gazed at him for a moment. "Apparently, my brother is trying to follow in my footsteps." John flashed him a warning glance, but Evan seemed to be studiously avoiding him. "Seeing as his housemates are all gay too."

Oh, I'm going to kill my brother. "Have you seen the menu for tonight?" John asked, desperately trying to change the subject. He could see Daniel wasn't happy by the nudges he was giving Evan.

"It looks really good," said Chris. "Grandma has really pulled out all the stops." John gave him a grateful smile. He glared at Evan, who smiled back at him sweetly. *Just wait 'til I get him alone….*

JOHN SMILED politely at the waiter who refilled his glass and made sure Brett's was replenished too. He sat back and sipped the wine. Dinner had been one delicious course after another. Brett was on the other side of the room, talking animatedly with a young man who John recognized straightaway as a footballer. He smiled to himself. *Looks like Brett's found our celebrity.*

"Brett is very good looking."

John turned to Evan and glared. "Did you, or did you not just out me to my boss?"

Evan pursed his lips. "Technically, no. I merely told him all your housemates were gay. I didn't say *you* were." His face took on an innocent expression that John knew only too well.

"What are you up to, Ev?" John had found it difficult to concentrate on enjoying the wonderful meal. His thoughts had been focused on Brett.

"Why are you worried?" Evan's face straightened immediately. He lowered his voice. "Are you concerned how he'll react if he thinks you're gay?"

John rolled his eyes. "Not everyone is as forward-thinking as Mum and Dad. There are some homophobic assholes out there, remember?"

Evan shook his head. "But Brett's not one of them," he said decisively.

"How can you know that? You've only just met him." John was trying hard not to be angry. "This is my job you're jeopardizing here. I have to work with him."

Evan tilted his head. "You like him."

John made an impatient noise. "You're not listening to me. I—"

Evan waved a hand. "You like him. Tell me I'm wrong." His eyes glittered. "And you know *exactly* what I mean."

John gulped. Evan was far too close for comfort. He took a deep, calming breath before speaking. "I'm just worried, that's all."

Evan made soothing noises. "I'm telling you, there's nothing to worry about. In fact…." His words trailed off as he gazed speculatively across the room at Brett, who was still deep in conversation.

"I know that look," Daniel said. "Baby, whatever you're planning, forget it."

Evan turned to his husband. "You know I love you, right?" Daniel lifted his eyebrows. "Well?" Daniel nodded. "And you trust me." It wasn't a question.

Daniel stilled. "Yes, I trust you." His eyes narrowed. "Ev?"

Evan took a deep breath. "Then I want you to ignore anything you see or hear for the next part of the evening."

"Why?" There was an edge to Daniel's voice that John hadn't heard before.

Evan took hold of Daniel's hands. "Because I'm about to lie my arse off, okay?" He fixed Daniel with an intense look. Daniel regarded him in silence for a moment and then nodded once. Evan sagged in his chair. "Thank you, sweetie." He leaned forward and kissed Daniel on the cheek. He met John's gaze. "This goes for you too. Don't believe anything you see or hear, all right? I'll explain later." He got to his feet and walked toward the bar.

John bit his lip. *I have a bad feeling about this.*

BRETT SHOOK Eric Lazenby's hand and walked back toward the table. He couldn't suppress the smile that spread across his face. The young footballer had been only too happy to help out. He'd even volunteered to do a training session with some of the older boys who were mad keen on football. *This could end up being our most successful charity event ever.*

Some of the tables had been cleared away to reveal the highly polished wooden dance floor. Couples were already moving slowly together around the floor. Brett stopped as he caught sight of Josh and Chris dancing together, their heads touching. *They look so beautiful.* The thought made his heart ache. It wasn't their physical beauty that caught his eye—it was the sight of two men in each other's arms, oblivious to the rest of the world. Their fellow dancers paid them no mind, which was refreshing.

"They look good together, don't they?"

Brett turned to Evan, who was standing beside him, his gaze fixed on Josh and Chris. "Yes, they do," he admitted.

He was surprised when Evan stroked a finger casually down his arm. He jerked his head back. Evan regarded him calmly, those piercing blue eyes so reminiscent of John's.

"It's okay," Evan said softly. "They can't see us." He trailed a finger up over Brett's bicep. "You obviously take care of yourself." Brett couldn't miss the almost purring note of approval.

He found his voice at last. "You're a married man." *And a very attractive one.*

"This is true." Evan locked eyes with him. "But we have an arrangement, Daniel and I."

Brett's heartbeat quickened. "Arrangement?"

Evan nodded. He moved his hand under Brett's dinner jacket and caressed his arse. Brett caught his breath.

"We have a very open marriage. He plays, I play...." That hand squeezed him gently. "And now and again, we invite someone else to play with us." Evan smiled invitingly.

Brett swallowed. *Oh, fuck....* It wasn't that he was immune to Evan's charms—if anything, his cock was like steel—and it certainly wouldn't be the first time he'd taken part in a threesome, not by a long shot. But it felt *wrong.*

"I... I'm going to have to decline, flattering though the offer is." He took a step back, and Evan slowly withdrew his hand. He cocked his head to one side.

"Well, I can't say I'm not puzzled by your reaction." Evan glanced downward to his crotch. "Because *that* doesn't lie." Brett's breathing grew more rapid. Suddenly, Evan's eyes lit up. "But maybe the wrong brother is doing the asking." He winked. "Is that it, sir?"

Brett forgot how to breathe altogether for a moment or two. *Fuck....* And then Evan's words sank in. *The wrong brother? John?*

And then Evan's whole manner changed. Gone was the flirtatious, sexy man who'd just felt him up. Evan regarded him with a gentle smile.

"It's okay, Brett. You can breathe now."

Brett stared at him. Slowly, his brain started to function again. "You... you...." He struggled to find the words. Realization dawned. "You and Daniel don't have an open relationship, do you?"

Evan shook his head. "He's my whole life."

Brett couldn't get his mind off Evan's question. "John.... Is John gay?"

Evan's smile increased in intensity. "That's something you'll have to ask him." He leaned closer and whispered. "But I think you already know the answer, don't you?" He straightened. "You might want to take a moment before you join us at the table. I think you need to calm down first." He gave Brett an apologetic look. "I'm sorry. I probably shouldn't have done that, but I couldn't help myself—I had to know." And with that, he walked off toward their table.

Brett stared after him, his thoughts still in disarray. Two things were burned into his brain. He'd just outed himself—and the man who had captured his interest was gay. Possibly.

Hopefully?

"WHAT THE hell was that about?" John demanded in a low voice when Evan sat down in the chair next to him. "What were you and Brett talking about?"

Evan gazed at him frankly for a few long seconds. Then he picked up his wineglass, took a long drink from it, and gave John a sweet smile. "Brett is gay." John caught Daniel's sharp intake of breath.

John stared at him. His mind grasped for words. "And you know this because...."

Evan shrugged. "I'm sorry, but he had my gaydar pinging right from the start. I had to do something." He caught hold of Daniel's hand on the table. "So I lied to him, just to see if I got a reaction." He took another drink from his glass and then grinned at them both. "And boy, did I get one."

Daniel shook his head. "You are a wicked, wicked man, and when I get you home tonight, you *know* your arse and my hand have an appointment, don't you?" His eyes gleamed. Evan didn't look perturbed by this announcement—in fact, John thought he looked delighted. John closed his eyes. *Not going to go there. I don't want to know.* His mind was still reeling from Evan's revelation. *Brett is gay. Oh, my God—Brett is gay.*

"John, what are you thinking right now?" Evan's question broke through.

He opened his eyes to face his brother. "That this changes everything."

And then he smiled.

BRETT KEPT darting glances at John throughout the rest of the evening. John appeared happy and relaxed. He joked with Josh and Chris and told Daniel some of the things his group had got up to in his first half term. There seemed to be no change in his behavior, and Brett came to the conclusion that Evan had said nothing. What disturbed him most was that this thought disappointed him.

You wanted John to know, didn't you?

Brett couldn't deny it. To have someone he could confide in, be himself with…. He couldn't get over this change of heart. For the first time in his life, he wanted to feel connected to another human being.

There is another alternative—Evan's told John, but John isn't interested.

His chest tightened. And wouldn't *that* be a kick in the nuts? *The first man I've wanted to get to know outside of a bedroom, and he doesn't want me?* Brett pushed the thought aside. He couldn't think like that—*wouldn't* think like that. He tried to take an active part in the conversations around him, but he was too distracted. Thankfully, no one seemed to notice.

At last, the evening drew to a close. It was nearly midnight, and the last guests were departing. Brett sat at the table, staring into his empty wineglass. *Now* what did he do?

"Good night, Brett. It was lovely to meet you."

Brett pulled himself together and smiled at Josh and Chris. He got to his feet and shook their hands. "It was lovely meeting you too. Good luck with your wedding—when you eventually get around to it." They smiled at him and walked toward the door.

Evan appeared beside him. "We'll have to say good-bye too. We're sharing a taxi with them." He held out his hand, and Brett shook it. Evan leaned closer. "Good luck," he whispered. He straightened and gave Brett a warm smile. Impulsively, Brett grabbed him and gave him a brief hug.

"Thanks." He released Evan and then shook Daniel's hand. Daniel's amused expression filled him with relief. He watched the couple follow Josh and Chris out of the room. Brett turned to face John. "You ready to go? I'm going to get a taxi home. I'd ask if you wanted to share it, but I don't know if we live in the same direction." And suddenly, his heart was pounding.

John stood up and moved closer, so close that Brett had difficulty keeping his breathing even.

"I was going to walk home, actually."

Brett frowned. "Really? It's a cold night. You could catch your death."

John shrugged. "It's only half an hour. Besides, I'm not ready for bed yet." He moved closer still. Brett watched him bite his lip, and then suddenly, he caught his breath as John pressed his lips against Brett's cheek in a fleeting kiss. John pulled away, his cheeks hot. "Good night, Brett. I'll see you Monday." One last smile and John turned to walk out.

"John." Brett reached out to stop him, grabbing his arm. John stopped and faced him. Brett took a deep breath and cupped John's cheek. He leaned in close and kissed him there, allowing his lips to linger. Brett pulled back and met John's gaze. His eyes were wide, the pupils slightly blown. Brett stroked his cheek. "Thanks for this evening."

"You're welcome." The words were barely a whisper. John pulled free and walked slowly toward the door. He paused and turned to face Brett, his hand on his cheek. Brett gave him a nod, and John walked out.

Brett sank into the chair, his heart beating rapidly.

Now *what have I started?*

He laughed to himself. *My heart is pounding, my pulse is racing, and I feel like I've just kissed a boy for the first time. This is bloody ridiculous!* After so many years of casual encounters, why should one fleeting kiss have him in such a mess?

Because this time, it's different. And you know it.

The thought stopped him dead in his tracks. And it was then that the panic started.

I can't do this.

CHAPTER 10

JOHN COULDN'T sleep. He was *way* too excited for that. He'd wandered home in a daze, oblivious to the chill wind that whistled around him as he walked along the quiet streets.

Brett kissed me.

Okay, so it was a brief kiss, but it was something.

He'd let himself into the silent house as quietly as he could and tiptoed up to his room. Once there, he switched on the bedside lamp, dropped onto the bed, and stared at the ceiling.

Wow. I never saw this *coming.*

He lay there for what felt like hours, while he ran over the entire evening in his mind, playing the last few minutes over and over again, as if it were on a loop. As an afterthought, he got undressed, going through the motions automatically. His last thought before sleep claimed him was that he couldn't wait to see what Monday would bring.

BRETT HATED himself.

He'd spent Monday avoiding John, limiting their interactions to shared glances across the staff room during the briefing or during the lunch hour in the dining hall. He'd done everything possible to avoid being alone with John. But he knew it was coming. His stomach churned.

John's going to hate me.

Finally. The bell had rung and the kids were long gone, not to mention the staff. He knew John hadn't left yet—his bike was still chained up. Brett could see it from his office window. He tidied his desk, knowing full well that he was simply putting off the inevitable.

You have to tell him. And now is as good a time as any.

Brett left the office and walked through the silent corridor to John's classroom. He peered in through the glass porthole. John was seated at his desk, staring out the window. Brett wasn't a vain man, but he could lay even money that he knew what—or who—was on John's mind. With a heavy heart, he turned the handle and entered.

John looked up, and his face erupted into a shy smile. "I've missed you today. You haven't been around."

Brett crossed the room to his desk. The hardest thing was not letting his emotions show. And when John's face fell, he realized how crap he was at hiding stuff.

"What is it?" John's quietly uttered words pierced the silence of the room.

"First off, I have to apologize about Saturday night." The words had sounded better in his head. He'd been rehearsing them over and over again all through Sunday.

John stilled. "A-apologize?" The sudden flash of pain that he couldn't hide was like a knife to Brett's heart. "Why are you apologizing? Saturday night was wonderful."

Oh, for God's sake, stop looking at me like that with those beautiful blue eyes.

"I'm sorry, John. I shouldn't have kissed you. And... and we can't take this any further."

Those eyes widened. "Why?" The word came out as a whisper. "We're not doing anything wrong. And we wouldn't be hurting anyone."

"It's not a matter of right or wrong. I'm your line manager. I can't line manage someone if I'm in a relationship with them." Brett strove to keep his voice even. He'd wrestled with this all through Saturday night, when sleep had eluded him. Sunday had been no better. Any way he chose to play it, this wouldn't work.

"But why not?" John demanded. "We'd keep it separate from school. I could do that." Brett could see the hope in John's expression. *Oh, fuck.*

"You think?" Brett's voice was gentle. "John, your face lit up like a Christmas tree when I walked into your classroom. You really think you can keep your feelings out of this during the school day?" He took a deep breath. "What it comes down to is this. If word got out about us among the staff, it could seriously undermine their confidence in my ability to act impartially. I could get accused of favoritism." John opened his mouth to speak, but Brett held up his hand. "Yes, I know you'd always act professionally here, as would I, but I have to think about the potential adverse impact on the school."

"Oh, God—you're really serious about this, aren't you?" The misery etched across John's face was more than Brett could bear.

"Look, at least we're stopping things now before they have a chance to develop into something more." The lie sounded plausible. Brett knew it was already too late for that—the memory of those soft lips on his cheek, the musky smell of John's cologne, everything about those precious moments was burned indelibly into his brain.

He looked at the floor, unable to meet John's gaze for a moment. "We need to put this behind us, all right? Because if we don't, it's going to make working together very difficult, and I wouldn't want anything to jeopardize what is a very important year for you." He raised his head and locked eyes with John. "So it ends here." He pushed out the words decisively. Without waiting for John's response, he turned and exited the classroom.

Just get me out of here. Because if I have to look into John's eyes one more time today, it's going to kill me.

JOHN LET himself into the house and went straight upstairs to his room. Everywhere was quiet. He knew Stu was on a flight to Orlando and Alec was working a late shift. It was Martin's turn to cook, but John had no appetite. He stripped off his cycle gear and grabbed a towel from the back of his chair. He was functioning on autopilot. The short journey home had been dicey. He hadn't kept his eyes peeled at the roundabout near the Apollo Theater, and he'd had to swerve to avoid colliding with an oncoming car. The driver had gesticulated angrily before driving off, but John knew he was the one at fault. He hadn't been thinking straight.

He leaned against the tiles, eyes closed, and let the hot water cascade down on him.

He doesn't want me.

It was the one thought that wouldn't leave him. Yeah, he'd listened to the logical excuses Brett had given. They all made perfect sense. But he couldn't get away from the inescapable conclusion that there must be something wrong with him.

Can he tell how inexperienced I am? Is that *it? Is there something wrong with me?*

John stood there, the water pouring off him as he mechanically soaped away the day. His hand drifted lower to his flaccid cock. God, Sunday morning he'd been so hard. The memory of that fleeting kiss had been enough to send his mind on a delicious journey, one where he'd ended up jacking off to a breathless fantasy of Brett. John's imagination had filled in the blanks as he'd tried to picture his mentor naked.

Not that I'll ever get to see the real thing. Christ, this is so fucked up.

He turned off the shower and toweled himself dry. When he got back into his room, he cast a baleful eye at his folder. There was work to be done, but he was in no mood to do it. What he really wanted right now was a drink.

He was on his third glass of white wine when he heard the key in the front door. "In here. Come join me."

Martin stuck his head around the door, and his eyes widened as he caught sight of the nearly empty bottle. "Wow. You've been busy." He came into the lounge, took off his suit jacket, and loosened his tie. "You going to leave one glass for me? Because I think you've had enough. Especially as this is a school night."

"Sure. You can have the last glass." John winked. "I can always open another bottle." He prided himself on the fact that his words remained distinct. Martin perched on the arm of the couch and regarded him, brow wrinkled.

"Okay, what happened?"

John raised his glass. "Congratulate me. I got dumped."

Martin's face fell. "Oh, fuck. He only kissed you on Saturday. He get cold feet or something?" He moved off the arm to sit next to John and peered intently at him. "John, put down the glass and talk to me, please."

With a sigh, John placed the glass on the coffee table and sagged into the couch, his eyes closed. "He doesn't want me." He felt Martin's hand on his knee, but he batted it away. John got to his feet unsteadily. "You know what? I've jus' realized I'm wastin' time here. Brett's not the only guy to take an interest. So if you'll excuse me, I'm goin' out."

Martin jumped to his feet. "Hon, I don't think that's such a good idea. You're not thinking clearly right now. How about I make us some dinner, and then you and I can watch some TV, try to relax?"

John shook his head. The more he thought about it, the more sense it made. And he knew *exactly* where he would go. He pushed past Martin and grabbed his jacket from the newel post at the foot of the stairs. After patting his pockets to make sure he had his wallet, he lurched down the hall and out the front door, dimly aware of Martin calling to him.

I know where to find someone who'll want me.

THE MUSIC pounded through his skull. The lights skewered through his eyeballs. John didn't recall Babel being this loud or bright, but then again, it might have had something to do with the drinks he'd been pouring down his throat since he'd walked into the club. And then of course, there were the three glasses of wine from earlier. He scanned the dance floor and the area around the bar. Disappointingly, there was no sign of the one man he wanted to see. He shook his head. Maybe this had been a mistake. His head ached like crazy.

"You can't keep away, can you?"

John lifted his head slowly to see Max standing in front of him, hands on hips. He was grinning.

"Hi, Max." John gave him a drunken little wave. "Have a seat, why don'tcha. Let's you and I get acquainted." He gave him a salacious grin.

Max's face straightened immediately. "Just how much have you had to drink?"

John scowled. "Why's everyone suddenly so concerned about my drinkin' habits?" He tried to focus on Max, who was looking a little blurry around the edges.

Max glanced in the direction of the bar, and his face cleared. "You stay there, and I'll be right back." John watched him walk off and then returned his attention to the glass in front of him—which was empty.

Time for another, he thought. Because he could still recall Brett's face as he told him they couldn't do this, so clearly he'd not drunk enough. Before he could stagger to his feet, Max was back again. He placed something in front of John.

John stared in disbelief. "It's a cup of coffee." He raised his head. "Black coffee? In a gay club?"

Max chuckled. "Trevor behind the bar is a mate of mine. And by the way, he won't serve you any more alcohol. You've had enough." He sat in the chair facing John and folded his arms across his chest. "Now drink it. It might make you feel a little better."

John glared at him. "D'you know what? I've 'ad quite enough of people tellin' me what to do today, makin' decisions for me." He tried to push the cup away, but Max lifted it out of his reach.

"The state you're in, you'll spill it." Max fixed him with a sympathetic look. "Okay, baby, talk to me."

"Don't wanna talk," John groused. He let his gaze roam up and down Max's lean body. Those tight black leather pants did little to hide the clear outline of Max's dick. John gave a sly grin and slid his hand over Max's tightly muscled thigh, on a direct route to his cock. To his surprise, Max grabbed his hand around the wrist and held onto him. He hauled John up onto his feet, grabbed the coffee, and marched him over to a quieter corner of the club. He pushed John down into a chair and then sat facing him.

"Uh-uh." Max shook his head. "We are not going down that road. If I do anything with you, it will be when you are sober enough to remember every second of it." John swallowed and sagged into his chair. Max pulled up his chair until their knees touched and then leaned forward, his weight over his elbows. "Now tell me what's going on—John, isn't it?" His voice softened. "What happened, honey?" He reached out and stroked John's cheek. The action was so gentle and carried out with such compassion that John had to stifle a sob.

"He doesn't want me," he bleated out. Max arched his brows, and John proceeded to tell him, between sniffs, everything that had transpired between him and Brett. Max listened carefully, never uttering a word. He passed John his cup of coffee, and John drank it down, the bitter taste a jolt to his system. When John had finished speaking, Max sat back and met his gaze.

"Baby, I'm flattered, really. But right now, you're in a pretty vulnerable state." He grinned. "I may be a bad bastard on occasion, but I don't take advantage of drunken virgins. It's not my style."

John's cheeks felt as if they were on fire. "But I'm not a virgin. I told you that before. I've had sex."

Max guffawed. "Women don't count. You're a virgin until you've had a dick in your arse."

John's mouth fell open. He pondered for a moment. "Is that why Brett doesn't want me? 'Cause I'm a v-virgin?"

Max laughed softly. "Only if he's crazy." He stroked John's hair. "Honey, I have no idea why this guy rejected you, but for what it's worth, I think he's a fool. You're gorgeous, and you're obviously a nice guy." He looked up over John's shoulder. "And you also have some pretty amazing friends." John cocked his head, and Max chuckled. "The cavalry has arrived."

John inclined his head to find Martin standing beside him, a look of sheer relief across his face.

"Oh, thank God." Martin gave a shaky laugh. "I've been so worried. I was imagining all sorts of things." He glanced across at Max, and his gaze took in the empty coffee cup. He smiled. "You've been taking care of him, haven't you?"

Max got to his feet. "Someone had to—it just happened to be me." He winked. "Now I think you should get this boy home. He's going to have one hell of a hangover tomorrow." He turned to walk away, but Martin grabbed hold of his hand and shook it.

"Thanks, Max. That was good of you."

Max shrugged. "It was nothing. John needed a guardian angel. Like I said—it just happened to be me." He released Martin's hand and helped John to his feet. He pecked him on the cheek. "Now go home and get some sleep. You'll probably feel like shit in the morning, but at least you're going home in the same state you arrived—intact." He shook his head. "Don't do this again, babe. There are lots of guys around here who don't have my principles, if you get my meaning." He gave them both a smile and walked off toward the bar.

Martin stared after him, lips parted. "Seems I got Max all wrong." He sighed. "Come on, let's get you home. And then you're going straight to bed. If you're lucky, you'll make it through the night without throwing up."

John groaned. He felt like shit.

And tomorrow, I'll have to face Brett again.

The thought did not improve his mood.

JOHN HELPED Alec clear away the plates after dinner while Stu made the coffee. He knew he'd been quiet all evening, but there was nothing to say. Brett had been cool with him on the few occasions they'd met in the corridor or on the way into assembly. Thank goodness they weren't due for a meeting until Friday. It would take him a few days to put Monday morning's conversation behind him and to put their professional relationship back on an even keel.

"So how was the head this morning?" Alec asked.

John groaned. "I'm guessing Martin spilled the beans."

Alec guffawed. "Like he was going to keep *that* a secret." He clucked his tongue. "Bad hangover, was it?"

John hung up the tea towel and stared at the tiled kitchen floor. "I'm not sure I'll ever be able to look Max in the face again." Not to mention the fact that he'd felt extremely unprepared for his lessons. Thank God Brett hadn't dropped in for a surprise observation.

Alec leaned against him. "It will get better, honest."

At that particular moment, John found it hard to believe. "I think it will be better for all concerned if I just try to forget the whole sorry situation ever happened." Of course, working with Brett in such close proximity wasn't going to be easy. *I guess this is where I find out what I'm made of,* he mused.

Alec was staring at him. "You really do like this guy, don't you?"

John's eyes met his. "Unfortunately? Yes." He grabbed one of the coffee mugs Stu had just filled and walked out of the kitchen. He didn't want to talk about it anymore. Once he reached his room, John sat at his desk and took out the sheaf of test papers from that morning. *Better get these marked*, he thought with a sigh. He'd hated the way he'd felt today, a feeling of not being in control.

This is what you get when you don't plan your day. He'd gotten through by the skin of his teeth—he wouldn't be caught out like that again. John put his head down and concentrated on his work.

Toward ten o'clock, he heard several pairs of feet on the stairs and a soft knocking at his door. "Come on in." He stared as all three housemates came into the room. Martin had a tray with mugs and a packet of chocolate biscuits. John sniffed. "Hot chocolate?" He couldn't help grinning. "Guys, I'm fine now, really. You don't have to mollycoddle me, you know."

Stu cleared his throat. "Actually, this is a council of war." The other two nodded in agreement.

John gaped. "A what?"

Alec plonked himself on the bed and made himself comfortable. "A council of war. We're your military advisors."

John chortled. "Okay, I'll bite. What exactly are you advising me on?"

Martin took the lead. "How you're going to drive Brett out of his tiny little mind." He winked. "By the time you're done, he'll be so hot for you he won't be able to keep his hands off."

John laughed—until he realized they were all deadly serious.

CHAPTER 11

"YOU'RE SERIOUS." John stared at his housemates.

"Extremely," Stu replied. "We are here to give you the benefit of our wisdom." He put the tray on John's desk and handed out the mugs. Then he sat down on the rug by John's bed and crossed his legs. Martin joined him.

"Just think of us as your three fairy godmothers," added Martin with a grin. "We're going to come up with a plan to have that man whimpering every time he sees you."

John almost sprayed hot chocolate over his desk as Martin whipped out a wand wound around with Christmas tinsel from behind his back and waved it over John's head. Martin chortled.

He thought for a moment about Martin's suggestion. John was dubious. "I can't do anything that would be seen as sexual harassment. You *do* realize that?"

Alec smiled. "Oh, we're not talking anything overtly sexual here. It's got to be little things that will build and build until he can't take it any longer—and all he'll want to do is take *you*." The others chuckled.

John grabbed a mug and considered the idea for a moment. "Well, what have I got to lose?"

Alec beamed. "Exactly!" He pinned John with a look. "Get your pen and paper ready. Seduction 101 is in session."

John couldn't help smiling as he reached for a notepad and pen. His housemates were wonderful. "Okay, what first?"

"First off, you aren't goin' to lay a finger on him," advised Stu. John quirked his eyebrows. "I mean it," Stu continued. "You're goin' to bring him to his knees with hot looks, touchin' yourself, suggestive actions—but you won't touch *him*."

"Imagine sitting in front of him, toying with a ruler," suggested Martin. "Running your finger along its length, glancing at his crotch, then back to the ruler. Let your finger slide until you've measured off about seven or eight inches. Then look expectantly at him."

"Try unbuttonin' your collar and loosenin' your tie, when it's just the two of you alone in that office after school." Stu's eyes sparkled. "And lowerin' your head and lookin' at him subtly through those long lashes."

"Licking your lips," interjected Martin.

"And then of course, there's the age-old trick—jealousy." Alec was really getting into this. "Maybe one of us could come to the school one evening, acting as though we're interested in you."

"Yeah." Stu's eyes lit up. "Let Brett think you've got someone who wants you."

"Tell him about Max," suggested Martin. "You could be telling him what happened during your weekend. Brett needs to stop seeing you as his new teacher and start seeing you as this hot young guy that he's about to let slip through his fingers."

"Yeah, but don't forget to share stuff about yourself," Alec put in. "He needs to see that you're more than a cute, sexy body. Brett needs to see the warm, sensitive man hiding beneath the hot exterior."

John gazed at the three men with their earnest expressions. "You really think all this will work?" And then Alec's words sank in. "I'm hot?" His cheeks were suddenly on fire.

Stu let escape a wry chuckle. "I keep forgettin' how innocent you are." He leveled a keen look at John. "It's no different to seducin' a woman. You pay him compliments, comment on his clothes...."

"Use his name when you talk to him," added Martin.

"And don't forget to carry condoms," mumbled Alec around a chocolate biscuit. John's eyes widened, and Alec giggled. He swallowed his mouthful and grinned. "I'm serious. You never know when the opportunity will present itself."

"Brett's not about to leap on my bones in school, is he?" John tried to ignore the image that arose instantly in his head—him naked on his back on that wide table in Brett's office while Brett plowed into him. John felt his hole clench. *Oh, God….*

"Well, not while the kids are around, certainly," Martin said practically. "But after school?" He waggled his eyebrows.

Alec was staring at John. "You think he's going to wait to fuck you until he's got you in a bedroom, don't you?"

John felt his cheeks grow hot. "No, but—"

"Some of the best sex I have ever had has been spur-of-the-moment, lightning-quick, '*For-God's-sake-fuck-me-now*' sex, when we both wanted it so badly we couldn't have waited a minute more." Alec's eyes glazed over.

Stu snickered. "*God*, yes, I know *exactly* what you mean."

John looked from Stu to Alec to Martin. "I don't have a clue, do I?" He hadn't felt this unprepared when he'd lost his virginity. It had been a simple case of Insert Tab A into Slot B, and it had been over relatively quickly.

Stu's eyes gleamed. "Hold that thought." He got up from the floor and darted out the door. Moments later, he returned and flung a book across the room. John caught it deftly and looked at the front cover.

"*The Joy of Gay Sex?*"

Stu chortled. "That's your homework, teacher. Call it a little bedtime readin'." He winked. "But there won't be a test on it." He sat down again next to Martin on the rug.

John studied the book for several long seconds. A thought occurred to him. He gazed at his housemates with a half smile. "I'm not sure how I feel getting advice about how to get my man from so-called advisors who don't have men of their own."

Stu laughed. "Oh, baby. Don't assume that because you don't see me bringin' anyone 'ome that I'm not gettin' any." There was a wicked gleam in his eye. "Trust me, I don't go without."

Martin nudged him. "A guy in every airport, right, Stu?"

Stu tried to look modest. "Well, not sure that I'd go *that* far, but yeah, I've had more than me fair share of hot guys. And as for not 'avin' a man of me own? Maybe one day I'll settle down, but right now, I'm 'avin' too much fun. Hell, I'm only twenty-seven."

John was fascinated. This wasn't a subject they broached often. "What about you, Martin?"

Martin laced his fingers behind his head and leaned back against the bed. He grinned. "I'm not as big a slut as Stu," he said with a sideways glance at Stu. Stu guffawed and gave him a mock punch to the upper arm. "There've been a few fellas, sure, but no one who made me go weak at the knees." He put his hand to his chest. "Certainly, no one who got in *here*." For a moment, his expression faltered, and John suddenly saw a side to Martin that he'd never glimpsed.

"But you want that," he said quietly. Martin's gaze met his, and for a few seconds, there was silence in the bedroom. Then Martin gave a lopsided grin.

"Maybe one day." The wistful note in his voice belied the expression on his face.

"And we all know what a hopeless romantic *I* am," Alec said with a half smile. Martin heaved himself up from the floor and joined Alec on the bed, where he hugged him tightly. Alec gave him a grateful look.

"You'll find someone. I'm sure of it," Martin reassured him. "Somewhere out there is a *very* tall, handsome guy who is looking for a sweet, generous man to top him. Someone who isn't afraid to explore his submissive side—and who wants to take care of you the way you deserve."

Alec stared at him openmouthed. "You really *do* know me, don't you?" There was a look of something akin to wonder on his face. He kissed Martin on the cheek. Martin's cheeks flushed.

"So, still happy to take advice from us?" Stu asked John with a wink.

John smiled. "I think I'm a very lucky man. And if I follow all your advice, Brett's not going to know what hit him."

He felt the ripple of excitement that ran through him. Brett might think it was all over, but John was now determined to make him change his mind.

And I can't wait to put all this advice into action.

MAYBE HE'S stronger than I thought.

Brett watched John from across the staff room as the staff filed in, ready for the morning briefing. John met his gaze and returned it with a confident smile. Brett had been prepared to find him quiet, withdrawn, maybe even a little upset. He certainly hadn't expected the calm young man who'd greeted him nonchalantly this morning as Brett had entered the men's room. John was in the middle of changing into his suit, and Brett had caught his breath at the sight of that tight, lean body as John buttoned up his crisp white shirt. Without the slightest hint of embarrassment, John had smiled and continued dressing, seemingly oblivious to Brett's presence. If anything, Brett was a little disconcerted.

He certainly seems to have got over it very quickly. For a brief moment, Brett was aware of a heavy feeling in his chest. *Am I so easy to forget?* Because in spite of everything he'd said, he couldn't get John out of his mind. *For God's sake, man, it was a simple kiss on the cheek—*get over it.

Brett ran through his notes briskly and efficiently. For some reason, he felt his gaze drawn continually to where John was sitting. The young man never took his eyes off Brett. There was nothing untoward in that focused gaze, but Brett found it strangely compelling. It was almost a relief when the briefing ended and he could escape to his office. Why John should have this effect on him, he had no idea—he only knew it unnerved him.

Throughout the day, he walked several times along the corridor where John's classroom was situated and glanced through the porthole. He loved the way John interacted with his pupils, and already he could see that the class was reacting enthusiastically to John's style of teaching. Hands shot up into the air as children strove to answer questions and be rewarded with their names on the whiteboard. Brett could see the gold star chart on the wall, already filling up. Brett had had his concerns about the group after their performance the previous year, but John seemed to have begun to turn them around.

Brett smiled to himself. *The man's a natural-born teacher.*

During break, he ran into Bev in the corridor. She was grinning widely.

"Have you seen how many shoeboxes John's group has already brought in?"

Brett broke into a smile. "I take it they're doing well?" It warmed his heart when the children showed how generous they could be. Their backgrounds weren't exactly affluent, to say the least.

"Doing well? He's already brought me fifteen boxes."

Brett was astounded. "How come there are so many?" Such a figure was unheard of.

Bev smiled fondly. "He went into a shoe shop in the Arndale shopping center and told them about Operation Christmas Child. They apparently gave him a load of boxes—which they brought round to the school, which is amazing. And then he sat in his room after school and covered every one of them in wrapping paper."

Brett was touched. The charity was very close to his heart. He'd spent his childhood in an orphanage—not that anyone in the school knew that—and he remembered vividly how dismal Christmas could be if no one made an effort.

"But he didn't stop there," Bev continued. "Some children were able to bring in a few items for the boxes, and for everyone else, he got them to bring in a minimum of one pound. Then he went shopping in Poundland. He came back with so much stuff." Her eyes shone. "I think he bought a lot of it himself, if you ask me."

Brett knew the store. Poundland was very popular with the poorest members of the school community. True to its name, everything cost one pound, and he knew some children spent their birthday money in there. But hearing how generous John was brought a warm glow to Brett's heart.

"It sounds like we may have a bumper crop of boxes this year." Brett was delighted. He'd shown the pupils a video of the boxes being delivered to children all around the world. He'd glanced around the quietened assembly hall, noting the smiles on his pupils' faces as they watched the obvious joy and delight that the boxes brought to their recipients. It did

K.C. Wells

them good to see that there were children in far worse circumstances than themselves.

Bev grinned. "Yes, indeed. And it's having a knock-on effect. Other classes don't want to be outdone, so there's some healthy competition going as to which group brings in the most boxes." She nodded to him and walked off toward the staff room. Brett watched her, his mind on John. He couldn't wait to see what his newest member of staff came up with for the charity day.

"I HAVE to say, I'm impressed." Brett shut John's folder and handed it back to him. "Your first assessment is going to be extremely positive."

John's face lit up. "Really?"

Brett laughed. John was such a modest man. In the last few weeks, Brett had been very impressed by his performance. The lessons he'd observed were all living up to the promise John had shown on his interview day. And Brett was relieved to find the two of them getting on so well. Any fears he'd had that his decision not to take things any further might have harmed their developing professional relationship had proved unfounded.

John relaxed into his chair and grinned. "Phew. I guess I can breathe now." His eyes sparkled.

Brett chuckled. He loved the way John's smile reached his eyes. He watched as John loosened his dark blue tie and undid his top button, revealing the creamy skin at the base of his throat. For a second, Brett found himself fantasizing about kissing him there, tracing his tongue over the silky skin of his collarbones. He shook himself mentally and forced his gaze upward. John was regarding him intently, and Brett had to fight hard to repress a shiver as John licked his lips, leaving them looking moist and soft. *Oh, God.* The urge to kiss that lush mouth was incredible.

With an effort, Brett dragged his gaze from the tempting view. He glanced up at the wall clock. "Hey, the weekend is finally here. Any plans?" Anything to get his mind off what his body wanted to do to John.

John stretched his arms above his head, and Brett suppressed a groan. The movement pulled the fabric of his shirt taut against his chest, and Brett could see the dark circles of flesh where John's nipples stood proud. *Christ, he has no idea what he's doing to me.* Right then, all Brett wanted to do was slip his hand under the desk and palm his stiffening cock.

"My housemates want to go to Babel tonight," John said. Brett knew of the club, although he'd never visited it. He viewed John's expression with interest. John pressed his lips together, and there was a sudden tenseness about his shoulders.

Brett cocked his head. "Don't you *want* to go? You don't seem tremendously keen on the idea."

John grimaced. "Oh, don't get me wrong. I love dancing, and there are always so many hot guys who want to buy me a drink or dance with me."

Brett's chest tightened at the thought of him dancing up close and personal with numerous faceless men. He could almost see John moving his body sensually against another man, lost in the rhythm of the music that pulsed throughout the club.

He cleared his throat. "Then what's the problem?"

John let out a sigh. "There's this one guy, Max, who's been, shall we say, very *attentive* lately." He shivered slightly. "He's proving very hard to resist."

The tight feeling in Brett's chest had morphed into a burning sensation. He clenched his teeth at the thought of this unknown Max with his hands all over John. Brett clamped down hard on the urge to tell John to be wary of him. *You don't have a clue what this Max is like,* he told himself sternly. *He could be a really nice guy, for all you know.*

A really nice guy who plainly wanted John. Brett didn't like that. Not one little bit.

A noise outside the office door startled him. It was already five thirty—there should have been no one else left in the building but the two of them. A rap on the door followed.

"Come in." Brett got to his feet. He wasn't worried—someone with malicious intent would surely not have knocked politely. He arched his eyebrows as the door opened and a man entered. He was about five eleven, with blond hair and blue eyes. The man looked around apprehensively, and then he beamed as his gaze alighted on John.

"There you are, hon. I thought I'd missed you."

John's face broke into a delighted smile. "Stu! What are you doing here?" He got to his feet and crossed the room to hug the new arrival warmly.

Stu gave him a lazy grin. "I wanted to surprise you. I was passin' the school, and I saw your bike, so I knew you were still around here somewhere." His gaze moved to Brett. "My apologies—you haven't finished your meetin'." Those cool eyes fixed on him.

Brett waved his hand. "Oh, don't worry, we were just finishing. And you are…?"

Stu came forward, hand outstretched. "Stu Benton. I share a house with John—well, me and two others." He returned his gaze to John. "You ready to go, babe?"

John smiled. "Just give me a few minutes to get changed into my gear and I'll be right with you." He glanced across at Brett. "If that's all right with you."

Brett nodded. "Certainly. You get changed—I'll entertain your friend." John beamed and exited the office. Brett turned his attention back to Stu. "I'm glad to see John getting on so well with his housemates—well, *one* of them, at least." He ached to know more. John had certainly seemed very friendly toward Stu.

"Well, between you and me, I'd like us to be more than housemates, if you get my meanin'." Stu winked. "I'm working on it, at any rate."

Brett sized him up quickly. Stu was tanned, and his skin had a healthy glow about it. He estimated him to be in his late twenties. He wore a sinfully tight pair of jeans that left little to the imagination. Brett's jaw ached, and it dawned on him why this might be—his teeth were still clenched.

He made an effort to speak calmly. "Oh, I see. I thought John already had a boyfriend," he said, lying through his teeth.

Stu quirked his eyebrows. "Oh, I suppose he's told you about Max. Well, Max might wish he were John's boyfriend, but that's as far as it's goin' to go if I have anything to do about it." He pursed those firm lips. "John needs lookin' after, and Max is *far* too predatory for my liking." He gave a start and glanced apologetically at Brett. "Sorry—that was rather forward of me. You must forgive me goin' on like this. It's just that John talks about you so much, I figured you and he might 'ave discussed this."

Brett was suddenly aware of a fluttery feeling in his belly. "John talks about me?"

Stu chuckled. "All the time. At home, it's 'Brett says this' or 'Brett said that.'" He tilted his head. "He obviously thinks a lot of you."

The words filled Brett with warmth.

John came back into the office, his backpack already nestled between his shoulder blades. Brett tried hard not to look at those firm thighs and the snug way his cycling shorts and black shirt clung to his body. "Have a good weekend," he managed to choke out. He sat down quickly and reached for a sheaf of papers. He hadn't the slightest intention of working, but he couldn't remain standing, not with his traitorous dick hardening noticeably.

John gave him a brisk nod and then smiled at Stu. "Let's go." Stu dipped his chin briefly in Brett's direction and followed John from the office. Brett waited until he heard them leave the building, and then he walked across to the window and peered through the blinds. He saw Stu kiss John on the cheek before the two men started to walk out of the grounds, John pushing his bike. Brett was startled to hear the noise that issued from his throat as he watched them. It was almost a growl.

Not for the first time, Brett questioned his decision. His body's reaction to John and his growing attachment to him threatened to overcome the logical part of his brain. No matter how many times he told himself he'd done the right thing, there was still this tiny voice in his head that wouldn't shut up.

You want him. Admit it.

Brett closed his eyes, shutting out the view of John and Stu. But he could still see John in his head. And now there was a dull ache in his chest.

Oh, fuck.

CHAPTER 12

JOHN GAZED with pride at the certificate on his classroom wall. Year Six had collected a total of thirty boxes, the highest number ever achieved by a single group. His heart had almost burst when he'd watched two children from the class go out to the front of the hall to be presented with their certificate. Brett shook their hands as the whole school applauded their efforts.

He gazed around the chaos of his room. The term had ended with a Christmas party for all the pupils. First, there had been a film shown in the hall, *The Muppet Christmas Carol*, and judging by the happy laughter and shining faces, it had been a good choice. Then all the groups had returned to their classrooms, where teachers had organized prizes for achievements throughout the term. The LSAs had been busy preparing the hall for the party, which had been a combination of food and games, and John had loved every minute of it.

As was typical on the last day of term, the children were allowed to leave after the party, and John was staggered to have received so many small gifts and cards from his class. He hadn't expected anything. The boxes of chocolates, squashy gifts that could *only* be pairs of socks or maybe gloves, and a couple of bottles of wine brought in by grateful parents now sat on his desk.

Heaven knows how I'll get this all home, he mused. He wondered briefly if Alec was at home. He might be able to cadge a lift in his car.

"Well, you've survived the longest term. Congratulations."

John swung around to see Brett walking into his room, a welcome smile on his face.

John gestured toward his heap of presents. "This was unexpected."

Brett gazed at the numerous gifts, and his smile widened. "Yes, I have a similar collection in my office." He tapped his watch. "Unfortunately, Mr. Wainwright, your day is not finished quite yet. You and I have an appointment to keep."

Oh, hell. John had forgotten. There was still the assessment to finish. "Will it take long? I wanted to ring one of my housemates to see if he can pick me up. I'll never get all this home on my own, and I don't have the bike today."

Brett looked thoughtful. "I tell you what—let's get the assessment completed, and then I'll drive you home. What do you say? There are only a few missing details, and then we can sign off on it."

John smiled. "That would be great." He looked around the classroom. "Can you give me about ten minutes to clean up in here? I don't want to leave it in a state over the holiday, and I told the cleaners I'd see to it. I didn't want them to stay late, not on the last day of term."

Brett regarded him warmly. "That was nice of you. Yes, sure. I'll be in my office when you're ready." He exited the room, and John took a deep breath. So much for all his efforts during the last weeks. They'd obviously had little effect on Brett. It was disappointing to admit defeat when the others questioned him about how his campaign was faring. And he'd tried *everything*, but Brett seemed oblivious to John's attempts at seduction.

Or maybe I'm just not cut out for it, he admitted to himself with sadness. He'd finally reached a decision. He was wasting his time pinning his hopes on a man who clearly had no interest in him. Brett had obviously been able to forget that initial attraction—maybe it was time John made a concerted effort to do the same. Because holding onto that hope resulted in nothing but an aching heart.

At last, the room was once more in its usual tidy state. He noticed the last box of doughnuts, which had remained unopened, one of his little gifts to his class. *Maybe* not *the wisest choice*, he mused, recalling the sticky faces and fingers that had resulted. It had taken several trips to the bathroom, but finally, everyone had removed all traces of jam and sugar. He picked up the box and grinned. Brett would undoubtedly have coffee brewing—these would be a pleasant treat.

Brett was seated at his desk, peering intently at the monitor, when John entered the office. The building was quiet. John loved these times when it was just the two of them. The light had already faded outside, and Brett had pulled the blinds. The warm glow of the desk lamp lit up his face as he worked.

"Got something to go with our coffee," John offered, holding up the box.

Brett looked up and grinned. "Oh, nice. Like we didn't get enough sugar at the party." He winked. He switched off the monitor and picked up the assessment document that sat on the desk. He brandished it in the air. "This makes impressive reading."

John glowed. "That's great." It was such a relief that his first term had been a success.

Brett poured out two mugs of coffee and brought them across to the table. They sat and relaxed, sipping the aromatic brew.

"Come on—hand one over." Brett pointed at the box of doughnuts.

John chuckled. "Yes, sir." He held open the box, and Brett helped himself to the sugar-covered delicacy. Brett bit into it, and John tried not to laugh at the sight of the jam oozing out over his chin. Brett gave him a rueful stare and wiped at the red stickiness but only succeeded in getting his fingers coated in it.

John couldn't help it—he burst out laughing.

Brett narrowed his eyes. "*Not* helping," he said firmly. John smothered another giggle and then took a bite of his own doughnut. Oh, hell—there was sugar *everywhere*. He licked his fingers and then caught his breath as he saw Brett's pupils widen and heard the hitch in his breathing. *Interesting.* Slowly, John sucked his finger deep into his mouth, his eyes fixed on Brett. He shivered as Brett swallowed, his lips parting. John licked the sugar from his lips, never taking his gaze off Brett. He felt the hairs stand up on his arms, almost as if the room were flooded with an electrical charge.

Brett put down his doughnut. He stretched his arm across the desk for the box of tissues, pulled one out, and then slowly wiped his lips, chin, and fingers clean, his eyes focused on John's mouth as he did so. Brett regarded him for a moment, and John was suddenly aware of his heart beating strongly, his mouth flooded with saliva.

"Do you have *any* idea," Brett began, enunciating every word slowly, "how difficult it's been these last few weeks to be around you?" He got up slowly from his chair and walked to the office door. To John's surprise, he locked it and then turned to face him.

John stiffened. His pulse raced. "What… what do you mean?"

Brett locked eyes with him. "I think you know *exactly* what I'm talking about. I couldn't get you out of my mind. It seemed like *every single* day you'd do *something* that made me want to touch you, lick you—" He licked his lips. "—fuck you."

John swallowed. Oh. Fuck.

Brett regarded him intently. "Yeah, you knew what you were doing, didn't you? How about all those times I'd walk into the men's room, only to find you either changing into your cycle gear, or even worse, *out* of it prior to taking a shower. Or putting on your suit."

John couldn't take his eyes off him. His mouth was suddenly devoid of moisture, and his stomach muscles tightened as Brett moved toward him. John let out a small yelp as Brett pulled him to his feet, his hands tight around John's upper arms. John trembled to see the intense expression on Brett's face.

"Brett, I—"

"Shut the fuck up," Brett growled, and then John gasped as his mouth was claimed in a brutal kiss that stole the breath from his body. He froze for a second—and then surrendered to those lips pressed against his, that tongue sliding into his mouth in an erotic exploration that left him gasping for air. He couldn't get enough. John moaned as Brett slid his hands over him, molding around his arse, pulling John tight against his hard body. John could feel Brett's erection, heavy and full, against him, and he couldn't stifle the low groan that rolled out of him as Brett ground his dick against John's rapidly stiffening cock. Brett didn't let up for a second. He kissed him hungrily, and John responded, their tongues sliding together in an increasingly erotic ballet as Brett devoured him.

Brett broke the kiss and stared into John's eyes as he reached down to stroke John's erection through his pants. John groaned once more, and Brett's eyes widened.

"Bloody hell, John—what have you *got* in there?" And then he grinned.

John gasped as Brett dropped to his knees, fumbled with John's button and zipper, and then dragged his pants and briefs down over his hips in one swift movement to reveal his cock, which rose up, hard and wanting.

Brett's grin widened. "Well, hel-*lo* there."

John's cheeks were scarlet. He'd always been embarrassed by the size of his cock at school. The appreciative gleam in Brett's eyes, however, was doing wonders for his self-esteem. Brett eyed his rock-hard dick and licked his lips.

"God, yes," John whispered.

Brett slid his tongue slowly over the wide head, lapping up the bead of precome that had already appeared at the slit—and then sucked him deep. John cried out as Brett's head bobbed enthusiastically over his shaft. *Holy Fuck*. It felt bloody *marvelous*. Brett grabbed his arse and propelled John deeper into his mouth, until John could feel Brett's throat muscles tighten around the tip. He heard Brett breathe through his nose as he worked his cock, bobbing faster, until suddenly John felt his skin begin to tingle. He placed his hands lightly on Brett's head and held him there while he began to thrust slowly into that hot, wet heaven. Brett moaned around his shaft, and his cheeks hollowed as he sucked him deeper. John froze as Brett made choking noises and started to pull out when he saw tears appear at the corners of Brett's eyes, but Brett growled around his cock and sucked all the harder. John's legs shook with the effort of remaining upright while Brett edged him closer to orgasm.

"Oh, fuck, Brett, you're going to make me come."

Brett pulled off him so abruptly that John whimpered. "So come," he gasped out, his voice hoarse. "Because I'm not finished with you yet." And he took John deep once more, only this time he grabbed hold of his arse and squeezed his cheeks tightly, causing John to cry out. Brett pushed a finger into his crease and brushed lightly over his hole. John shuddered, and his legs trembled. When Brett eased the pad of his finger slowly inside him, he couldn't hold back any longer. He arched his back as his dick pulsed come down Brett's throat, his hands on Brett's shoulders for balance. Brett drank him down hungrily, his finger still lodged firmly in John's arse, until John was leaning over him, weak at the knees.

Brett released his half-hard cock and sat back, pulling his finger free and gazing up at John with eyes glazed with lust. He gave him a wicked smile that set off the fluttering in his belly with a vengeance. Brett rose to his feet and drew John to him in a slow, searching kiss that made him quiver all over. He could taste himself on Brett's tongue. When at last he broke the kiss, Brett removed John's jacket and tossed it over the back of a chair. John stood there immobile, his gaze never straying from Brett as he undid the buttons of John's shirt and ran his hands over John's chest and abs. John shuddered anew as he thought about what was to happen next. Brett turned John to face the table and pushed him until he was bent over it, his cheek pressed against the smooth grain, his spent cock pointing down to the floor.

John gasped as his bare torso made contact with the cool surface.

"Stay there. Don't move."

He froze and then listened as he heard Brett move across the office toward his desk, hearing soft noises that he couldn't distinguish, then the sound of a drawer opening and closing. And then Brett was back at the table. John heard the sound of a belt being undone and the unmistakable noise of a zipper. He held his breath, hardly daring to breathe as Brett leaned over him, his chest tight against John's back. Brett nipped at his neck, making him emit a tiny yelp. Brett's breath was warm against his ear.

"I've wanted to fuck you since you first walked into my office this summer," Brett whispered, making John shiver, his hands flat against the table. He wanted to say something, to tell Brett to be gentle, but he couldn't get the words out. Brett pushed up his shirt and kissed down his spine. John exhaled sharply as two slick fingers pressed slowly into him. "I need to warn you, this isn't going to last long," Brett breathed into his ear. "I'm on the edge already. I'll try to hold back as long as I can, but you have me so worked up right now, I'll probably shoot my load as soon as I'm inside you."

Tremors rippled through John as those fingers twisted inside him, stretching him, paving the way for Brett's cock. *Fuck, he's about to screw me, and I haven't even seen his cock.* Although he was shaking in anticipation, John felt a pang of regret. It wasn't how he'd imagined his first time would be. He didn't have time to dwell on that thought as the sound of foil tearing suddenly filled the quiet room. He caught his breath. *Oh, God—this is really going to happen.*

"Reach back, spread yourself for me." Brett's harsh command had him obeying without thinking, and he pulled his cheeks apart—and then froze as he felt Brett's hot, all too solid cock press against his hole. John tried not to cry out as Brett pushed forward with his hips, slowly easing his way into his body.

"Oh, fuck—you're like a furnace in there. And so tight. My *God*, you're tight."

John's face burned, and then he forgot his shame as Brett's groin met his arse and Brett was as deep inside John as it was possible to be. Now the burn was inside him. He gritted his teeth, determined not to reveal how much this hurt. He bit his lip in an effort to keep in the cries that begged to escape.

And then Brett began to move.

Slowly at first but then gaining momentum, Brett started to slide in and out, his hands gripping John's hips, his fingers digging into the smooth flesh. He grunted, hips snapping forward with greater speed, and suddenly, he insinuated a hand around John's cock, which lengthened almost instantly.

"Oh, my God, you feel so good."

Brett's words filled him with joy. And then the burn had eased off, morphing into something distinctly more pleasurable. John shivered, but this time it was different. He rose up onto his elbows, and Brett grabbed hold of his shoulder, pulling him back almost savagely onto his dick. John didn't need prompting. He pushed back, fucking himself on that rigid column of hot flesh.

"Oh, hell." John dropped his head toward the table and moaned as Brett's cock connected with his prostate, setting off explosions inside his head. "There. Don't stop," he panted and then cried aloud as Brett speeded up, pistoning into him, each thrust now slamming into his prostate.

"Oh, fuck, about to come," Brett gasped out. His hand tugged at John's now hard-as-steel cock, and John felt his second orgasm roll through him, his body tightening around Brett's dick as he pumped come over Brett's hand and onto the floor. Behind him, he felt Brett become rigid. John could feel the pulse of Brett's cock deep inside him as he came, Brett's breathing harsh and loud against his ear. John collapsed onto the table, panting. His body ached, he was sore, and he felt utterly exhausted—and *bloody hell*, he wanted to do that again. As soon as he recovered sufficiently.

Brett eased out of him and pulled him upright. He turned around to be greeted by a succession of slow, sensual kisses as Brett stroked down his arms and back. John pressed against him, raising his arms to wrap them around Brett and draw him closer. He cupped the back of Brett's head and intensified their kiss, and Brett responded with a low moan. That soft stroking along his arms was just perfect, a slow, steady motion as Brett explored his mouth with a leisurely tongue.

John sighed into Brett's mouth, and Brett pulled away, his gaze fixed on John's face. "That was a happy sound."

John smiled. "I was just thinking—if I'd known that sex between two men could be so good, I wouldn't have waited this long to experience it for myself."

Brett froze. "What?" John frowned at the abrupt change. "Are you telling me this was your first time?"

John became still. He met Brett's gaze head on. "Yes." He swallowed as Brett's face changed. All of a sudden, it was as if a mask had slipped into place.

"And you didn't think to say anything?" Even the timbre of Brett's voice had changed.

John pulled free. An alarm bell was ringing in his head. "I-I wanted to, but I got carried away in the heat of the moment." He tilted his head. "Does it matter? I really enjoyed it." He reached up to cup Brett's face, but he moved away. John's heartbeat raced as Brett pulled off the condom and grabbed tissues to wipe himself. "Brett?"

Brett dropped the used condom and tissues into the wastepaper bin beside the table and then tucked his flaccid cock into his pants. He gave John a quick cool glance. "You'd better get dressed."

John's mind was racing. He had no idea what had just happened, but it was like Brett had become a stranger. John fumbled with the buttons on his shirt and hastily pulled up his pants and briefs. He waited for Brett to give him a clue, *anything* that told John what was going on in his head.

Brett ran a hand through his dark layers of hair. "Look, this isn't right."

John stared at him, aghast. "What?"

Brett wouldn't look him in the eye. "This isn't going to work." He sounded almost angry. "Nothing's changed here. I'm still your line manager, and we still can't do this."

"Isn't it a bit late for that?" John's voice rose. "Considering what we just did?"

Brett finally met his intense gaze. "It was a moment of insanity. It shouldn't have happened. And it *won't* happen again." He bit out the words with a decisive air. He looked around the room at the desk, the table, anything but John. "Why don't you go get your stuff from your room, and I'll take you home." He pulled his jacket from the back of his office chair and slipped it on. John stared at him in consternation for a moment and then grabbed his jacket. He unlocked the office door and went through the silent corridor to his room. His mind was a whirling mass of confusion. He found a couple of plastic bags and hurriedly stuffed the gifts into them before returning to Brett's office. Brett was already standing by the main door, giving his watch impatient glances.

"Let's go," he said curtly.

Thankfully, it was a very quick journey. John wasn't sure if he could have stood the painful silence for longer than the few minutes it took to reach his front gate. Brett pulled the car up to the curb where John indicated and then sat waiting, the engine still running, his eyes fixed on the road.

John opened the car door and then reached over to grab his bags from the backseat. He paused as he was about to remove himself completely from the car. "Brett, what—"

"Have a good Christmas." Brett snapped out the words with a finality that was unmistakable. John barely had time to withdraw his head and close the car door before Brett revved the engine and the car took off down the street. John watched the red glow of its taillights in utter dismay.

What the fuck just happened here?

CHAPTER 13

JOHN TURNED the key and let himself into the brightly lit hallway. He could hear Alec humming away in the kitchen. John dropped the bags to the floor and grabbed the newel post for support. His whole body was shaking. There was so much going on in his head at that moment, he couldn't process it all.

"I thought I heard you come in." He could hear Alec coming from the kitchen. "It's just you and me tonight, so I—" His words died as he caught sight of John. Alec dashed forward and gripped John's upper arm. "What happened? You look *awful.*"

John didn't know where to begin. His emotions were too raw, too close to the surface. He was afraid that if he opened his mouth, it would all pour out of him in a torrent.

Alec moved in front of him. "Sit down before you fall down." He pushed gently at John's shoulders until he sank onto the second stair. Alec crouched before him, his brow wrinkled. He placed a hand on John's shoulder. "Did you get fired? Because it has to be something momentous to have put that look on your face." He bit his lip. "Did Brett fire you?"

John barked out a bitter laugh. "No—he fucked me." He heard the hitch in Alec's breathing. John tried to swallow, but the lump in his throat made that difficult.

The crease between Alec's eyes deepened. "I don't understand." He squeezed John's shoulder. "Then why are you...." His eyes grew large and round. "Oh, that fucker. He dumped you again, didn't he?" His nostrils flared. "And here was I thinking it was only me around here who had bad luck with men." He rubbed John's shoulder gently. "Come with me, hon. Let's go upstairs, and then I'm going to run you a bath."

John's brain couldn't keep up. "A bath?" he repeated stupidly.

Alec gazed at him fondly. "Trust me. Right now, you're feeling a little sore, correct?" John winced at the reminder. He was more than a little sore, and the physical discomfort only served to heighten the mental anguish that threatened to overwhelm him at any moment. He took one look at Alec's upturned face with his pained stare and then gave a slow nod. Alec helped him to his feet, and they went up the stairs, Alec leading the way. Once in the bathroom, John felt lost as Alec opened the taps fully to fill the bath with hot, steaming water. He grabbed a bottle from the shelf below the window and poured a capful of its contents into the stream from the hot tap. The scent of lavender filled John's senses. Alec left the taps running and turned to John.

"Let's get you out of those clothes."

John was too dazed to feel embarrassed as Alec parted him from his clothing and then helped him step into the bath. Alec turned off the taps. John sat down carefully and winced as the hot water made contact with his hole.

Alec nodded sympathetically. "I remember my first time, hon. The bath will help, honest." He gave John a gentle smile, picked up his clothes, and carried them from the bathroom.

John sat in the bath, hugging his knees. He couldn't believe it was possible to go from one extreme of emotion to another in so short a timeframe. He stared at the bathroom mirror, fogged by steam, and tried to work out the tangle of confused thoughts that were colliding inside his head. *How could I have got it so wrong?* He felt so… numb.

Alec returned with a small glass of amber liquid. "Drink this," he said as he handed it to John. He knelt beside the bath and leaned his arms on the side, his gaze fixed on John.

John knitted his brows as he looked into the glass. "What's this?"

Alec tapped his nose. "Something that will make you feel a little better. I have to be honest here, you're worrying me. You look like you're in shock." He leaned closer. "It's Stu's VSOP brandy that he brought back from his last trip to Paris." He sat back and gave John an encouraging stare. "Sip it slowly. Let it warm you."

John wrinkled his nose as he took a cautious sip, gasping as the fiery liquid hit the back of his throat.

Alec nodded. "More."

John regarded the contents of the glass, tipped it up, and drained it in one swallow. His throat burned, and his eyes watered. He leaned back, his head resting against the edge of the bath and closed his eyes. He felt Alec remove the glass from his hand.

"It's okay, you know, if you don't want to talk about it."

The warm tone of Alec's voice, the note of concern.... Suddenly, it was all too much. Tears slid from beneath John's eyelids and rolled down his cheeks. He couldn't stop them.

"Oh, hon, it'll be all right."

John opened his eyes. Alec was regarding him anxiously. He reached for a washcloth, poured body wash onto it, and proceeded to rub it over John's chest and shoulders, moving in slow circles. The motion was soothing. Alec said nothing but simply took care of him. John wiped his eyes, sat up and leaned forward as Alec washed his back, squeezing the cloth out, letting the warm cascade of water run down over his skin. He let Alec minister to him, the young man's face fixed in an expression of concentration as he washed away every trace of Brett's touch.

When all the soap had been rinsed from his body, Alec helped him to his feet, pulled the plug, and wrapped him in a thick towel. He took John's hand as he stepped carefully from the bath and stood him on the bathmat while Alec rubbed him down. At last, when he was dry, Alec led him into John's room and switched on the bedside lamp, which cast a warm glow over the bed. Alec pulled back the duvet, and John slid between the soft layers, his head coming to rest on the thick pillow. Alec pulled the duvet up over his shoulders and then lay down beside him on top of it, his arm draped over John protectively.

Alec said nothing but simply held him. John let Alec's warmth seep into him, lulling him into that wonderful state where the world became hazy and sleep beckoned with welcome arms.

"Sleep, hon. Just let it all go and sleep."

Alec's softly spoken words were a gentle intrusion, and at last, John's troubled mind found some peace as he drifted off to sleep, Alec snuggled around him.

BRETT SAT in his armchair, his eyes staring, unseeing, at the glow of the TV screen. In his hand was a glass of scotch. It was ten o'clock, and he felt far from sleep. He glanced around at his lounge, devoid of any sign that Christmas was fast approaching. Brett usually waited until the end of term to put up his decorations, but he was in no mood to be festive.

God, what a bastard I am. What a complete and utter bastard.

He took a long drink of the warming liquid and grimaced. It was his third, and as yet, it hadn't brought the mental obliteration that he craved. In his mind, he still saw John's distraught expression as he'd driven away.

He closed his eyes, as if that would force the image from his mind—only to have it replaced with the image of John as he lay facedown on the table with Brett's cock thrusting into that exquisitely tight arse. Except now he was seeing it from a different perspective. He didn't know if the low cries were of pleasure or pain. He couldn't tell anymore. Guilt clouded his judgment.

If only I'd known. He took another drink and thought for a moment. What would he have done differently, with hindsight?

I'd have taken my time. I'd have spent hours in a bed with him, kissing, stroking, touching…. I'd have fingered him and then rimmed him until he was begging me to get inside him. I'd have made sure that he loved every second of it. I certainly wouldn't have fucked the shit out of him on my office table, that's *for sure.*

The noise level on the TV increased, and Brett picked up the remote and switched it off. He'd wanted the distraction, but nothing seemed to work, not the TV, the booze….

I didn't even ask him if he wanted *to be fucked, for Christ's sake. I just fucking took him.*

Okay, so it was how Brett liked it—hot and dirty, fast and furious—but not what he would have wanted for John's first time, had he known. And that was another thing—the way he was thinking about John. Yeah, so he'd been blinded by lust, until his brain was so fogged all he could think about was being balls deep in John's arse. But now, this wanting to take care of John, it wasn't *him*. It wasn't how Brett treated his bed partners.

Why is John so different? Because he *was* different—Brett couldn't deny that any longer. The man was starting to get under his skin.

Maybe it's because I see him every day at work. Maybe that's *why he's on my mind.*

But it still didn't answer the question as to why Brett should feel such confusion.

The phone rang, shattering the silence. Brett stared at it for a moment or two, debating whether or not to answer. As it rang for the fifth time, he reached out and grabbed the receiver before the answering machine switched itself on. He waited for the caller to identify themselves.

"Brett? You there?"

Brett closed his eyes. *Of all the times….*

"Luke, what can I do for you?" He hadn't heard from his former mentor for a while. It was only the thought of all Luke had done for him that kept him on the line.

"I imagine you're breathing a sigh of relief and having a well-earned drink, now that the term is finally over." Luke sounded as jovial as ever. "The autumn term is a bastard, isn't it?" He gave a wry chuckle.

"Oh, yeah." Brett took a long drink of scotch, enjoying the burn of the alcohol. "A bit late for calling, isn't it?"

"Yeah, I'm sorry about that, but there was something important I wanted to discuss with you, and I didn't want to forget."

Brett sighed. "Look, it's great to hear from you, Luke, it really is, but now is not a good time."

"Oh, God—you haven't got someone there with you, have you?"

Brett stared into his glass. *Unfortunately, no*, he thought. "No, I'm alone." He heard Luke heave a relieved sigh.

"Oh, thank God. I suddenly had visions of me interrupting you and a lady friend."

"Nope, still single." And for the first time, the words weighed heavy on his heart. "And I'm sorry, it's just that it's been a long day and I'm really tired."

Luke's tone changed. "Right, I won't keep you," he said briskly. "I just wanted to let you know about something I felt was right up your street. HMI are recruiting for new blood, and I thought of you straightaway."

Brett frowned. "Luke, why on earth would I want to join the illustrious team of Her Majesty's Inspectors for schools? I have a school of my own to take care of, remember?"

"I should—I had to push you to *apply* for the bloody position, as I recall." That wry chuckle again. "You've been head there for, what, five years now?"

"Four," corrected Brett. "This is my fifth year." He took a slow sip of scotch.

"And you're only thirty-three. Do you know how *rare* it is to be your age and in the post of head teacher for *four years*?" Luke's voice softened. "Brett, have I ever steered you wrong? I remember when I promoted you to deputy head. You were only twenty-seven, but *God*, man, you were *so* ready for it."

Brett knew he was right. He'd only been teaching for five years when Luke Parton, his head teacher at the time, had pushed him to accept the management position. And Brett had jumped at the chance. Luke had nurtured him, taught him so much—and then two short years later had pushed him to apply for a headship.

"I'm not sure I'm ready to leave Ardwick just yet," Brett admitted. "There's still so much to do."

Luke laughed. "You forget, I've been keeping an eye on you. You've turned that school around, Brett. It was in special measures when you took over, and look at it now. It's the flagship primary school of the whole Greater Manchester area. You should be very proud."

Right then, Brett wasn't feeling remotely proud.

"I just want you to think about it, okay?" Luke urged. "I think it's the right time for you. More importantly, I think you could do great things as an inspector—and who knows where you might end up? It would certainly be a great stepping stone into Whitehall."

Brett barked out a laugh. "Why in hell would I want to walk *those* hallowed halls? All those government educationalists who hand down policies from on high, and most of them have never set *foot* inside a classroom."

"But that's my point," Luke said patiently. "Think of the difference you could make. You could finally begin to change the system—from the inside."

Now Luke had his attention. "But that could take years," Brett said slowly, in an attempt at rationalizing the idea.

"So? You're thirty-three! You've got time." He heard Luke's gleeful laugh, and it warmed him. The man had a point. It was simply the wrong time to make it.

"Luke, like I said, I'm tired, too tired to think about this clearly right now."

"But you *will* think about it, won't you?"

Brett could tell from his tone that Luke wasn't about to give up on this easily. He smiled to himself. "Okay, I'll think about it. That's as much as I can promise, all right?"

"Good enough." He could hear the note of satisfaction in Luke's voice. "And now, I'll let you get back to whatever it was you were doing when I rang."

Brett didn't want to go back there. The thought of the hurt on John's face....

"Actually, I think I'll have an early night." He thanked Luke, wished him a merry Christmas, and then said good night. As he replaced the receiver, it crossed his mind briefly to call John.

What on earth would I say to him?

As he got up, switched off the lights, and made his way upstairs to his bed, it occurred to Brett that he'd irrevocably damaged his relationship with John. So badly that perhaps there was no coming back from this.

God, I hope I'm wrong.

SATURDAY MORNING, and for once, everyone was home. John sat at the round kitchen table, sipping his coffee while Stu and Martin slaved away, putting together a cooked breakfast. They were uncharacteristically quiet—not really surprising for Stu, as he'd gotten in very late. Alec was laying the table. John wanted to thank him for last night, but he didn't know how to start. He'd awoken alone later than usual, the December sunshine pouring in through the curtains. It hadn't taken long until the memory of the previous evening's events intruded. John tried to push them from his mind. *I can't go there. It hurts too much.*

It was only when breakfast had finally been cleared away that John got up the courage to speak. "I take it Alec's told you what happened." There was a moment of silence.

"There wasn't much I could tell them," Alec admitted.

"Can you talk about it?" Martin asked him with an anxious expression. Stu's face bore a similar look.

That did it. There was no *way* John was going to have his housemates pussyfooting around him for the next two weeks. He took a deep breath. He told them what had taken place in Brett's office and then about Brett's almost instantaneous change of heart.

"Wait—he went all cold on you when you told him you'd been a virgin?" Stu's eyes blazed. "And then he gave you the silent treatment?" John saw the veins in his neck twitch. "And to think I liked him." His hands clenched as they lay on the table.

"Well, at least you know your seduction methods worked," Martin joked feebly. John could tell he was trying to lighten the mood.

"Rather *too* well, I'd say." Alec spoke quietly. He looked across at John. "You had me so worried last night."

John gave him a grateful smile. "Thank you, by the way. You were great."

Alec leaned closer, until their foreheads touched. "You're welcome, hon. You just needed looking after."

"Am I allowed to ask how it was?" Martin tilted his head to one side.

"Martin!" Stu and Alec's voices rose in unison.

"I was only *asking*," Martin said indignantly. "I mean, we all know what your first time was like, Stu."

They all laughed at that. The evening they'd spent discussing their sex lives had proved illuminating for John—and very entertaining.

John decided Martin had the right attitude. Besides, he was twenty-four, not some eighteen-year-old boy. *Time to man up.*

"Up until the moment when he became this whole other person? It was good, really good." He shivered as he recalled the feel of Brett's fingers inside him, Brett kissing down his spine as he fucked him, that muted heat inside when Brett climaxed.

"I'm glad," said Alec with a shy smile. "I'd have hated it if you'd had a bad experience, on top of everything else that happened."

John stared at his coffee mug. "But after today, I really don't want to talk about it. It's just too painful." He still couldn't believe Brett could have treated him in so abrupt a fashion. To fuck him and then tell him it was all one big mistake.... *God, that hurt.*

"Understandable." Martin gave him a decisive nod. "It's going to be bad enough when you go back in January, especially if you have to work with him organizing this charity day of his."

John's mouth fell open. "Oh, God—I'd completely forgotten about that." The thought of it was enough to make him panic. The preparations were proving difficult. "And there's so much to be done." He stared gloomily at the table. "I wish he'd never asked me now."

"Can you request a change of mentor?" Stu wanted to know. "Because otherwise it's goin' to be really awkward."

"I need to think about that." For the life of him, John couldn't think of who could replace Brett.

"Are you going to see your parents at Christmas?" Alec asked.

And that was yet another thing John didn't want to think about. Christmases at his parents' house were always happy events, full of laughter, relatives coming round to visit.... John wasn't sure he could stand that.

"Ev and Daniel are going to visit them on Christmas Day. I might just go with them and then come back here." John couldn't contemplate staying there. "Will you all be here?"

There were nods around the table.

"Martin's goin' to see the olds for a few days, but then he'll be back. Alec's on his own, so he'll be here the whole time." Stu squeezed Alec's shoulder as he spoke. John knew from past conversations that Alec had been an only child whose parents had been killed in a car crash when he was at university. Alec grasped Stu's hand and smiled.

"And of course, I'll be here. I've nowhere else to go, have I?" Stu said brightly.

John saw through the plastered-on smile to the pain behind Stu's words. He couldn't begin to understand the hurt Stu must have felt, having his parents reject him because of his sexuality. He watched Martin put his arm around Stu's shoulder.

Stu turned to Martin and mouthed, "*Ta, mate.*"

"In that case, we'll do our best to give you a really nice Christmas," said Alec with a brisk nod. Stu and Martin murmured in agreement.

John smiled at the three men around the table. He couldn't have picked three finer housemates.

All I want for Christmas is to forget this mess. Not the sex—as far as John was concerned, *that* part was unforgettable. But as for what happened afterward....

I won't make the same mistake twice. I won't let Brett get to me.

The trouble was, he already had.

CHAPTER 14

"I REALLY don't want to go, Ev," John said for maybe the third time. His brother was being particularly insistent.

"Look, it's a Christmas party, it's one evening," pleaded Evan in his ear. "There'll be me and Daniel, Josh and Chris, some of Josh's friends from medical school, some other people, the four of you...." John shook his head and smiled to himself at that last part.

"What about Sean and Michael?" Evan hadn't mentioned them. In fact, he hadn't talked about the couple in ages. "Won't they be there?"

"No, Michael's taking them to Oxford for Christmas. His mum's had the flu really badly, so he and his sisters are going to take care of her for a while." Evan sighed into the phone. "And I think the change might do them good." There was a brief pause before he forged ahead. "Anyway, we were talking about you. Have you even mentioned it to the others?"

"Yes."

"And?"

John laughed. Evan wasn't going to let it go. "Okay, you got me. They all want to go, and they think I should too."

"See? It's not just me." Evan's triumphant tone brought a smile to his face.

"All right, all right, we'll *all* be there. If that's what it takes to get you to shut up about it." He chuckled to hear Evan's whoop of delight. "You're nuts, you *do* know that?"

Evan fell silent for a second. "I just think you need to do something fun. You've seemed so down the last few times we've talked. And I know we agreed not to mention his name, but—"

"Then don't mention him," John interjected. "I mean it."

"Okay, bro." Evan's voice quieted. "But I *still* think he's treated you like—"

"Ev!" The word came out more sharply than he'd intended. His brother fell silent. "Look, I know you mean well, but I *really* don't want to talk about him, okay?"

"All right." Something in Evan's voice told John the message had finally got through. "So we'll see you all tomorrow night, right?"

"Yes." He said his good-byes and disconnected the call. He stared at the phone. At least Evan hadn't suggested inviting Brett, thankfully. Christmas had come and gone, leaving John thoughtful and low. He couldn't shake the blues that hung around him like a shroud. He'd done his best to be cheerful with his housemates and family, but he had the distinct impression that no one was fooled for an instant. His mum had given him more than her usual amount of hugs, and his brother Aaron had been particularly kind.

Maybe they can see it, John mused. *Is it possible to see heartache, to sense it, even when someone's trying like hell to hide it?* He only knew that the closer the new term drew, the more panicky he felt.

Maybe the party will do me good. Maybe I need to get really drunk and forget about it all, for one night at least.

Then he laughed. Like *that* was going to happen. He went downstairs to the kitchen to inform his housemates that they *were* going to the ball, after all.

"EVAN TELLS me you're organizing a charity event for your school," Chris said as he poured a glass of wine for John. All the other guests were in the lounge, and the sound of laughter floated out along the hall.

John groaned. "Oh, God, can we *please* not talk about this?" He took the proffered glass and drank half of it.

"Hey! Steady on. You'll be pissed in no time if you carry on like that." Chris's brow furrowed.

John snorted. "That's the whole idea." He was surprised when Chris took the glass from him and put it down on the kitchen worktop. "I was drinking that!"

Chris gave him a patient look. "Talk to me and you can have it back. What's up?"

John huffed. "Brett asked me to organize the day, yeah? Well, so far, apart from Brett inviting that football player, I've had no ideas, and no one else at the school has come up with anything either." He stared hopefully at the wineglass.

Chris laughed and wagged his finger. "Not yet, you don't. So, you need to come up with some ideas that will raise money. Is that it?" John nodded. "Well, in that case, I might be able to help you."

John stopped dead. "Really? How?"

Chris smiled. "Remember that ball you came to?" John arched his brows. As if he could forget. "Well, that was organized by my grandma. She does a lot of fund-raising for her foundation. If anyone will have ideas, it will be her. Especially if her foundation ends up getting some of the cash you raise." He winked.

John gently bit his lower lip. "D'you really think she'd help?"

Chris grinned. "Trust me—if it means money for her beloved foundation? She'll come up with lots of great ideas." He reached into his jeans pocket and pulled out his phone. "In fact, why don't we ask her right now?"

John put out his hand to stop him. "Chris, think of the time. It's late." And if Chris's grandmother really could help, the last thing he wanted to do was piss her off.

Chris thought about it for a moment. "You're right. I'll tell you what. I'll call her in the morning and get her to set up a meeting with you before you go back to school. How's that?"

John gave him a wide smile. "That sounds like a great idea. Thanks, Chris."

Chris grinned. "No problem." He picked up the glass of wine and handed it to John. "And you look much happier."

John felt as though a weight had been lifted off him. All he'd wanted was some ideas, and it looked as if that was a definite possibility. "How about we go and join the others?"

Chris's grin widened. "Now *that* sounds like a great idea. It is a party, after all." He patted John on the arm. "It'll be all right, you'll see." He exited the kitchen, armed with a bowl of snacks. John followed him into the lounge. Stu looked across the room and beamed at him.

"Where you been? Get over here—you're missin' all the fun."

John joined his housemates. Maybe it was about time he relaxed and enjoyed himself. Everyone seemed to be sitting down. Evan and Daniel were reclining on a beanbag on the floor, Evan leaning back against his husband, Daniel's arms wrapped around him. John joined Stu, who was cross-legged on the rug, Alec leaning against him. Martin swung an arm around John's shoulders and gave him a quick hug. John caught Evan's eye and smiled. He was going to do his best to have a good time. Evan nodded encouragingly.

"Why are you sat all the way over there, gorgeous? Why not come sit next to me?"

John looked across to where a young man with dark, curly hair and blue eyes sprawled on the couch near Josh. He patted the space on the couch next to him. John quirked his eyebrows, unsure if he was the one being addressed. The guy's eyes gleamed.

"Yeah, you with the sexy blond hair and the come-to-bed eyes." He grinned.

Josh leaned across and whacked him on the thigh. "Ben, behave."

Ben gave him a quick glance. "You go back to your fiancé, mate." He turned that wide smile on John once more. "Well, how about it?"

John felt his cheeks flush. "I'm fine here, thanks." He looked at Evan. "What are you all doing, anyway?"

"Debating which game to play," answered Daniel in his deep voice. "Ben over there wants to play Spin the Bottle."

Ben gave a wicked chuckle. "Yeah, but only if I get to play with Evan's older brother." He gave John a salacious wink.

John looked around the room once more and did a swift mental calculation. There were about twelve to fifteen men in the lounge—and all of them gay. Six of the men were in couples—Evan and Daniel, Josh and Chris, and Josh's friends Om and David. And when he looked again, John noticed that maybe it was heading for four couples. The young man seated on the floor near Ben's legs was giving Ben some very keen glances. *Can't Ben see that?* John mused.

"How about Truth or Dare?" suggested Stu. "That can be a lot of fun." He waggled his eyebrows.

"I've heard of that, but I've never played it," said Om. "How does it work?"

Stu rubbed his hands together gleefully. "Right, then. We'll need a bottle." He peered at the coffee table in the midst of them and grabbed an empty wine bottle. "Can we get this table out of the way? We're goin' to need the room."

Two of the other guests, Kyle and Connor, lifted the table clear and then sat down once more. Everyone was more or less seated in a circle. Stu shuffled on his knees into the center, the bottle in his hands.

"Okay, to start, I'm goin' to spin this once, to determine who's goin' to ask the first question, and then that person spins again, to decide who answers it. You can choose Truth, where you get asked a question and you have to reply honestly—or Dare, if you don't like the sound of the question. After the first go, the guy who answered spins the bottle. He gets to ask the question, and whoever the neck of the bottle is pointin' at, he has to answer it, and so on. Everyone with me so far?"

There were nods from around the round.

"But, to make it a little more interestin'"—Stu reached behind him into the backpack he'd brought along—"every time it spins and it's your go, you have to drink down a shot of this." He held up a bottle of Patron Tequila and grinned. "I found this on my travels to Orlando recently." The room was filled with an equal measure of groans and chuckles. Chris got up and left the room, only to return moments later with a shot glass.

John stifled a groan. He hoped to God he didn't have to answer many questions—he'd already downed quite a bit of wine. And when he was drunk, his inhibitions seemed to fly out of the window. Evan was watching him, and there was a distinct look of amusement on his face. *Oh, hell*—his brother could tell a few tales about what happened when John got drunk.

Then he took another look around the room. Most of the guests had had a fair bit of alcohol too.

Maybe I should just go with the flow and have some fun, he thought.

Stu spun the bottle on the carpet. After a few rotations, it came to a stop, its neck pointing toward Martin, who cackled wickedly. Stu crawled back to his position on the rug next to Alec, and Martin spun. This time it pointed to Chris, who sat upright, swallowing. Josh had his hand on Chris's knee. Stu tossed the unopened bottle to Chris, who poured himself a glassful. Grimacing slightly, he upended the glass and downed the drink in one. Shuddering, he placed the bottle on the floor. There were snickers from the onlookers. Chris laughed.

"Don't know what *you're* all finding so funny—it might be *you* next." He winked and then faced Martin, his back still rigid.

Martin stroked his chin. "Who was the first person you ever kissed?"

Chris sagged into the couch, clearly relieved. "The guy who's sitting next to me." He turned to Josh, a beautiful smile on his face. Josh beamed and then leaned over to kiss Chris slowly, taking his time. There were calls and whoops as the kiss progressed, especially when Chris let out the tiniest of moans as Josh kissed down his neck. John watched Chris shiver as he broke the kiss. His cheeks were pink.

Chris grabbed the bottle. "I'm going to ask the question before I spin." He glanced around the room. "And I want to know—" He paused dramatically. "—how old were you when you first sucked a cock?" Laughter erupted as he spun the bottle.

John found himself holding his breath, silently praying for the bottle to miss him. He didn't want to admit this was something he'd yet to do. Someone on high apparently took pity on his discomfort, as the neck pointed to Stu.

Martin snorted. "Oh, I can't *wait* to hear this." Stu arched his eyebrows as he reached for the tequila and poured himself a measure. He tossed it back and shuddered. Then he grinned at the surrounding men.

"I was thirteen, and his name was Billy Henshall," he announced proudly. Everyone burst into laughter. Stu gazed keenly around the room. "And *I* want to know… boxers or briefs?" This elicited giggles from some of the more inebriated partygoers. He spun, and the bottle came to a stop—

facing John. Evan let out a loud cackle and then covered his mouth with his hand. John shot him a warning look.

Stu handed over the bottle and glass, and John poured himself a drink. He took a deep breath. A few of the guys started a low chant, "*Drink it, drink it,*" and he quickly drank down the tequila. He coughed and spluttered as it hit the back of his throat. There were cheers from some of the men. John lifted his chin and said, "Briefs," biting out the word. He knew why Evan had laughed. His brother knew *exactly* why John couldn't wear boxers.

John got up on his knees and surveyed the room. He spoke slowly, careful to enunciate every word clearly. "My question is, what is your fantasy guy like?" It wasn't too risqué a question and one he felt comfortable asking. He spun the bottle and smiled when it pointed to Alec. He handed Alec the tequila and glass. Alec drank it down with little fuss and then sighed.

"He's about six feet, blond, with slim hips and dreamy blue eyes. And all he wants to do is take care of me and love me." John was surprised when this was greeted with a chorus of soft sighs of approval. Then Alec winked. "And he's a total submissive who loves getting fucked—especially when I tie him to the bed." Raucous laughter greeted his words, and Alec grinned widely. His eyes gleamed mischievously. "My question is, who in this room would you like to make out with?"

As John listened to the quiet chuckles that followed Alec's question, he became aware that the tequila bottle was being passed around. It seemed everyone was taking a swig. *At this rate, the party could prove very entertaining—or dreadfully embarrassing.*

Alec spun the bottle, and it pointed to the young man on the floor near Ben, James. He stared at the bottle, his cheeks on fire. James ignored the offered glass and took a chug of tequila straight from the bottle.

As he fastened the cap, he turned to look at the man behind him on the couch. "Ben," he said with a decisive air. There was a loud burst of applause, which died away as the partygoers saw Ben's reaction.

Ben's eyes widened—and then his pupils enlarged slightly. He edged off the couch to sit on the floor next to James and appeared to study his face intently for several seconds. The room fell silent. All eyes were on the two men as Ben reached out and cupped James's jaw in his hand, pushing his head back against the seat cushions. John could hear the change in James's breathing immediately. He watched, fascinated, as Ben stroked his tongue over James's lips and James opened for him. Ben plunged his tongue into James's mouth with a groan and then moved to straddle him.

It was as if someone had turned up the thermostat by several degrees. The air was suddenly erotically charged as Ben devoured James in an intense kiss, rolling his hips sensually. When he grasped James's hands and placed them on his own arse, John could see how much both men were clearly into it. Restrained as he was, James was pushing up with his hips against Ben, and his hands squeezed Ben's arse. Definite sounds of approval rumbled out of Ben.

The breathing around John was charged, and he glimpsed more than a few guys palming their dicks. He was already half hard. Watching the two men was extremely arousing. But as he watched them, John felt his body flush cold. *That's what I wanted—with Brett.*

"There's a room upstairs if we're bothering you," Evan said sweetly, addressing Ben and James. Laughter followed, and at last, the two men on the floor broke off their impassioned kiss, to the sound of rapturous applause. Ben didn't return to his seat on the couch, remaining instead by James's side. John noticed James's hand as it crept into Ben's.

John grabbed the tequila and drank from it, welcoming the blurring of his emotions that came with it. He didn't want to think about Brett.

The game proceeded apace, the laughter more frequent as the guests drank freely. Stu had the misfortune—or *not*, depending on the point of view—to have the bottle point to him a few times.

His answer to the demand for the most outrageous place he'd ever had sex had John's mind reeling. "In the pilot's cockpit." When someone demanded to know how that could be done, Stu had winked and replied, "Very carefully."

Daniel began the applause, grinning widely, and Stu had taken a drunken bow.

Kyle's question to Stu brought a brief burst of lucidity that penetrated the alcoholic fog enveloping John's brain. It hadn't been too difficult to notice the looks Kyle had been giving Stu all night. A blind man could have spotted them. But Kyle's question gained an interesting reaction.

He spun the bottle first, and when it pointed to Stu, his eyes lit up.

"Have you ever done something sexual with one of your housemates?"

Stu stopped dead, and in that moment, John was suddenly aware of Alec's rising blush. Stu swallowed. "Actually? I think I'll take a dare."

There were several gasps, but Stu kept his eyes on Kyle, steadfastly avoiding Alec's direction.

Kyle's eyes gleamed. "I dare you to strip off in front of us and stand on one leg, while rubbing your belly and patting your head at the same time—for fifteen seconds." Applause greeted his words, and it was clear everyone thought Stu would refuse. Stu got to his feet and went to stand in the center of the group. He faced Kyle as he slowly undid his black silk shirt. The mood changed as a few of the men began to hum the theme to *The Stripper*, more and more joining. Stu paid them no mind. He dropped the shirt to the floor, revealing a wide chest covered in a dense carpet of thick, curly hair. John was used to the sight—the cry, "*Stu, put some clothes on!*" was a common one around the house. The humming grew louder as Stu slowly popped free the button on his jeans and lowered the zipper at a snail's pace. But when he wriggled out of his tight black jeans and his very erect, thick cock sprang up, the noise in the room grew exponentially. Stu stepped out of his jeans and wiggled for them, his tight arse cheeks jiggling only slightly. John couldn't believe how bold Stu was, and he wondered how much alcohol it would take for him to get up enough courage to do something *half* as brazen. Then he snickered to himself. About as much as he'd already imbibed, probably. John was pleasantly drunk, and it was a great feeling.

Stu paid the noise no mind as he stood on his right leg, his left leg bent at the knee, his foot resting on his calf. The trouble began when he tried to complete the hand actions. Kyle began to count off the seconds, and Stu struggled to make his hands work at the same time, as well as keeping his balance. It simply wasn't happening. Within seconds, he started to wobble, and seconds after that he ended up on his back, legs in the air—on top of Kyle. The laughter proved infectious as Stu lay there, helpless, tears of laughter in his eyes, his stiff dick waving about as he struggled to right himself. So when Kyle bent low over him, licking his lips, it was no surprise to John that another chant broke out.

"*Kiss him, kiss him, kiss him….*"

Stu looked up at Kyle, his face poised above him, and then glanced around the room with a nonchalant shrug. "If I must," he said, eyebrows arched—and then pulled Kyle down into a passionate, sensual kiss that brought on more applause, which grew even louder when Kyle slid a hand down Stu's torso to wrap around his cock. Stu gave a full-body shudder, and his hips rolled up off the floor, pushing his dick through Kyle's fist. John cast a surreptitious glance in Alec's direction. The young man was watching the pair, a smile fixed on his face. But for one infinitesimal moment, their eyes met, and John saw a spark of some stronger emotion in those expressive green eyes. It passed so quickly that John was almost convinced he'd imagined it. After a couple of minutes of passionate making out, Kyle moved his hand away, and Stu broke off the kiss with a gasp. He grinned up at Kyle and stroked his cheek. Kyle returned his grin. Stu rolled over onto his front and crawled back to his space on the rug, where he would have remained naked, if Martin hadn't grabbed his clothes and thrust them in Stu's direction with a wide smile. Stu looked extremely pleased with himself as he wriggled into his jeans.

The tequila bottle was virtually dry, and it was decided there would be one more question. John leaned heavily against Martin, who chuckled loudly in his ear.

"You've managed to escape unscathed, I see." For which John was profoundly grateful. Not that he hadn't enjoyed himself, but the prospect of answering a question in his present state had worried him. His relief proved short-lived. Ben spun the bottle for the final time, and the neck pointed clearly at John. *Oh, fuck.* John prayed it wouldn't be anything as embarrassing as some of the questions that night—*Have you ever taken part in a three-way? Have you ever fucked bareback? Do you spit or swallow?*—although his lack of experience meant that most of those questions would have been simple to answer. He struggled to hold himself upright, which was a task in itself. The world was suddenly a much hazier place.

"Can you suck your own dick?" Ben asked with a wry chuckle.

Evan snorted and then covered his mouth with his hand.

Josh laughed. "Yeah, we know *Daniel* could do it. But let's face it, with a cock as long as your husband's, that's not exactly difficult, is it?"

Evan was laughing openly now, and John was shooting him warning glares. Unfortunately, Evan wasn't paying him any attention. Evan nodded, wiping his eyes.

"Yeah, that's true enough." He gave Daniel a warm glance. "You *do* have a very big dick, sweetie." Daniel's cheeks were crimson. Evan met John's anguished stare. "But my brother's cock? Is in a *whole* different league…."

Heads swiveled in John's direction. He froze.

Stu's eyebrows shot up. "Oh, really?" He gave John a look full of admiration. "You been hidin' your light under a bushel, mate?" He winked. "Or should that be hidin' your cock in your briefs?"

Ben guffawed. "*Now* we know why he doesn't wear boxers." He squinted at John's crotch. "Just how big *is* that baby? And how do *we* know you can suck it?" His eyes sparkled. "Prove it."

And just like that, the chanting began. "*Prove it, prove it, prove it….*"

Oh, fuck.

John was so going to kill Evan.

CHAPTER 15

JOHN GAZED around at the chanting men. Evan was grinning at him, as if daring him to refuse. For one moment, the thought was tempting. The chanting grew louder. *Oh, for God's sake, it's a party and you're here to have fun*, he told himself sternly.

"Fuck it," John said and got to his feet. The applause was tumultuous but died away as he fumbled with his jeans.

"I'll give you a hand with that, if you like," Connor offered with a wink. Everyone laughed, John included. John pushed his jeans to his ankles. His cock was already poking its head above the waistband of his black briefs.

"Fuck, John, how big is that monster? You're not even fully hard yet." Stu's voice sounded awed.

"We measured it once," Evan said. His eyes gleamed. "Mind you, that was a few years ago." He grinned at the assembled men. "It was ten inches." Gasps rippled around the room, and John felt his face heat up. He reached into his briefs and shyly pulled out his cock.

"This might make things easier for you." Connor was suddenly kneeling before him, sliding John's briefs slowly past his hips to join his jeans. He eyed John's lengthening cock with an appreciative glance—and a quick lick of his lips.

"I think I can manage it from here," John said with a drunken chuckle. He could feel his cheeks glowing. He began to pull at his dick, feeling it harden almost instantly. This whole situation was surreal. Connor hadn't moved from his kneeling position in front of John. He gazed up at him, eyes shining. John tugged at his dick, coaxing it to full length, trying not to look at the deep brown eyes that never left him. Connor was cute.

"Nah, you *definitely* need a helping hand there," Connor said—and all of a sudden his hand was around John's cock, moving from tip to base in a wickedly slow motion that had John as hard as granite. John inhaled sharply and stared down at Connor with wide eyes. *Oh, fuuuuuck....*

"Oh, my God, I can't watch someone give my brother a hand job," Evan groaned and turned his head to Daniel's chest. Laughter greeted his words. Daniel chuckled and stroked his hair.

"You stay there, baby," he said soothingly. "I'll let you know when Connor's done his stuff." He winked at John. "Although I think John's enjoying Connor's brand of help far *too* much."

John's cock poked up toward his navel, and he reached down to grasp Connor's hand around the wrist. "I think you've helped enough."

Connor pouted. "Aw, and I was just beginning to enjoy myself, too." He winked—and then leaned forward to deliver a swift lick to the head of John's cock before hurrying back to his place next to Kyle. John let out a strangled gasp, and Connor leered at him.

"Okay, let's see you suck that baby," Ben said, and he began a slow hand clap, which had everyone joining in. Evan pulled away from Daniel's chest to peer at him.

I can't believe I'm actually going through with this. John pulled himself together and got down on the floor on his back. He went into a shoulder stand, his body bent almost in two. His feet touched the floor behind his head, his jeans and underwear bunched around his ankles, his rigid cock pointing down toward his head. He licked it, which earned him a round of applause. It was a bit of a struggle, but he strained his head up off the floor to suck the head into his mouth. The applause was deafening.

"Oh, my fucking God, you did it." Stu was laughing and applauding enthusiastically. Alec shook his head and chuckled. John released his dick with a loud pop and righted himself, his face on fire. As he hitched up his briefs and jeans to dress himself, the men patted him on the shoulders and back. John had never done anything like that in his life—and it felt amazing.

Evan edged over to him, wiping his eyes and laughing. He hugged John tightly.

"Well, I have to say, I never thought you'd go through with it, big brother—"

"*Very* big brother," interjected Ben with a snicker. Others joined in and laughed.

Evan ignored him. "But I am suitably impressed. Not just with the cock sucking—though the fact that you managed it was pretty mind blowing—but with the way you let yourself go with the flow." He gazed fondly at John. "You look like you had fun."

John smiled. "Yeah, I did." And it had been exactly what he'd needed.

The party drew to a close as one by one the guests took their leave, taking taxis that Evan had thoughtfully prebooked.

When it was time for the housemates to leave, John grabbed Evan and hugged him. "Thanks, little brother. I had a great time."

Evan smiled. "Yeah, me too—although I never want to see that again as long as I live. All right?" He leveled a firm stare at John. "And you know what *that* refers to, don't you?"

John blushed. "Ev!" And then he thought, *Two can play at that game.* He winked. "Just like *I* never want to have to listen to the sound of Daniel fucking my little brother in the room below me." He watched Evan's mouth drop open. Behind him, Daniel burst into laughter.

"Nicely played, John." He leaned close to Evan's ear. "I *told* you it was a bad idea, but would you listen?" Daniel wrapped his arms around Evan's chest and held him close. Evan seemed stunned.

"Come on, taxi's here," said Martin, pulling at John's arm. The four housemates said their good-byes and stumbled down the little path into the waiting black cab. Martin and Stu were talking animatedly all the way home, perched on the pull-down seats. Next to John, Alec was quiet. John took hold of his hand and squeezed. Alec gave him a brief but warm smile. Fifteen minutes later, they were home, each man heading for their respective rooms. John stood in front of the wardrobe door as he undressed. He caught sight of himself in the mirror and grinned.

Well, you certainly enjoyed yourself tonight. And it was true. It had felt so good to let go of everything. He gazed at his reflection, instantly recalling the feel of Connor's hand around his cock, the appreciative look in his eye as he'd regarded John, the feeling of being wanted, desired. There'd been no doubting *that*.

Then why doesn't Brett want me? What the fuck is wrong with me?

And just like that, all the enjoyment he'd gained from the evening fled him, leaving him feeling hollow inside. He hadn't wanted Connor—but he *did* want Brett. He closed his eyes, and suddenly, he could feel Brett's mouth on his, that bruising kiss that had left him wanting more. He squeezed his eyes tight, but he could still feel Brett's hands on him as he powered into John, making him cry out.

Oh, fuck, this isn't helping. He threw back the duvet and climbed into bed, curling up in a tight ball. *What will it take to get him out of my mind?* And it wasn't just the sex; that was what made it worse. Brett had gotten under his skin. It was everything about him—the way his face lit up when he smiled, the way he gestured with his hands when he spoke, the reassuring glances he gave when they were discussing John's progress....

I can't keep doing this. It'll drive me mad.

John hugged himself, huddled in a fetal position under the duvet as he shut out the world—and hopefully, all thoughts of Brett. His last thought as he finally succumbed to sleep was that from now on, work would be his focus—work, the charity event, passing his NQT year....

Anything but Brett.

"OKAY, GRANDMA, do you need anything else before I disappear and leave you two alone to talk?" Chris asked as he set down a tray with a teapot, cups, saucers, milk jug, and a plate of delicious-looking biscuits on the coffee table.

Margaret Marriott reached up to cup her grandson's cheek tenderly. "Thank you, Christopher, but it seems you've thought of everything." Her eyes lit up when she saw the biscuits, and she smiled. "Josh bought these, didn't he? That boy knows my tastes."

Chris laughed and kissed her cheek. "I'll be in the kitchen if you want me." He gave them both a nod and exited the lounge.

Margaret settled back into the armchair with a wince. "I swear each winter is harder to deal with than the previous one."

John smiled. "If Chris has got your age right, I think you're doing very well, Mrs. Marriott." He knew Margaret was approaching eighty. The old lady certainly didn't look it. She was dressed immaculately in a suit of fine dark blue wool, a paler blue silk scarf wound around her neck. Her white hair lay coiled in neat curls, and those blue eyes regarding him were bright. John had the impression that behind those eyes was a sharp mind, for all her years.

He poured out two cups of tea and handed her one. She sipped it, a small smile of appreciation twisting her lips. Then those eyes were focused on him.

"So, young man, you've been tasked with organizing your school's charity day, and you need some advice."

John admired the way she got right down to business. "Yes, and by the way, thank you for agreeing to meet here." It had been Chris's suggestion that she come to their house.

Margaret beamed. "Oh, it was no trouble. Besides, these days I see so little of my grandson that it's a wonderful opportunity to visit him and his lovely fiancé." She sighed. "Engagements and wedding talk seem to be in the air, what with all the changes in legislation allowing for marriage equality. My personal assistant, Ellis, just proposed to his boyfriend, Rhys, and they're *so* excited." She tut-tutted. "Though it *has* proved difficult to get Ellis to concentrate on his work. He gets this faraway look in his eyes, and I know *perfectly well* that he's thinking about his fiancé and *not* about my schedule." Her eyes sparkled with amusement. "Now, suppose you tell me what you've organized so far, and then we'll put our heads together and see what else we can come up with. I have lots of ideas."

John sighed. "That sounds great. The only problem is, I've had so few ideas."

"Well, it seems to me that you need events for each group that the children are capable of running, which should include resources that they can produce themselves. Those will appeal to their relatives and the local community and would typically require small amounts of money to participate. Then you need activities that the staff could organize, aimed at raising larger amounts. I would also suggest getting local businesses involved, if they can, maybe with stalls. It would mean them donating stock, but it would all be good publicity. Make sure you get the press involved."

John nodded, scribbling furiously in his notepad. For the next thirty minutes, they discussed various ideas, discounting some but coming up with some really great events. John was amazed at how Margaret's mind worked.

"You're really good at this," he said as he handed her the plate with the biscuits.

Her cheeks pinked. "Why, thank you, John. I've been running the foundation since my husband died. His was the brain behind everything, so I've had to learn a lot since his death." She focused her gaze on him. "Have you decided upon the charities that will benefit from your event?"

John chuckled. "Not all of them, but the foundation will definitely be a major recipient."

Her face glowed. "Oh, that's wonderful. We're finding there are more and more people requiring our help these days." Her smile faltered. "I find the increasing need for food banks quite alarming. It makes me so angry. At one end of the spectrum, you have bank executives paying themselves huge bonuses, while at the other, there are so many people who can't even afford to eat."

John knew the foundation aided underprivileged kids and the homeless. He poured out some more tea. "I think it's a great idea of Brett's—Mr. *Sanderson's*—to organize a day like this." He felt his heart stutter briefly in his chest. He didn't want to think about Brett.

Margaret regarded him keenly. "Tell me about yourself, John. All I know of you is that you're Evan's elder brother." That sparkle was back. "I must say, I pity you growing up with that young man. He must have been quite a challenge."

John laughed. "Evan was a pain when he was little. Though I must admit, these days, he's been extremely supportive." The thought warmed him. Knowing Evan was there for him was a real comfort.

Margaret's eyes gleamed. "I sense a story here. Not that you should feel any pressure to tell me anything," she hastened to add. "I know old ladies can be notoriously nosy." She gave him a wink.

John liked Margaret immensely. She reminded him of his own grandmother, who'd been a wonderful part of his life when he was growing up. There was something about her that made him feel very comfortable.

"Evan was the first person to know that I was gay," he admitted. Margaret's fond mention of her PA and her supportive comments about gay marriage led him to think he could be honest with her.

"Ah," she said with a smile. She regarded him intently. "And yet you're not happy right now, are you?"

John was stunned. *She can* see *that?* His mouth fell open.

Margaret gave him a fond look. "My dear boy, I've lived a great many more years than you. Is it so surprising that I can recognize pain when I see it?" She reached across and wrapped a wrinkled hand around his. "You don't have to tell me—as long as you *do* have someone you can confide in. Shared pain is sometimes easier to bear." Her affectionate expression brought a lump to John's throat, and for a moment, he couldn't speak.

"Th-thank you," he stammered at last. "I'm lucky—I have some fantastic housemates, and they're supporting me through this. But…." His voice hitched. "I'm sorry, but I really find this hard to talk about."

Margaret squeezed his hand. "Then don't," she said practically. "We're just going to finish our tea and biscuits while you entertain me with stories about Evan as a little boy." Her eyes gleamed. "Because I'm positive you have a lot of entertaining stories about *that* young man."

John laughed, the ache in his heart easing slightly. "You have *no* idea."

They spent a very pleasant half hour conversing over tea and biscuits, and John was sorry when Margaret glanced at the neat gold watch on her wrist and sighed.

"Unfortunately, my time is up. Ellis will be ringing me any second now, demanding to know if I'm ready for my next appointment." She gave John a warm smile. "It has been a pleasure to meet you, John. And I look forward to attending your event."

John's eyes widened. "You're coming?"

Margaret grinned. "Seeing as my foundation will benefit from your efforts, I think it only polite to be there. Besides, I love attending such events." Her eyes met John's. "I take it you don't object?"

"Oh, no, not in the least," John said hurriedly. It was a comforting thought that Margaret would be on hand, if he were honest. "School starts on Monday, and I'll walk in there with a list of ideas to share with everyone. You've been a real help."

Her cheeks pinked once more. "Oh, it was nothing. To be honest, it was lovely of Chris to suggest us meeting like this. I must thank him for a delightful morning."

A melodic chime came from her handbag, and she reached into it, withdrawing a phone.

"Yes, Ellis, I'm ready. The car is on its way? Excellent. Yes, I'll be there. Ellis? You're fussing." She shook her head. John loved the humorous glint in her eye. She listened intently for a moment. "That's wonderful. I'll see you shortly." She finished the call and chuckled. "That boy can be *such* a mother hen." She grasped John's hand once more. "I hope things sort themselves out for you, John. You deserve some happiness."

He gave her a grateful look. *Happiness would be good.*

The brief image of Brett's smiling face that surfaced in his mind brought a fresh jolt of pain.

Not going to go there.

CHAPTER 16

"I DIDN'T expect to hear from you." Elliott sounded sad on the phone.

"Yeah, well, let's just say things didn't work out and leave it at that," Brett said shortly. "Can I book my usual room for the February half term?" He was in dire need. He'd spent the Christmas holiday drinking far too much and feeling sorry for himself. Christmas was always a bad time, one he simply endured.

It might have been really different this time if you'd had someone to share it with.

Brett closed his eyes to shut out the thought.

He could hear Elliott leafing through his diary. There was the briefest of sighs. "I should tell you we're full, y'know. *You* were the one who wanted to break out of this cycle, after all."

"But you're not going to, because you're a businessman, and far be it from you to turn away a paying customer." He waited patiently.

Elliott huffed. "Okay, you got your usual room. Though I'm still waiting for the day when you walk through my doors with your arm around a guy. I'll be that chuffed, you'll be having the room on me."

Brett snorted. Elliott might have a wait on his hands, if *that's* what he was holding out for. "Thanks, Elliott. I'll see you in about six weeks' time. Have a good start to the year."

"You too, mate." He hung up.

Brett wrote the booking in his diary. It was good to have something to look forward to, a reward for getting through the next half term. He wasn't sure what to expect the following morning when term started. It had crossed his mind once or twice that John might ask to be taken off the charity event, maybe as a way of getting back at him. But then he'd dismissed it. John was utterly professional, *that* much Brett knew already. No, the younger man would most likely work really hard to make the day a success.

God, it's going to be bloody awkward.

Brett had spent most of the holiday being angry with himself. Angry for allowing himself to be blinded by lust. Angry for throwing logic and common sense out the window. But mostly, angry that he couldn't get John out of his mind. The man haunted him. Visions tortured him, visions of the smooth, creamy skin of John's back as Brett had caressed it, his cock plunging into that tight furnace inside him. He kept seeing his hands gripping John's hips as he fucked him. The one set of images that seemed to stay with him the longest were those of John's face. John smiling, laughing, biting his lip when he was concentrating....

Oh, for God's sake, let him go. You fucked up—literally.

Brett closed his eyes. Like he needed reminding.

THE STAFF room was crowded, everyone buzzing as they talked animatedly about their holiday. Brett always loved the start of the spring term. Batteries recharged, the promise of spring in the air.... It would have been the perfect start to the new year, but for one thing—John wasn't looking at him. In fact, John was looking *anywhere* but in Brett's direction.

Well, what the fuck did you expect?

Brett had arrived at his usual time. The first thing he'd done was put on the coffee, and then he'd stood by the window, mug in hand, watching for John's arrival on his bike. He knew the young man wouldn't be late. Sure enough, ten minutes later John had arrived—but not on his bike. He'd gotten out of a Mini, but not before he'd leaned across and given the driver a peck on the cheek. Brett had gotten a good look. It wasn't the guy who'd come to the school that day, but another one. *Probably another of his housemates*, he surmised. John seemed to be awfully close to them. And then it struck him. *Maybe he's in a relationship with one of them by now.* The thought sent a rush of cold flooding through his body. Brett had watched as John walked around the car. The driver's gaze had gone toward Brett's window, and there was no mistaking the flicker of hostility in those eyes, even at *that* distance. Oh, hell. *This is* not *going to be good.*

Brett hadn't seen John at all that morning. He'd remained in his room, probably getting everything ready for the day. Brett had heard the mechanical whir of the photocopier in the staff room above him, and he'd been sorely tempted to go upstairs, looking for any excuse to see John. But common sense had prevailed. *Just leave him alone. You're going to have to speak with him eventually. It can wait.*

Brett glanced at the clock. "Okay, people, let's get started, shall we?"

A hush fell over the assembled group of people, and all eyes turned to Brett, including John's. What Brett wasn't prepared for was the look in those blue eyes. The light that Brett had loved seeing there was gone.

I did that. It wasn't a good thought.

Brett ran through his notes, including the message he'd taken from the police that morning. Carl Meadows had attempted to see his son during the last week, in spite of the restraining order his wife, Anna, had taken out. It had not been pleasant, and Brett was making sure that all staff had a photo of Carl in their rooms. He urged them to be vigilant. Anna was panicking, it seemed.

"Just remember—if you see this man anywhere near the school, do *not* approach him. Get on your phone and let me know. I've got a direct number for the detective in charge of the case, and they'll be here as soon as possible. Keep your eyes peeled during breaks and lunchtimes, before school as the kids are arriving and at the end of the school day." Brett turned to Michelle Fielding, the Year Two teacher. "Michelle, make sure you know where Wayne is at all times, all right? And be sure to keep him with you until Anna turns up for him when school is over." Michelle nodded, her expression grave.

Brett shuffled his notes. "Anything else from anyone?"

John got to his feet. "Actually, I'd like to talk to everyone, if I may." He held a sheaf of papers in his hands.

Brett waved him forward. "Certainly, John." He ignored the brief pang as John stepped up to the front of the room, studiously avoiding Brett's gaze. John gave everyone a tight smile.

"Morning, all. As you may remember, Brett asked me to take charge of the charity event, which takes place toward the end of this month. With that in mind, I've prepared notes for you all." He held them out to Bev, who took them with a warm smile and proceeded to hand them out to all the staff and LSAs. "There are lots of activities listed, and I'd like you to discuss these with your group and choose one. Obviously, we can't have two groups running the same event, so I'm afraid it will be first come, first served. Tell me as soon as you can which activity you'll be undertaking. If you need resources, please get a list to me ASAP and I'll sort those out for you. You'll see that there are also staff activities for you to get involved in. Please don't be shy, people—we need as many of you as possible to take part in this if we're going to make a success of it."

Brett was impressed. John's delivery was professional and confident, and the notes looked thorough. Brett felt a flush of pride. It had been the right decision.

"I've also given some thought as to which charities should benefit from the day. I don't know if many of you are aware of the Marriott Foundation and the sterling work it does with underprivileged kids and the homeless"—there were immediate nods from around the room—"but their CEO, Margaret Marriott, will be attending on the day." Murmurs of approval filled the room. "And of course, Brett has arranged for Eric Lazenby to be our guest of honor for the day. He's agreed to run a training session for some of our children. It might also be an idea to have parents pay to play football with him on the day, with the highest bidders getting the opportunity." John smiled at the teachers before him. "Now, I do realize that this might not appeal to many of you here"—his female audience laughed—"but I'm sure you can think of *someone* who'd like the chance."

Trish Stetman, the Year Four teacher in charge of sports, snorted. "Speak for yourself, John. *I* want to play with Eric." Laughter greeted her words, and she winked at the ladies. "I'm going to be raiding my piggybank for this event." The laughter increased.

Brett held up his hand. "Okay, that's it. Time to get ready for the day. Can I just thank John for the wonderful work he's done so far to make this event successful." A round of applause followed his words, and John looked around at his colleagues with a shy smile.

Brett clapped his hands together. "Work time." He put out his hand to stop John as he moved away, but the young man ignored it and walked off, talking with Trish. Brett pulled his hand back quickly, his chest tight. Any fears he'd had that he'd damaged their professional relationship had just been confirmed.

And you have no one to blame but yourself.

FOUR THIRTY and the school building was quiet. Brett sat in his office with a mug of coffee and peered at his monitor, where the application form for the position of HMI was displayed. He couldn't deny he had all the necessary qualifications and experience, but still, something held him back. The thought of leaving the little primary school, if he proved successful, was one that filled him with mixed feelings. He liked the way his team worked together, and what they'd already achieved had been incredible. The school was fast becoming the heart of the community.

The soft knocking at his door startled him. "Come in."

Brett's heartbeat increased as John poked his head around. "Do… do you have a minute, Brett?" The hesitancy in John's voice was a step in the wrong direction.

Brett waved him in and gestured toward the coffee machine. "You want one?" John nodded and went to pour himself a mug. Then he grabbed a chair from around the table and pulled it over to Brett's small desk. Yet another backward step. Normally, they would sit at the conference table.

Yeah, like he's going to sit at the table you fucked *him on.*

Quickly, Brett minimized the document on the screen and picked up his mug.

"How's today gone? Anything happen that I need to know about?"

John shook his head. "A pretty straightforward day." The atmosphere in the office was tense. John seemed unable to sit still for more than a moment, crossing and uncrossing his legs, smoothing the fabric of his pants, and even scraping his hand through his blond layers.

Brett was aware of the fluttery, empty sensation in his belly. His skin tingled. Something was coming.

John studied his mug for several long seconds and then raised his head. "Look, we have to talk."

Brett's heart sank at the lifeless tone of John's voice. "Go on," he began cautiously.

John's gaze met his. "Is... is there anyone else who could be my mentor? For obvious reasons, I'm not happy with us continuing as we were." His eyes flicked for the briefest of seconds toward the table before returning to Brett.

Brett flinched. He should have anticipated this. "Is that really what you want?" he asked quietly.

John locked eyes with him, and the breath died in Brett's throat to see the pain there.

"Can you honestly tell me you don't feel awkward about... about what happened?" That intense gaze rested on him for a moment before John dropped his chin toward his chest, his cheeks flushed.

Oh, God, did *he*.... All of a sudden, Brett wanted John to see what lay in his heart.

"John, I can't begin to tell you how much I regret what I did." John jerked his head up. Brett cleared his throat. "Perhaps I should make myself clear. I am so very, very sorry for the way in which I...." He couldn't bring himself to say the words. What *could* he say? *The way I fucked you? Took you on my office table?*

John's eyes never moved away from him, his body rigid in his chair.

Brett sighed. *Time to be honest.* "I found you very attractive. I still do." He watched John's pupils react. "But I shouldn't have abused my position in that way. I allowed lust to cloud my judgment. And there hasn't been a *single day* since then when I haven't bitterly regretted my actions." He lowered his gaze to stare at his mug. He couldn't look at John right now. "I have only to close my eyes and I'm back there, watching myself...." He swallowed. "What I did was reprehensible. I screwed up the rapport we'd established, the professional relationship that we'd worked so hard to...." His words died away, and he took a deep breath before raising his chin to look once more at John. "And I killed any chance there might have been of something... more."

There was an ache in his chest as he spoke. He meant every word of it. No man had ever gotten to him in the way John had.

John stared at him, eyes wide. "My God, you mean that," he said in a hushed tone.

Brett nodded. "But I still stand by my original decision. I have to be seen to be impartial, John. Objective. Above reproach. And being in a relationship with you... it would leave me open to possible accusations from the staff, the governors...." He sighed. "And yes, there isn't a day goes by when I don't think about how different things might have been."

"But it wouldn't be against the rules, would it?" Brett's heart quailed at the hopeful note in John's voice. "I mean—"

"Please, John, don't." Brett clamped down hard on the emotions that John engendered in him. He couldn't afford to think like that. "It already hurts too much."

John studied him intently for a moment and then took a long drink of his coffee. The silence that built up in the little office was almost tangible.

"I've changed my mind," John said at last. Brett's brow furrowed. "I don't want anyone else for my mentor. I think...." He looked Brett in the eye. "I think we're professional enough to get past this. Besides, no one here knows me like you do." He attempted a weak smile.

"Are you serious?" Brett could hardly dare believe it. "Do you really think we can do this?"

John nodded. "I think we both know where we stand, don't you?" That smile faltered. "I'm not assuming for one minute that it will be easy, but I'm sure we can find a way through this."

To Brett's ears, the words made perfect sense and seemed very plausible. But the light that had gone from John's eyes spoke louder. The younger man was hurting. And that was down to Brett.

"How about we talk through *this*," Brett said, picking up John's notes for the charity day. John was right, after all. Time to draw a line under recent events and move on.

Even if it hurts like hell just to look at him. Brett, when you fuck up....

JOHN PUT the kettle on and stared out through the kitchen window at the bare garden beyond, his thoughts miles away from his task.

"You haven't said a word since I picked you up outside school."

John turned to face Alec. He gave him an affectionate glance. "Thanks for that, by the way."

Alec shrugged. "There was no way I'd let you handle your first day back on your own. It was just lucky my day off fell that way." He walked over to where John stood and gestured with his head toward the kettle. "It *has* boiled, y'know." A grin flickered across his face.

John poured the boiled water over his tea bag and waited as it infused. His mind was still focused on Brett. He couldn't believe how open the man had been with him.

"Okay, what happened?" John arched his eyebrows, and Alec smiled as he spoke. "Well, it's obvious *something* did." He narrowed his eyes, and his smile died. "You spoke with Brett."

John nodded. "And it was certainly… illuminating." He ran through their conversation.

Alec pursed his lips. "So he felt bad, did he? Good."

John reached out to lay a hand on Alec's arm. "Just for a second there, I got the impression…." His words trailed off, as if the mere act of voicing his thoughts would somehow jinx them. Alec was staring at him, head tilted to one side. John sighed. "I got the impression that Brett wanted us to be together." He met Alec's gaze head on.

Alec's mouth fell open. "You're serious." John gave a slow nod, and Alec's eyes widened. "Bloody hell, you still want him. After everything that man did, you still want to be with him, don't you?"

John's chin trembled, but he maintained eye contact. "Yes." The word came out as a whisper.

Alec's expression softened. "Oh, hon. You fell hard, didn't you?"

John turned away to focus on the tea. "I don't know what you mean."

Alec laughed softly as he turned John to face him. "You're talking to someone who's stood exactly where you're standing now. I know how confusing it can be, the range of emotions that are raging through you right now, the desire to be wanted, needed… loved."

John caught his breath, unable to look away from the expression of compassion on Alec's face. "Yeah, you *do* know how I feel, don't you?"

Alec pulled John to him in a tight hug. "It does get better, honestly," he said into John's ear. "But the chances of it getting better with Brett? I have to be honest here. They're remote." He released John and stepped back, his expression earnest. "And the last thing I want you to do is pin your hopes on a man who in all likelihood is going to let you down. Life's too short, hon. Let this one go." He fixed John with an unflinching gaze.

John gave a brave smile, far braver than he actually felt. "You're probably right. Plenty more fish in the sea. But to be honest? Right now, I'm too busy and in no mood to go fishing."

The fond look Alec gave him warmed John. "There's no rush. Give it time." He patted John's arm and exited the kitchen.

John sipped his green tea and watched Alec go. No matter what words came out of his mouth, his heart was still telling him the same thing.

I want Brett. Even if Alec was right, it didn't stop John hoping.

$\mathcal{C}$HAPTER 17

"SO HOW are the preparations coming along?" Margaret asked him.

John hunched his shoulder to keep his phone lodged against his ear as he piled the chopping board and knife into the sink, then ran the hot tap and soapy water filled the bowl.

"Things are going well. We're on course to have everything ready on time." Thankfully—there was only one week remaining until D-day.

"Good, good." John could hear the note of satisfaction in her voice. "Oh, and I saw the piece in the *Manchester Evening News*, giving advance notice of the day. You did well there. Publicity is essential, and you've given the public some indication of what to expect. Have local businesses got on board as you'd hoped?"

John wiped his hands and reclaimed his phone. "Yes, in fact, more responded than I'd anticipated." If everything went to plan, it was going to be a fantastic event.

"That's excellent news." John could tell over the phone that Margaret was smiling. "And on a more personal note, how are *you* doing?"

"Me?" John was genuinely puzzled by the question. "I'm fine."

"Then you've got over whatever it was that was making you so unhappy?"

John stopped dead, the question catching him unawares.

Margaret sighed down the phone. "I thought not."

"How… how do you do that, Margaret?" The old lady was amazing.

"John, my dear boy, I can hear it in your voice. I only wish there was something I could do to help."

He smiled. "You've done so much for me already. This event is going to be brilliant because of you."

"Perhaps, but success won't bring you what you're looking for."

John closed his eyes. He couldn't shut out the delicious fantasies that had pervaded his dreams during the last few weeks—Brett thanking him for all his efforts before drawing him closer to kiss him and then tumbling them both into the huge bed that magically just *happened* to be there…. He and Brett, curled up together on the couch in front of the fire…. He shivered.

"Maybe not, but it will be good for the school, and right now, I'd rather concentrate my efforts on that."

"You're a good man." He detected a note of satisfaction in her voice. "And I've taken up far too much of your time." He thanked Margaret for the call and then hung up before returning his focus to preparing the dinner. All the housemates were home for a change, and it was his turn to cook. As he opened the fridge to get the meat, he heard a key in the front door.

"What are we having tonight?" Martin called out. "I'm starving."

John chuckled. "You're always starving. And it's pork steaks marinated in light soy sauce with garlic and paprika, and roasted veggies." The colorful vegetables were already in the oven, drizzled with groundnut oil. He grabbed the plastic container that held the steaks from the fridge and set it on the worktop.

"Hmmmm." Martin's murmur of appreciation drifted along the hallway. He appeared in the doorway, loosening his tie, his jacket and shoes already removed. "I'm ready to eat now." He crossed the kitchen, clearly on a course for the fridge. John picked up the wet knife from the sink and brandished it.

"You are *not* going to snack. You'll spoil your dinner."

Martin snorted. "Yes, Mum." He held up his hands and gave a good-natured grin. "Okay, okay, I get the message. No snacking." He glanced back up the hall. "Are the others home?"

John nodded. "Stu's in his room on his phone, and Alec's in the shower. You'll have time for one when he gets out. The veggies take forty minutes in the oven." He opened the fridge and pulled out the bottle of rosé. "But in the meantime, how about a glass of wine?"

Martin's eyes gleamed. "*Now* you're talkin'." John poured out two glasses and handed one over. He took a sip of the chilled wine and sat down at the table. Time to relax before cooking the steaks.

Martin joined him and leaned back in his seat, watching him closely. "Things aren't getting any better, are they?" John cocked his head. "At school," Martin added.

John huffed. "You know what? I don't want to discuss this."

Martin held up his hands defensively. "I'm sorry. I'll shut up." He took a drink of wine and studied the tabletop.

John let out a sigh. This wasn't an unfamiliar topic. "Look, it's not you, all right? I'm just fed up of moping around, my head full of thoughts about a man who clearly isn't going to make a move on me. Maybe Alec's got the right idea after all. Maybe I should just let this one go." His heart ached even as he said the words. *Easier said than done, yeah?*

Martin's expression was full of sympathy. "Perhaps it's for the best."

John regarded him fondly. "Which is precisely what you've all been saying for weeks now—only I haven't been listening, have I?"

Martin put down his glass. "John, we're just concerned. We do know what you're going through. There's not one of us who hasn't nursed a broken heart at one point or another." He narrowed his eyes. "Except maybe Stu. I can't see *anything* getting to him. That boy is too thick-skinned."

John wasn't so sure. There was a lot about Stu that the flight attendant kept well below the surface. A coping mechanism? Perhaps.

"So what's the plan? Get dressed up in your tightest jeans and go on the pull in Canal Street?"

John laughed. "No, thank you. I think I'll stick with managing to get through one single day without thinking of him. If I can do *that*, it's a start."

Martin stared. "Oh, fuck—you *have* got it bad, haven't you?"

John shrugged, ignoring the clenching in his stomach. "Enough, all right? We need a new rule in this house. *No More Talking About Brett.*" He attempted a smile, although he had a feeling Martin would see straight through it.

"That sounds like a good rule," Alec said as he came into the kitchen, his brown curls still damp from the shower. "I vote yes." His eyes lit up as he spied the glasses. He let out a groan. "Wine—*God*, yes."

Martin chuckled as he opened the fridge to retrieve the wine. "Bad day?"

Alec winced. "Long shift—and yes, a bad day. We got called to a shooting."

Both John and Martin became still. "Really?" Martin said with an incredulous stare.

Alec nodded. "Day over. Don't want to talk about it." He took the glass that Martin had poured for him and took a long drink. He closed his eyes. Martin gave him a quick squeeze around the shoulders, and Alec smiled gratefully. He gazed inquiringly at John. "Okay, when's dinner? I'm starved."

John shook his head. It seemed he wasn't the only one who wasn't feeling talkative.

BRETT STOOD at the main gate, watching the children pour out of the doors, surge across the playground, and spill out onto the pavements in their eagerness to go home. Parents, relatives, older siblings—people waited outside the gates to collect their young charges. He watched Michelle by the outer door of her classroom, little Wayne by her side. She spoke with parents, but her gaze constantly moved to and fro along the street, ever vigilant.

"Brett, have you got a minute?"

Brett turned to Bev, who was standing behind him. There was a distracted air about her.

"Certainly. Here or in my office?"

Bev replied immediately. "Your office, please."

He gave a nod, and after giving one last glance at the departing children, he led the way back into the building. When they got into his office, he gestured toward one of the two comfy chairs along the wall and then took one.

"Okay, what's up?" He kept his manner brisk, although he was dying to know what was coming. Bev had never asked to speak with him privately.

She twisted her hands in her lap. "It's about John."

Brett arched his eyebrows. "Is there a problem?" His heart stuttered briefly in his chest.

"I'm not sure, but I think so. He's seemed really low these last weeks. I wondered if you'd noticed the same thing. I mean, you probably have more dealings with him, as his mentor." She bit her lip. "And I'm not the only one who's noticed. Michelle and Trish both said the same."

"Oh? I can't say he's seemed particularly depressed." Brett delivered the lie smoothly. He'd had similar concerns. John wasn't the same person. But if others were starting to notice, then maybe things had gotten worse.

"We thought maybe it was something to do with the charity event. He's put in an awful lot of work for it. Has he mentioned any issues to you?" Bev gazed at him inquiringly, her brow wrinkled.

Brett shook his head. "No, and when we've discussed it, it seems everything is going well." That much he was sure of. He knew in his heart what was troubling his newest member of staff, and he fervently wished he could go back in time to erase the damage he'd done.

Bev's brow cleared. "Well, that's good, at any rate. I just thought I'd mention our concerns."

Brett regarded her closely. "You like him, don't you?" Bev's cheeks heated up. *Oh, wow.* It wasn't as if Brett hadn't foreseen this—a few of his staff had definitely started paying John more attention of late. *Poor ladies. They'd be so disappointed if they knew….*

"He's a nice guy," she said simply, her eyes not meeting his. She cleared her throat. "In that case, I'll be off. Thanks, Brett, for listening." She got up and headed for the door, and he went with her. She paused at the threshold. "Do you have a meeting now with him?" Brett nodded. "Then please pass him a message from Trish. She says to tell him she's found the stocks." She grinned.

"Stocks?" Brett repeated with a frown. And then it came to him. The stocks for the charity event. "Ah, that's good. Although we still haven't had anyone volunteer to do *that* particular event." He winked.

Bev laughed. "I'm not surprised. Good luck trying to find two ladies who are keen to be put in the stocks and have soapy sponges thrown at them, in deepest, darkest *January* of all months." She grinned. "Personally, I think it should be our only two *male* members of staff who get that honor. It would be the gentlemanly thing to do." Her eyes gleamed.

Brett grinned back. "Oh, you think so? I tell you what—I'll suggest it to John. If he says yes, *I'll* say yes. How's that?" He shrugged his shoulders. "Can't say fairer than that." He held out his hand, and Bev shook it firmly, her smile still evident. She walked off along the corridor in the direction of her classroom. Brett closed the door after her and sat down at his desk, his thoughts on John. He was dismayed that others had noticed the change in him. It didn't bode well.

Ten minutes later, John was at his door, folder in hand. Brett wanted John's evaluations on his latest lesson observation. Thankfully, John was a total professional. Each time Brett sat in on one of his lessons, John seemed to forget he was there and focus on his teaching. Brett knew from experience just how difficult a task that was, and the fact that John was able to accomplish it in spite of their past was a credit to him. Their discussion was brisk and to the point—and nothing like their meetings pre-Christmas. *That* John had been relaxed and cheerful, able to laugh and joke with him. This new John was quiet, even cautious, and the differences made Brett heart-sore.

As their meeting drew to a close, Brett remembered to pass on Trish's message. For the first time in a while, John's face creased into a genuine smile.

"I was hoping she'd come through. Otherwise, we would've had to cancel the sponge throwing."

"Hmm, about that." Brett fixed him with a hard stare. "It has been suggested—by *whom*, I shan't say—that you and I should be the victims. I said I'd mention it." He watched for John's reaction.

John stroked his chin. "The kids would love it, of course. The chance to throw things at the head teacher? Oh, yeah. If we say yes and advertise it as soon as possible, I can see them lining up with their pennies for *that* one." He chuckled. "Not to mention most of the staff as well." He met Brett's gaze. "All right—count me in. But there'd better be something hot to drink afterward, because we'll be *freezing*." He grinned.

Just for a moment, Brett saw a glimpse of the John who'd gotten under his skin. *God, I've missed him.*

"Let's add it to the final list of events that you're sending to the *Evening News.* That way, everyone knows what to expect next week." He couldn't believe the day was almost upon them. All John's hard work was about to pay off, hopefully.

John nodded. "I'll e-mail them the finalized list now," he said, getting up from his chair. "If that's everything?" He paused, his eyes on Brett.

Brett opened his mouth to reply—and then closed it. He decided on a brisk nod instead, and John left the office. Brett took a steadying breath. He'd wanted to say something, *anything*, that might have made John feel better, but for the life of him, he couldn't think of a single thing.

You know what you really *wanted to say, don't you?*

Brett knew. It had been on the tip of his tongue to tell John it had all been a mistake, that he'd been an idiot—that he wanted him. But his desire was overruled by logic yet again. Although now a tiny part of his brain was asking questions.

Could you be with him and keep it a secret?

If anyone found out, what's the worst that could happen?

For God's sake, man, don't you want to be happy?

And isn't it about time you were?

Brett clenched his hands into fists at his sides.

He stared out of the window, watching John as he walked out onto the road with his cycle, his backpack snug between his shoulder blades. John hefted himself onto the seat and set off down the road. Brett followed his progress, his eyes never straying.

If only there was a way.

THE SCHOOL hall was alive with noise. Every available inch of space was taken up with tables and stalls, and people crammed into the room, straining to get a view of each activity.

Brett had never seen so many parents and relatives attend a school function. So many people had stopped him in his progress through the hall to say what a fantastic event it was and to offer their congratulations. There were stalls set up by the local baker, selling cakes and different types of bread. The deli from around the corner in the nearby shopping center was doing a roaring trade, for which Brett was profoundly grateful, seeing as their profits were all going to charity. One class had produced a treasure map and was selling off squares. Another class had all made birthday cards for sale. Yet another had a huge jar full of sweets, and visitors were invited to pay to guess the total number. Everywhere he looked, money was changing hands.

"It looks like being a marvelous success, Mr. Sanderson," a cultured voice said next to him.

Brett glanced to his right to where Margaret Marriott was standing, gazing around the room, a wide smile on her face. Her head barely reached his shoulder.

"It certainly does," he agreed. In the midst of all the organized chaos, he spied John, who was making sure everything ran on time. The greatest crowd had gathered at Eric Lazenby's table, where the young footballer was signing autographs, helped by Trish, who was taking bids for the chance to play football with Eric later on in the year when the weather improved.

Margaret nodded toward the crowds. "And getting that young football star to help out was inspired. You are to be congratulated."

Brett gave a half bow. "Thank you, but the credit for all this goes to John. This is the result of all his efforts." Brett couldn't have been prouder of John. He watched as Margaret sought out John in the middle of the hall.

"I agree. It has been a pleasure working with him on this venture." She sighed. "If only his private life were as successful."

Brett stiffened. "What do you mean?" His heart raced.

Margaret's expression grew serious. "I know from what he has told me that you are his mentor." Brett nodded. "Maybe he would open up to you." She paused and then waved her hand. "Forgive me. I shouldn't have spoken. It's none of my business, at any rate."

"No, please," Brett interjected. "Say what's on your mind."

Margaret pursed her lips. "It simply occurred to me that he might speak more freely with another male than he would with an old lady. Especially another male whom he trusts."

"About what?" Brett held his breath.

She fixed him with a steady gaze and lowered her voice. "That boy is dreadfully unhappy. If you ask my opinion, someone broke his heart."

Brett became aware of the heavy feeling in his stomach. He couldn't move. He could only stare at John across the hall. That face was burned into his brain. *Oh, fuck—could I have been so blind that I couldn't see what was right under my nose?*

John had been in his thoughts, his dreams, his fantasies.

But not once had he considered that he might have figured as heavily in John's.

A sharp intake of breath brought him back to Earth with a bump. Margaret stared at him, her eyes wide, her expression accusatory.

"But you already know that, don't you, *Mr.* Sanderson?"

Brett swallowed. His heart pounded. He didn't dare speak. He was too afraid that every word out of his mouth would only confirm what the sharp-eyed old lady clearly suspected. He felt the hairs lift on his arms and the nape of his neck.

Margaret's eyes widened. "My God. You're as unhappy as he is." Her gaze went from him to John and then back to him. "Oh, my." And then her expression softened. "I see."

Brett froze. "I… I don't know what…." Words failed him.

Margaret studied him in silence for a moment. Then she smiled kindly at him. "Some words of advice, Mr. Sanderson—*Brett.* Life is short. That may sound strange, coming from an old lady fast approaching eighty, but believe me, as you get older, life slips by at a faster rate. And there is nothing worse to live with than regret." Her gaze alighted on John. "He is a warm, caring young man. And when he opens his heart, he will blossom even further—with the right person by his side." She glanced at Brett. "Take that from someone who has seen *all* kinds of love, Brett." She gave him a knowing smile. "These eyes see a lot, yes. That's one of the benefits of old age—there is little that surprises me anymore."

Brett was dizzy, his knees shaking. He had never felt so naked before someone as he felt in that moment.

Margaret laid a frail, wrinkled hand on his arm. She lowered her voice once more, and Brett strained to hear her. "If you have it in your power to make that young man happy—and yourself for that matter—then I suggest you do something about it. Find a way. Because there is *always* a way, if you want something badly enough." She locked eyes with him. "It all depends how badly you want something, of course." There was that knowing smile again as she withdrew her hand.

Brett was ready with the lie, to tell Margaret she was barking up the wrong tree, but he couldn't bring himself to do it. It felt… wrong. Out of the corner of his eye, he noticed John making his way toward them across the hall. John tapped his watch as he drew near.

"It's time we got changed for our soaking session." John's lips twisted into a half smile.

Margaret chuckled. "Oh, I'd forgotten. I saw the stocks out in the playground as we arrived. I certainly don't want to miss this. Neither will the photographer from the *Evening News*."

Brett's heart was pounding so strongly, he thought it was about to explode from his chest. He breathed deeply. "Okay, let's do this."

John smirked. "Just remember—it's all for a good cause." He winked at Margaret. "At least, that's what I'll be telling myself next week when I'm in bed with the flu as a result." He exited the hall.

Brett met Margaret's gaze. "Thank you for the… advice, Mrs. Marriott."

She gave him an affectionate look. "You're very welcome, Mr. Sanderson. I hope it proves useful." And then she smiled. "Now go and get ready for the little darlings who are lining up to soak you." Her eyes sparkled with amusement.

Brett bobbed his head and turned to leave the hall just as Trish announced over the PA system that it was time to "*get those wet sponges ready*." The loud chorus that greeted her words left him in no doubt that he and John were about to be on the receiving end of some very enthusiastic volleys. As he hurried along to the men's room, his mind was turning over Margaret's advice.

There is always *a way—if you want something badly enough.*

The questions that faced him now were, just how badly did he want John?

And what was he prepared to do about it?

CHAPTER 18

As BRETT walked into the men's room, John was taking off his pants and pulling on a pair of shorts and a T-shirt. He looked up and gave Brett a wary smile. "I brought some old clothes to wear, seeing as they're going to get soaked." He stepped into a pair of sweatpants.

Brett reached for the bag he'd left there earlier and took out similar items. He gave a half smile. "Yeah, I had the same idea." He removed his tie and began to unbutton his white shirt. He didn't look at John as he spoke. "You *do* realize we're going to freeze out there?"

John snickered. "I'm still amazed you agreed to do this."

Brett straightened as he dropped his pants and then slipped on his shorts. "Well, you were right. I couldn't see many kids passing up the chance to throw wet sponges at me." He shuddered dramatically. "I only hope Trish is kind to us and uses warm water."

John laughed, and the sound was music to Brett's ears. He looked over at John. The young man wasn't as relaxed as he sounded. There was a rigidity to him that saddened Brett. Margaret's words were still ringing in his head. *Just how badly do I want this?* He recalled his conversation with Elliott, telling him that there had to be more to life than mindless fucks with anonymous men. *I want more than that.* He stared at John, and his heart skipped a beat. Could *I have it... with John?* The mere idea set his pulse racing. He couldn't take his eyes off John, who sat there, tying up his trainers, oblivious to Brett's internal turmoil. *Oh, for God's sake*, say *something to him....*

"John...." For a moment, his nerve failed him.

John glanced up and became still. "Yes?" Brett heard his breath hitch.

"John, I just wanted to say... I'm sorry."

A look of mild surprise crossed John's face, and then his expression hardened. "You've already apologized."

"No," Brett insisted. "Please, let me finish." John's eyes met his, and he gave a brief nod. "I miss the way we were together, before I—" Brett swallowed. "—before I did something really stupid." He watched as John's face contracted as if in pain. "Not that us having sex was stupid, don't get me wrong." *Fuck, this is difficult.* Brett struggled to find the words to express what was in his heart. "But the way I chose to go about things, *that* was stupid, and the way I treated you after, well, that was downright cruel."

John seemed to be holding his breath, his gaze fixed on Brett.

"What I'm trying to say—and making a real mess of it—is that I want us to go back to how we were before I fucked up. I've made you unhappy. Hell, I've made *both* of us fucking miserable. But I want to put things right." Brett took a deep breath. He'd never been this hesitant his entire life. "Can... can we start again, please? And... and see where things take us?" Those last few words had him eyeing John anxiously. *Please... please say yes....*

John stared at him, lips parted, eyes shining. Slowly, he exhaled.

"Yes," he said at last. "I'd like that." He took a step toward Brett— just as someone rapped loudly on the door.

"Are you two ready? You won't *believe* the crowd that's waiting for you!" Trish sounded positively gleeful.

"And that's our cue," Brett said reluctantly. He smiled. "Ready?"

John nodded, a shy smile spreading slowly across his face. "Ready."

Feeling lighter than he'd felt in a long while, Brett followed John out of the men's room and along the corridor to the main door that led onto the playground—where both men stopped dead.

The playground was full of children, all beaming and holding up their hands, showing their coins. Adults too—there were lots of adults crowding around the wooden stocks, awaiting them with wide grins.

"D'ya know, I've always wanted to throw stuff at a teacher," called out one parent, and laughter rippled through the crowd. Trish was waiting by the stocks, looking almost apologetic.

"I had no idea it would be *this* popular," she said with a gesture toward the queues of people lined up. "I've already sent Bev off to find more buckets."

Brett swept his gaze over the hordes. "How much are we charging for this?" he asked John out of the corner of his mouth.

"Fifty pence for three sponges," John replied.

Brett grinned. "We're going to make a *fortune*." The two men regarded each other, and then both cracked up. "Come on—no putting it off any longer." He clasped John's hand briefly, and they walked over to the stocks. Trish had put down one of the rubber exercise mats so they could kneel on the ground while she unfastened the hinged top of the stocks and fitted their heads and hands through the holes.

"Comfortable, gentlemen?" Trish asked as she fastened the top securely in place. Her eyes gleamed.

"Trish, you're enjoying this far too much," Brett grumbled. He eyed the space between them and the waiting crowd, a distance of about ten feet. "I don't suppose we can move them back a little?" he asked hopefully.

Trish let out a playful gasp. "Why, Mr. Sanderson—you have to give the public a *chance* of hitting you, at least." She waggled her eyebrows.

The first children stepped forward, brandishing their money, all smiling happily. As the first sponges sailed through the air and landed on the ground in front of them, John twisted his neck to peer at Brett. "Maybe this won't be so bad after all."

Brett glanced at the tall boy from Year Six who was holding his sponge at the ready, a very determined look on his face. Brett groaned. "Think again." He gasped as the sponge landed on top of his head, and warm water soaked his hair, running down over his face. Brett shook his head, but seconds later, another sponge found its target. He caught sight of Margaret standing to one side with the photographer, who was snapping away merrily. Margaret was laughing.

"I shall... remind you of... this, John, when it's... time for your... final assessment," Brett gasped out, his words punctuated by the sound of sponges landing at their knees, water spattering their clothes.

John guffawed as he took another sponge to the head, his blond hair plastered to his face. "Smile for the camera, sir." He grinned, and Brett couldn't help laughing.

In spite of the cold wind that whipped around his soaked body and the water that chilled immediately after making contact with his skin, Brett managed to grin throughout the experience. He gave several loud groans each time a fresh bucket of water appeared, much to the delight of the children. And there were some fathers whose aim was frighteningly good—unfortunately.

"Some of our kids could be future bowlers for the England cricket team, based on today's performance," he managed to stammer out through chattering teeth.

John chuckled, although there was a tinge to his lips that told Brett he'd probably had enough. Trish seemed to think so too. She blew her whistle and declared the event finished, much to the dismay of the children who were waiting, their sponges ready.

Brett glared at one child. "Philip Jones, you've already had five tries. Don't think I haven't noticed." The boy giggled. "And I *will* remember this." He was pleased to see Philip gulp. The crowds began to disperse, and Trish released them from the stocks. Both men were shivering.

"Let's go and grab a quick shower to get warmed up," Brett suggested. "We need to be ready for the last few events." John nodded. They hurried along to the men's room, and once there, they huddled next to the radiator as they stripped off the soaked garments clinging to their icy skin. Brett glanced surreptitiously at John as his lean body emerged—and was suddenly conscious of John doing the same.

Brett straightened and stood nude before John, focusing on his mouth. John faced him, trembling.

"Your lips are almost blue," Brett whispered, reaching across and running his thumb over them. Shudders rippled through John, and his breath caught. Brett edged closer. "They need warming up." He leaned forward and brought his mouth to John's in a tentative kiss. John froze, hands by his sides, and then Brett felt the change in him as he relaxed, his hands coming up to rest on Brett's shoulders as he responded to the kiss. Brett cupped the back of John's head and parted his lips with his tongue, exploring him slowly, loving the low moan that rolled out of him. This kiss was nothing like their first. *But it's how that kiss* should *have been*, Brett thought ruefully.

The sound of voices in the corridor had Brett pulling back, breaking the kiss. John was staring at him with wide eyes, lips still parted. Brett cupped his cheek and ran his thumb along John's jaw.

"We can't do this now," he urged. John nodded, but Brett could see the disappointment burning in those blue eyes. "Let's shower and see this day through to the end, okay?" John gave him a shy smile, and Brett kissed him impulsively on the tip of his nose. He got into one of the two shower stalls and groaned as the hot water cascaded down onto his cold body. He laughed to hear similar sounds emanating from John's stall. As he let the water warm him thoroughly, Brett found himself trembling. *Where had that come from?* He hadn't been able to resist the pull of that sensuous mouth. Thoughts clamored in his head, telling him he was being reckless, that such actions were dangerous, but he pushed them aside. Listening to the logical part of his brain hadn't brought him happiness, had it?

So go with your heart, he told himself. *Maybe it's time to do things differently.*

JOHN COULD hardly keep still. His heart had almost stopped when Brett kissed him. He couldn't believe it was happening. And as he showered in the stall next to Brett's, he was conscious of the thin wall separating their naked bodies. For one beautiful moment, he imagined being bold enough to step into Brett's stall. He'd tried not to look at Brett as he'd stood there naked, but now John wanted to see the man in all his glory, to touch him, kiss him all over. Then reality bit.

You're in school, for goodness sake. A parent could walk into the men's room at any moment. Hell, they could have done that *while he was kissing you.* And then he laughed quietly as the sheer enormity of Brett's actions hit home. *Wow.*

They'd gotten dressed quickly, not looking at each other. John knew his face was hot—he could feel his cheeks burning. As they'd left the men's room, Brett had paused at the door for one infinitesimal moment and given him a brief smile before hurrying along the corridor to the main hall. That smile did wonders. *He doesn't regret it*, John exulted. He walked to the hall, feeling as if he were walking on air.

The final events of the day were almost a blur. He was aware of the crowds finally dying away, until only a few stragglers remained. Emily Taylor was in Brett's office, totaling up their takings for the day. The stalls were packed away, and John was pleased to see very little remaining on the stands—it had been a resounding success.

Margaret came over to speak with him before she left. She clasped his hand in hers and tilted her head up to smile at him.

"You did really well," she assured him.

John grinned. He couldn't help it. The combination of the day's success and Brett's tentative but promising kiss filled him with joy that threatened to bubble out of him at any moment.

Margaret gave him a knowing look. Her smile increased. "I am *so* happy for you," she said at last, her gaze meeting his. John wondered for a second or two if she was referring to more than the fantastic events of the day, but he quickly rejected that idea. There was no way she could know what had passed between Brett and himself. Impulsively, he hugged her and felt a chuckle reverberate through her.

She gently disengaged his arms and reached up to stroke his cheek. "Sweet boy."

John could feel the blush that heated his cheeks. "Thank you for all your help and advice. When we have a final figure, I'll make sure Brett invites you into school to present a check to you."

Her eyes lit up. "That would be wonderful. I look forward to it." She said good-bye and walked carefully to the main door where a young man in a sleek gray suit was watching her anxiously. *That must be Ellis*, John surmised. Ellis grinned at Margaret and held out his arm, which she took. One last wave to John and Margaret was gone.

"That is one remarkable old lady."

John turned to Brett and smiled. "Yes, she is." He glanced around at the now deserted hall, and all of a sudden, he felt weary. "You know, I'm glad we organized this day to be held on a Friday. I'm not sure I could have faced coming to work after this."

Brett chuckled. "I know exactly how you feel. I'm exhausted, and all I did was have countless wet sponges thrown at me." He winked and then looked at his watch. "Time to go."

John felt a jolt of disappointment. He wanted more. *Oh, well....* "Yeah, you're right."

"So how about I run you home? You must be tired too. Did you come to school on the bike this morning?" Brett inquired.

John shook his head, although inside he was rejoicing that they weren't about to be parted *just* yet. "I was going to walk home."

"Oh, no, you're not," Brett said decisively. "Not after everything you've done today. Give me five minutes, and I'll be ready to go." He walked off to his office, leaving John standing by the door, his mind in a whirl. His phone vibrated in his jacket pocket. It was Stu.

"How'd it go?" Stu demanded. "And are you ready to come home? Alec says he'll come get you. We've made somethin' special for dinner, to celebrate your day."

For the umpteenth time, John reminded himself how lucky he was. "That's sounds great, but tell Alec he needn't bother. I have a lift." He peered along the corridor, but there was no sign of Brett. Something occurred to him. "Stu, is there enough food if I invite someone to stay for dinner?" He crossed his fingers.

Stu chuckled. "Oh, there's plenty. Martin went overboard." There was a pause. "Who you invitin'?"

John took a deep breath before answering. "Brett."

There was suddenly silence at the other end of the phone. Then finally Stu spoke. "You *are* jokin', right?"

John glanced toward Brett's door. He spoke quickly. "Look, I haven't got time to tell you, 'cause he'll be out any minute, but something's happened, all right? You're going to have to trust me on this." Still silence. "Stu, *please*," he implored. "This... this is important. And you need to tell the others, okay?"

Stu huffed. "I think you're askin' for more heartache, meself." He let out a tired sigh. "Okay, okay, we'll act like you know what you're doin'. And yeah, I'll tell them to be on their best behavior."

John heaved a sigh of relief. "Thanks." He heard Brett's door open. "Okay, gotta go. I'll be home soon." He disconnected the call and pocketed the phone just as Brett appeared. John clamped down on the frisson of excitement that ran up and down his spine.

He hasn't said yes, yet.

BRETT SWITCHED off the engine and dropped his hands to his lap. John had said nothing during the quick journey, and Brett was painfully reminded of the last time he'd taken John home.

But this time is different.

It certainly was. The air in the car seemed to be electrically charged. Brett was sure that if he touched John with even a single finger, there'd be a spark. The hairs on his arms were upended. *Something's coming….*

"Thanks for the lift," John said, breaking the silence.

"It was the least I could do." Brett didn't want to go. In normal circumstances, he would've asked if he could come in, but their history made that bloody awkward. *Have I ever felt this unsure of myself around another man?* Then he laughed to himself. *Everything* about John was different. But he couldn't sit there and say nothing. "Look, I should go." He forced out the words, even though leaving was the last thing he wanted. He placed his hands on the wheel.

To his surprise, John reached across and grabbed his hand. "Don't go."

Brett turned his head to look at him. John's expression was earnest. "What?"

John tightened his fingers around Brett's. "Stay for dinner. There's plenty."

For one brief moment, hope swelled within him. Then he remembered. "I'm not sure that's a good idea," he said gently. "I don't think your housemates would be all that pleased to see me." He recalled with perfect clarity the look of hostility that had flashed in his direction that cold morning weeks ago.

"But *I* want you to stay," John insisted. "And don't worry about my housemates. They'll be fine about it, trust me."

Brett wanted to, with all his heart.

A rap on John's window made them both jump. Stu was leaning down, peering in at them. John lowered the window.

"Why are you two sat out here in the freezin' cold?" Stu hugged himself. "There's a fire goin' and hot food in the house. Come on, crazy people, get your arses in there!" His gaze went to where John's hand was still wrapped around Brett's, and a slow smile crossed his face before he beat a hasty retreat up the path to the front door.

Brett took a moment to collect himself. Stu's reaction had been unexpected. John was regarding him in obvious anticipation. And in the end, the decision was a painless one.

"I'd be delighted to stay for dinner," Brett said with a smile.

John's happy expression sent warmth radiating throughout his body, along with something else—a feeling of hope.

CHAPTER 19

"D'YOU WANT some more moussaka, Brett?" Martin asked, holding out the serving dish.

Brett groaned. "I couldn't eat another mouthful. I'm stuffed." He pushed his plate away and leaned back into his chair. The meal had been delicious. Stu had been correct—Martin had made plenty of it. And at least the atmosphere had warmed a little during the course of the dinner. Despite John's assurances, Brett's reception had been on the frosty side. Stu had been fine, and Brett had been grateful when he'd made several attempts to bring him into the conversation. But Martin had given him some very cool stares when he'd first walked into the house, and as for Alec, the young man had made no attempt to hide his dislike.

What none of them had counted on was John.

From the minute John led Brett into the house, he'd made it plain that Brett was there at his invitation and that he was very happy about it. He'd made lots of eye contact throughout dinner and had gone out of his way to send plenty of warm glances in Brett's direction. Brett had sat next to him, and throughout the meal there had been brief moments when their hands had touched, sending a shiver through Brett. The contact was fleeting yet deliberate, and Brett had quickly realized that John was sending a message to his housemates. To their credit, they were quick on the uptake, although Alec was slowest to respond.

"I'll go and see if the fire needs building up," John said. "We've got plenty of logs in, haven't we?"

Stu nodded. "And I'll put the coffee on."

John stood up and squeezed Brett's shoulder as he passed behind him on his way out of the kitchen. No sooner had he exited the room than Brett found himself the object of intense scrutiny. It was no surprise to him that Alec was the first to speak.

"I'll make this quick," Alec began in a low voice, his jaw set. "If you hurt him again, you'll have the three of us to contend with. That man has been through enough, thanks to you." He speared Brett with his unflinching gaze.

Stu reached across to grasp Alec's upper arm. "And you need to treat John's guest with respect," he advised. "Haven't you cottoned on yet, thick boy? Or were you too busy lookin' daggers at Brett all through dinner to see what was happenin' under your very nose?"

Alec frowned. "What are you talking about?"

Martin snickered. "Those two didn't stop touching all through the meal. And Brett didn't exactly look unhappy about it." He gave an apologetic glance in Brett's direction. "You'll have to forgive Alec. He gets very protective about John."

Brett shook his head. "There is nothing to forgive. I'm glad John has friends like you three in his corner." He turned to Alec. "And I have no intention of hurting him. You must believe that. I only ask that you give me the chance to prove it." He let out a sigh. "I don't blame you for mistrusting me, not after everything I've put John through, but please believe me when I tell you that things have changed." He stared at Alec, willing him to see the truth of his words.

Alec regarded him closely. Several seconds passed. Brett could hear the odd noise coming from the lounge as John piled logs onto the fire. At last, Alec seemed to relent.

"I guess I'll have to trust you," he said grudgingly. "And I can't deny that John is the happiest he's been in months." Martin and Stu murmured in agreement.

Brett hadn't missed the change in John either. He'd seemed so relaxed as they'd eaten.

"What are you all doing in there?" John called out. "How many of you does it take to make coffee?" Brett could hear the amusement in his tone.

Alec grumbled, "Well, don't keep him waiting." But finally his eyes met Brett's and he grinned, albeit reluctantly.

Brett returned his grin. "Yes, sir." He got to his feet and cast a last glance in Alec's direction before exiting the kitchen. He found John sitting on the rug in front of the fire, staring into the flames. The room was furnished with two fat armchairs, a rocking chair, and a large couch, which looked very inviting. Brett sat down on it and patted the seat cushion next to him.

"How about you sit up here with me?" he suggested.

John's face lit up, and he got up from the floor to walk over to Brett and sit beside him, perching on the edge of the cushion. Brett settled back and smiled at him. "Maybe you'd be more comfortable if you leaned against me." Despite his relaxed appearance, Brett's stomach was rolling as he found himself in unfamiliar territory. For all his experience in the bedroom, he'd never once snuggled with another man. He waited to see how John reacted.

John stared at him for a moment, his expression unreadable. Brett's mouth was suddenly dry. Then a slow smile spread across John's face, and he snugged up against him, his arm reaching across Brett's belly, his head on Brett's chest. Brett fought hard to keep from showing his relief. Instead, he put his arm around John, letting his hand drape over his shoulder.

What does it say about me, that at thirty-three I should find this such an alien experience?

Brett didn't want to think about that. He focused on the warmth of John's body radiating through his layers of clothing. He took in the sound of John's breathing, synchronizing it with his own, and the act of doing that brought a layer of calm that settled over him like a fine, soft blanket. He breathed in John's scent, warm and heady. As he gazed down at John, cuddled up to him, Brett realized with a shock that the younger man looked totally at home there.

It's as if he's meant to be there, in my arms.

The revelation shook him so much that he didn't hear the three men enter the lounge. The first he knew was when Alec's soft gasp alerted him to their presence. Brett didn't move. All he wanted was to enjoy the moment.

"Aw, look at the lovebirds, Martin."

Stu's teasing tone made Brett look up. Stu gave him a wink. He placed two mugs of coffee on the low table in front of them. Brett caught his eye and mouthed, *"Thanks."* Stu smiled and then curled up in one of the armchairs, his eyes on Martin, clearly waiting for a response.

Martin snorted. "You're just jealous." He walked across the room and switched on the TV.

Stu guffawed. "Yeah, right. What about you? When's the last time *you* brought a date home, eh?" He waggled his eyebrows. "Oh, wait a minute—you're not home that often, are you?"

It was obvious to Brett that the banter was all good natured. He tightened his arm around John, who simply snuggled up that little bit closer. *God, this feels good.*

Martin quirked an eyebrow. "What's your point, Mister 'I'm-just-off-to-New York-Paris-Orlando-somewhere-else-unpronounceable'?" He snickered.

Stu threw a cushion across the room, which hit him on the arm. "My point is, you work too hard."

Alec was curled up in the wide rocking chair, hugging a plump red velvet cushion. His attention seemed to be divided equally between Stu and Martin.

"What do you do, Martin?" Brett asked. He knew next to nothing about John's housemates. He glanced at the three men. Of the three, Stu was definitely the most confident—at least, that's the way it seemed. *But then again, things aren't always what they seem, are they?*

Martin…. He couldn't get a handle on Martin, whereas Alec seemed to be an open book. Brett was glad the hostile glances had eased off. He wanted to get to know the three men. *Especially if I'm going to be around here a lot.* The thought was both warming and terrifying.

"I'm an assistant manager for a men's clothing store in the Arndale Shopping Center," Martin said before sipping his coffee.

Brett raised his eyebrows. Martin seemed young for management. "How long have you worked there?"

"Been there three years. Before that I was a trainee manager in another branch—I went there right after I got my degree—but then I got promoted." Martin shook his head, a wry smile on his face. "And now I'm up for promotion again."

Alec sat up straight. "You never said! Since when?"

Martin sighed. "Head office wants me to take on more of a management role, but I'm not sure. I'm actually thinking of looking in another direction."

Stu put down his mug and stared at Martin. "You've kept this dead quiet."

Brett watched this interchange with interest. The housemates were clearly very close, but the surprise on Stu's face was unmistakable. Beside him, Brett sensed John following the proceedings quietly.

"What are you thinking of doing?" Alec asked.

Martin picked up the TV remote and muted the sound. He gazed at the fire for a moment before replying. "I've been considering applying for a post as a buyer. It'd mean traveling, which would be great. And I have the qualifications for it, after all."

Brett was intrigued. "What's your degree in?"

Martin smiled. "Fashion design—specifically, menswear."

Both Stu and Alec snorted.

"What's so amusing?" Brett couldn't hold back the question.

Stu grinned. "Martin and clothes. Just ask him how many wardrobes he has, Brett."

"Yeah, and *then* ask about the stash of clothes in the attic," suggested Alec with a mischievous smile.

Martin huffed. "I can't help it if I like clothes."

Stu chortled. "You '*like*' clothes? Now *there's* an understatement."

"But he *loves* the staff discount," added Alec with a wink.

Brett chuckled. He loved this.

Martin shrugged. "You're both jealous."

Stu laughed. "Oh, immensely. I mean, you see what I go to work in. Red is so not my color." His face straightened. "But back to my first point.

With your hours, you don't have time to date. You work most Saturdays, Sundays too. What about time for a relationship?" His expression softened.

Martin smiled at him. "Right now, the job's more important. I can think about finding a partner when my career is sorted out." He speared Stu with a look. "And you can talk, Mister Mile-High-Club." He laughed gently, and Stu joined him.

Brett looked across at Alec. There was an expression in those green eyes that spoke of sadness. "Are you okay, Alec?" Even if the young man hadn't exactly welcomed him with open arms, that didn't mean *Brett* couldn't extend the hand of friendship.

Alec looked up, surprise written plainly across his face. Then his expression morphed into something far more friendly. "I'm fine, really. It was just all this talk about work and relationships." Brett tilted his head, and Alec sighed. "Let's just say, the atmosphere where I work isn't fun right now." He stared at his empty coffee mug.

Martin got up from his armchair and moved quickly to the rocking chair. He knelt beside Alec and put his arms around him, hugging him.

Alec closed his eyes when his cheek pressed against Martin's as he whispered into Alec's ear. "It'll all work out, Alec. You'll see."

Brett felt John stir in his arms. He pulled John closer to himself and placed a gentle kiss on top of his head. Brett swore he could hear John purring. He caught sight of Alec's eyes widening as he watched this. Brett gave him a brief smile. Almost instantly, Alec returned it. The atmosphere in the room lightened perceptibly, and Brett felt himself relax fully into the couch.

The rapport between the housemates was wonderful. He loved how protective Martin was toward Alec, toward *all* of them, really. And Brett was convinced that beneath the brash Mancunian exterior, Stu had a big heart—one that had probably been broken more than once. As for Alec, he might have appeared tough at times, but there was a vulnerability that must draw men to him.

As the evening wore on, Brett grew more and more relaxed. He noted that John had hardly participated in any of the conversations, which concerned him—until he caught sight of John's pleased expression and realization dawned. *He's giving them time to get to know me. This obviously matters to him.*

Brett smiled to himself. *Maybe this will work, after all.*

JOHN WAS in heaven.

There was no other word for it. He cuddled up to Brett's firm body and pressed his ear to Brett's chest, feeling the reassuring, rhythmic thump of his heart as it reverberated through him. Brett tightened his arm around him, and John almost sighed with happiness. The man he'd been dreaming about for months was finally holding him, and it felt *wonderful*.

Don't go overboard, he told himself sternly. *It's just a bit of cuddling on the couch.* But it was difficult to contain the elation that coursed through him. This was Brett cuddling him. John had no idea what could have happened to bring about such a sea change in Brett, but whatever it was, he thanked God for it. From the moment Brett had spoken to him in the men's room as they'd changed, John had felt a tingle of anticipation, the feeling that something momentous had occurred. But to find himself being held like this was something he'd never foreseen.

Stu's huge yawn broke through his reveries. "Well, I have an early flight tomorrow, so I think I'll call it a night." Stu stretched his arms above his head and got up from his chair.

"You do?" Martin said, his brow furrowed. Then it cleared quickly. "Oh—you do—yes, I remember now." John watched a glance pass between the two men. "Oh, and I have to get to the shop early tomorrow—I have a stock delivery to check in." Martin got to his feet and smiled at John and Brett.

John was trying not to laugh. His housemates were about as subtle as a train wreck. He kept his face straight as the two men glared at Alec, who was apparently slower on the uptake. John watched as the penny dropped.

Alec unfolded himself from the rocking chair. "Well, I'm on an early shift tomorrow, so I supposed I'd better go to bed too." He gave Brett and John a bright smile and a totally unconvincing yawn.

"I'm sorry you all have to leave us," Brett said, frowning. "Thank you for a very pleasant evening."

"You're welcome," Stu said with another bright smile. "No doubt we'll be seeing you more often now." He fixed Brett with a look that John couldn't decipher.

Brett gazed back at him. "Count on it," he said quietly. Stu gave him a nod, and the three men traipsed out of the room. John listened as they went upstairs, making remarkably little noise.

For a moment, the only sound in the room was the crackling of the logs on the fire. Then Brett chuckled.

"Just so we're clear on this—I didn't swallow a single word of that."

John laughed. "Oh, thank God. I'd have been worried if you had." He turned his face up to look at Brett directly.

Brett cupped his cheek. Dark brown eyes regarded him, and John suddenly found it difficult to breathe normally.

"Besides, I'm very grateful," Brett added. "Because now at least I get to do this without an audience." And then he kissed him, their mouths meeting in a soft union of lips and tongues.

John melted into the kiss, *lost* himself in it as Brett made love to his mouth—it was the only way to describe what Brett was doing to him. This was how he'd *dreamed* kisses would be, and to find himself in Brett's arms, making out with him, was almost too much to take in. He stroked Brett's face, growing bolder with each passing second as he explored Brett with his tongue, exulting in each heady groan that he pulled from Brett's lips. His body tingled with exhilaration. He didn't want this moment to end—until Brett changed gears, and then *everything* changed.

John pushed out a low moan as Brett shifted position on the couch until he was lying down on his back, and then pulled John on top of him. The kisses didn't slow up for a second. Brett's hands were in his hair, his fingers carding through the layers, moving lightly over his scalp and sending shivers running down his spine. Then hands slid down his back, stroking him slowly, sensually. Brett's touch was light, but John was aware of every stroke of his fingertips as his body hummed along with the erotic melody Brett was creating.

And now he was aware of Brett's hard length, pressing up to grind slowly against his own stiffening dick. John's pulse raced as Brett stroked his tongue slowly in and out of his mouth, keeping perfect time with the deliberate rocking of his hips. John groaned and pushed against Brett's chest, breaking the kiss to stare down at him.

"Can you feel how hard you're making me?" he whispered.

Brett slid his hand up to the back of John's head. Their eyes locked. "Just tell me you want this, that it's not just me about to have my wicked way with you."

John chuckled and then dropped his head low to whisper into Brett's ear. "I'll make it really easy for you to understand. I want you to take me upstairs to my room, undress me, and then I want you to fuck me." He pulled back so Brett could see his eyes. "Is that plain enough for you?"

Brett's face lit up in a slow smile. "As daylight." He reached down to cup John's arse with both hands and squeezed, pulling him tight against his groin. His mouth was suddenly on John's neck, sucking the warm skin there.

John gasped. "If you keep doing that, we're going to end up fucking right here on this couch."

Brett broke away, and his eyes glittered. "Oh, I like it—the possibility of your housemates walking in on us at any moment. I *love* living dangerously."

John let out a soft whine of impatience. "But the condoms are upstairs, along with the lube."

Brett became still. "So where's this room of yours?" He thrust up with his hips, and John let out a low cry as their cocks rubbed against each other.

He scrambled off Brett, grabbed his hand, and tugged him upright. He didn't trust himself to speak, he was so turned on right then. Brett laughed gently as John almost dragged him from the room. All he could think about was getting the two of them naked—and *now*.

CHAPTER 20

JOHN HAD no idea how they managed to get up to his room without falling or making a huge racket. He only knew that once his bedroom door closed behind them, Brett changed gears yet again. John trembled as Brett slowly undressed him, kissing each new bared area of skin, until he felt like he was going out of his mind.

"What are you *doing* to me?" he asked hoarsely. "You're driving me crazy here."

Brett kissed his neck below his left ear, and John shuddered. He could feel Brett smiling against his skin.

"I'm taking my time, like I should have done the first time," Brett murmured into his hair. "There's no rush. We have all night." Those lips touched his ear, and Brett's breath tickled him. "And I intend having you again and again tonight." John couldn't keep in the shiver that rippled through him. Brett's hand slid lower to caress John's erection with a single finger. "Not to mention taking this magnificent dick inside me."

John froze. "You... you want me to fuck you?" Warmth spread through him as the idea took root.

Brett pulled away and began to unbutton his shirt, his gaze never leaving John's face. His pupils were huge. "Oh, God, yes." He grasped John's hands and brought them to his shirt. "Undress me," he said huskily.

John's fingers trembled as he undid the buttons, feasting his eyes on the wide chest that came into view. He ran his hands over the hairy pecs, edging lower to circle Brett's nipples with his fingers. He watched, fascinated, as the skin pebbled and those tiny nubs became taut. Brett's lips parted, and he exhaled slowly, his eyes closing.

"You like that?"

Brett let out a low whine. "Don't stop."

John took that for a yes.

He grew bolder in his explorations. Lowering his head to Brett's chest, he licked at a nipple, flicking it with his tongue. Brett's whine became a full-blown moan when John sucked the nub into his mouth while he played with the other, tweaking and twisting it. Brett's hips bucked.

"Oh, fuck, John."

And then John's head was grabbed, and their mouths met in a heated kiss. John fumbled with the button and zipper on Brett's pants as he struggled to part him from them. Brett simply held on, taking his mouth in a brutal claiming that left John gasping for air. He could feel Brett almost dancing as he tried to free himself from the pool of clothing around his ankles. Despite Brett's intentions to slow things down, it seemed they were both eager to get to the naked part.

At last both men were nude. Brett held him close, sliding his cock over John's with a sensual roll of his hips while he ran his hands over John's arse, murmuring appreciatively.

"Bed, now." That husky quality in Brett's voice was making John harder.

John broke free to pull him by the hand to his bed. He fell backward onto the soft duvet, Brett tumbling with him to end up by his side, laughing.

"What's funny?" John wanted to know.

Brett smiled. "I love the fact that we're both really eager." His expression grew serious. "I want this to be everything that a first time *should* be, not how it was before Christmas."

John became still. "I meant what I said that day. I really did enjoy it." He covered Brett's hand with his own. "You have *no* idea how many times I've thought about that day." Brett stiffened and tried to pull away, but John held him firmly. "I'm not talking about what happened afterward. I close my eyes and remember how you felt inside me. The way you kissed me. Your mouth on my cock. The memory is so clear in my head." John lowered his voice. "There… there hasn't been anyone else since…."

Brett closed his eyes. "Oh, God, John, if I'd known you were a virgin, I would have done things *so* differently."

John kissed him lightly on the lips, and Brett opened his eyes.

John smiled. "Then show me."

BRETT DIDN'T know where to begin. A gorgeous man beside him, nude—with a very erect, long, thick cock. *Oh, yeah, you know where to start, all right.*

Brett wrapped his hand around that long cock and moved slowly from root to tip, feeling John shudder beside him.

"Your dick is beautiful," he said quietly as he pushed back the foreskin to reveal the wide flared head. He pumped his hand faster, noting the precome that had already begun to make an appearance. He slid his fingers through it, spreading it over the hard cock, making it glide smoothly through his fist. John's breathing changed, and he shifted onto his back, his hips giving tiny thrusts as he pushed up from the bed. Brett took a moment to admire the younger man. John was slender around the waist and across his hips, but not too thin. His chest was virtually bare, and there was the merest hint of downy blond hairs leading toward his navel. But the rigid cock rising from between John's long, slim legs was amazing. Brett had never been with a guy with a cock as big as John's. He could probably have placed both hands around it and still not have covered its whole length. And it was wide enough to have his hole clenching at the thought of taking it inside him.

John's lips were parted, his eyes focused on the motion of Brett's hand. "That feels good," he admitted. He licked his lips as his gaze moved toward Brett's cock. "Can I touch you?"

Brett caught his breath. "Yes, *God*, yes." He swung around until his dick was level with John's mouth, those pink lips tantalizingly close. John moved onto his side, and Brett shivered as a tentative hand enveloped his cock. "*Ohhh*, that's good." John's grasp grew firmer, and he worked Brett's dick faster, breathless gasps accompanying his efforts.

Brett eyed the thick cock before him and couldn't wait a minute longer. He sucked the wide head into his mouth and felt the shudder that coursed through John—and then fought hard to breathe as John copied him and wet heat surrounded his cock.

Brett moaned loudly around John's cock as John sucked him deep. Their heads bobbed faster as they licked and sucked, and Brett found it hard not to choke as John pushed with his hips. John's hand and mouth worked in tandem, and Brett knew it wouldn't be long at this rate before he'd be spilling his come into that hot mouth. And he wanted to be deep inside John when he came.

Brett pushed his hand between John's thighs to seek out that hot little hole. John hooked a hand under his thigh to lift his leg higher, and Brett zoomed in on John's crease. John groaned around his cock as Brett rubbed over the puckered ring of muscle, pressing into it lightly. He pulled his mouth free of John's dick and grabbed his cheeks, spreading them to reveal his prize. John gasped, and Brett's cock slid free as he traced a line with his tongue down over John's balls to arrive at his hole. He could hear the hitch in John's breathing as he licked over John's entrance with a flat tongue before licking around the rim. Brett's cock was forgotten as John shifted onto his back. Brett straddled his chest to press his tongue slowly against the tight little pucker that resisted him. He could feel John thrashing beneath him, and it only made him work harder. He wanted John to unravel completely before he sank his cock into that hot, tight heaven.

"*Ohhhhhhh.*" John trembled under him. Brett could see the muscles in his thighs jumping as he licked into John's hole. John was becoming unglued. Brett pushed a single finger into that tightness until it was up to the knuckle. "Oh, fucking *hell*…. God, Brett… that's…."

"If you can still talk, then I'm not doing this right," said Brett with a chuckle, and he pulled his finger free—only to slide in two fingers this time. John arched up off the bed, and Brett pushed down with his body before returning to his task. His fingers moved easier now, and John was pushing down hard on them. And suddenly, Brett didn't want to wait any longer.

He swung around to kneel between John's parted thighs. John's gaze was fixed on him, his eyes shiny, lips parted.

"Now, Brett, please. Condoms… in the top drawer."

John's breathless plea had his dick hardening even further. He leaned toward the bedside cabinet, yanked open the drawer, and pulled out a strip of condoms and a bottle of lube. With one hand, he pumped his cock slowly, his eyes on John. He couldn't ever remember being this hard, this *eager* to be inside someone. He let go of his hard-as-steel dick to unroll a condom over it and then snapped open the bottle to dribble the viscous liquid along his length. John was pulling gently at his own cock, eyes fixed on Brett's face.

"God, need you inside me," John breathed. He drew his knees up to his chest, and Brett inched closer until the head of his dick came to rest at John's entrance. He gazed at the young man, barely able to contain his desire to thrust into him with one solid push. John was shaking visibly. "Now, Brett. In me, want you in me."

Brett pushed forward slowly, holding his breath as his dick sank into the tightest, most perfect place in the whole world. John's heat seared him, welcoming him home.

"My God, how you *feel*...." Brett lowered his chest to meet John's and hooked his arms under John's knees. Their mouths were inches apart, and John's gaze was begging him. Brett took his mouth in a gentle kiss that built in intensity as he began to thrust into John, slowly at first but gaining in momentum as they found their rhythm. John rocked up from the bed, meeting his every thrust, until the erotic sound of skin slapping against skin rang out in the quiet bedroom.

And then another soundtrack took over as John began to moan softly, his cries in time with Brett's grunts as he slid deeper inside him. When Brett sat up and grabbed John's ankles to spread him wider, rolling his hips to force his cock into that tight channel, he knew exactly when he connected with John's prostate. John's eyes rolled back in his head, and the breath was almost punched out of him. Oh, *fuck*—the *sounds* that John was making pushed Brett closer to the edge. He grasped John's dick and tugged and then gasped as he felt John's channel tighten around his cock.

"Really close, John," he managed to gasp out.

"Oh, God, me too."

Brett's hips were almost a blur as he pushed him relentlessly toward his climax. John's dick stiffened in his hand as he came, pumping come in an arc over his chest and abs, his cries of ecstasy ringing out, echoing around the room. Brett gave a hoarse shout as John's channel milked his cock. He pulsed into the condom, his balls emptying themselves until there couldn't have been a drop left in them.

John reached for him, and Brett sank down onto his damp chest, the stickiness spreading between them. His arms came to rest on either side of John's head as their lips met, the kisses slow and tender. Brett's cock was still buried in John's body, the connection between them unbroken. John shivered beneath him, jolted by aftershocks, and as his body's grip on Brett eased up, Brett began to move slowly inside him with a gentle motion. Brett stretched out on top of John, nuzzling into his hair and the soft skin at the base of his neck. No words were uttered, only tiny noises of contentment that said so much more. His cock finally slipped free of John's body, and he rolled them both until John lay beside him, wrapped in his arms, breathing more easily. Brett eased the condom off his cock and dropped it onto the floor before enveloping John once more in his arms. He could feel the come on their bodies, but cleaning up could wait—he didn't want to lose this moment.

And then it hit him, and the enormity of the thought was enough to send a flush of adrenaline tingling through his body.

It didn't happen. Oh, my God—it didn't happen.

Where was that familiar itch? He felt no burning need to get out of there. Gone was the usual desperate urge to get rid of his sexual partner. Astounded, he gazed at John, who lay there, eyes closed, looking sated and at peace, his head upon Brett's chest. What shocked him more was the thought that John looked as though he was exactly where he belonged—in Brett's arms.

Brett didn't dare move, as if he feared the slightest motion would somehow break the spell. He was overwhelmed by the feeling of… *rightness*, as if his life had been missing one vital piece all these years, and it had finally slotted into place.

"That was perfect," John murmured against his chest, his arms reaching around Brett to hold him close.

Brett couldn't have chosen a better word.

Perfect.

JOHN CAREFULLY rolled over in bed to look at the man asleep beside him. He'd woken up to find Brett curled around his back, his arm draped over

John's waist. John had craned his neck to look at his alarm clock. It was still early. He lay there, gazing at the sleeping Brett, taking in the smooth skin of his forehead, the faint shadow of a beard, the full lips.

I still can't believe he's here in my bed.

Memories of their night together were still fresh enough to harden his cock at the thought. John wrapped his hand around his dick and slid the silken skin back and forth. He couldn't believe how... *wanton* he'd been. It was the only word that fitted. *Was that really me demanding to be fucked harder?* His cheeks heated as he recalled shouting out as Brett pounded into him from behind, John holding onto the headboard. *There was* definitely *nothing virginal about* that *performance*, he thought ruefully. Then he grinned. *And I loved every minute of it.*

His gaze was drawn to where the duvet tented. *Oh, Brett has wood.* Which gave him a wicked idea.

John reached toward the bedside cabinet for the lube and slicked up his fingers. He knelt up on the mattress and pushed a finger into his arse, which still felt loose from their fucking only a few short hours ago. He slid in another and worked his hole, remembering how Brett had stretched him for his cock. Then he grabbed a condom. *Now for the tricky part.*

Carefully, he drew back the duvet, anxiously watching for any sign that Brett was about to wake up, but his lover was sound asleep. Brett's dick rose into the air, a thick seven inches. John's hole tightened at the thought of that solid rod of flesh filling him. *All in good time.* He tore the foil square as quietly as possible and then brought the rolled condom to Brett's rigid cock. He began to unroll the latex down over Brett's length, his gaze darting to Brett's face now and then, but nothing. *Wow—he must be a really sound sleeper.*

John slicked up his hand and slid it over the granite cock before straddling Brett's hips very slowly. He could feel the blunt head of his dick pressing against his hole, and he reached back to ease it into him, holding his breath as the wide glans popped through the ring of muscle. John didn't dare breathe as he lowered himself fully onto the erect cock.

"If you think I'm not going to wake up when a cute guy covers my dick with a condom," Brett said quietly, making him jump, "then you really *are* deluded." He chuckled. "Did you *really* think you could sit on my cock and I wouldn't notice?"

John paused halfway down, jerking his head up to stare at Brett, who stared back, looking very alert. "How long have you been awake?" John demanded to know and then gasped as Brett pushed up slowly with his hips, filling him completely.

Brett grinned. "Oh, since you wriggled *ever* so carefully out of my arms." That look in his eyes sent warmth flooding through John. "I loved having you there, by the way."

And then Brett's eyes gleamed as he grabbed hold of John's hips to hold him in place while he fucked up into him, stealing John's breath.

"But to open my eyes and find you riding my cock—now *that's* the way to wake up." Brett grabbed hold of John's hands and laced their fingers together. Their eyes locked. "So ride me, baby, and make it good, because this isn't going to last long. I'm already on the edge. Your arse feels too good."

John grinned. "Yes, sir." And he rolled his hips and rode that cock until both men were panting breathlessly, unable to hold back any longer. They came together, their joyous shouts mingling as Brett filled him with heat, connecting them once more. John collapsed onto Brett's damp chest, breathing heavily and with a delicious ache.

"Yeah, *that's* the way to wake up."

JOHN SNUGGLED up against Brett, loving the way it felt as Brett stroked his hair. Cleanup complete, condom taken care of—John had already come to the conclusion that postcoital cuddles were *the* best kind. He didn't care what the time was because he had no intention of moving ever again.

"We can't stay here, you know. We'll have to get up eventually," Brett murmured into his hair.

John sighed. "Oh, don't spoil it. This is heavenly." He stroked the fur-covered chest beneath his head, loving the way Brett caught his breath when John strayed too close to his nipples. Yeah, Brett was *very* sensitive there. "Don't you like lying like this? Just the two of us, the house empty?" He could hear nothing from beyond his bedroom door.

Brett slid his hand down to cup his cheek, turning John's face up toward his. "I love it," he said softly, before kissing John on the forehead.

His eyes sparkled. "Are you always this gullible? Or has sex addled your brain? Not that I'm complaining—I think it's adorable."

John knitted his brow. "Huh?"

Brett chuckled. "Do you *really* think we're alone?"

And then John caught it, the unmistakable sound of footsteps on the stairs. His eyes widened as there was a loud rap on the door.

"I'm comin' in, and I'm not about to cover my eyes, so I hope you're both indecent." Stu sounded in a good mood.

John grabbed hold of the duvet to yank it up over them, but Brett stilled his hand. "It's okay," he said with a smile.

The door opened, and Stu walked in bearing a tray loaded with two mugs of steaming coffee and a plate with a pile of hot buttered toast and a full English breakfast. The smell made John's mouth water.

Stu was grinning. "Good mornin'," he sang as he placed the tray carefully at the foot of the bed. He looked at them, and his eyes lit up. "Oh, God—don't *you* two look damn good in bed together?"

"Oh, wow," said Brett as he eyed the tray. "Talk about being spoiled."

John couldn't believe Stu's nerve. "Whatever happened to privacy?" Brett seemed totally unfazed by the intrusion.

"You've lost that privilege!" Martin shouted from outside the room. Brett gave John a puzzled look, and John shrugged his bare shoulders. "I only gave you one house rule when you moved in here, and you shot *that* one all to shit last night. Several times, I might add." John could hear him laughing.

"Yeah, why'd you think I brought you the full works for breakfast?" Stu said with a grin. "We figured you needed to replace all the energy you spent last night. And it *was* all night—we heard *everythin'*."

Oh, God. John felt the heat bloom in his cheeks. Brett was looking at him, an amused expression across his face.

"Er, I think we were a little noisy last night," John suggested. Brett smirked.

"A *little*?" Alec popped his head around the door, his face wreathed in a wide smile. "Oh, boy—talk about an understatement." He met Brett's gaze and grinned wickedly. "Brett, next time you decide to stay the night, I suggest you supply us all with earplugs." Then he looked at John and Brett in the bed, and his expression softened. "Oh, wow—our baby's all grown up."

John's mouth fell open.

Brett burst into a peal of delighted laughter. "Okay, thanks for the breakfast, but that's it. Seeing as *you* are supposed to be on a flight to God knows where," he said, pointing at Stu, "and Alec is supposedly on an early shift at the hospital—oh, and Martin is taking care of a stock delivery—you can *all* disappear and let us enjoy this delicious-looking breakfast and wonderful-smelling coffee without an audience." He gave Stu and Alec a mock glare. "Because if you're not out of here quick, last night's noise will be as *nothing* compared to what happens next." He winked at John. "I'm sure we can arrange something suitable, don't you think?"

John stared at him for a moment and then burst out laughing.

"You're going to fit in *perfectly* around here."

CHAPTER 21

BRETT STARED impatiently at the clock on his office wall. *Surely, everyone's gone by now?* He dragged his gaze back to the sheets on his desk. The day had crawled by.

He couldn't get over how wonderful the weekend had been. He hadn't left John's house until late Sunday night. He'd been on the point of leaving three or four times, only to spy John's beautiful face or find John regarding him with a look of pure longing, and then all thoughts of leaving fled his head, and he was tugging John up the stairs to his room and shutting the world outside.

God, how many times did we fuck? He was amazed that John's hole wasn't raw. He closed his eyes to focus on the memory of John lying beneath him, legs wrapped around Brett's waist as Brett slowly penetrated him again and again, taking him to the brink of orgasm, only to ease off and begin the delicious slide into him all over again, until both were shaking, desperate to come.

And it wasn't just the sex that was memorable.

Brett had never felt so utterly relaxed. Stu hadn't lied—he had a flight later on Saturday—and Martin had gone in to work before lunch time, so Brett and John had spent a lovely Saturday afternoon with Alec, playing Scrabble. Brett couldn't believe the difference in the paramedic. Alec had laughed and joked with him, and Brett found himself warming to the younger man.

But the best part had been spending time with John. They'd curled up on the couch on Sunday morning, talking about so many things—John's family, Brett's early days as a teacher, even Brett's life in the orphanage. That last topic had surprised the hell out of Brett. He'd been able to talk about those days with relatively little pain. It was a part of his life that he rarely spoke of, and yet he wanted to share it with John. To have John lying there in his arms, listening intently to him, and then hold him tight afterward….

The office door opened, and John stepped in, smiling. "It's just us," he confirmed.

Brett heaved a sigh. "Then lock that bloody door and get over here."

John locked the door and then hurried across the room to step into Brett's outstretched arms. Their lips met in a hungry kiss.

"God, I've been waiting all day to do this," Brett murmured before taking John's mouth in another eager kiss. His hands stroked under the smooth jacket to cup John's arse and pull him tight against him. "I've missed you today."

John responded eagerly. "*God*, yes. I kept watching the clock once I finished my preparations for tomorrow, just wishing that everyone would get the fuck out of here so I could go and kiss my boyfriend."

Brett chuckled as he slid his lips down John's soft throat. "Boyfriend?"

John threw back his head and groaned softly. "Well, how *else* would you describe—oh, fuck, Brett, do you *know* what you do to me when you kiss me there?" He shivered in Brett's arms as Brett kissed that spot under his ear. "You're not playing fair," he whined breathlessly. "You *know* we can't do anything here, and *you're* the one who said we shouldn't do anything during the week."

Reluctantly Brett broke the kiss. "You're right, of course. I'm being very selfish." He kissed John softly on the lips once more and then stepped back. "Though I'm starting to rethink the whole 'let's behave during the week' idea," he added ruefully.

John stroked his cheek. "And *you* were right. Imagine how little work I'd get done if you came round to the house on a weekday."

There *was* that. "So I'll have to content myself with stolen kisses when everyone's gone home?"

John nodded, his arms coming around Brett to hold him tightly. "But then the weekend? I'm all yours," he whispered before kissing Brett deeply, sliding his tongue between Brett's lips. It was Brett's turn to groan.

"Do you know how hard I am right now?" he murmured against John's mouth.

John chuckled. "No—and I'm not about to find out. Because right now I have to go and get changed into my cycling gear so I can go home, where I'll work my arse off to make sure everything gets done in advance, so I can spend every waking minute of my weekend in bed with my lover." He paused to catch his breath.

Brett became still. "I like that word—*lover*."

I have a lover. After so many years of fucking strangers, one-night stands in hotel rooms, hurried sex in bathrooms.... Brett finally had someone in his life. *And damn, it feels good.*

"At least we'll have the half term week together," John said quietly, releasing Brett from his embrace. "Thank God's it's only a week away."

Half term.... Brett suddenly had a wonderful idea. He looked at John and grinned.

"Fancy a trip to the south coast?"

"YOU STILL haven't told me why Brighton," John said as they got out of the taxi in front of the smart-looking hotel, its many windows gleaming in the February sunshine. He looked up at the frontage and smiled. "This looks nice."

"It *is* nice," Brett said with a smile. "And be patient—I'll tell you all about it later." His chest tightened. The one thing they hadn't spoken of was Brett's past sex life. Brett figured John was too embarrassed to ask questions. And as for him, it had taken a lot of soul-searching before Brett had come to the decision that John needed to know everything about him.

He looked at John's profile as they walked up to the main door.

He has no idea how much he's changed my life.

Brett pushed through the revolving glass door and led John into the light, airy reception area. He'd discovered this place by accident one visit when he'd sheltered from a violent storm. Seven years later, he was a regular. *But this time is different.*

His face lit up as he spied Elliott behind the main desk.

"Come with me. There's someone I want you to meet," he murmured into John's ear as he slipped his arm around his waist. John reacted with surprise to the gesture, but Brett smiled reassuringly at him. "Trust me—we can be ourselves here." He watched as the penny dropped and John's look of concern melted away.

Elliott was deep in conversation with the receptionist, but he looked in their direction briefly and his eyes widened. A huge smile spread across his face, and he bounded from behind the main desk to walk toward Brett with outstretched arms.

"I am so very, *very* happy to see you." Elliott beamed. He threw his arms around Brett and hugged him tightly before holding out his hand to John. "And I am delighted to meet you, sir. More than you'll ever know."

John shook his hand, his gaze meeting Brett's for a moment. There was a questioning look in his eye as his hand was grasped in a very enthusiastic handshake.

Brett smiled. "But he *will* know, Elliott. Because I'm going to tell him." He watched as this last item filtered through.

Elliott's eyes grew round. "In that case, would you two do me the honor of joining me and my partner for dinner one night this week? Not down here—in our apartment upstairs."

Brett's grin was so wide, his cheeks ached. "We'd be delighted."

"I LOVE hotel rooms," sighed John as they lay under the soft cotton sheets.

Brett stroked his arm languidly. "Why's that?"

John wriggled contentedly. "What's not to love? This bed is supremely comfortable—not to mention silent."

Brett chuckled. "Well, we certainly road tested it, didn't we?" They'd been in the room five minutes before John was tearing his clothes off, and two minutes after *that*, John had been on his knees before Brett, sucking his cock like a starving man. Not that the blowjob had lasted all that long before Brett had bent his lover over the bed and fucked him until they both came explosively, their loud cries echoing up to the high ceilings.

"And through there is a fantastic bathroom with a whirlpool bath big enough for two—which we *will* be making full use of later," John stressed. "And of course there's in-room dining, so we needn't leave this room for the entire week." He sighed happily. "Yeah, I *love* hotels."

Brett laughed. "Don't you want to see Brighton? It's got a thriving gay night life."

John snorted.

"If I want to see gay bars and clubs, I can go to Canal Street with Evan and Daniel anytime I want." He rolled on top of Brett and stared down at him. "All I want to see this week is you."

The expression in those blue eyes was making muscles jump in Brett's stomach. He cupped John's head and drew him closer to kiss him softly, the kiss slowly intensifying.

John reached down between them to stroke over the head of Brett's cock. "Where's the lube?" he asked huskily.

Brett's already firm cock twitched. "Under the pillow with the condoms." John arched his eyebrows, and Brett chuckled. "What can I say? With you around, it pays to be prepared."

John sat up and straddled him. He reached behind him to rub Brett's cock over his hole. "And that's something else we need to talk about."

"What's that?" Brett was finding it difficult to keep up. All he wanted to do bury his dick in that gloriously tight heat until he was balls deep.

"Ditching the condoms." John's eyes glittered.

Brett froze. He couldn't help it. There was only one thought colliding in his head at that moment. *Too fast. This is happening too fast.* He searched for the right words—*any* words— but his brain seemed to be on a go slow. He saw the light die in John's face as he stared down at Brett beneath him.

John paled. "Well, I don't have to ask what you think of that idea, do I?"

"What?" Brett gaped. *For God's sake —say something....*

"And here was me thinking you wanted this relationship to be something permanent." John barked out a bitter laugh. "Looks like I got *that* wrong." He moved off Brett, climbed off the bed, picked up his jeans from where they'd been tossed onto the floor, and proceeded to wriggle into them.

Brett watched him in horror, unable to move. "What... what are you doing?"

John grabbed a sweater and pulled it over his head. "Getting out of here. I need some fresh air." He shoved his feet into his trainers.

Finally, Brett got his limbs to move. He swung his legs off the bed. "John, don't go, please. We need to—"

John held up his hand. "Look, I'll be back, okay? I... I just need a little time to get my head on straight." He picked up his phone from the small table by the window and went to the door. He gave Brett one last glance and then left the room.

Brett flopped back onto the bed, his arms across his face.

What the fuck?

He couldn't believe things could have gone downhill so fast. Now all he could do was hope that John calmed down enough so Brett could let him know what was going on in his head.

JOHN SAT on the promenade wall, gazing out to sea. The wind was coming inland with an icy bite, but John hardly noticed. He stared at the burned-out shell that had once been the pier, but his thoughts were solely of Brett.

I really thought he wanted this as much as I did. Apparently not. John closed his eyes as the wind picked up, but he could still see Brett's expression. It wasn't so much that Brett clearly hadn't considered the possibility of going bareback—it was his reaction to the idea. The man had looked like he was in shock.

Did I get this wrong? Was I making too much of what we have? John couldn't think straight. *God, I need some advice right now.* He pulled his phone from his pocket and stared at it for a moment. There was only one person he could call.

As the call connected he could hear laughter in the background.

"Hey there, bro. What are you doing calling me? Aren't you supposed to be having a dirty week in Brighton?" The cheerful note in Evan's voice was so welcome right now.

"Ev, can we talk?" He listened as the noise died away, only now he swore he could hear birds singing.

"I've come out into the garden," Evan explained. "It's a bit quieter out here. What's wrong?"

John couldn't hold it in. "Ev, I think I've fucked up."

Evan groaned. "You *can't* have. You two have only been together a week. What did you do?"

He spilled out the whole mess, fighting to keep calm. "I really thought he'd want this. I mean, I know it's a big decision, but I thought if we were going to be together, that…." He paused. There was silence at the other end. "Ev? You still there?"

"I'm thinking of how best to word this."

Oh, God, that sounds ominous. "Have I overreacted?"

Evan sighed. "John, you two have been having sex as a couple for one week. *One week.* And you've just asked him to consider doing something that most couples wouldn't even *think* of until they'd been together for a *lot* longer."

John could see how that might have freaked Brett out. "Oh, God."

"But it's not just that," Evan went on. "What do you know of his sexual history? Has he had many relationships? Were any of them really serious? Has he ever had any scares? Does he get tested regularly?"

John fell silent. It suddenly occurred to him that that was a lot about Brett that was a complete mystery.

"I'm going to take your silence to mean that you don't know any of that. Would I be wrong?"

John exhaled slowly. "No, you're not wrong."

"Then what you need to do is stop wasting time talking to me and go and talk to your boyfriend," Evan said patiently. "Who is probably going crazy right now, wondering where on earth you are and *how* on earth he can fix this." He gave a wry chuckle. "Slow down, bro. Take your time. And talk to each other." John heard a noise in the background. "I'll be right in, sweetie. Just talking to John."

"I'm keeping you from whatever you're doing. Thanks for the advice, and say hi to Daniel for me," John said.

"I will—now *you* need to go talk to your man," Evan said firmly. "Send Brett our best wishes, but do it *after* you've sorted all this mess out. The next time we speak, I want to hear that everything's okay. Understood? Sort this." He said good-bye and disconnected the call.

John absently put the phone back into his jeans pocket and shivered as a particularly strong gust of wind came off the sea. He twisted around to stare up at the hotel.

Time to sort his mess out.

He let himself into the room with the key card and found Brett dressed, sitting in one of the two velvet-covered armchairs in front of the window, staring out at the view. Brett turned his head and gave him a cautious smile. "You're back." John couldn't miss the look of relief on his face. "Come sit down for a minute. I need to talk to you."

John approached him and took the other chair. "Actually, those were going to be *my* first words," he admitted. He noticed Brett was rubbing the arms of the chair. When Brett wouldn't look him in the eye, John realized with a shock that his lover was nervous. "What is it?"

Brett took a deep breath. "I need to… I want to share something with you."

John was suddenly aware of the empty feeling in the pit of his stomach. "Go on."

"I want to tell you about a… someone I know, Rob." John arched his eyebrows, and Brett held up his hand. "Please, let me talk. Everything will become clear."

John sat back into his chair, and Brett gave him a grateful smile.

"Rob has been coming here for seven years, and he visits about six or seven times a year, usually for a week, sometimes longer." Brett swallowed. "All he had was his job—and this place."

John wanted to get closer, to touch him, but there was something about Brett that told him to give his lover space.

"Well, every night he spent here, there would be a different guy in his bed. And as soon as they finished fucking, the guy was out the door. That was how Rob wanted it."

John couldn't help but think that it sounded like a very lonely way to live.

"A few months back, Rob finally had enough. He started to think there had to be more to life than faceless fucks. He talked to a friend, who asked if there was anyone in his life who could possibly be more to him than just a good fuck." Brett's eyes finally met his. He gulped. "I told him there was, but he was straight. And then, of course, later I found out how wrong I'd been."

John registered the change of pronoun—and then he stiffened as the words finally sank in. "You... you're Rob." His eyes widened.

Brett nodded, his gaze fixed on John's face. "That was my name every time I came here. It was the only place I allowed myself to be out. I used to live for the times I spent down here. But it wasn't enough. I wanted more."

He sat forward and reached for John's hands. John gave them instantly.

"I need you to understand. Until you, I'd never had a relationship. Fuck, I'd never even *cuddled* with a guy." Brett was shaking. "Having you in my life is absolutely *huge*—and it's only been one week." He laughed nervously, his voice quavering. "For the first time in my life I'm in a relationship, and it scares the *hell* out of me."

John groaned. "And then I go and ask you to make a huge commitment. No wonder you freaked."

Brett let out his breath in a long exhale. "Oh, thank God—you get it." He left his chair and knelt at John's feet, staring up at him before laying his head on John's lap, his eyes closed. "I thought I was going to lose you."

John caught his breath. He stroked Brett's short hair and rubbed across his shoulders. "Can I ask you something?"

Brett lifted his head to meet his gaze. "Anything."

"Were you safe?" John felt his cheeks warm, but Evan's questions were still ringing inside his head.

Brett nodded. "I've never had unprotected sex. And I get tested regularly." He reached up to cup John's cheek. "As for your suggestion...." John opened his mouth, but Brett silenced him with a single finger across his lips. "Let me finish. I'm not saying no, all right? But you need to give me time to get used to this—to us." He smiled. "I love it that there *is* an 'us,' by the way."

John returned his smile. "Take all the time you need. I'm not going anywhere." He bent down and kissed Brett tenderly on the lips. Slowly, without breaking the kiss, Brett got to his feet and pulled John up from the chair into his arms. John clasped his hands loosely around Brett's neck and deepened the kiss, which grew more intense. Brett stroked his hands down John's spine, making him shiver. When John felt his hand slide under the waistband on his jeans to squeeze his bare arse, the shiver became a full-body shudder.

Brett pulled away to gaze at him, pupils blown. "Come to bed." His voice was husky. "We've got a few hours until dinner." He leered.

John laughed as Brett backed up to the bed, his fingers already busy as they relieved him of his sweater. "Why, Mr. Sanderson, *whatever* can you have in mind?"

Brett's wicked chuckle told him that whatever he was planning, John was going to enjoy it.

CHAPTER 22

"HAVE YOU enjoyed your stay in Brighton?" George asked John as he handed out cups of coffee. Elliott was close behind him with glasses of brandy.

Brett snorted. "He hasn't seen anything of Brighton except the view from our window." John's cheeks were a lovely shade of pink.

Elliott tut-tutted. "Stop embarrassing the poor lad, Brett, or else you'll find me telling him a few tales about *you*. And you know what an excellent, *long* memory I have." He smiled sweetly.

John turned to look at Elliott. "Really? That sounds like it might be a fascinating conversation." He grinned wickedly at Brett.

George snickered. "Nice one, love," he said as he slipped his arm around Elliott's waist and kissed him on the cheek. Elliott gave him a quick peck on the lips before going into the little kitchen.

Brett leaned back into the worn, comfy couch and let out a sigh of contentment. "I love your apartment, George." He glanced around at the cozy space. Everywhere he looked, there were photos of the two men, along with little bits and pieces, clearly objects that had special significance for them. Another couch faced them, the two separated by a thick rug and a low square coffee table in a dark-stained oak. A fire blazed away behind the grate in the fireplace.

George sat down on the opposite couch and smiled as he gazed around the room. "We like it," he said simply. "It's not as grand as some of the rooms in the hotel, but it's home."

Brett gave John a glance and lifted his arm in invitation. John cuddled up to him, a contented smile on his face, his gaze going to the dancing flames.

Elliott came out of the kitchen and sat down next to George, who immediately put his arm around him and pulled him close. Elliott laid his bald head on George's arm and gazed across at Brett, a lazy smile playing about his lips.

"You're looking good there, Brett."

Brett smiled and raised his brandy glass. He studied the two men before him. He had a rough idea of Elliott's age—maybe in his early forties—but he estimated George to be at least ten years older, his hair graying at the temples. All through dinner, Brett hadn't been able to take his eyes off the pair. They just… fit each other.

Maybe that's what being together for eleven years does for you, he thought. They seemed so very comfortable with each other. He watched as George leaned across to kiss Elliott softly on the mouth. The way Elliott's eyes lit up as he looked at his partner made Brett all warm inside. *God, they look so in love.*

Elliott leaned against George and met Brett's gaze. "I suppose this means I'm going to be seeing less of you," Elliott said with an exaggerated sigh. Then he winked. "And I'm absolutely delighted about it."

"I don't think you should stop coming here altogether," John said suddenly. "I mean, it's good to be able to get away from it all now and again, isn't it?"

Both Elliott and George nodded. "I'll always have a room for you," Elliott said. "Any time you feel you need to escape, just give me a ring. Besides," he said with a wink, "I don't think you'll be on your own, will you?" His gaze flickered toward John.

Brett kissed the top of John's head. The same thought had already occurred to him. But as he watched the older couple together, an idea began to take root, one that refused to go away. And as the evening progressed, it suddenly dawned on Brett that maybe he needed to share it with John.

He couldn't wait to see John's reaction.

JOHN SWITCHED on the bedside lamp and pulled back the duvet.

"I like Elliott and George," he announced as he undid the buttons on his shirt. "They seem very well suited."

Brett had to agree. He went to draw the heavy curtains across the window to shut out the night sky and then turned to face his lover. John's skin glowed warmly in the lamplight, and Brett stood still, watching as he lowered his jeans, revealing the firm curves of his arse. He caught his breath as John's cock was freed from its confines. Half hard already, it was a thing of beauty that never ceased to draw his admiration. John became still and looked up at him, a faint smile on his lips.

Brett gazed at him. "You're beautiful," he said softly.

John's eyes widened. "Men aren't beautiful," he said, a blush staining his cheeks.

Brett crossed the room to stand before him. He drew his hand slowly down John's arm, trailing his fingers across the firm belly with its downy blond treasure trail before lowering them to stroke his dick. He felt rather than saw John's reaction to the gentle caress.

"Oh, yes, men can be beautiful too," he said quietly. "Right now you are the most beautiful man I've ever seen." He loved the way John's face heated up, the eager way he helped Brett to undress, the sexy way he bit his lip when he found Brett watching him, the way his breath caught when Brett's heavy cock brushed against him.

Brett got into bed, pulling John with him. "It's our last night," he said with some degree of sadness. Tomorrow they'd travel back to Manchester and the real world would beckon, but for now he wanted to put aside any thoughts of work and concentrate on the gorgeous man in his arms. He lay on his back, and John stretched out on top of him, their bodies fitting together in a way that was fast becoming familiar. Brett reached up to stroke John's cheek as John nuzzled into his neck.

"Can we talk for a sec?"

John lifted his head and looked Brett in the eye. "Of course."

Brett rolled John onto his side and then mirrored his body with his own. "I was looking at Elliott and George tonight, and I found myself thinking something that wouldn't leave me alone." John's brow creased, and Brett leaned forward to kiss him quickly on the mouth. "Not a bad thought, so don't worry. I simply found myself wishing for what they have."

John sighed. "They fit each other perfectly, and they seem so happy together."

Brett nodded, his eyes never leaving John's face. "And I want that—with you."

John stilled, his blue eyes wide. His lips parted, but no sound came forth.

Brett cupped his chin and kissed him softly on the mouth. "I watched them together, and all I could think of was that you and I are a pretty good fit too. I know we haven't been together long, but I want to see where this leads."

"Me too," John said in a low voice. But Brett hadn't finished.

"So I think we should get tested. I'm not saying we need to go out and do it next week, but if things are still going well in a month or so, then yes, let's get tested." Brett cocked his head. "What do you think?"

John grinned. "Works for me." His expression softened. "Yeah, that sounds good." And then he grabbed Brett's upper arms and pulled him on top of him, spreading his legs wide so that Brett came to rest between his thighs. Brett could feel the heat of John's cock as it nestled against his own. He slid his hand down to stroke over John's balls, watching John's pupils enlarge as he pressed against his perineum, only to move lower to where that tight little ring awaited him. The plaintive whine that escaped from John's lips when Brett pulled his hand away was adorable.

"We have all night," he muttered, dropping his head lower to take John's mouth in a gentle kiss that didn't stay gentle for long. Before minutes had passed, he was attacking that beautiful mouth with a hunger that John was obviously experiencing as well, as the two men writhed against each other. Sharing his thoughts seemed to have unleashed something almost primal in John. Their passionate coupling went on long into the night, both men seemingly desperate to hold on for as long as possible, until their orgasms could no longer be held at bay.

Brett's last waking thought as he curled up around John, the duvet a warm cocoon around them, was that a week spent sleeping with his lover in his arms was definitely not enough.

He wanted more.

JOHN BUSTLED around the classroom, picking up books and pencils and tidying them away, before making sure his resources were ready for the following morning. He cast a longing glance at the wall clock. Another hour and he'd be in Brett's arms.

He chuckled to himself as he sat at the desk and wrote down the results of his class's latest test in his markbook. *My life is getting predictable.* In the six weeks since their visit to Brighton, his days had fallen into a pattern. The weeks flew by as he spent his hours teaching, marking, preparing resources, and evaluating his progress. He was spending more time in the evenings on schoolwork, but all that hard work paid off when the weekend arrived and he was able to spend more time with Brett. Their time together was precious. Even the relatively short times they shared at the end of the school day were something to be treasured. The only thing was, they had to be so careful. John knew Brett was unhappy about the situation. Nothing had changed, after all—if their relationship was discovered, there would be hell to pay.

John put down his pen and stared out at the street beyond his classroom.

Will it always be like this?

He loved those stolen moments with Brett, but if he were completely honest, John was growing tired of the sneaking around, the brief snatches of time, the need to be careful.

I want to be able to walk down the street with him at my side and not have to worry in case anyone from school spots us. I want us to be able to go out to a club and not fear the consequences of being seen together.

And then something struck him so forcefully that it sent his mind reeling.

I want a life with him.

"You look deep in thought."

John gave a start. Bev stood at his classroom door, her coat over her arm.

He shrugged. "Sorry, I was miles away. You off now?"

She nodded but then stepped into his room. His mind groaned. *Oh, not now.* All he wanted was for everyone to go so he and Brett could share a coffee and a quiet moment together in the safe haven of Brett's office.

Bev approached his desk, and John gave her a closer look. *She must be going on somewhere from school*, he thought. Her makeup looked freshly applied, and she'd changed out of her gray skirt and white blouse into a short dress that clung to her. She came around his desk and leaned against it. A heady perfume tickled his nostrils.

"I was wondering if you'd like to go for a drink when you finish," she said, smiling at him.

John waved his hand over his test papers. "Sorry, but I'm going to be here for at least another hour." He glanced at the clock. It was only 4:10 p.m. Then it hit him. *A drink—at this time?* He glanced up and saw the disappointed expression she tried to hide. He gave her an apologetic smile. "Another time, maybe," he said diplomatically.

Bev gave him another bright smile and patted his arm. "I'll hold you to that." She straightened and walked toward the door. "See you tomorrow, John. Try not to work *too* hard." He could hear her chuckle as she walked along the corridor. He heaved a sigh of relief and concentrated on the task in hand.

Get this done and then you can see Brett.

That had him smiling again.

"I TAKE it we're alone?" Brett said as he heard the key turn in the lock, his eyes on the screen in front of him. Seconds later John's arms slipped around his waist as his lover hugged him from behind.

"I thought they'd never go," John groaned quietly. He kissed Brett's neck, and Brett closed his eyes, leaning back into John's embrace. "I've been watching the clock for the last hour. All I wanted to do was get in here and kiss you."

Brett chuckled. "And what makes you think I *want* to be kissed?" he teased. John pulled away, and Brett sighed at the break in contact.

John snorted. "I turned down a drink with Bev Waverley to sneak in here and kiss you, I'll have you know."

Brett swung around on his chair to stare at John. He quirked his eyebrows. "Oh, really?" He grinned. "Did she really ask you to go for a drink with her?"

John walked over to the coffee machine and poured himself a mug. "Yep. She turned up in my room just over an hour ago."

Brett thought for a moment. "Was that the first time Bev's asked you to go for a drink with her?" He watched John's forehead crease as he thought about it.

"Actually, now you come to mention it…. She's asked me a few times." Brett shook his head and bit back a smile. The crease between John's eyes deepened. "What?"

Brett snickered. "You really don't see it, do you?" The look of genuine puzzlement on John's face was adorable. Brett got up from his seat, walked over to where John stood, mug in hand, and kissed him on the lips.

John tilted his head. "What *are* you on about?"

Brett stepped back and met John's gaze head on. "Bev has the hots for you." He grinned.

John's eyebrows shot up. "No way." He gaped.

Brett laughed. "John, you're a gorgeous man. Why would she not fancy you? And she's not the only one, believe me." He winked. "You have quite a *few* admirers."

The look of dawning horror on John's face was comical. "But… I've never given her any… I mean…." His face twisted. "You're serious, aren't you?"

Brett nodded. "But don't worry about it. If you keep turning her down, she'll get the message. Just make sure you do it nicely." He noticed John's brow was still wrinkled. John bit his lip. Brett softened his voice. "What is it, baby?" He put his arms around John and drew him closer.

John rested his head against Brett's shoulder. "I hate this," he said in a small voice. Brett could feel the tension in John's body.

"What's wrong?" Brett murmured into his hair. "This isn't like you."

John nuzzled into his neck, his breath warm against Brett's skin. "I hate all of it. All this sneaking around. Not being able to be myself. Having to be so careful. Knowing that what we're doing could get us both into a lot of trouble." He raised his head and looked Brett in the eye. "You seem to cope with it all so much better than me."

Brett kissed him softly on the mouth and then gave him a gentle smile. "You think? Then I'm a bloody good actor. I hate all this just as much as you do." In the last few weeks, he'd found himself questioning what he wanted out of life. And spending more time with John was definitely on his mind. Their relationship was blossoming, and Brett knew in his heart that things couldn't stay as they were. John's words confirmed his own feelings. They both wanted more and were unable to do anything about it.

Well, that's not quite true, is it? There is something I could do—but it would mean changing everything. And am I prepared to step out of my comfort zone and face an entirely different future—with John at my side?

The more Brett thought about it, the more he realized he needed to take steps. As careful as they were being, it was only a matter of time until someone at school said or heard something—and then God help them both.

I should never have started this, he thought. *I had the right idea when I tried to push him away.* Then he looked at the man before him. Try as he might, he couldn't regret the change John had wrought in his life. *He's brought such happiness into my world. And now? I can't live without him.*

That last thought made the decision easier. It was too late for regrets, but it wasn't too late to put plans in motion that would allow them to have a future together.

He kissed John once more and then patted him on his arse. "I think you need to go home now."

John's face fell. "Already? I wanted a little longer with you."

Brett caressed his cheek. "I know, but I still have things to do here. So go home, get some work done, and spend a quiet evening relaxing with the boys. I'll call you later, I promise." He led John to the door and unlocked it. "Who's at home tonight, by the way?"

"Everyone but Stu—he's in Paris."

Brett sighed wistfully. "Paris. Lucky Stu." He kissed John on the mouth, a tender, lingering kiss. "We'll go there one day, just the two of us."

John opened the door and gave him a brief smile. "Yeah, that sounds nice. One day."

Brett pushed him out into the corridor as playfully as he could manage. "Now go home and stop distracting me with this tempting body." He gazed intently at his lover. "I'll phone you tonight when you're in bed. You can distract me all you want then."

John smirked and then nodded. "Later." He turned and walked slowly to his classroom.

Brett came back into the office and sat down at his desk. He called up his web browser on the screen and went to his bookmarks. He stared at the words for a long time before finally clicking the link.

Her Majesty's Inspector (HMI) and Senior HMI vacancies.

Brett began to read.

CHAPTER 23

"GOD, STU, I don't know what I'd do without your foot rubs."

John groaned as he lay there sprawled on the couch while Stu sat at the other end, manipulating his tired feet. Those nimble fingers working his arches and the balls of his feet? *Heaven.*

Stu chuckled. "What on earth have you been doin' today? You look worn out."

John rubbed his face. "Well, I suppose it *is* my fault...."

Alec looked away from the TV and laughed. "Now, why does *that* not surprise me? What have you done now?"

John rubbed his eyes with the heel of his hand. "I sort of promised Trish Stetman that I'd help her with organizing the School Sports Day and Swimming Gala in May."

All three men snorted loudly.

"See, you made such a good job of organizin' that charity event that now *everyone* wants your skills," Stu said with a grin. "So what was so tirin' today?"

John sighed. "When my class got wind of the fact that I was involved, they got it into their heads that *they* have to be the best group for both days. They don't want to show me up, apparently."

"Aw, that's sweet," Martin said, smiling, from his position curled up in one of the armchairs.

"Yeah, but that means they want to practice every chance they get, so every day during the lunch times we're out on the field, practicing for the three-legged race, the egg-and-spoon race, the sack race...." John let out a long moan. "And last week, they used their swimming lesson to practice for the gala. They are such a *competitive* lot! I swear, they're going to wear me out."

"Do the staff have to take part in these racing events?" Alec asked.

John sat up, pulling his bare feet free of Stu's hands. "Yes—and that's another thing. Because there's now a *male* teacher in the school, the rest of my colleagues are telling me I can't race against them. They claim it would be unfair."

"Well, doesn't that let you off the hook?" Martin demanded to know.

"That's what I thought—until some bright person said in the staff meeting on Monday that there should be a race just between me and Brett." He groaned. "So we're going to race for a length of the swimming pool."

Stu was giggling. "Ooh, racin' against your boyfriend—*and* your boss. You'd better let him win."

John's back was suddenly rigid. "No I bloody won't! I'm going to give it my best shot."

"Brett's, what, nine years older than you?" Alec asked. John nodded. Alec grinned. "Well then, you should be able to wipe the floor with an old man like that."

John laughed at that. "I'll try not to beat him by *too* wide a margin," he said. "He might decide to take out his revenge in bed." He gave a wicked little chuckle and then sagged back against the seat cushions. "God, I am so glad the Easter holiday starts on Friday." Only one more day and he'd have two weeks—*two whole weeks*—with Brett. It was all that was keeping him going lately.

"You two have any plans?" Stu asked, getting up and picking up the empty coffee mugs from the table.

John stretched his arms into the air. "He talked about spending part of one week in Brighton." The three men began whistling and making suggestive noises. John shook his head. "And *this* time we might actually make it out of our room." Spring had made an unusually warm entrance this year, and the thought of getting to go for a romantic walk on the beach was uppermost in John's mind. There'd been a few similar thoughts too.

I know what set me off thinking like this, he thought. He and Brett had made an early morning trip to a clinic a couple of weeks ago to get tested. When Brett had suggested it, John had been overjoyed. It had been on his mind to ask, but after their conversation in Brighton, John wanted Brett to make the first move. And the fact that he'd done so had got John thinking.

Where does Brett see this relationship going?

John knew he found it easier to say what he was feeling than Brett did, which made life a little difficult sometimes. John had to hang back and not share *everything* that came into his mind—especially when it came to how he felt about Brett. But he knew how *he* wanted things to go. He just wasn't sure when would be the right time to tell his boyfriend that he was falling in love with him.

THE NOISE in the classroom was increasing by the minute as home time neared. All the children were excited for the coming holiday, especially when John had brought out first solid chocolate eggs in white crisp shells, then food colorings. Everyone was sitting around in little groups, decorating their eggs to take home. John gazed around at the happy faces, all the children engrossed in their task. The eggs idea had been Alec's brainwave.

John's learning support assistant, Mandy, was beaming as she looked at the scene. "This is lovely, Mr. Wainwright." Then she smirked. "But I think it will be a miracle if some of these eggs actually make it home."

John was inclined to agree. He glanced at his desk and bit back a groan. "Oh, hell," he muttered under his breath. "Trish isn't in today, and she asked me to take the letters about the Sports Day and Swimming Gala to all the staff, to make sure the kids took them home today." The letters were sitting in a neat pile on his desk.

"Do you want me to take them round to the classrooms?" Mandy asked. "There's still fifteen minutes left until the bell."

John thought about it quickly. "Actually, I've got a better idea. Could you watch the class for a minute while *I* do it? That way, if the kids have any questions I can answer them."

Mandy nodded cheerfully and then gazed around at the happy, smiling faces. "They'll be fine with me."

John squeezed her arm, grabbed the sheaf of letters, and dashed out of the room. He went into every room and made sure all the children understood about giving the letters to their parents or guardians. As he went along the corridor to the last class, Michelle Fielding's Year Two classroom, he glanced at his watch. *Five minutes to go.* He knew from past experience that people rarely stayed late on the last day of term. *Even better—I get to kiss Brett all that much sooner.* The thought made him smile.

He entered Michelle's classroom with a wide grin on his face. Michelle looked up from where she was kneeling next to a little boy and smiled when she saw him.

"I was wondering if you'd forgotten about the letters," she said, her eyes gleaming. "There are only a few of the kids in here who can swim, by the way, so I'll only need about five letters."

John nodded and handed her the sheets. Behind him, he heard the door from the corridor open and close—and then he caught sight of Michelle's face. It was white.

John turned around to see a tall man, thick and muscular, wearing faded scruffy jeans and a denim jacket, his hands stuffed into the pockets. John recognized his face immediately.

Oh, fuck—Carl Meadows.

John stood very still. "Can I help you?" He was amazed at how calm he sounded. Behind him, he heard Michelle get to her feet.

Carl scanned the room. "I've come for me son, Wayne," he said gruffly. He peered past John to the corner where John knew Wayne was sitting. "Let's go, son."

John held up his hand. "I'm sorry, Mr. Meadows, but we *are* aware of the restraining order that's in place." He gave a quick look at the children. They were all staring at Carl. "Can we step outside into the corridor to discuss this?" He kept his voice even.

Carl stared at him, his eyes cold. "I've got nuffin' to discuss wi' you. I just want me boy." He took a step forward.

John held up both hands. "Mr. Meadows, I really must ask that we discuss this somewhere else. If you'd just like to come with me, I'll—"

"I'm goin' nowhere," Carl gritted out. "Not without the lad. And you don't want to get in me way." He pulled his hand free of his pocket—and pointed a gun at John.

John felt his heart skip a beat. He found it difficult to breathe. "It's Carl, isn't it? Carl, you need to put the gun away." He spoke slowly, careful not to make any sudden moves. John was aware of the noises coming from the children. Some were starting to cry. John fought to keep calm, but his heart was hammering.

"Seein' as I'm the one wi' the gun, I don't think *you* get to tell me what to do, okay?" Carl kept the gun pointed at John. "Now, let Wayne leave wi' me, and no one gets 'urt."

A few of the children began to sob loudly.

John felt a wave of dizziness wash over him. He swallowed and then tried to keep his tone light. "Carl, you don't need these kids to be in here. How about if my colleague, Miss Fielding, takes them outside? I'll stay, but I think it's better if they go. You're beginning to scare them." He hoped there was enough of a father in Carl to make him see reason. The children's sobs were increasing.

Carl's gaze went to Michelle and then back to John. "Okay," he agreed grudgingly, and then he waved the gun. "But Wayne stays." His eyes bored into John.

John swallowed once more and then gave a slow nod. "Michelle," he said quietly, without turning his head, "why don't you lead the children out into the playground? It's nearly time to go home anyway." He regarded the children with a bright smile. "Okay, kids, you need to stand up quietly and go with Miss Fielding." He twisted around quickly to seek out Wayne. The little boy was staring at his father with huge eyes. "Come here, Wayne." John extended a hand toward him.

Wayne hurried to take John's hand but then hid behind him. John could feel the little boy trembling. He watched as the children made their way through the glass door that led out onto the playground, Michelle holding the door wide for them. When the last child was through, she gave John one final panicked look and then let the door close gently behind her.

John brought his attention back to Carl. That gun was still pointing in his direction, but John noted how Carl's hand shook. His face was ashen, and John could see the beads of sweat that had popped out on his brow.

Oh, God. He looks more nervous than I am—which could be a blessing or a nightmare.

BRETT TIDIED away the folders from his desk with a satisfied smile. He wasn't going to give school a second thought during the next two weeks. He leaned back and laced his fingers behind his head, his mind focused on John. The idea of spending two weeks together sent a tingle of anticipation through him. Funnily enough, it wasn't the thought of sharing a bed with John that occupied his thoughts, but the prospect of doing more mundane things together. Brett wanted to take him out to dinner, somewhere quiet and intimate. Maybe they could go see a film or a play, or perhaps take a picnic and go off into the countryside. He just wanted to be with his lover.

The thought made him smile. Eight months ago, he'd have laughed at the idea of doing stuff like that with a guy. *And yet look at me now.* Okay, so he knew their bubble could burst at any minute, but right now? Brett was happy. *Really* happy for the first time in his life—and it was all because of John.

His office door burst open, startling him from his pleasant thoughts. Emily Taylor dashed into the room, her face pale and panic stricken. Brett was on his feet in seconds.

"What's happened?"

Emily was shaking. "You need to call the police, Brett, right now. Carl Meadows is in Michelle's classroom, and he has a gun."

Shitshitshitshit.... "Oh, God. He's in the school? What about the kids? Are they in there with him? What about Michelle?" He reached for the phone to dial 999, but his stupid fingers wouldn't cooperate.

"John got him to allow Michelle to bring them out. He's—"

Brett's heart gave an almighty thump in his chest. "*John*? What was John doing in there?"

"Apparently he'd gone in with some letters. Carl has him at gunpoint."

He froze, the receiver hanging loosely in his hand. Waves of panic coursed through him.

Emily's eyes widened. "Brett—the police?"

Come on, Brett. Get it together. He dialed 999, his hand trembling. When he got through to the operator, he quickly gave her the details as clearly as he could. He answered her questions, listened intently for a minute, and then hung up. "They're on their way." Brett pulled on his jacket and was about to follow Emily out of the office when he spied his phone on the desk. He grabbed it and scrolled through to find the landline number for John's house.

Please—let one of them be home.

The phone rang for a while before Stu answered. He sounded a little groggy. "'Lo? Who's this?"

"Stu, it's Brett. John's in trouble." Brett's voice quavered.

Stu reacted fast. "Tell me."

Brett filled him in as quickly as he could. When Stu told him he was on his way, Brett knew better than to try to dissuade him. Those boys were John's family. He hung up and ran out of the office to find Caroline Westmore, the Year One teacher from the room next to Michelle's, waiting for him at the end of the corridor that led to her room. She was twisting her hands together and biting her lip.

"The police are on their way," he informed her. "What's been done so far?"

"Brett, we've got all the children outside," she began, her voice shaking. "Parents are already outside, of course, waiting for them. Michelle's a mess. She's been doing her best to keep the kids calm, but I think she's in shock."

Brett looked over Caroline's shoulder to the door of Michelle's room. There was no sound coming from the classroom.

"If only we knew what's going on in there." Brett's stomach was churning. He didn't want to contemplate how badly things might turn out.

"Brett, the police have arrived. They're outside, and they want to talk to you." Emily sounded a little calmer.

Brett took a deep breath, forcing himself to push aside the fear that threatened to overwhelm him.

"Let's go talk to them," he said. "I want to talk to Michelle as well." He led Caroline and Emily out of the building, his heart quaking as he offered up a silent prayer.

God, bring him out of this alive.

JOHN COULDN'T take his eyes off the gun. The more he watched Carl, the more convinced he became that Carl was as terrified by all this as he was. And John couldn't stand there and do nothing.

"Carl," he began, keeping his voice low and even, "please, put the gun down."

There was a sheen of sweat on Carl's cheeks and forehead. "No. I... I need it."

"No, you don't," John insisted, as gently as he could. "You're really scaring Wayne." The little boy was clutching John's arm, his eyes huge and bright, no color in his cheeks. John could hear his breathing, shallow and fast. John raised his gaze to look Carl in the eye. "Is it loaded?"

"I don't know. I don't think so. Not sure." Carl's hand trembled as he tightened his fingers around the grip. A strong smell of sweat was emanating from him, and John watched as he wiped his forehead with the back of his hand. He could see how fast Carl's heart was beating by the pulsing vein in his neck. His eyes were wild. "Okay, the kids have gone. So let Wayne come over 'ere, an' I'll get out of yer 'air." His gaze lowered to where Wayne was hiding behind John. "You need to come wi' me, son."

John took his courage in both hands. "Look, you know I can't let you walk out of here with him."

Carl jerked his head. The gun wavered in his hand. "Do you know 'ow long it's been since I've seen 'im? Twelve months I were inside— twelve bleedin' months!"

"What were you in prison for, Carl?" John spoke quietly, hoping this would rub off on Carl. He'd read somewhere that using a person's name could help build rapport.

Carl's eyes became dull. "Assault, causing a disturbance, resistin' arrest—I went on a bingin' session wi' me mates and got 'ammered." His face twisted. "I were only ever violent when I got drunk. I never laid a 'and on the kid, never." His eyes blazed.

"I believe you," John said softly.

"Anna weren't so lucky. Seems the more I drank, the worse it got." There was a sudden expression of pain in Carl's eyes. "It were just 'istory repeatin' itself."

"What do you mean?" John tried to keep him talking. He knew the police had to be on their way, if they weren't already there.

Carl became still. "In prison they make you go to therapy sessions, and they get you to talk about your childhood." He swallowed. "And they made me realize that I were only doin' the same thing as me dad did when I were a lickle kid."

"Your dad used to get drunk and become violent?" John was beginning to see Carl in a whole new light, and for the first time since he'd arrived in the classroom, he saw Carl not as a hardened criminal but as a desperate man.

"Yeah," Carl said. "And there were no way I wanted me lickle boy to go through what *I* did." His chin dropped. "I know what I did was wrong, and all I want to do is make it up to Anna." The eyes that met John's were tortured. "But 'ow can I do that when she won't let me near 'im?"

"That's why you wanted to see her."

"Yes," Carl breathed. "I just want to put things right. I wanted to tell her… I haven't had a drink since I got out. I'm sober, and I'm goin' to stay that way." His eyes were filled with pain. "Just wanted to put things right," he repeated softly.

"But this isn't the way to do it, Carl," John said slowly. "Can't you see how much you're scaring your son?" John tried to keep the focus on Wayne.

"She wouldn't let me see 'im!" Carl blurted out, his free hand rubbing the back of his neck.

"I know, I know." John spoke softly.

Carl couldn't take his eyes off the little boy, who wouldn't even look at his father. "When I were in prison, I wrote to her, asking for photos, just so I could see my lickle boy. She never sent nothin'." He gazed imploringly at Wayne. "I love you, son." He looked stricken when the boy edged farther behind John, starting to cry.

Carl stared forlornly at his son. "She wouldn't even let me in the 'ouse. All I got were letters from her lawyer. Lawyers!" he spat out in disgust. Then his face softened as Wayne's sobs grew louder.

"Carl, this isn't the way to go. Surely you can see that." John swallowed. He felt weak at the knees but did his best to stand up straight and still. His heart felt as if it was about to explode, it was beating so fast.

"I couldn't think of nuffin' else!" Carl wailed. All trace of calm had fled. "I thought maybe if I 'ad a gun, I could...." His words died away. "What am I sayin'? I wasn't thinkin' straight."

"Carl, think now." John put his hand down to stroke Wayne's hair, feeling the boy shaking, his tears easing off. "Think what your little boy is going to remember about today."

Carl froze. "What... what do you mean?"

"Even if you get out of here, what's he going to remember? His dad, waving a gun. He's seven, Carl. He won't forget this, trust me."

Carl lowered his arm slightly. "You think?"

John nodded, encouraged. "Supposing that gun *is* loaded, and it had gone off and hurt one of the children—or, God forbid, Wayne. Could you live with that, knowing you'd hurt a child?" John took a step toward him. "I don't think you've ever shot anyone in your life. Am I right?"

Carl barked out a nervous laugh. "Never even 'eld a gun 'til today. I borrowed it off a mate."

John breathed easier. Carl was sounding more and more like a guy who'd fallen in with the wrong crowd. But he was still a man with a gun.

"There's still time, Carl," he said, thinking fast.

Carl's eyes met his, wide and scared. "What d'you mean?"

"If you leave the gun in here and walk out with me and Wayne, the police might take it easier on you. If no one gets hurt and you give yourself up." John glanced toward the window. "They'll be out there by now. They'll know you have a gun, so we're talking an armed response unit. What's better, Carl—to walk out of here with your hands up and go peacefully with the police, or walk out with that gun to find rifles trained on you?" Wayne's little hand tightened around John's. "What do you want your son to remember of this day?"

Carl's gaze lowered to his son. "I just want to see me boy," he whispered. The hand holding the gun fell down to his side.

"Carl, how about you leave the gun here? I'll let the police know that you're coming out unarmed."

"How?" Carl regarded him hopefully.

John took his phone from his pocket. "I can call Mr. Sanderson, the head teacher. He'll be out there with the police. I can tell him to make sure the police know. What do you say?" He held his breath.

Carl thought about it for several long seconds. "Yeah, do it," he said at last. He placed the gun on the table nearest to him, and John could have wept with relief. Fingers trembling, he speed dialed Brett.

"Are you all right?" Brett's voice, low and urgent, filled his ear. John drew in a deep breath through his nose, clamping down on the surge of emotion that coursed through him at the sound of his lover's words.

"I'm fine," John said quickly to reassure him. He heard Brett exhale slowly. "Can you tell the police that we're all coming out but that Carl is going to leave his gun here in the classroom. He'll be unarmed, and he hasn't hurt us."

"Thank God." Brett's voice shook slightly. "I'll tell them now." His voice dropped to a whisper. "I just want you out of there and in my arms."

"Me too." John kept his tone even, but his heart soared to hear Brett's words. "We'll be out in a minute." He disconnected the call and looked at Carl. "The police are being informed as we speak."

Carl nodded, his Adam's apple bobbing as he swallowed.

John held Wayne's hand tightly. "You're doing the right thing, Carl. I think we should all walk out together. Wayne's mother will be out there, waiting for him."

Carl's jaw tightened, but he gave another brisk nod. "Okay. Let's do this."

John walked over to the glass door, Wayne holding onto him tightly, keeping close by his side. He could hear Carl walk up behind him. Just before he pushed open the door, Carl placed a hand on his shoulder, and John had to work hard not to jump, he was so keyed up.

"Can… can I say somethin' to Wayne before we go out there?"

John nodded, and Carl dropped to his knees before the little boy. John felt him tense up immediately, and he put out a hand to stroke Wayne's curly hair.

Carl gazed at his son. There was no denying the love in those eyes. "Daddy…. Daddy loves you, Wayne. Okay?"

Those big brown eyes, swimming with tears, stared at Carl, and his full lower lip trembled. "O-okay, Daddy." Carl regarded him in silence for a moment and then reluctantly got to his feet.

"Okay, let's go outside."

John pushed open the door and grasped Wayne's hand. Impulsively he held out a hand to Carl. "Let them see," he urged. "We'll hold our hands up so they can see you're no threat."

Carl nodded, all trace of bravado gone. His face was devoid of color as he took hold of John's hand, and the three of them stepped out into the bright sunshine.

CHAPTER 24

JOHN COULDN'T believe the sight that awaited him when he stepped into the playground. There were police everywhere. Yellow police tape stretched between the school gates, and inside it were police officers dressed in black, crouching with rifles in their hands, their eyes trained on the door where John, Wayne, and Carl had just emerged. Beyond them the street was packed. John counted two black police vans, three police cars, and an ambulance. That last one sent a chill right through him. The street immediately outside the gates had been cordoned off, but crowds of people stood behind the yellow tape, talking animatedly. He could make out the faces of the staff, their expressions anxious, and next to them, several parents, clutching their children. *Where's Brett?* John couldn't see him, and his stomach rolled heavily.

What he hadn't expected to see was the van from Granada TV—or the guy with the camera pointing toward them.

"Oh, fuck." Carl's whispered expletive from beside him brought him sharply back into the moment. Wayne's small hand tightened around his.

"Ready?" John said quietly. "We're just going to walk slowly over to the officers, hands in the air, all right?" He could almost feel the fear that was rolling off Carl in waves. John was aware of the tide of nausea that rippled through his body. *Almost there....*

"Okay." Carl's voice was small. John raised their joined hands, and they walked slowly over to where the police officers knelt.

"Lower your rifles." A voice rang out across the playground, and John turned his head to see what was unmistakably a more senior officer striding toward the crouched men. He could feel the clamminess of Carl's hand in his. But John's heart began to pound as he looked beyond the officer to see... Brett. His lover stood rock-still, his gaze trained on John.

John pushed down the euphoria that surged through him. *Later.*

"Wayne!"

A female voice, full of anguish, cut through the air. John saw Wayne's mother, Anna, straining to push past the female police officer who was holding her back. Her hand stretched out toward her little boy, her fingers clutching at the air.

"Mum!" Wayne pulled free of John's hand and ran toward her, his arms held up. At last, the wall of men parted and Anna ran forward, sweeping up the little boy into her arms and holding him tight. John's chest constricted as he saw the tears that ran down her cheeks. She kissed Wayne's hair fervently, then his cheeks, her eyes closed. Wayne locked his arms around his mother and held on tight.

John felt Carl's hand tighten around his until his grip was almost painful. In spite of the terror that Carl had put him through, John's heart went out to him.

"There's always hope. Don't give up," he murmured. Carl turned his head slightly to meet John's gaze, and John was shaken to see his eyes shiny with unshed tears. "Use the lawyers—let Anna see that you've changed. It may take time—and they may send you back to prison for this, you have to be ready for that—but eventually, she has to see how much you love that little boy."

As if he'd heard John's words, Wayne turned round at that moment and looked at Carl. His big brown eyes were fixed on his father. John's chest tightened as Carl raised his hand to wave at his son. When Wayne gave a tentative wave, John could feel the tremors throughout Carl's body. He heard the tiniest noise, as though Carl were holding back a whimper.

"See? There's always hope."

Carl nodded as two police officers approached them, handcuffs in hand. He took a deep breath and then stepped forward, releasing John's hand and holding his in the air. John saw Carl straighten up and square his shoulders as one officer cuffed his wrists and then led him toward the gate. Carl inclined his head slightly as he passed Anna and then stared forward as he was pushed into the back of a black police van. His eyes met John's, and Carl bobbed his head briefly before the door closed, shutting him off from view.

John was overwhelmed by a sudden giddiness that coursed through him. He closed his eyes and drew in a deep breath through his nose. *It's over.*

"Mr. Wainwright?"

John focused on the officer. "Yes?" He struggled to breathe evenly.

"We'd like you to come to the station and give a statement."

John nodded and went to follow him—until he saw Brett striding purposefully across the playground, eyes locked on him. The man had never looked so good. Brett came to a dead stop in front of him, his hands clenching by his sides.

"I think I aged twenty years in the last twenty minutes," he said in a low voice. His face was pale and drawn.

John opened his mouth to reply, but Brett got there first as he pulled John roughly into his arms and kissed him on the mouth, lips pressed tightly against his. John had no time to think and reacted instinctively—he brought his arms up to lock around Brett's neck and clung to him, eyes closed as Brett continued to kiss him, his hand reaching up to cup John's cheek.

The kiss seemed to spin out as time stood still—until someone cleared his throat.

John's eyes flew open, and just like that, sanity was restored. They broke apart, both men's chests heaving.

"Later," whispered Brett. He turned to the officer, whose cheeks had flushed bright red. "I'll bring him to the station. Is that okay?"

The officer coughed. "Er, yeah, that'll be fine." He spoke quietly into the radio fixed to his jacket and then stepped aside as Brett placed his hand around John's upper arm and led him toward the gate—where the cameraman stood, his camera trained on them.

"Oh, God." John felt his legs go weak. "I think you just outed both of us." He nodded toward the camera. "And for the local TV station."

Brett let go of his arm and reached down to grab John's hand. "Then this isn't going to matter to anyone, is it?" His fingers tightened around John's.

John scanned the crowd. Shocked faces stared back at them, mouths open, expressions of incredulity, some smirks and grins—and one tall young man nearest the police tape stared at them both, beaming. John sagged with relief. "Stu's here."

Brett tightened his grip. "I called him. I couldn't think what else to do."

As they reached the tape, Stu ducked under it and seized John in a tight hug.

"Oh, thank God," Stu breathed. "I've had Martin and Alec ringin' me nonstop. You scared the shit out of us!" He let John go as his phone warbled. He grinned. "See what I mean?" He glanced at the screen, and his grin almost split his face in two. "Oh, fuck—seems you two just made the four o'clock news."

John gulped. This wasn't good.

Brett leaned into him. "Breathe, baby. We'll deal with the fallout later. Right now, we need to get you to the station to get the statement out of the way. Then I'll take you home. And I'm not leaving your side for a minute." He gave Stu a tight smile. "That okay?"

Stu nodded. "Go do what you have to, then bring him home. I'll have dinner waiting." He clasped John to him in a brief but firm hug, paused, and then did the same to Brett before jogging back to his car, which John could see parked beyond the police cordon.

John caught the dazed look on Brett's face. In spite of the fluttery sensation in his belly, John leaned close and whispered into Brett's ear. "Welcome to the family, babe." As he straightened, he saw a small group of people approach the tape. His colleagues' faces wore similar expressions of relief, although Bev seemed to be holding herself quite stiffly. He didn't have time to think about it as he was pulled into enthusiastic hugs.

"Oh, thank God." Michelle looked drained. "I was so frightened, John. I had visions of you coming out of there in a body bag."

John allowed himself to be held, several women reaching for him at once. He couldn't help but note their expressions as they looked back and forth between him and Brett, as though they couldn't quite believe what they were seeing. He waited for one of them to say something, but Brett took matters into his own hands.

"Ladies, I'm going to whisk John away to the police station now, so if you'll excuse us." He gave them a tight smile. "Go home, please. And try to relax over the holiday, okay? I know this isn't the ideal start, but do your best to put it from your minds. John and Wayne are safe, thank goodness, and no one was harmed. Drama over."

There were several relieved smiles, although Bev's seemed strained. Brett took hold of John's arm and led him toward the car park. John found it hard to breathe as a police officer passed him, holding the gun in a clear plastic bag. The whole situation felt so unreal. It was as if John was watching it all taking place, but at a distance. Brett said nothing but reached across to squeeze his hand as John fastened his seat belt in the car.

"Let's get this over with," Brett said quietly, "and then I'll take you home. You must feel out of it right now." He gave John a sympathetic glance.

"*Out of it* is the perfect description," John said with a shake of his head. "Come on—let's go." He leaned his head back and closed his eyes.

Well, the shit has well and truly hit the fan this time.

BRETT FOLLOWED John up the path to his front door. He'd been very quiet on the way home from the station. In fact, Brett had watched him as the officer took down his statement. They'd allowed him to sit with John when they'd seen the state John had been in. He seemed to be functioning on autopilot. The whole time they were sitting in the little interview room, cups of undrinkable coffee chilling on the table before them, all Brett wanted to do was gather John in his arms and tell the world to get lost. He wanted to keep touching him, as if to reassure himself that John was really there, that he *had* made it alive out of that nightmarish situation. Refraining from doing so had put Brett under a real strain, and right now, it wouldn't take much to break the tenuous hold he had on his emotions. He wanted John in his arms, in a bed, naked, vital, alive....

John fumbled with the door, and they stepped into the hallway. Stu came out of the kitchen, his relief obvious. He moved quickly to grab both of them in a hug and then stepped back, his voice rough.

"So fuckin' glad you're home. Martin's runnin' late, but he'll be home in about an hour, and Alec's shift finishes in about thirty minutes. So dinner will be a little late."

Perfect. "Great. Now we're going upstairs. See you at dinner." Brett didn't mean to be short with Stu. He just didn't trust himself to speak, he was so keyed up. He grabbed John's hand and headed for the stairs, not waiting to hear Stu's answer. *God, I just need to be alone with John.* John said nothing but allowed himself to be dragged to his room. When Brett pushed him inside and shut the door behind them, he noted the dazed look on John's face.

"Come here." Brett took John in his arms and kissed him, unable to wait a second longer. John didn't hesitate. His hands gripped Brett's shoulders as Brett deepened the kiss, drinking in John's scent. John shuddered, the tremors running through his body, and Brett knew instantly that all wasn't well. "It's okay, baby, let it out," he soothed. "I've got you. It's over." He helped John out of his jacket, led him over to the bed, and sat him down, rubbing his back slowly, watching as John grew calmer.

John let out a long exhale and leaned against Brett's arm. "I was so scared."

The words pierced the quiet of his room. Brett put his arm around him and kissed his hair. "I know, baby. I wasn't kidding earlier when I said I'd aged twenty years." He stroked John's cheek and kissed him softly on the lips. He leaned, their heads touching, and closed his eyes. "I was shaking like a leaf the whole time, but what really killed me was that I couldn't tell anyone what was going on in my head. I wanted to yell at the top of my voice, 'That fucker has my lover in there!' just so *someone* knew what I was going through." Brett opened his eyes and tilted John's face toward him. Their eyes met. "I kept thinking, 'He can't die, he can't—not without me telling him—'" His throat seized up. It felt like there was a lump the size of an orange in there, making it hard to breathe.

John's eyes widened. "Telling me what?"

Brett inhaled slowly before letting out the words he'd never said to another man in his life.

"I love you."

The words hung there in the silence that followed, before John's face erupted into an expression of joy that made Brett's heart soar to see it. *Oh, thank God....*

"I love you too." John's eyes were shining. "I wanted to tell you how I felt, but I was afraid...."

His voice faltered, and Brett cupped his cheek. "Of what?" he asked softly.

John gave a nervous laugh. "Oh, God, where do I start? I've never been in love before. I kept asking myself, 'How do you know what you're feeling is love and not just lust?' Then I wondered if my emotions were just in a tangle because you were the first man I ever...." Brett loved the blush that bloomed on those cheeks. "But most of all I was afraid of telling you in case you didn't feel the same way."

Brett stared at John in silence for a moment, and then he pushed him down onto the bed, moving with him until he was leaning over John, their faces almost touching. Brett could feel the warmth of John's breath on his cheek as he continued to stare into his lover's eyes.

"I love you," he repeated quietly as he let his hand drift down the front of John's shirt. He eased his fingers under the fabric to free each button, hearing the hitch in John's breathing as he made his way lower, until John lay there, his shirt pulled apart, his chest bare but for the blond fuzz on his belly that pointed the way to where Brett wanted to be. Brett moved his head lower to suck John's left nipple, teasing it with his teeth, loving the way John arched up off the bed, his mouth wide.

Brett raised his head to look at John while he trailed his hand over the downy belly to the impressive bulge of his crotch. He cupped it, rubbing gently, watching as John pushed up into his hand. John's lips were parted, his pupils blown, his gaze fixed on Brett.

"Let's make love." Brett chose his words deliberately. No fucking on the menu. Later? Definitely.

John let out his breath in a slow release. "Oh, God… yes. Yes, I want that too." Then he gave a slow, sexy smile. "Brett? Lock the door, please."

Brett dialed back his arousal. This was a time for taking things slowly. "Good thinking." He got off the bed, went to the door, and turned the key in the lock. Something on the floor caught his eye, and he bent down to pick up the long white envelope. When he saw the postmark, he grinned. *Perfect timing.*

He walked over to the bed, where John was slipping off his shirt. "You might want to open your mail," Brett said with a smile. He handed over the envelope and then removed his jacket.

John peered at it for a moment. "Stu must have shoved this under the door." He opened it and withdrew the single sheet. Brett watched his expression as he stared at it uncomprehendingly. "What am I looking at here?"

With a chuckle Brett took the sheet from him and glanced at its contents. *Oh, yeah.* "It's your test results. I got mine this morning too." He tossed the sheet onto the floor behind him. "Guess what? You're clean. And for that matter, so am I." He didn't take his eyes off John as he slowly unbuttoned his shirt and slipped it from his shoulders. John's eyes were glazed. Brett unfastened his belt and pushed down his pants and briefs and stepped out of them. John watched his striptease with clear enjoyment.

Brett climbed onto the bed and crawled on all fours to where John lay, still wearing his pants. Brett quirked an eyebrow.

John smirked. "Oh, yeah, the socks really do it for me." He snickered.

Brett arched his eyebrows. "Mmmm, note to self. Socks are a passion killer." He leered. "In which case, I'd better take them off, because passion is exactly what I had in mind." He spread John's legs slowly and edged between them to squeeze the erection that was clearly begging to be let out. "I want this inside me, bare," he uttered in a low voice. "I know we haven't done that yet, but right now, I really need you inside me."

John became very still. Brett could hear the change in his breathing. He could see the outline of John's cock as his lover's erection strained against the zipper. Brett felt his hole clench at the thought of taking that long, thick cock inside him. He enjoyed being fucked, but John's length presented him with a whole new level of challenge.

"Brett?" John's voice broke through his delicious musings, and he looked up at his lover—and stopped dead. The tears that Brett had known would come eventually were trickling down the sides of John's face. His breathing had become more ragged. "Hold me?"

The need in John's voice tore at him, and Brett didn't hesitate. He knew there was time to make love later, but right now John needed to feel safe in Brett's arms.

God, I need him too.

CHAPTER 25

BRETT LAY down next to John and pulled him closer, wrapping his arms around his trembling body. He could see John was trying to hold back the tears.

"Let it all out, baby," he urged. "This is your body's way of coping with the stress you were under. The adrenaline's worn off, that's all."

John buried his face at the juncture where neck met shoulder, shudders rippling through him. Brett could feel the quiet sobs that racked his body, and he simply held John close to him, breathing slowly and evenly, until eventually, John's breathing synchronized with his.

John craned his neck to look into Brett's face. "M-men don't c-cry," he sniffed, wiping his eyes with the back of his hand.

Brett chuckled. "Oh, trust me, all men cry at some point. And crying doesn't make you weak. It's far better to release all that stress and tension building up inside you than to keep a lid on it. Far healthier in the long run too." He kissed John's cheek. "Be honest—that feels better, doesn't it?" John nodded, and Brett smiled. "Good. I'm amazed you got *this* far before it all came flooding out. I listened when you gave your statement. I think you were incredibly brave. And be under no illusions—it's because of what you said to Carl that you're here in my arms right now." His gut clenched. He didn't want to think about how events might have turned out.

"Do you really think so?" John asked softly, staring up at him. He was calm at last.

Brett nodded. "You kept your head, you got him talking, you kept him focused on Wayne. It was the right way to go." He pushed out a long sigh. "I have no idea what will happen with Carl, but I hope that one day he gets to play a part in Wayne's life again. And *if* that happens, it will in some part be down to your actions today." He pulled John on top of him and cradled his head in his hands, gazing into his eyes. "I am so proud of you."

John studied his face in silence for a moment, and then he smiled. "I love you."

Brett stroked his cheek and then rubbed his thumb across John's lips, his cock stiffening when John sucked his thumb into his mouth, those blue eyes totally focused on him. There was no mistaking the erotic intent behind John's actions.

Brett bit his lip as he held back a whimper. "How do you do that?" he asked in wonder. "One minute you're blushing, unable to say that I was the first to fuck you—and the next, you're sucking—"

John stopped his words with his hand. Brett's eyes widened.

"Baby, too much talking," John whispered, and he slid his hand away, only to bring their lips together in a long, drawn-out kiss that went from lukewarm to raging inferno in a matter of seconds. Brett could feel him fumbling with his pants as they kissed, neither man willing to break the connection.

With a gasp Brett broke away and pushed John onto his back before grabbing his pants and pulling them roughly down John's legs. That gorgeous cock bobbed before him, long and thick, and Brett was momentarily distracted from his task. He licked his lips.

John laughed. "Oh, no you don't. Get my pants off—only one of us is naked, remember?"

Brett grinned as he freed John's legs and pulled off the dark gray socks, tossing them over his shoulder, making John laugh once more. He crawled up John's body, heading back to the stony dick that awaited him. He paused above it, blowing across the head, feeling John shiver beneath him. He raised his gaze to meet John's.

"I have to be honest here. I've never taken a cock this big inside me."

John arched his eyebrows. "Really?" Brett nodded. A slow smile spread across John's face. "Then get it nice and wet, babe, 'cause you know where it's going next."

At his words, Brett's anus contracted, and he bit back a low moan as John held his rigid cock with one hand while he guided Brett's head with the other, until his dick was pressing against his lips, demanding entrance. Brett sucked the wide head into his mouth, relishing John's low groan of pleasure as he took him as deep as he could without gagging. John rocked his hips, pushing up with small thrusts, Brett's head held firmly in place.

"Oh, fuck, that's good," John gasped out.

Brett relaxed his throat and took John deeper, making him moan all the more, his hips moving faster. *God, the taste of him.* What he wasn't prepared for was John pushing him off and then tugging him urgently until he was straddling John's head, knees wide apart. John grabbed his arse and spread him, and Brett let out a low cry as John began to lick and suck his hole, pressing his tongue ever deeper into his channel. Brett clung to the headboard, his body shaking, as John subjected him to a relentless rim job. His dick pointed straight up, already leaking copious amounts of precome. The erotic sounds that filled the room only served to ramp up his arousal, until he was aching to be filled.

"God, John, *please*," Brett begged. He groaned with relief when John ceased to tongue-fuck him. His cock was hard as steel. He moved to straddle John's hips, his breath catching as he felt John's dick slide through his crease and brush over his hole. John reached blindly for the lube and thrust it into Brett's hands. Brett slicked up his fingers and pressed them slowly into his hot channel, twisting and stretching himself in readiness. John watched him, his breath leaving him in short gasps as he stroked Brett's thighs.

"Ready for me?"

Brett pulled his fingers free and reached behind to position John's dick against him. His eyes met John's. "Ready." And then he sank down slowly onto that thick rod, his gaze never leaving John's as he was filled for the first time with hot, bare cock.

"HOLY *FUCK*."

John choked out the words, hardly able to draw breath as his dick was enveloped in a tight, silky furnace. He held onto Brett's hips, anxiously watching his face for a sign that he could move. Because *God*, he wanted to move. Above him, Brett held his breath as he inched lower. Oh, *fuck*—the heat inside him. Brett's eyes went wide.

"Oh, my fucking God," he groaned. "I swear I can feel your dick nudging my tonsils." He pushed out a shaky laugh, which John felt all around his cock. Brett stared down at him, and a slow smile crept across his face. "My God, you feel good inside me. *Huge*, but so damn good."

John was barely holding on. "Please, Brett, I have to—" The rest of his words were lost as Brett's channel tightened around him. John's eyes rolled back, and he couldn't hold on to the breathless cry that was forced out of him. "What the fuck did you just do?" Brett's eyes gleamed wickedly, and whatever it was, he did it again. Then he slipped his hands under John to pull him into a sitting position. Their faces were inches apart, both men breathing heavily.

John couldn't hold back any longer. He grabbed Brett's shoulders and forced him down onto his cock, at the same time pushing up with his hips. Brett groaned loudly, and John cried out at the sensation.

"Christ, John, move!"

Brett raised himself up slightly, and John grabbed his hips, holding him in place as he began to thrust up into that tight arse, hips rolling. He'd only managed a few thrusts before he pushed Brett onto his back, his dick momentarily released. Brett pulled his knees up, and John guided his cock back to that heavenly hole, pushing in until he was buried up to the hilt in glorious, tight heat.

"God, *yes*!" Brett yelled, eyes wide.

John pulled almost all the way out, only to thrust forcefully into Brett's channel, pushing loud cries from his lover. He propped himself up on his hands, arms locked, and began to fuck Brett in earnest, hips snapping forward as he slid again and again into the tightest, softest place imaginable. Brett let go and wrapped his legs around John's waist, his hands grabbing John's arse to propel him deeper, urging him on with whimpers and low cries that grew in intensity until Brett was hoarse.

All too soon, John felt his balls draw up. "Close, Brett," he gasped.

Brett only nodded, eyes huge as he grasped his dick and began to tug it rapidly. John pinned him to the bed, hips pumping, cock going deep as he thrust into him all the way. Brett's arse tightened around his shaft, pulling them both into orgasm.

"Oh, *shit*," John wailed as his cock swelled briefly inside Brett before pulsing come into him, back arched as he froze, their bodies tight against each other. Brett howled as his dick erupted, covering his hand with his seed. John's elbows gave out, and he collapsed onto Brett, their mouths meeting in fervent kisses as their bodies rode out jolt after jolt of ecstasy, until finally they lay panting, Brett's arms coming up to wrap around John and hold him close.

John had no idea how long they lay like that. He didn't care about the sticky come that sandwiched them together. All he cared about was the man beneath him, whose lips eagerly sought his own. Brett stroked his back with gentle hands as their kisses grew less heated and more tender, until John felt totally melted.

"You need to pull out, babe," Brett urged him.

"Why?" John groaned. He didn't want to move ever again.

"Because you're going to look bloody funny going down to dinner wearing me on your dick, *that's* why."

John sighed. "I could start a new fashion trend—cock gloves." He grinned at Brett. "You're the hottest, tightest glove I've ever worn."

Brett chuckled. "I'm the *only* glove your cock has ever worn." He reached up to cup John's head, pulling him down into a soft, loving kiss. "Did it feel good?"

John rolled his eyes. "Do you have to ask?" He returned the kiss and then began to ease out of Brett, his softened dick shiny with come.

"Oh, God—I can feel you trickling out of me," Brett breathed. John stared at his lover's hole, fascinated, as his come was pushed out. Brett smiled. "There'll always be part of you inside me."

John loved the sound of that. And he couldn't wait to try it for himself.

BRETT AND John were stretched out together on the couch—Alec had insisted. "You two need to be close tonight." Brett wasn't about to argue, and it warmed his heart that it had been Alec's suggestion.

John was still shaken by the ear-bashing he'd received, first from Evan, then from his mother. Brett had understood their frantic concern, but they hadn't witnessed the state John had been in. Evan had calmed down reasonably quickly and had promised to visit soon. John's mother had been another matter. Once John had reassured her he was still in one piece, with everything where it should be and in working order, then the tears had come, audible even to Brett. But when John had begun to look stressed out, Brett had taken things into his own hands. He'd removed the phone from John, introduced himself calmly to his mother, and then explained that John was still a little fragile. That got her attention. Brett told her John would call the following day when he was feeling more himself. He'd finished the call, turned off the phone, and pocketed it before taking a surprised John once more into his arms. Nothing else was said about it that night.

Dinner had been quiet. The three housemates had said nothing of the day's events while they ate, but once the dishes had been washed and put away and everyone was sitting in the lounge with mugs of coffee, it hadn't taken long until the subject was brought up. Martin was the first to speak, and John told them everything. The other two had interjected now and again with questions, but mostly they'd let John tell his tale. When he got to the part about the gun, there had been horrified gasps. Brett had simply tightened his arms around John, reassuring him of his presence.

As the evening drew to a close, John turned in his arms to look at him closely. "You *are* going to stay, aren't you?"

Brett was aware of four pairs of eyes watching him. He smiled and kissed John on the mouth before replying. "You just try and stop me," he said quietly. John sagged into his arms, his relief plain, and it was clear from the glances between the other three that they were happy with his response.

If I had my way, I'd never let him out of my sight again.

The thought took his mind off in countless directions. He hated the thought that once the holiday was over, they'd have to go back to the way things had been during the last term. Three nights a week with John sleeping in his arms, making love long into the night, and when they awoke, spending the whole weekend together—they didn't compensate for the four nights the lovers spent apart. *I'm getting greedy in my old age*, he thought. *I want more.*

Then there were his uncertain plans for the future. He'd had a reply from HMI to say his application had been received and that he would hear from them in due course. *That could mean anything*, he reasoned. He wasn't going to think about it. *Let's just wait and see.* A more pressing issue was what would await them both after the holiday. Brett was a realist. He knew there was no way he could carry on now as John's line manager. He'd already given thought as to who could replace him and what measures he could take to ensure John passed his NQT year without question.

As to his continuing as head teacher, a lot rode on the reaction of his staff. If *one* of them felt his relationship with John meant that Brett was unable to act impartially where his lover was concerned, there would be problems. Brett had done his best to ensure he'd acted fairly at all times, but he knew it was human nature to read more into a situation than actually existed.

No use worrying about this now, he argued with himself. *You have two weeks with him. Enjoy them to the full.*

Brett intended doing exactly that.

JOHN HAD been lying in bed, watching Brett sleep, for an hour now.

Sunday morning should have been a peaceful start to the day, but as John awoke, all he could think of was that tomorrow was the new term. He'd edged his way carefully out of Brett's embrace and rolled over to lie on his side and stare at his lover, relaxed in sleep. John took the time to study the face he'd come to love. Brett looked younger asleep than his thirty-three years.

He sighed internally. *I don't want this dream to end.* Because the last two weeks had felt like a dream. Brighton had been lovely. He'd gotten his walks along the beach with Brett, the two of them holding hands. He could understand why Brett liked going there. It was a gay Mecca of sorts. To walk along a street, their arms around each other, was heaven.

The rest of the holiday had been spent just being themselves. Cooking a meal together for the house, which had been great, especially when John realized that Brett was far better at cooking than he was. And yeah, there'd been some teasing about that from the others. Plus he'd gotten to spend more time at Brett's flat, where they could make love without fear of anyone making jokes about earplugs the following morning. John didn't know if it was because he was still new to sex, but as far as Brett was concerned, he had a ravenous appetite. He couldn't get enough of the man. And although he'd loved topping Brett, he'd already begun to realize that he much preferred it when Brett made love to him. He loved it when Brett took him roughly, when sex was fast and dirty. But better still was when Brett made slow, sweet love to him, their lovemaking lasting long into the night. And then the bliss of being awoken the following morning when Brett slid inside him again, John still wet with his come.

"Do you know how beautiful you are first thing in the morning?"

John surfaced from his sensual reflections to find Brett awake, looking up at him, a faint smile playing about his lips. John leaned over—*fuck morning breath*—and kissed him lightly on the lips. Brett pulled him into his arms, rolling until John was straddling him. When he wrapped his hand around both their erections, grinding them together sensually, John let a low moan escape.

"Want to tell me why you sighed a moment ago?"

John didn't. He didn't want to think about the following day, not when Brett was squeezing their dicks together like that. "It's nothing, honest." He arched his back, pushing his cock through Brett's fist. "Besides, how can you expect me to think when you're doing this?"

Brett grinned and pulled him down into a kiss before reaching for the lube. "Ride me, baby," he said, his voice husky.

John took the lube from him and slicked up Brett's erect shaft. As Brett slowly pushed up into him, his cock sliding in easily, John let out a sigh of sheer contentment.

"With pleasure."

Tomorrow can wait, he thought.

$\mathcal{C}$HAPTER 26

THE FIRST thing Brett noticed was the lack of chatter.

Monday morning briefings, especially right after a holiday, were not the quietest of affairs. Everyone was usually relaxed, eager to share what had taken place during the time away from school. It often took Brett a minute or two to get silence.

Not today.

He took his usual place in front of the room and glanced around at his staff.

No one is looking me in the eye. Shit….

John sat next to Trish Stetman, looking anywhere but at Brett. He knew why. They'd talked about this the previous day, both agreeing not to draw any attention to themselves. But apparently the present situation called for straight talking.

Brett cleared his throat and was relieved to find people looking in his direction.

"Good morning, everyone. I had intended to start the meeting with Trish giving a briefing about this month's sports events, but I think there's something much more important that needs to be addressed first." That had their attention.

Brett put down his sheaf of notes on a nearby table and regarded his staff for a moment before speaking. He was relieved not to see any hostility in the faces before him. *Thank God for that.* He'd hoped he knew his staff well enough to be sure of a homophobia-free reception, but the possibility was always there.

"First of all, I'd like to thank you for the way you responded to the emergency. You were calm, you acted swiftly, and your handling of the children was wonderful. It was a scary afternoon, and I'm sure we are all relieved that it ended peacefully." There were nods and murmurs of agreement all around the room. "The police have been in contact. Carl Meadows is back in Strangeways prison awaiting further outcomes from the incident." That was the easy part. *Now for the tough bit….*

Brett took a deep breath. "Okay, as I'm sure you were able to work out, John Wainwright and I are in a relationship." That started the murmurs going. "I realize that as his line manager, this puts me in an awkward position, and therefore I will be stepping down from my role as his NQT mentor. As the most senior member of staff in the school after me, I would like to ask Trish Stetman if she would take on this role for the remainder of the academic year. She can, of course, refuse, in which case I would ask for the local authority to provide a mentor." He looked across at Trish, who straightened in her chair.

She nodded briskly. "Yes, I'll do it, Brett."

Brett gave her a grateful smile. "Thanks, Trish." He returned his attention to the rest of the staff. His eyes gleamed. "I'm sure I don't need to add that my love life is not for public discussion around the school, just as yours wouldn't be. I would ask that you act as professionals and do not speak of this where you can be overheard. It only remains for me to stress that John and I will conduct ourselves professionally at all times. If you feel this is not the case, or you think that this will in some way impact negatively on the school, then you must of course take this matter up with the proper authorities, namely, the governing body."

He paused to take a breath. The atmosphere in the staff room had changed slightly. The ladies in front of him appeared more relaxed, which told him he'd taken the right tack. John had been apprehensive about laying everything out in this way, but Brett knew it was better to be transparent.

"Are there any questions?" He looked around expectantly and was pleasantly surprised to see smiles directed at him from all sides. Well, *nearly* all sides. Bev had a poker face, which he found a little unnerving.

When no questions were forthcoming, he gave the floor over to Trish and stepped to one side, determinedly not looking in John's direction.

This is going to be so hard, he thought to himself. But he knew he had to be seen to be above reproach. Otherwise, there was always the possibility that he or John could be asked to resign from their posts.

Trish handed out sheets with details of the sports day, with all the races listed.

"By the end of this week you should have a clearer idea of which kids will be participating in each race," she said, running her hand through her short-cropped auburn hair. "The LSAs will be officiating as timekeepers and recording all the results. Can I ask that you have your groups out on the field at least fifteen minutes before the first race? Please stay with them, unless you are participating in a race—and for goodness' sake, get them to cheer their friends on!" Chuckles followed this request. "Remember—this is supposed to be fun. The long-range weather forecast promises a fine day, with no rain—thank God."

Everyone laughed at this. Manchester was well known for its rain.

"Which brings me on to the Swimming Gala later this month. Letters have gone home, and the children should be bringing in their slips to tell us if their parents will be attending. Victoria Baths has very kindly offered us the use of their gala pool with its viewing gallery again, but space is limited." Trish paused. "And I'm sure I don't have to remind you that we want as many staff as possible to take part in both events. And no cheating in the blindfold race." She grinned and looked pointedly in Michelle's direction. "Yes, Miss Fielding, I do mean you. I saw you last year, sneaking a peek under your blindfold."

Michelle's cheeks were scarlet as she glanced around at her colleagues, who nudged her, giggling.

Brett stepped up once more. "Thanks for that, Trish. If you have any questions regarding the sports events, please contact Trish or John, who is acting as her assistant. And that's it from me. Have a good day, people." He gave them one last smile and then headed into the small staff kitchen to grab his mug. Trish stopped him at the door, her hand on his arm.

"Can we have a quick chat in your office before school starts?" she asked.

Brett glanced at the wall clock. "Yes, that's fine. Come on." He stood to one side to let her exit, noting a few of the ladies heading in John's direction. John's gaze met his, and he managed a nervous smile before giving his attention to Caroline Westmore. Brett went to his office, Trish following him, and closed the door behind them. He turned to face her. "What can I do for you?" He cleared his throat.

Trish smiled. "Relax, Brett."

Brett expelled a long breath and leaned back against his desk. "That was nerve racking."

"I can imagine." She gave him a speculative glance. "Are you sure you want me to do this? The mentoring bit, I mean."

Brett nodded as he went to the shelf and pulled out John's NQT folder. "And I'm going to be a pain, I'm afraid. Can you fit in at least two or three lesson observations this term?" He handed her the folder. "All the documentation is in here, all correct. His observation sheets and evaluations are there, but it occurred to me that I could be accused of bias. So if you can observe him, you'll soon be able to tell if I was giving valid judgments."

She nodded. "I understand. Your first priority is to see that John passes this year based on solid evidence. That's fine. I don't expect there will be any problems. We'd have heard by now if there were any issues."

Brett knew what Trish meant. If a teacher was having problems in the classroom, with either his or her teaching methods or with classroom management, word got around fast. Children talked to their parents—and parents were quite vociferous when it came to their children's education. Brett breathed easier, knowing Trish was up to speed.

"Of course there *is* something I have to say here," Trish said with a twinkle in her eye. Brett tilted his head, and she grinned. "Congratulations, Brett. You make a lovely couple."

He laughed. "I didn't expect that." He held out his hand, and she shook it. "Thanks, Trish." He inclined his head toward the staff room. "So, do you think our news has broken a few hearts in there?"

She guffawed. "Oh, there are going to be some very disappointed ladies in there, now that John's definitely off the market."

Brett quirked his eyebrows. "And does that include you?"

Trish met his amused gaze with a cool stare. "Not me, Brett. His plumbing is all wrong, as far as I'm concerned." She winked.

Brett stared at her with wide eyes. "Oh, you're kidding." She looked back at him with an innocent expression. Brett chuckled. "Well, you learn something new every day."

Trish shrugged. "Not something I share with everyone, but hey…."

Brett nodded. "I appreciate it. And thank you for trusting me." He glanced at his watch. "I'll let you go. It's nearly time to get started." He inhaled deeply. "Battle stations."

Trish smiled and exited the office. Brett heaved a sigh. The staff meeting had gone better than he'd expected. Only time would tell if there would be further repercussions. And in the meantime, he'd have to play things very carefully at school, where John was concerned.

At least we'll have the weekends together, he reasoned. Trouble was, that wasn't enough anymore.

THE NOISE in the gala pool was deafening. Most of the races had been run, and only the staff races were left. John was standing by the deep end, feeling self-conscious in his Speedos. There was no sign of Brett yet. John looked up to the gallery where his class was sitting with Mandy, and he grinned. The kids had made a banner with the words, "Go Mr. Wainwright!" and a gold medal on it. There had been a jubilant mood in his classroom during the last two weeks. Year six had done very well in the sports day. The only thing was, they wanted to do equally as well in the swimming gala. Two pupils stood up and waved the banner excitedly, and John gave them a thumbs-up. The class cheered.

John cast a quick glance at the results board. There were some impressive times there. Only two more pupils needed to achieve their length certificate and the whole class would be the first to achieve Brett's target. Peter Simon and Kathy Jones were the last two, and he knew Kathy was spending her Saturdays at the pool, really trying to get up the confidence she needed. Peter wasn't bothered, and his classmates were pushing him to make an effort. They wanted to be the first class to leave where every pupil could swim the length of the pool.

"Ready for this?"

John turned to look at Brett—and then hastily grabbed his towel to hold it in front of his crotch. Brett in a tight pair of black Speedos was a sight to behold. Brett arched his eyebrows and smirked. John looked around quickly before speaking in a low voice. "Do you know what effect the sight of you in those trunks is having on me?"

Brett shrugged nonchalantly. "Thought I'd try to psyche out the competition," he said with an evil smile. He looked around at the lively pool. "It seems to have been a great event. It's just the ladies' race left, then ours." He glanced at the female staff, who were approaching the pool, and burst into a huge smile. "Oh, bless her."

John followed his gaze and grinned. Emily Taylor had come out of the changing rooms in a bright purple swimsuit. What drew the laughter and applause from the audience was the round red nose she wore and the bathing cap covered in sunflowers, not to mention the flippers on her feet.

"She said she'd agreed to wear something different for a laugh," John said with a smile. The pupils loved Emily. She was always patient and kind with them when they came to the office.

John watched as Emily clambered down the steps into the pool, while the other ladies stood at the edge, poised to dive. The whistle went, and the whole school began cheering as the women swam the length of the pool. John was laughing to see Emily doing a sedate breaststroke, head held high, while the others did a front crawl, churning up the water. He wasn't surprised to see Trish touch the wall first, and the loud cheer that greeted her win only served to prove how popular she was. Emily was the last to finish, but the applause for her was tremendous.

"Our turn," Brett said with a smile. He walked over to the pool edge and shook out his arms to loosen up. John took up a position a little distance from him. They bent over, ready to dive.

As the whistle went, John dived cleanly into the water and surfaced, going straight into his front crawl. He clawed at the water with strong strokes, feeling great—and then he saw Brett. The man was already ahead. John put a spurt on, thrashing through the water, legs kicking strongly, but he couldn't catch him. When John reached the wall and stood up in the shallow water, breathless, Brett tapped his wrist as if to say, *what kept you?* He was grinning. John felt exhausted, but Brett looked hardly out of breath.

They climbed out of the pool and made their way to the deep end, dripping. John grabbed his towel and began to dry himself off.

"Okay, kids, let's hear it for Mr. Sanderson and Mr. Wainwright!" Trish said into the loudspeaker. The applause was deafening as the children got to their feet, hands clapping, stamping their feet, with John's class holding aloft their banner. Both he and Brett took a bow, and then Brett grasped John's hand around the wrist and held it up. Brett winked at him.

John shook his head. So much for beating the "old man."

BRETT HANDED out drinks from the tray and sat down next to John. The little pub was new to John, a small, cozy corner tucked behind Debenhams department store. Brett had invited the staff for a drink after the gala, once the children had gone home. All the ladies had come along, with the exception of Bev. She'd cried off, saying she had plans for that evening that required her getting home ASAP. John was surprised but not particularly unhappy about her decision. In the last two weeks, Bev had been different. She no longer chatted with him first thing in the morning when he came to get a coffee from the staff room. In fact, he'd hardly seen anything of her. It was almost as if she was avoiding him.

They pulled two tables together, and everyone sat around on the padded benches or the comfortable chairs. Brett made it clear he expected John to sit beside him.

"We're not in school, babe. This is our time." Brett winked. John felt his cheeks heat up at Brett's endearment, but the low chuckles and sighs from the others went a long way to making him feel more comfortable. This was the first time they'd been together as a couple with the staff, and he hadn't been sure what to expect. Certainly not the warm looks and affectionate glances that came their way.

Brett raised his glass to Trish. "To my wonderful sporting events organizer." Trish blushed. "Thank you for all your efforts. The sports day was great, but I think this was the best swimming gala we've ever had since I've been here." There were murmurs of agreement. Everyone lifted their glasses to Trish and echoed Brett's toast. John took a long drink of his cold cider. It was a good thing he intended walking home. He wanted to stay with Brett as long as possible.

I guess it'll have to do until the weekend, he thought with an internal sigh.

"On the subject of the swimming gala," Trish began, leaning back into her chair, "can I just say what a really impressive performance you gave, Mr. Head Teacher, sir."

"I'll say," Michelle huffed. "You streaked down that pool!"

"I'm saying nothing," John said with a slight shrug. "Seeing as he wiped the floor with me." He met Brett's gaze. "I didn't have a clue you were so strong a swimmer."

Brett mimicked his shrug. "I had a good day."

Trish spluttered into her pint of lager.

"Did it go down the wrong way?" Caroline asked, concerned.

Trish was laughing. "John, you did very well, seriously. But *you*...." She stared at Brett. "I was so impressed by your speed, not to mention your swimming style, that I got curious." Her eyes sparkled. "I looked you up, Brett."

"Oh?" Brett said indifferently, but John knew him too well to be fooled. Brett looked distinctly uncomfortable.

"Hmmm, and I think John for one will be very interested in what I found. Manchester University Swim Team, 2000-2003—their all-time champion swimmer was one Brett Sanderson."

Several pairs of eyes looked in Brett's direction. There was a stunned silence.

"Oh, hell," Brett muttered and took a very long drink of his Coke.

John stared at him in amazement before hitting him on the arm. "You could've *told* me, you sod!"

Brett gave him a wide-eyed, innocent stare. "But, baby...."

"Don't you '*but baby*' me," John growled. "Here was I thinking it was going to be a really easy win, and you're a bloody *ringer*!" He speared Brett with a look.

Trish burst out laughing. "Oh, dear, Brett, I don't think you're getting any this weekend."

There was a moment's silence before the ladies sitting around the table collapsed into snorts and giggles.

Brett gave John an apologetic glance. "I'm sorry. Yeah, in hindsight, maybe I should've said something."

John looked into those warm dark brown eyes and melted. He couldn't stay mad at Brett for long. Brett got under his skin.

"Go on, kiss and make up, you two," Caroline suggested with a gleam in her eye.

Brett grinned and beckoned to John. "Come here."

His cheeks on fire, John edged closer until Brett's thigh was touching his. Brett leaned across and kissed him chastely, their lips pressing together, warm and soft.

"Wow," Michelle said, her gazed fixed on them. "That was...." Her words trailed off.

Brett broke the kiss, and John leaned against him. "Show's over, folks," Brett said softly.

John looked around the table at his colleagues. He'd been dreading the return to work, but so far it had been painless. The only downsides were Bev's cooler attitude toward him and the distance between himself and Brett when they were in school. They could still meet at the end of the day for a coffee and a few kisses, as long as there was no one around. But Brett was so careful whenever they met in the hall or on the playground. No one mentioned anything in the staff room. It was almost as if it had never happened.

John could cope with anything, as long as he had time with Brett at the weekends and those stolen moments at the end of the day. Okay, so he wanted more, but for the moment, he had to be satisfied with what he had.

It can only get better, he surmised.

Famous last words.

CHAPTER 27

JOHN WALKED around the classroom, glancing over his pupils' shoulders as they worked, heads down, everyone concentrating. It was an end-of-module test to check on their progress. John smiled to himself. They were a good little group. He would miss them when they all left at the end of July to go on to high school.

He heard the door open, and, glancing up, he was surprised to see Trish Stetman, looking unusually solemn.

"Mr. Wainwright, could you go to Mr. Sanderson's office, please? I'll be staying with your class until you return."

There was something in her voice, something John couldn't decipher. He straightened and gave her a brief smile. "Certainly, Miss Stetman. They have ten minutes left before the end of the test. Mandy has the next activity ready for them." John looked quickly at Mandy, who was sitting next to Philip. She bobbed her head once and then went back to her task.

John picked up his jacket from the back of his chair and went out the door. As he passed Trish she gave him a quick smile before giving her attention to his class. John walked swiftly along the corridor to Brett's office, pulling on the jacket as he did so. Something was up; he could feel it.

When he got to the office, Emily smiled and picked up her phone. "Mr. Wainwright is here." After a moment, she replaced the handset, stood up, and said, "Please go into the office, John."

John's scalp was prickling. He walked into the office and came to an abrupt halt when he saw the Chair of Governors, Mary Lacey, sitting at the conference table. There was no sign of Brett. She stood up to greet him.

"Good morning, John. Please, have a seat."

John sat down, his stomach quivering. Behind him, he heard the office door close, and then Emily joined them at the table, a notepad in her hand.

"Morning," John said quietly. The hairs were standing up on his arms under his shirt.

"I asked to meet with you because certain allegations have been made against you."

Cold hit him and spread throughout his body. "Allegations?"

Mary nodded. "The purpose of this meeting is to acquaint you with those allegations. Emily Taylor is going to take minutes, and you will be provided with those later. Okay?" Her expression was unreadable.

"Yes." John's stomach churned. "Please, go on."

Mary consulted the sheet in front of her. "The governing body received a complaint that alleges you have benefited from preferential treatment here at the school, because of your relationship with Brett Sanderson." Her face was impassive.

The cold hand around John's heart was suddenly like ice. He struggled to maintain his composure.

"Furthermore, it alleges that your pupils could be at risk by having a… homosexual as their teacher." Her mouth twisted with distaste. Whether it was because of him being gay or because she didn't like what she was saying, John couldn't tell.

"Those allegations are complete crap," John blurted out. "I—"

"I can tell this is a shock to you, John." Mary's expression was suddenly softer. "But I have to investigate any such allegations, as I'm sure you understand." He nodded, feeling numb. "So here's what will happen. I am going to appoint Trish Stetman to investigate this fully. She will conduct interviews with staff and pupils and will then write a report of her findings." She paused, looking him in the eye. "Now, obviously, this will be awkward if you are in school, so I propose to suspend you immediately. You'll be on full pay, of course."

John reeled. *Suspended?*

"A supply teacher will be brought in to cover your lessons. I want this cleared up as quickly as possible, as I'm sure you do, so I will be asking Trish to have her report ready by the end of this week. During your suspension, you must not speak with any staff, pupils, or their parents about this case. Is that understood?"

"Yes." John found it difficult to think. His mind was racing. *Who in hell has done this?* Mary's next words sent his heart plummeting.

"Brett Sanderson has also been suspended, and I will be investigating his case." She stood up and waited for John to get to his feet. "Please make sure that Emily has your school keys and laptop before you leave. She will go with you now to collect these, and then she will escort you from the building. Any communication between you and the school must be conducted through her. Is that understood?"

John nodded, unable to speak. He felt dizzy. Mary gave him a tight smile and then led him to the office door. As he went through it, she laid a hand on his arm.

"Try not to worry about this, John. You haven't been suspended because we believe you to be guilty of the allegations. It's actually to make things easier for you. This way we can clear things up a lot faster. Emily will contact you if Trish needs to see you to go through anything she turns up in her investigation, all right?" Her face was kind.

He nodded and exited the office, Emily right behind him. He walked slowly along the corridor, his mind still reeling. Emily walked in silence. When he entered the classroom, Trish looked up and gave him a sympathetic smile. He couldn't return it. He couldn't think straight. He walked over to his desk, picked up the laptop bag and backpack, and went back to the door where Emily was waiting for him. The class had finished their test and were all chatting excitedly about how they'd done. John tried to smile at them, but his heart felt too heavy. He closed the door and handed Emily the bag, then reached into his pocket to give her his keys.

"That's everything." Numbness spread through him in a slow tide.

"Did you come to school on your bike this morning?" Emily asked.

John shook his head. "It was a lovely morning, so I decided to walk." They went along the corridor toward the main door. As they reached it, John turned to Emily. "Em, what could happen here?" He felt the bile rise in his throat as if he were going to be sick.

She met his gaze. "If Trish thinks there is a case to answer, then she will recommend a formal disciplinary hearing, when you'll have to go before the governors. Do you belong to a union?" John nodded. "Then I would advise you to contact them and apprise them of the situation. If it comes to a disciplinary, you'll need representation." Then she smiled. "But it won't come to that, I'm sure. If Trish finds nothing, then you'll be reinstated."

"What about Brett?" John couldn't contemplate what his lover was going through at that moment.

"The same procedure for him," she replied. Then she took hold of his arm. "This will all get cleared up, John. And in the meantime, you need Brett."

John stared at her. "She said I can't talk to any staff."

Emily stared back. "About the case. As long as you two don't discuss the case, you can see him. But you didn't hear me say that, okay?" Her eyes twinkled. "Now go home and try not to worry." She squeezed his arm. "It'll turn out all right."

John wished he shared her confidence. He said good-bye and then began to walk slowly along the road, his feet feeling heavy. He went along as if in a dream, oblivious to the traffic and passersby, functioning on autopilot. In his head, he was going over and over again all the things Mary had said. What hurt the most was the allegation that basically his kids were in some kind of danger because he was gay. *What the fuck?* He wouldn't have believed it possible that someone could even have made such a suggestion. And he really wanted to know who had made the complaint.

He reached the front door and fumbled with the key. As he stepped into the hallway, he couldn't miss the sound of Stu singing in the shower. Stu had returned home late the previous night from a New York flight and had probably just woken up. John walked into the kitchen and mechanically began to set up the coffee machine. His mouth was dry. By the time the coffee was bubbling, he heard the shower switch off. John stared out of the kitchen window at the small garden beyond. The flowers were in bloom, and he could see the butterflies hovering around them.

"What the hell are you doin' here?"

John turned his head. In spite of his worries he had to smile at the sight of a naked Stu, towel in hand. He couldn't help it. Stu was such an exhibitionist. He smirked as Stu wrapped the towel around his waist and came across the room to him.

"Somethin's wrong, yeah?" Stu's eyes were filled with concern.

John sighed. "Wait 'til you hear this." He relayed the morning's events.

Stu stared at him aghast as John poured out two mugs of coffee. "Oh, fuck, mate. That's terrible. Have you spoken to Brett yet?"

"Just about to," John said, taking out his phone. He speed dialed Brett's number, and within two rings Brett answered. "Hey there. I hear you've had an eventful morning too."

"Where are you?" Brett asked urgently.

"I'm home." John couldn't hold it in any longer. "Brett, I need you."

"I'll be right over." And then he was gone.

"Can you two see each other while you're suspended?" Stu asked, his forehead furrowed.

"As long as we don't discuss the case. But seeing as we're both suspended, I don't see what they could do about it anyway." All John knew was that he needed Brett.

Stu put down his mug and tugged John into a tight hug. "I'm here for you, mate, both of you." He pulled away and glanced at the dinner rota on the wall. "I know it's supposed to be your turn to cook tonight, but bugger that—me and Alec will cook. You spend the rest of the day with Brett, and we'll feed you, all right?"

John returned Stu's hug. "Thank you. That's really nice of you." He had the *best* housemates.

"And if Brett's on his way, maybe it would be better if I put some clothes on, eh?" Stu said with a wink. He took his mug with him and exited the kitchen. John sat down at the table and sipped his coffee. *What a mess.*

Fifteen minutes later he heard a car pull up outside, and he hurried to open the front door. Brett was walking up the path, his brow wrinkled. As soon as he'd stepped into the hallway and pushed the door closed behind him, John was in his arms.

"I'm so, so sorry I got you into this mess," Brett murmured into his ear.

John pulled back, wide-eyed. "You have nothing to apologize for, do you hear me? You did everything you could to be fair and unbiased. You were honest with all the staff." He kissed Brett firmly on the mouth. "This is *not* your fault."

Brett smiled, the creases across his forehead easing. He ran his fingers through John's hair and then along his jawline. "How did I get to be so lucky?" he mused. He brought their lips together in a tender kiss and then wrapped his arms around John, holding him tightly against that firm body. "We'll get through this, baby, I know it."

John nuzzled his head against Brett's neck. "Yes, I'm scared. But I know I've done nothing wrong—nor have you, for that matter." He craned his neck to look Brett in the eye. "Take me to bed? I just want to hold you, a duvet over our heads, for an hour or two."

Brett's eyes lit up. "Sounds perfect." He released John from his embrace and then took his hand to lead him up the stairs. "Let's go shut out the world for a while."

John knew it wouldn't solve anything, but in that moment all he wanted was to be naked in Brett's arms, to feel his warm breath on the back of his neck.

And let's face it—I have nowhere else to be right now.

The thought made his chest tighten.

"THEY CAN'T fire you both, can they?" Alec asked as he cleared the dishes from the table.

Brett leaned back in his chair. "To do that, they would have to prove gross misconduct, and they have no evidence of that." He caught John's worried gaze and grasped his lover's hand. "They have no evidence, and besides, you and I both know that second allegation is total crap." He lifted John's hand to his lips and kissed it softly. John smiled.

"But what about you?" Martin demanded. "Can they fire you for having a relationship with John?"

Brett turned in his seat to face Martin. "Having a relationship with John doesn't break any rules. What puts a spanner in the works is that I'm his line manager, his mentor. Obviously someone on my staff thinks I've displayed favoritism in some way. If they feel that I can't remain impartial where John's concerned, then they have a right to complain."

"But you *have* remained impartial, haven't you?" Alec looked outraged.

Brett gave him a grateful smile. "Yes, and if Mary Lacey does this by the book, she'll soon see that." He bit his lip. He knew what the outcome might be, but he didn't want to think about that. If his plans worked out, then it wouldn't be an issue.

"What are you not saying?" John's eyes narrowed.

Brett's stomach did a slow roll. *I should've known—he knows me too well already.* He leaned forward, his elbows on the table, chin in his hands. "There is the distinct possibility that they will ask John to look for another position—in other words, leave the school. Or they could ask the same of me, for that matter."

John became very still. "They could do that?"

Brett shrugged. "Whatever happens, they'll be reluctant to allow us to keep on working together." He locked eyes with John. "We have to be prepared for that, babe."

"So they can't fire you, but one of you could end up havin' to look for another job?" Stu's face twisted in anger. "This stinks, it really does." There were murmurs of agreement from Alec and Martin.

"Look, I can't say too much, but I'm looking into something that might mean it won't come to that."

All eyes turned to stare at Brett.

"What?" John demanded. "Why can't you tell us?"

"Because it's not one hundred percent certain, okay?" Brett said firmly. "You'll have to trust me. If I hear anything, you'll be the first to know."

He hoped to God things worked out. He didn't want this whole sorry state to have a negative impact on John's promising career. And then it struck him. He cared more about John's future than his own.

Well, fuck. *Looks like I'm well and truly in love.* And then he chuckled to himself. *Like there was ever any doubt.*

JOHN WAS going out of his mind. It had been four days since he'd been sent home, and he was climbing the walls. It was the thought of not knowing how things were progressing. He hadn't heard a word from Trish, but he had no way of knowing if that was a good or a bad thing. The logical part of his brain kept telling him it would all be sorted out. Only trouble was, he wasn't sure his brain knew what it was talking about.

He lay on his bed, staring at the ceiling. At least he and Brett had been able to spend some time together. He could tell that Brett was finding it a strain too. They didn't talk about the case, but it was always there, the elephant in the room.

His phone warbled beside him on the bedside table. John smiled when he saw Brett's name.

"Hey there, I was just thinking about you." The truth was, John thought about Brett all the time.

"Have you checked your e-mails recently?" Brett asked. His voice sounded strained.

John sat up immediately and went over to his desk where his laptop sat. "No—why?" he asked as he booted up the computer and logged onto his e-mail account.

Brett sighed down the phone. "Because I've had an e-mail from school, so I figured you might have too."

John was about to ask more, but an e-mail caught his eye. "Oh, God—you're right."

"Open it."

John could hear the note of urgency in his voice. He clicked on the e-mail and quickly read it. A wave of relief crashed through him. "Oh, thank God."

"Good news?"

John could have cried. The feeling of lightness that surged through him was wonderful. "They're not taking it any further. They've concluded there's no case to answer, and they're reinstating me." He peered at the attachments. "It looks like they've sent me all the documentation."

"That might make interesting reading," Brett said dryly. He expelled a breath, the sound like a rushing wind in John's ear. "Baby, I'm so pleased for you."

John was so overcome with joy at the outcome that he almost forgot Brett's original words. "What about you? What did yours say?" There was a silence at the other end. "Brett?"

"My hearing is set for next week," Brett stated quietly.

Oh… fuck.

"Oh, God, I don't know what to say." John was horrified.

"Say you'll be there."

"What?" John's mind raced. "*Can* I be there?"

"If I tell them I want you there, then yes. Besides, the outcome will affect both of us."

John didn't hesitate. "I'll be there."

"Thank you." The note of gratitude in Brett's voice tugged at his heart. "I feel better knowing you'll be at my side."

Warmth flooded through him. "We'll face this, Brett—together."

CHAPTER 28

JOHN STRAIGHTENED his tie for what must have been the fourth time, until Brett reached across and stopped his hand in midaction.

"Leave it. You look fine."

John huffed. "This waiting is killing me." He stared at the floor of the reception area. "How long could this take?" Brett's hearing was due to start in about ten minutes. The school was quiet as all the pupils were in their classes.

John couldn't believe how calm Brett was. He'd spent the night at the house with John and had left early that morning to go home to get ready. John had expected to see some nerves displayed, but Brett seemed remarkably unruffled. John was anything but calm.

"What's bothering you? Out with it." Brett spoke in a low voice.

John wanted to touch him, even if it was just to hold his hand, but this was neither the time nor the place. "I don't want to see her. She's going to be in the meeting, isn't she?"

Brett didn't have to ask who "she" was. They'd talked of little else ever since John had seen the statement Bev had written. At least he knew now who had made the complaint.

"I'm not sure. I don't think so. Trish might be there." Brett turned slightly so that he was facing John. "Baby, I'm going to be all right. Just trust me, okay?" His deep brown eyes were warm.

John regarded his lover for a moment and then nodded. "I'll try." He shook his head. "How can you be so calm about all this? They're going to decide on your future in there."

Brett smiled. "Maybe not."

Before John could make anything of this enigmatic statement, the door opened and Emily appeared. "If you'd like to come through, gentlemen?"

They got to their feet and entered the office. On one side of the table were two empty chairs, obviously for them. On the other sat Mary Lacey and two people unknown to John. At the end of the table was a well-dressed woman with a notepad. Emily entered the room behind them and took a seat at the opposite end of the table.

Mary Lacey stood. "Please, sit down." Once they were seated, she carried out the introductions. "On my left is Elizabeth Forrest, a parent governor, and on my right, Tony Davenport, the vice chair of governors. Emily Taylor will be taking the minutes, and Sarah Makinson is here as the human resources adviser to the governing body."

John and Brett gave polite nods to everyone. John's heart was pounding.

Mary took the floor. "John, you are here at Brett's request, as he is allowed to be accompanied. Before we start, can I say how pleased I was that the allegations against you proved to be groundless, and that I am very sorry for any discomfort this caused you. We received a great many letters of support from staff and parents."

John acknowledged this with a nod. He'd seen the letters as part of the investigation report. It gave him so much pleasure to read how greatly the parents and staff valued his contribution to the school.

Mary cleared her throat. "Which brings us to the situation before us. Strictly speaking, there is nothing that says two members of staff cannot be in a relationship. But when one is the line manager of the other, this is clearly a conflict of interest. For instance, Brett has the authority to make decisions on expenditures that affect John, for example, any applications for courses for his continuing professional development, pay recommendations, etcetera. This, of course, might mean a possible breach of the local authority's financial regulations."

"Can I say something at this point?" Brett interjected. Mary nodded. "As soon as staff became aware of our relationship, I stepped down as John's line manager."

"We are aware of that," Mary said, "but the fact remains that this relationship only came to light as a result of the dreadful incident involving Carl Meadows. We are not naïve, Brett. It had obviously been going on for some time before that. The only reason you saw fit to step down was because you basically outed yourselves in the aftermath of that day."

Brett fell silent. John knew there was nothing he could say.

"But I feel I should point out that there is no evidence to substantiate Bev Waverley's claim that you showed favoritism toward John in any way. In fact, we have reason to believe her complaint was based not on a desire to bring unfair practice to light, but rather to pursue her own... *personal* agenda."

John frowned. What the hell did that mean? And then suddenly things clicked into place. Bev asking him out for a drink on several occasions, her strained expression after the police had taken Carl away and Brett had kissed him, the reluctance to speak to him....

What do they say? "Hell hath no fury...." For all John knew, Bev might be homophobic. But to do all this, simply to get back at them? *I didn't really know her at all, did I?*

"But notwithstanding there being no evidence of any misconduct on your part, Brett," Mary said, gazing frankly at him, "we are still left with an untenable situation, in that the two of you cannot remain working together in the same school."

John caught his breath. *Oh, hell....*

"We are therefore left with two options, the first being that John is transferred to another school within the authority."

John's heart sank. He loved working at the little school. He thought of all that he'd achieved during the last ten months. *And for what?* he thought bitterly. He was surprised when Brett took his hand under the table and held it tightly.

"However, this would leave us with another problem. As head teacher, Brett, you have to be seen to show sound, reliable judgment. The local authority relies on you to act in the school's best interests. Clearly, at least for the start of this relationship, you were unable to do this. Therefore it is our judgment that you continue to be suspended and that Trish Stetman steps in as acting head teacher until such a time as you can find another position."

Brett coughed. "I agree with the appointment of Trish as acting head. I think that's an excellent choice. However, there is no need to continue with my suspension." He reached into his pocket and withdrew a long white envelope. "I would like to take this opportunity to tender my resignation." He placed it on the table before Mary. John's mouth fell open. *What the fuck?*

She became still. "Brett, you need to think about this. There's no need—"

Brett held up his hand. "Please, allow me to finish. This morning I received notification from HMI that I have been appointed as an inspector, my contract to begin in September."

John froze as he tried not to gasp. Okay, so it was fantastic news—but news Brett hadn't deemed fit to share with him.

Mary's face broke into a smile. "Brett, that's wonderful. May I congratulate you. I'm sure you will be a valuable asset to the team of inspectors. And please ensure that any reference requests are sent to me. It would be a pleasure to write, believe me." She got to her feet and reached across the table to take Brett's hand and shake it firmly. Brett gave her a warm smile and then shook hands with her fellow governors.

She held out her hand to John. "And you will be expected back in school on Monday morning, John." He shook her hand, nodding absently.

Emily stood and opened the door for them to leave.

John's head was in a spin. *That was it? All that angst for less than fifteen minutes?* He still had his job, but Brett wouldn't be coming back. He walked out of the office feeling shell-shocked. *I know Brett said to trust him, but how could he keep something this big from me?*

Once they were alone, Brett turned to face him. "Let's get out of here. We need to talk."

John could only nod. Brett led the way out of the building and down the narrow side street that came out onto the main road. John hadn't got a clue where he was going—until he looked across the road at the park. Brett grasped John's hand and walked across the road through a break in the traffic and into the peaceful park. He pointed to the first empty bench in sight.

"Let's sit there for a while." Brett sat down, the noise of the traffic blurring into the background. Birdsong could be heard above the faint roar.

John sat beside him, his thoughts still in a whirl. Brett had only just sat down when John couldn't wait any longer. He rounded on Brett. "Why didn't you tell me?" There was a painful tightness in his throat.

Brett sighed. "I found the letter from HMI waiting for me when I got back to the flat this morning," he explained. "I know I should've spoken to you about this before, but—"

"Why didn't you? This is fucking important!" John was trying not to yell, but it still burned that Brett had kept this to himself.

Brett took his hand, although John tried to tug it from him. "I didn't want to say anything in case it all came to nothing," he said patiently. "I didn't want to raise your hopes."

"But you must have had an interview," John reasoned. Brett fell silent. "So when was it?"

"Two weeks ago," Brett replied quietly.

John quickly thought back. "Two weeks ago… the head teacher's conference in Birmingham?"

Brett nodded, his expression grave. "Only, there was no conference. I went to London." He took John's other hand. "Baby, I'm sorry."

"You didn't tell me," John repeated. "I can't seem to get past the fact that you hid this from me." At last his heartbeat seemed to return to normal.

"And I will never hide something so important from you ever again," Brett said, his gaze fixed on John. "I give you my word."

"You're leaving." Now that the hurt was fading slowly, his mind fastened on the reality of the situation.

"Yes, but you're not. You have a promising career ahead of you, and that school is only the start." Brett squeezed his hands.

There was a sudden pain in John's chest. "Fuck, Brett, this sounds like…."

"Like what?" Brett's expression grew anxious.

John could hardly bring himself to say the words. "Like you're saying good-bye," he whispered, the words just about audible over the hum of traffic.

To his surprise Brett's face erupted into a beaming smile. He leaned forward.

"Oh, you don't get rid of me that easily, Mr. Wainwright." Brett's sexy smile was doing things to John's insides. "And just so we're clear? Yes, I may be leaving this school, but I am not leaving you. And whenever I am not off traipsing round the country as an inspector, I will be with you." He kissed John on the lips. "So… you don't have to be at work until Monday, which gives us—" He glanced at his watch. "—sixty hours to play with." He got to his feet, still holding John's hands, and looked John in the eye. "Let's go back to my flat, where we won't be disturbed by naked flight attendants." He winked.

John leaned closer and kissed Brett, not giving a flying fuck that they were standing in the middle of a public park. "Sounds like a plan." Brett took his hand, and together they walked back to Brett's car.

"WHOSE IDEA was this?" Brett spoke loudly above the music that pulsed through Babel.

John grinned. "Theirs!" He pointed to his housemates, who were standing at the bar, glasses in hand. The three men looked across and raised their drinks, wide smiles all round. John lifted his glass in return. "They said we couldn't let today go without celebrating." He pulled Brett closer. "So, what do you think?" Brett arched his eyebrows. "About this place. You haven't been here before."

Brett looked around the dance floor at the variety of bodies on show. "Nice view," he said with a leer. John belted him on the arm. "Ow! You asked!" Brett rubbed his arm, an exaggerated look of pain on his face.

John let out a low growl, and Brett collapsed into laughter. He pulled John into his arms and kissed him firmly on the lips. "I can look, but there's only room in my heart for one man."

Just like that, John melted. "You know how to get round me, don't you?"

Brett smiled against his lips. "Baby, this is not 'getting around you.' This is me telling you the truth, plain and simple." He kissed him, letting his lips linger, setting John's heart racing.

Fuck, he can arouse me in a heartbeat.

John broke the kiss with a low moan. "What you do to me."

Brett grabbed his hand and slid it down over his belly to the crotch of his tight black jeans. John swallowed. Brett's cock was a solid lump of flesh behind the zipper. Brett pressed John's hand against his full, heavy erection. "Right now I'm thinking of what I'm *going* to do to you when I get you in bed tonight." Brett moved his hand away, only to cup John's arse and pull him closer, grinding their dicks together in a slow, sensual rotation.

"If you don't stop that," John gasped out, "you're going to have me coming in my favorite jeans."

Brett released him and stepped back with a grin. "Oh, we can't have that. But by the time you get to school on Monday morning, you're going to have difficulty walking straight, if I get my way. I'm thinking of chaining you to the bed, all weekend." He gave John a wicked smile.

Despite the images Brett's words conjured up, something else registered. John felt as though someone had plunged him into icy cold water.

Brett cupped his face tenderly. "Babe, what is it? What just happened?" His gaze was full of concern.

John bit his lip. "It just occurred to me that Monday is going to be bloody awkward."

"Why should it be?" Brett asked. "The staff are all behind you."

"Not all of them." John's heart felt heavy.

"Oh, love." Brett took John in his arms. "Listen to me. If I were Trish, the first thing I would be doing on Monday morning is having a word with Bev. There's going to be a lot of animosity toward her when it gets out that she was the one who complained to the governors. And they're not stupid. They'll work out why she did it. I think she might find life rather difficult if she stays there."

"They can't fire her."

"That's true," Brett admitted, "but Trish might point out that maybe a transfer to another school might be the best route." He shrugged. "That's not to say Trish will do that, but it's what I'd do. You have a lot of support in that school, and word gets around quick." He kissed John on the lips. "Don't think about it now. Let's enjoy this evening." He glanced at John's glass. "And I'll help by getting you another drink." He gave John one more kiss, this time on the cheek, and then headed toward the bar.

John watched him cross the club, admiring the wide shoulders and narrow waist, shown off beautifully by the dark blue silk shirt stretched across his back. *What a gorgeous man—and he's all mine.*

"You look happy." Alec sidled up to him and leaned against his arm, glass in hand. Stu and Martin joined him.

John gave his housemate a quick one-armed hug. "I am." Alec beamed.

"Don't look now," Stu said with a grin, "but someone's giving you a really good lookin' over." He tilted his head toward a point behind John.

Before he could turn around, a familiar voice rumbled in his ear. "Hi there, beautiful. Haven't seen you here for a while."

John shook his head and smiled. "Hi, Max," he said as he turned around to face him.

Max's face lit up. "Well, you look better than the last time we met. You were crying into your tequila about some guy. Who was he again?" He stroked his chin.

"That would be me."

John smirked as Max whirled around to face Brett, who was standing behind him, carrying two pints.

Brett handed John a glass and then crooked his eyebrows. "You must be Max. I'd recognize you anywhere from the description John gave me." John was trying hard not to chuckle.

To his surprise, Max's face erupted into a huge grin as he turned to look at John. "Congratulations," he said softly. "You got your man after all." He leaned forward and kissed John's cheek. "I'm happy for you, John." Max held out his hand to Brett, who shook it. "And I'm very pleased to meet you." He gave the group a nod and then walked off toward the bar, a smile across his lips.

"I can't leave you alone for five minutes without some guy hitting on you, can I?" Brett's eyes gleamed with mischief. John felt his cheeks heat up. Brett put his arm around John's waist and pulled him close. "You are far too sexy for your own good, Mr. Wainwright."

"Oh, God," groaned Stu. "It's gonna be another earplugs night, guys." Martin and Alec chuckled.

Brett suddenly put down his pint and faced the three men. He took a deep breath.

"Guys, I love you. I think you're a wonderful group of men, and the way you support John is truly fantastic."

Alec flushed but Stu merely shrugged. "What can I say? We're a great bunch."

Brett smiled. "Yes, no argument there. But there are only so many times I can put up with seeing Stu's naked arse first thing in the morning when he comes out of the bathroom and I'm going in." Martin snorted. Brett turned to John. "So there's only one solution as far as I can see."

"And what's that?" asked John, curious.

Brett locked eyes with him. "Live with me."

John froze, his heartbeat racing. "What?"

Brett moved closer and lowered his voice. "Move in with me, live with me, shack up with me—are there any more ways I can say this?" Before John could react, Brett kissed him slowly and thoroughly on the mouth, dipping his tongue briefly between John's parted lips. He pulled back, his eyes shining. "Share my life, John," he whispered, the words barely audible above the music that thrummed through the club.

"Yes," John whispered breathlessly, reaching up to touch Brett's face, his skin tingling. "Oh, God, yes." Warmth radiated throughout his body.

Brett's smile was so wide John felt it would split his face in two. "Oh, thank God." He wrapped his arms around John and held him close. "I love you."

"Love you too." John quivered as he tried to control the elation coursing through him.

"Oh, great," muttered Martin. John twisted in Brett's arms to stare at his housemate. Martin blushed. "Oh, don't get me wrong, guys. I'm really happy for you, and I know the others feel the same way."

"Yeah, we do," said Alec quietly, his eyes bright. Stu was grinning.

"But?" demanded Brett, his arms still around John.

Martin gave a sad smile. "I'm being selfish, I suppose. I don't want to lose John. And we have to start looking for another housemate."

"You never know," John said with a wink. "The next one might be even better."

"Impossible," murmured Brett, kissing his neck. John shivered.

"Can I write the ad this time?" asked Alec. "We can make it really specific."

"Yeah!" Stu's eyes twinkled. "I can see it now. '*Wanted—tall, sexy sub.*'" Alec's cheeks were suddenly bright red.

"Or how about '*Wanted—Slut.*'" Martin chortled. "Someone to give Stu a run for his money." He winked at the others.

Stu shrugged. "He can try." Alec and Martin guffawed.

"I think whoever comes to live with you will be a lucky man," John said loyally. He looked from his housemates to the man who held him. "Though he'll have to go a long way to be as lucky as I am." He gazed at the man he loved.

Nah, he thought. *Not possible.*

Born and raised in the north-west of England, K.C. WELLS always loved writing. Words were important. Full stop. However, when childhood gave way to adulthood, the writing ceased, as life got in the way. K.C. discovered erotic fiction in 2009, where the purchase of a ménage storyline led to the startling discovery that reading about men in love was damn hot. In 2012, arriving at a really low point in life led to the desperate need to do something creative. An even bigger discovery waited in the wings–writing about men in love was even hotter....

The laptop still has no idea of what hit it... it only knows that it wants a rest, please.

K.C. can be reached via e-mail: k.c.wells@btinternet.com, on Facebook: http://www.facebook.com/KCWellsWorld, or through comments at the K.C. Wells web site: http://www.kcwellsworld.com. K.C. loves to hear from readers.

Learning to Love Series from K.C. WELLS

http://www.dreamspinnerpress.com

Collars & Cuffs Stories from K.C. WELLS

COLLARS & CUFFS
AN
UNLOCKED
HEART
K.C. WELLS

http://www.dreamspinnerpress.com

Collars & Cuffs Stories from K.C. WELLS

COLLARS & CUFFS

TRUSTING
THOMAS

K.C. WELLS

http://www.dreamspinnerpress.com

Collars & Cuffs Stories with PARKER WILLIAMS

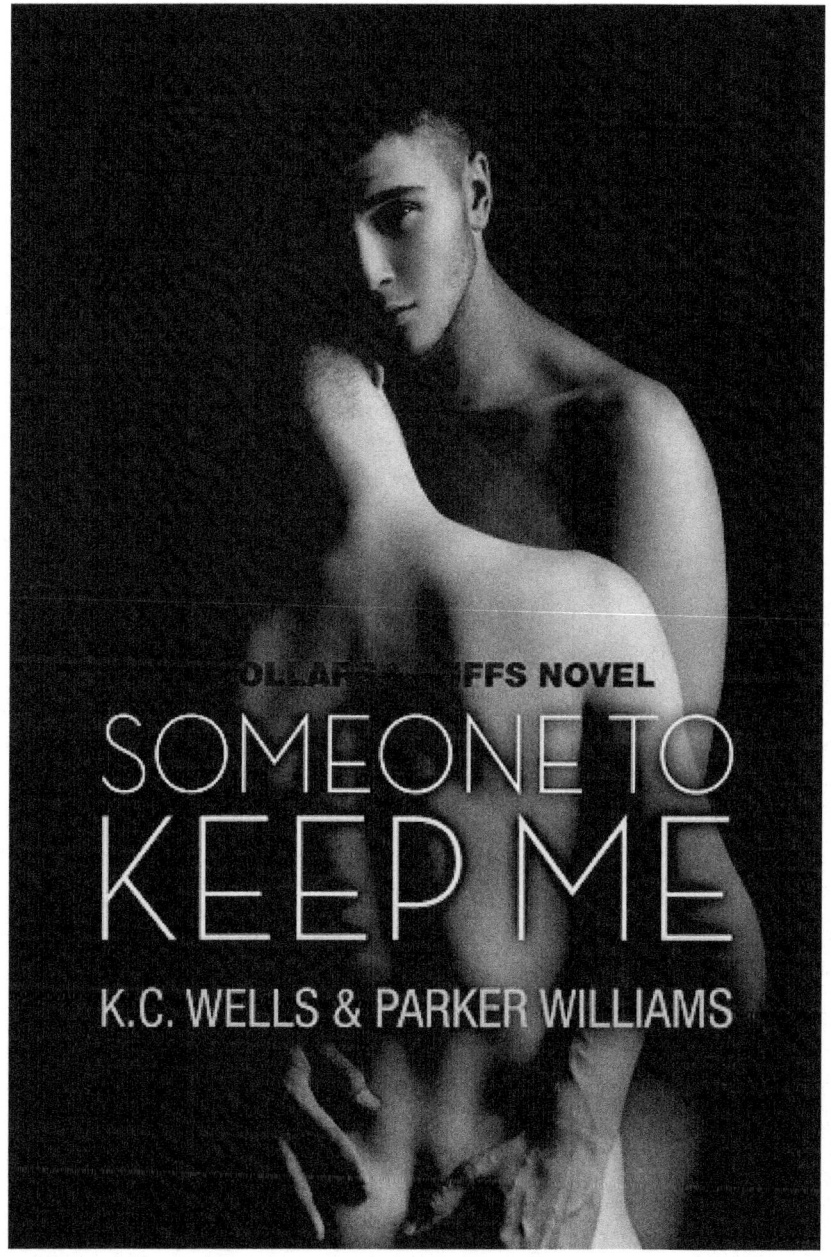

http://www.dreamspinnerpress.com

Printed in Great Britain
by Amazon

36054159R00159